COURTING DOUBT AND
DARKNESS

J. M. WEST

MILFORD HOUSE

an imprint of Sunbury Press, Inc.
Mechanicsburg, PA USA

MILFORD HOUSE

an imprint of Sunbury Press, Inc.
Mechanicsburg, PA USA

For information about special discounts for bulk purchases, please contact Sunbury Press Orders Dept. at (855) 338-8359 or orders@sunburypress.com.

To request one of our authors for speaking engagements or book signings, please contact Sunbury Press Publicity Dept. at publicity@sunburypress.com.

ISBN: 978-1-62006-548-8 (Trade Paperback)

Library of Congress Control Number: 2015931373

FIRST MILFORD HOUSE PRESS EDITION: May 2018

Product of the United States of America
0 1 1 2 3 5 8 13 21 34 55

Set in Bookman Old Style
Designed by Lawrence Knorr
Cover by Lawrence Knorr
Edited by Amanda Shrawder

Continue the Enlightenment!

Dedicated to
All my ancestors and family
who have made a difference.

Winter Snow

Nature—the kitchen goddess
Who sprinkles snow dust,
Like sifting powdered sugar
Winter's gift of sweet silence!
                    —J.M. West

"One has to abandon altogether the search for security, and reach out to the risk of living with both arms. One has to court doubt and darkness as the cost of knowing. One needs a will stubborn in conflict, but apt always to total acceptance of every consequence of living and dying." —Morris L. West

PROLOGUE

Carlisle Police Department's Senior Detective Christopher Snow hammered the Wrangler's brakes to avoid blowing through the red light on R 15 south of Lewisburg. "Shit!" Glancing in his rear view and side mirrors for any flashing lights and cocking his head to catch a siren's whine, he huffed a sigh when none materialized. Oh, he could flash his shield, but that wasn't setting much of an example.

The recorder on the seat beside him shifted. Snow picked it up, leaned over to open the glove box and tossed it in. His thumbs drummed the steering wheel, waiting impatiently for green while traffic piled up behind him. Unease gripped his gut, and experience had taught him to pay attention. "What spooked that woman during our interview?" he mumbled. "What had she gained from her husband's death? Her inheritance seemed typical." The query about her job caused her to break eye contact and cross her arms defensively across her chest. "Why? Because she knows more than she's telling." He talked to himself a lot since he'd ordered his wife and partner, Detective Erin McCoy, who usually accompanied him, to man the war room and feed him information when he needed it. "Damn it, woman, why can't you follow orders?" He had also assigned his former partner Reese Savage to assist Mac, since the Chief relegated him to desk duty.

Neither answered the phone in Conference One when he called for a background check on Greer. CPD had consolidated the case files, data, listed info on white boards on their homicide and two other related ones—at the RV parked along the Susquehanna near Winfield and the Safety Coordinator's body at the West Enterprises' Williamsport well.

1

Worry forced him to accelerate. He dialed HQ again and left a terse message for both. "I need to know what I'm up against!" Part of the Marcellus Shale zone beneath Penn's Woods, West Enterprises' active well was 'fracking,' or shattering the shale with millions of gallons of water, sand and over 500 chemicals miles underneath the surface to free the natural gas and oil, which then flowed to the surface through the horizontal pipes and up the vertical well, to be delivered to consumers.

He dialed Mac's cell. It went to voicemail. "This is important; neither you nor Savage are at HQ working this case? Where the hell are you?" He snapped the clamshell shut. "You're both insubordinate, so you'd better have a damn good explanation for your absence!" When his cell chirped, he checked the caller: HQ. "About damn time."

Snow hit talk. "Hello? Where the hell have you two been?"

Savage explained that they'd gone to BWI to arrest Abigail Benedict for the murder of Mindy Murphy. Then he put Mac on speakerphone to summarize Sienna Greer's arrest record, which included a DV incident, several DUIs and a road rage incident.

"Chris, where are you exactly?" Erin asked.

He dialed back his anger and gazed at the water. "About twelve miles south of Lewisburg." The river, a beautiful silvery ribbon slipping downstream, the sun playing upon the waves. Silver and gold reflections darted back and forth, refracted into a thousand dancing crosses of light. What he wouldn't give to spend a few hours...

While the Susquehanna distracted him, a blue semi barreled out of nowhere, bearing down on him, gaining ground quickly. Though there was room to pass, the trucker just mowed down the highway toward his Jeep. He checked the rear-view mirror as the cab loomed into view. Too late, he floored his accelerator as he veered into the outside lane, the truck following.

Suddenly, squealing breaks and metal smacking metal followed, crunching and what sounded like

2

dragging. His last conscious thought was Mac yelling into the phone. "Describe your location!"

1

After a three-hour workout with Shadow and a quick
lunch of cottage cheese and cantaloupe, Erin collapsed on
the recliner, the puppy lying beside her on an old blanket,
gnawing energetically on a marrowbone. Erin picked up
the spiral-bound volume again. Maybe she'd missed
subtleties during the first reading of Abigail Flowers's
Master's thesis last summer while she was busy relating
to its argument and conjuring futile *what-ifs* regarding
her own mother's whereabouts. The detective was
convinced that it contained the answer to the Flowers'
family dilemma and to Mindy Murphy's murder.

The Absent Mother

The English language dominates England—and thus North
America and Australia and its territories because "the hand
that rocks the cradle rules the hearth." Despite foreign
invaders, from the Romans to the Saxons and monarchs like
the Hanoverians from foreign shores, the English language
thrived. Today, it is the dominant language of global commerce,
literature, politics, social intercourse, and academia, as well as
English and American history.

We agree that by chance, circumstance or choice, the
mother has power in the home, but if she removes that hand
and abandons her role, will the child run wild like Golding
portrayed in *Lord of the Flies*, Twain in *Huckleberry Finn* or Lee
in *To Kill a Mockingbird*, and the numerous orphaned
protagonists in fairy tales? Is it accurate to conclude that
civilization is just a thin veneer hiding humankind's savagery?
Whether the mother's absence is physical or psychological,
whether literal or metaphorical—or even if such absence is
only the child's perception, then the conclusion must be valid.

Pardon the generalization, but usually mothers civilize
children and men. However, if the mother is absent, the social

and moral fabric rends and eventually disintegrates, as evidence in our cultural and literary history attests. Look how Ralph and Jack war over their island, how quickly the conch rules are ignored and chaos ensues. Or the orphan Huck Finn whose adventures down the Mississippi would probably not have occurred had he a mother to watch after him. Had his mother lived, perhaps Jem might have been spared the vicious, crippling attack in *To Kill a Mockingbird*.

For evidence to support my thesis, I will quote experts and include examples like Scout, *Huck Finn*, pertinent fairy tales, i.e. Snow White, Cinderella and Peter Pan, as well as television shows in which mayhem reigns when a mother's stabilizing influence is missing. Finally, I shall add my family history to the scale.

Also, women on "the mommy track" do not fare well in the face of feminism. Many feminists have spun gold and furthered careers by analyzing the negative effects of patriarchy: women's voices silenced, views and contributions marginalized, their bodies either a sexual object (whore), idealized (virgin), revered only in her acceptable role as wife/mother. For example, Virginia Woolf's metaphor, the 'magical garden of women' (digging the ground, sowing seeds, and planting bulbs) rejuvenates the Mother image, supplanting a social order that fails to nurture females. The garden symbol embodies the power in fertility, creativity and identity once celebrated in many pre-Christian cultures like many former Native American matriarchies. Does this garden signify the loss of security once the infant leaves the Mother's womb or the pleasure principal Freud so fondly posits as our subconscious drives? Feminists lament the masculine world of violence in competitive sports, destruction in war, and corruption in politics. They claim the paradigms in traditional education valorize the masculine and marginalize the feminine. While these issues indicate divisive perspectives worthy of attention, I leave them to their discourse.

For my purposes here, I need look no farther than my own family, which I will cite as a cautionary tale. I argue that the absent mother may indeed wreak havoc in the female psyche, but a present father actively engaged in childrearing provides not just an antidote but also a role model for survival.

5

***

Erin put down the thesis and pinched the bridge of her nose. The baby was kicking, she had a kink in her neck, and the racket from installing the sunroom screens and sliding glass doors was giving her a headache. Savage held the frames while Chris slid them into grooves. The pneumatic percussion of the air gun pierced her skull. Sonja Hamilton's husband, Ozzie, was laying the pavers that led around to the front of the bungalow. She couldn't see the Lieutenant; Les must be supervising. She released the recliner's footrest, pushed up and waddled to the kitchen for a glass of iced tea. She intended to return to reading and highlighting, but the doorbell pealed. Shadow leaped to her feet, barking. "Easy. Friend." Yet the dog heeled by her side as Erin opened the door.

Looking wilted in a charcoal suit with briefcase in hand, the Cumberland County ADA stood on the threshold looking apologetic. His chestnut waves and long, pleasant face suggested late thirties. He had bushy eyebrows and periwinkle eyes; a row of freckles marched across his Roman nose. Perspiration beetled down his temples in the unseasonably warm Indian summer. He looked longingly at her iced tea as he extended his hand. "Remember me? Chase Lawson. Sorry I didn't call first, but we need to review my questions for Monday's trial. As you know, defense counsel has entered a not-guilty plea in your kidnapping, and you are the major—indeed, the only, eye-witness." Erin motioned him inside and sidled over to the fridge, poured another glass of tea, and handed it to him. He eased himself onto the sofa, pulled a MacBook from his briefcase and booted it up.

"On what grounds?" Erin asked. "The evidence is compelling! And Detective Fields also witnessed my abduction."

"Hmm. Think he was unconscious. Diminished capacity."

The doorbell chimed again. A delivery boy balanced a stack of large pizza boxes emitting enticing aromas of spicy sausage, pepperoni, onions and peppers. "Around the side of the house." She pointed right and returned to her perch and addressed Lawson. "A specious defense. The cashier in the Adams County Camp Store, an Amish Farmer named Lapp, and my husband can testify that Lyons impersonated me after incarcerating me in a Michaux State Park cabin. Did you subpoena Abigail Flowers? She's in the video at the scene, though somewhat impaired, in my view. With luck, her testimony can implicate her sister, though you may need to offer her immunity." Ah, thank goodness, the outside pounding ceased. She eased onto the recliner, raised the leg rest to relieve her swollen ankles.

Chris appeared in the doorway, sawdust dotting his tee. "Pizza, babe? You OK?" He held out a slice on a paper plate, nodded at the ADA, making eye contact long enough to let him know he was on the premises.

"No, thanks. I had lunch. I sliced watermelon and cantaloupe—in the fridge—for you guys." She smiled at her husband's thoughtfulness, his nearness a comfort. At one time, the idea she needed protection would have raised her hackles, but since her abduction, she'd changed.

"Thanks. Yes, I'll get them. Let me know if you need anything," Chris said, chomping down, and then turned into the kitchen, retrieved the melon platter and carried it out to the volunteers.

Erin returned her attention to Lawson. "Would you like a piece?"

"No thanks. May I call you Mac? I'll peruse Ms. Benedict's deposition later, sure. When I put you on the stand, first I'll ask if you can identify your assailant and kidnapper. Then I'll trace the events that show animosity between you and Dr. Lyons at work."

"Abigail's real name is Flowers, and Ms. Lyons doesn't have an M.D. or PhD, so her title is Ms. Lyons." Erin stipulated. "I wouldn't characterize it as animus."

Lawson stopped typing and looked up. "What then?"

7

"We differ in our interpretations of events of the incident; I discharged my weapon, killing the shooter at a Virginia crime scene last year to save my wounded partner and our interviewees. Virginia State Police and CPD's IAD declared it a 'clean shoot'; she countered that decision and assigned me to desk duty. I filed a complaint, resulting in IAD investigating her." Mac tried to keep her voice even. "They found discrepancies in her resume and work history."

"But the kidnapping was a direct consequence of that incident at work. Wouldn't you agree?"

"Not entirely. Apparently, she had designs on my husband as well. I would consider that the primary impetus for wanting me sidelined or out of the picture."

"You want me to open that can of worms?" Lawson leaned back against the sofa and drank his tea, then saluted her in thanks with the empty glass and set it down on the coffee table. "Think the defense will bring it up?"

"I doubt it," Mac answered. "But you should; it goes to motive."

"I'm not so sure about that, especially since her husband's reappeared. It's prejudicial and unlikely to sway the jury in any case." His eyes returned to the text on his laptop, reading. "She claims you entered the bar and made unwarranted sexual advances on Detective Snow on the evening of—"

"You'd have to ask my husband about that; he didn't seem to mind." Her face heated at the memory of her brazen behavior. She restrained herself from telling Lawson what he could do with his impertinence. Lyons's behavior was so clearly antagonistic towards her. "I gave him an answer to his marriage proposal."

"You want me to put Snow on the stand? I will, but that testimony will not paint you in a positive light."

"I'm not the one on trial," Erin said.

"No, but your credibility may be. All right. Let's back up." Exasperated, Lawson glanced at the ceiling for patience, stretched his arms and laid them across the back of the sofa, fidgeting as if constrained. "Mind if I take off my jacket?" Without waiting for an answer, he wrestled it off, folded and laid it aside, unbuttoned and rolled up his shirtsleeves and settled back against the cushion. He leveled watery blue eyes at her. "Here's what we'll do. I'll ask the questions as pertinent events unfolded. Let me walk you through your testimony about the kidnapping. Just give me your answers, without digression or editorial comment." He rummaged through his briefcase for his notes and started tapping on his laptop. "Then we'll move into the office dynamics and then relationships. I will subpoena Lapp and..." Again, he checked his legal pad. "...the cashier at The Camp Store. Then I'll put similar questions to Detectives Snow, Savage and Fields. Sonja Hamilton's also on my list. Try not to worry about the others' testimonies."

"And Corey Kauffman, the K-9 instructor, can testify; he was at the cabin where I'd been incarcerated," Erin added. "My dog Shadow tracked and led them to me." Shadow's ears pricked up at hearing her name; she aimed a low growl at the prosecutor. Erin gave her a hand signal to stay.

Carson sighed. "This will be a lengthy session if I can't ask my questions."

"I've testified in trials before." Erin nodded at him to go ahead.

"Yes, I'm aware of your record. Let's run through these."

***

After the ADA left, Erin let Shadow out the back door, measured dog food into her dish, replenished her water, and deliberated about what to fix for dinner. Feeling too tired to wrestle with the trial issue, she strolled back out to whistle for the puppy.

She watched her father-in-law apply mortar and sink chunks of limestone into the end wall of the sunroom below window level while keeping an eye on Shadow.

9

Apparently, this task had fallen from father to son across the generations because he clearly knew his business. First he laid out the stones and then daubed on the mortar. "See, what you have to do is fit each stone into place quickly, press, then add the next, like a puzzle." He pressed a triangular stone onto the wall, and picked up another, repeating the process, tapping with his trowel handle. "If I need a smaller piece..." He indicated the hammer lying beside the stack of stone. "How does it look?"

Erin smiled. "Fine, just like the rest of the bungalow. You'd never know it's a new room; it blends in well. Thanks for helping."

"Well, the stone's from the original barn's foundation." The elder Snow smiled, satisfied at his own efforts then continued. "We saved them."

When Shadow returned, they padded indoors; the dog plopped down on her dog bed for a nap. Erin was tempted to do the same but freshened up with a quick shower instead and then slipped on a clean oversized tee and knit shorts. In the kitchen, she marinated chicken in Italian dressing, lemon juice and garlic and then rinsed and chopped vegetables for a salad. Tossed the veggies in a glass bowl with the lettuce and grated parm over the top, covered it and put it in the fridge. Set the table. And returned to Abby's case study:

The Absent Mother

Early on, my mother was physically present but seemed elsewhere mentally. Even though she fawned over my elder sister, daydreams colored her days. She loathed taking us shopping and allowed us to run around in clothes smeared with blobs of peanut butter and jelly or dribbles of spaghetti sauce. While she enjoyed cooking, culling recipes and baking, the over-all daily grind overwhelmed her. Her behavior recalls the Zombies' lyrics, "...she's not there." Her eyes often glazed over and gazed into the distance, perhaps yearning for a better life. Rarely did she live 'in the moment,' attend to or support my efforts or needs. At times, she joked on the phone to her friends, "There's nothing wrong with a little wholesome neglect. The kids are resilient; they'll manage." Often that meant April had to watch me, which my sister eventually resented.

When my father came home from work, mother whined, nagged or became lethargic, expecting him to assume the household duties. And the more chores he shouldered, the less she did. Cracks and fissures finally split into a full chasm. One summer day, in the space of eight hours, she packed up kids and household and moved out, which marked a downward spiral of denial, shock, resentment and ire, which she directed at me. Blatant insults like "I should leave you at the side of the road, you worthless brat" and "Sean's little sissy" were daily epithets.

And even though April was her darling, mother drifted away.

***

A bit later, Chris came in, bent over the recliner to kiss her cheek, sweat dripping off his body. "I'll shower first, then turn on the grill."

"Anyone staying for dinner?" asked Erin.

"Just you and me, babe." He disappeared. Followed by the sound of running water. After a dinner capped with melon slices, Chris led her into the bedroom. He'd draped a pale green sheet over a vertical quilting frame on the far side of the bed. Her eyes swiveled to the Nikon mounted on a tripod facing the bed beside an open umbrella lined with aluminum foil to bounce back the light. Behind her, Chris peeled off her tee and shorts.

"What's this?" Erin asked.

"A photo shoot. I want pictures of my wife."

"Like this?" She gestured at her body in the eighth month of pregnancy, her distended abdomen round and solid.

"Absolutely. You're my fertility goddess. You're my Eve, the mother of our son. You've never looked sexier. I want to record this event—the first photo in our family album."

"You're kidding. Like I'm carrying a bowling ball here." Erin wasn't sure about this. "Who will see these photos?" She certainly didn't want them online—or anywhere else, for that matter. She didn't feel sexy; she felt fat and bloated; her rings no longer fit her swollen fingers. Lassitude weighed upon her every motion—she felt like she was wading through Jell-O most days, carrying twenty-five more pounds than usual.

"No, I'm serious; the wedding photographer gave me the idea. Think about the magic of his conception. Know why it was breathtakingly spectacular?" Chris's hand caressed her rounded abdomen from behind as he unsnapped her bra and laid it aside, cradling her heavy breasts.

"Hmm, because we were needy? No, I gave my all. You reciprocated." She turned and leaned into him, and tilted her head back for a kiss, which he delivered gently, fingertips stroking her back.

"You held nothing back, surrendered totally, ceded control—a first. You initiated our lovemaking, and let me love you unconditionally; your ardor burrowed into my heart. I know how difficult that must've been."

On the contrary, she recalled how easy, spontaneous, and eminently satisfying that moment had been. "The boudoir photos were for your eyes alone. I'm not comfortable doing this." Erin frowned. "Who's going to see it?"

"Just me—or us. I don't understand why you'd object. A pregnant Demi Moore posed naked before the world on the cover of a magazine."

"Well... I don't know. I wouldn't do that. I'm not a celebrity."

"Tell you what. After I'm done, you'll have the final say; delete any shots you're uncomfortable with, and I'll print them from our computer and hide them in a photo album. But I'd like to hang one where we can see it every day." He nodded at the wall opposite the queen-sized bed where his leaf carving hung. And winked at her.

"Well, okay to the photos in an album." She surmised it'd be all right if the photos were private. "No to the wall display. FYEO."

Thus her husband turned photographer, posing her, pulling stands of her tousled roan hair forward over her breasts as she lay on her left side, her hand propping up her head. "Bring your right knee forward a little, rest it on the bed." Behind the camera, he studied her through the viewfinder, adjusted the lens. Then he shook his head and backed away, muttering "too stiff" and knelt by the bed to kiss her and trail his fingers down her side. "Look right here, babe, and think of sex in the shower," referring to the time when Chris had brought her home from the hospital after the Valentine's Day snowstorm. She'd sustained injuries detaining a suspect during a road rage incident.

Images of water sluicing over them, kissing, body touching body, slippery-clean with soap relaxed Erin. Her right arm cupped her round abdomen as Chris adjusted the lens—his hands, his attention, and the angle of his shoulders all focused on composition. He snapped two more.

"Hey, that's more than one!" Erin sat up.

"You want a choice don't you?" he asked reasonably, taking another. "Can you sit in a lotus position?" He ducked out to the kitchen; she heard the snick of a match. Bearing a lighted candle, he put the glass jar in her hands. The candle flame climbed up the wick, eating air. Click. "Now stretch your arms out: fill the frame." She rested the candle on her crossed feet, arms akimbo, tilted her head and studied him perusing her. Click.

"Now let's go outside, around the corner by the lilac bushes for some Nature shots." Chris blew out the candle and set it aside while pulling Erin up. Then folded the tripod legs and shouldered the camera.

"Are you nuts? I'm not trouncing around outside naked. You're not. What if someone sees us? They'd report us for exposing ourselves!"

"Not on our private property. We're surrounded by trees!" He leaned the camera and tripod in the corner and stripped off his boxers. Took the camera up again, headed out back through the garage's side door. Erin hesitated, shrugged and then skirted the foot of the bed, tugging the sheet down to drape around her and then followed her uninhibited husband, curious now.

Outside, the air had cooled; a pleasant dusty twilight greeted them; half a golden yolk broke across the horizon. A faint aroma of smoke from burning leaves tinged the air. In the gloaming, autumn leaves bled crimson, rust, orange, and yellow-gold. "Come on, while we still have some natural light." Working quickly, he hummed while setting up the camera. Erin twirled the sheet, which swirled around her and draped like a shawl, then fell from her shoulders, the ends caught in her arms. The camera clicked away.

"Chris, I wasn't ready!" She covered her breasts.

"Freeze. I want that profile."

"Does that camera have an automatic timer?" she asked.

"Of course."

She crooked her forefinger, motioning him to her. "I want you in the photo." He stepped in and reached for her. "Is this arrow aimed at me?" she teased as he put his finger under her chin and tilted her face to his to look into her eyes. Click.

"Aimed at your flower. Look at me." The naked affection in his bourbon eyes squeezed her heart and warmed her womb.

"Freeze." She said, as her right hand stroked him. "My turn. You've been touching, teasing and tempting me for the last hour." Click.

"Whoa!" Rounding the corner of the garage, both hands thrown up, eyes popping, skidding to a stop,

Savage exclaimed, "What an eyeful! You guys need to take it inside. Or I could join you." He stood rooted to the spot, gawking at them, grinning. Erin groped awkwardly for the sheet to cover her nakedness, her neck and cheeks burning. "No wonder Dispatch can't reach you! Come on; we've got a homicide at Letort Spring."

"Go ahead," growled Snow. "I'll meet you there in five." Shouldering the tripod once more, he ushered Erin, too mortified to say anything, through the door. Having been discovered by a colleague, their behavior seemed foolish, adolescent.

What if that had been Chris's parents? Would Savage tell his buddies at CPD? Erin wondered nervously.

"FIVE? Take ten," Savage replied. "I'm your driver. The body's not going anywhere."

After the men left, Erin pulled on a long-sleeve tee and pajama bottoms, let Shadow out to tend to business while she made a cup of tea to settle her qualms and scanned the photos with some trepidation. Surprisingly, most were tastefully composed. The pale green backdrop and duvet highlighted her auburn hair and milky skin. The revealing one with the candle she deleted. She really liked the one with the sheet whirling around, her face partially turned to the camera, her body merely a silhouette behind the sheet. At the second to last one with both in the photo, she stopped and stared. The light had caught her solitaire and fractured—five lines broke the plane; Chris's finger on her tipped chin, their profiles conveyed the tenderness, a subdued, shared passion that signified the heart of their marriage. Except the area from waist to mid-thigh, his tanned skin was several shades darker than hers; the planes of his toned body contrasted with her rounded one. Definitely her favorite, she wanted a copy of it. The last one she also deleted because of the impish expression on her face and his wide-eyed surprise, like he'd swallowed a fly.

***

15

On the eleven o'clock news, a local team converged on the crime scene along the Letort Spring Run—near the Carlisle Post. In the sepia twilight, the camera panned to the bridge connecting a trail to the park, catching the yellow tape linking the trees along the bank. An attractive reporter's breathy voice spoke: "Elena Michaels reporting live at the scene. Carlisle Homicide detectives are pulling a woman's nude body from the creek. Dr. Haili Chen, the coroner, is attending. Others are wading in the stream, ducking under the bridge, gathering evidence. This may be a first—and hopefully last—homicide here in this bucolic park where families picnic, play, and hold reunions. We'll have more on News at Daybreak. Now back to the studio."

Erin clicked off the TV and sighed. Violence as entertainment: She felt uneasy about the media's intrusion at murder scenes; absent the facts, broadcasters speculated. What if a family member saw and recognized the victim—though, in this case, the cameras were too far away for close-ups.

Sighing, she pushed herself off the recliner, took the puppy out for her last potty call for the evening, usually for fifteen minutes of Shadow romping around, sniffing the dried grass and snorting through leaves for little critters she could antagonize, or better yet, enjoy as a midnight snack.

Back indoors, she clicked her fingers and pointed to the dog bed in the mudroom. "Bed, Shadow. Might as well go to sleep. Chris will be out until who knows when, and I want to be alert for court tomorrow, prepared for the unexpected." Shaking her head at the asperity of Lyons's not-guilty plea with all the evidence aligned against her, Erin devoted ten minutes to her bedtime rituals. She mentally reviewed the questions Carson had asked earlier and promised herself to try for objectivity rather than the acidity she'd displayed earlier.

2

Judge June Acorn called the court to order. The attorneys made brief opening statements to the jury, as to the offense and outcome desired by the prosecutor and defense.

Dressed in a navy suit, white shirt and a royal blue tie, ADA Lawson called Detective Erin Snow to the stand. "For the record, if you would state your name," he said after she took the witness chair and was sworn in. The jury waited patiently. Someone cleared his throat; another coughed; papers rattled. Straight ahead, the DA was seated at the table next to Lawson's. To the right, Alison Lyons sat straight and prim in a white shirt and black pencil skirt. Beside her, defense attorney Denise Wilhelm, wearing a taupe suit over a chocolate satin blouse and sensible two-inch brown heels, wrote on a legal pad before her. The one white wave in her sienna hair stood out in dramatic contrast.

"Detective Erin McCoy Snow."

"How would you like to be addressed?" Lawson asked.

"Excuse me?"

"Don't the men on the CPD force call you Mac, short for McCoy?"

"That's correct. Detective is fine." The next few questions established her place of work, home address, and her duties at CPD. He walked her through the events leading up to her kidnapping.

"Detective, is your alleged assailant in the courtroom?"

She nodded her head toward the defendant's table. "Yes. The defendant, Alison Lyons."

"And how can you be certain? Wasn't your assailant masked and totally covered in a black ninja suit?"

"I noticed the platinum hair and heard her voice."

"How did you recognize her voice?"

"She spoke to her sister, Abigail Flowers/Benedict, who was also at the scene."

"So you knew your assailant personally?"

"At that time, Ms. Lyons worked as the part-time psychologist for the Carlisle Police Department."

"You're seeing a psychologist?"

"It's required any time a detective uses deadly force at a crime scene, as I had at the Virginia shooting."

He reviewed the Virginia incident to which Erin referred to give the jury a background and context for what would follow.

"Can you clarify the location of your kidnapping?"

"Our domicile on Lisburn Road."

Wilhelm leaped to her feet. "Objection. Evidence hasn't been established. 'Alleged kidnapping.'"

"It's prima facie," responded Lawson, backing to the table to lift a disc case for all to see. "I'd like to enter into evidence the recording of Detective Snow's kidnapping, which we will show later." People rustled in their seats. Lyons looked startled at the news.

"Overruled. Continue." Judge Acorn frowned at Wilhelm.

Lawson repeated the question.

"I was taken from our Lisburn Street bungalow on June eighth."

"Where you live with your husband, Detective Christopher Snow?"

"Yes, sir."

"Why do you think the defendant kidnapped—" Lawson began.

"Objection. Presumption of innocence until—" Wilhelm started.

"Sustained. Rephrase, counselor."

"Why do you think Alison Lyons came to the Lisburn Road premises?"

"To remove me so she could have Chris to herself."

Wilhelm popped up again while the gallery twittered. "Objection—hearsay! Move to strike the witness's last statement and declare her a hostile witness."

"Overruled. Detective McCoy's a seasoned police officer and the only eye-witness," countered the judge, glaring at the defendant's table. Lyons sat stone still, head bent and lips pursed into a tight, thin line. Her hands kneaded a white handkerchief.

Methodically, Lawson ran through his questions, tracing the events that led up to the CPD celebration after Snow closed the Bender case, in which a man sexually assaulted and murdered his sister-in-law while his young niece shivered in her mother's locked car until police arrived. Lawson picked up a sheet of paper. "Let me quote the defendant's own words: 'Detective McCoy entered the bar and made unwarranted sexual advances on Detective Snow at his closing party.'" He paused.

"Is there a question in there, counselor?" asked Judge Acorn.

"Yes, your honor." Lawson approached Erin. "Was Ms. Lyons romantically interested in your husband?"

"Objection. The couple wasn't married then. Suggesting otherwise is prejudicial," Wilhelm said.

"Sustained." The judge sighed. "Rephrase."

"I'll move on," Lawson tossed the file onto the table and exchanged a look with the DA, who resumed taking notes.

"I'd like to answer the question," Erin volunteered.

"All right. Did Ms. Lyons show an interest in Detective Christopher Snow?"

"Yes. They had a history."

"Will you please elaborate what you mean by 'history?'"

"They'd hooked up a few years ago."

"OBJECTION!" yelled the defense counselor. "Hearsay! Move to strike!"

"Sustained."

"And did you make 'unwarranted sexual advances' toward Detective Snow?"

"You should ask him." Restless spectators gaped at her. Whispers buzzed from mouths to ears along the rows.

"And the result?" Lawson asked.

"You can see for yourself," Erin indicated her swollen belly; everyone in the courtroom gasped or guffawed and would gossip about it later. The judge slammed her gavel down while Alison jumped to her feet yelling, "You damn liar!"

"This court will come to order!" The judge warned the witness. "No more of that, Detective! Wilhelm, control your client. Her next outburst will be followed by her removal from court!" She then turned to Mac. "Detective McCoy, avoid such innuendoes in the future. Court is a solemn affair—not entertainment. Continue."

"Yes, your honor." *But that's not all,* Erin wanted to add, *this defendant is guilty of more than kidnapping; I just can't prove it yet.*

Lawson covered the remainder of questions they'd rehearsed; her testimony provided facts about being trussed up in the cabin, freeing herself, garnering provisions, escaping and fleeing. As they proceeded, he entered the macramé rope with Erin's DNA, CSU photos of the scene, including the yawning escape hatch, the recovered belt loop from her jeans and her teal teardrop earring into evidence. Plus CSU found her detective shield in Lyons's beach house trash. Wilhelm objected to Erin's semantics repeatedly. Finally, Erin narrated the events on the video, jurors and spectators groaning at Fields' thwacking. Silence reigned as Mac's inert body, awkwardly bent, was trundled out on a handcart, her hair flopping over the edge like Raggedy Ann. Finally dismissed, she exited the courtroom as Lawson called Detective Christopher Snow, who had been sequestered in an anteroom with Zachery Fields and Sonja Hamilton during Erin's testimony.

Mac hurried home to give Shadow a workout on equipment that CPD members had assembled and erected in the woods behind the bungalow: a three-foot section of thirty-inch PCP pipe, partially buried and covered with bark; three upright tires lashed together; a ladder leading to a platform three feet off the ground with a slide on the other side with splash-down in the kiddie pool (until frost); a woodpile, a squat hunter's blind with a stuffed scarecrow inside, and eleven acres of woods—a host of hideouts for bits of clothing and contraband for Shadow to find. Kauffman had given Mac an ounce of weed and snow for her puppy to sniff and search. For the next workout, Erin would hide the drugs for Shadow to find. Afterwards, the pup crashed in the mudroom.

The K-9 training contest loomed in two weeks—right before Halloween. Shadow's workouts grew longer as her attention span increased. She located Erin's sneakers, Chris's ratty football jersey from high school, Erica's old slippers, a garden trowel rubbed with marijuana, a piece of a frayed baby blanket and other objects. Shadow could also follow hand signals well, except for "Leave it!" Seemed the dog was just too curious to let an interesting or noxious odor alone; her whole body quivered with each new find, alive or dead: a wounded robin hopping under the holly bush, painfully dragging a damaged wing or a butterfly hovering over the St. John's Wort. Shadow had gulped a quaking baby bunny before Erin could utter a word. In the creek, trout scuttled swiftly away when Shadow leapt for them. When curious children approached, Erin explained, "Shadow isn't a pet but a police dog in training. You should never approach a strange animal, not knowing what its reaction might be." Since the shepherd wagged her tail, she usually let the child pat the puppy's back.

As usual, the other handlers who'd be attending the training exercise were men. "Well, stand aside, men; look out world, here we come!" No longer nimble in this advanced stage of pregnancy, Mac would have to rely on voice commands and hand signals. She hoped Shadow would concentrate and pass the tests, since she couldn't go on an actual mission until Kauffman certified her. Erin started putting the pup through basic commands in public: at schools, in mall parking lots and along downtown sidewalks.

The halter leash gave Mac more control and more warning whenever the dog grew distracted or ignored her commands. She planned to take Shadow to lunch at The Ragged Edge, her dad's coffeehouse, when she met her former college roommate in Gettysburg. The outdoor patio would be an excellent test of the dog's response to the distractions of the noise, conversations and pedestrians hurrying along the sidewalk. And the million tourists who streamed into her hometown to soak up the ambiance, stroll through the town and outlets to shop and eat, visit the wax museum, take the ghost tour or trail through Dwight and Mamie Eisenhower's home—commenting on the couple's separate bedrooms—and attend the Civil War reenactments in July. The year-round denizens who lived, worked, and attended college there, many who depended on tourists, complained about the added traffic and strangers who wandered around reading brochures, checking events or any number of other activities. But they knew who buttered their bread.

"All the more to test Shadow's attentiveness," Erin said aloud.

3

Finding homemade marina sauce in a Mason jar in the fridge, Erin thawed and boiled ravioli, drained and layered it in a casserole dish. She nuked the sauce, poured it over, grated cheese over that and eased it into the oven. A basket by the door held the last of the garden veggies. Deciding to sauté squash, peppers, scallions and corn, she selected one of each. "Do thank Erica for these," she reminded herself.

The Jeep rumbled into the drive around seven p.m. Chris stopped in the mudroom, tugging his tie from his neck and peeling his shirt off to splash soap and water on his face and hands. Entering the kitchen, he hugged his wife. "Hmm. Something smells heavenly. Hey, I'll do that." He slid a butcher knife from the block and chopping board from the cabinet and thinly sliced the vegetables. He raked them into the pan once the olive oil wrinkled, adding a dash of sea salt, pepper and a shake of Italian seasoning. He poured iced tea while Erin set the table.

"Were you in court all afternoon?" Erin cut her pasta and forked in a mouthful. "Erica made this delightful sauce; it was waiting in the fridge. It's superbly seasoned with oregano, garlic, onion and basil. I ought to feel guilty. She spoils us."

"Hmm. She and Dad make vats of it, can or freeze it—and viola: Italia in a jar! No, Savage and I combed over the crime scene again and then went to our Jane Doe's postmortem. Not much to go on: she was stabbed but has no defensive wounds; either she was unconscious or accosted from behind. Her body was in the water for hours. The only distinguishing mark is a tattoo on her left ankle. She looks Native American—her long black hair had tangled in the tree roots under the bridge. Five-seven.

High, sharp cheekbones, a dusky complexion. I'm guessing she was dumped after she was killed." He shook his head as if to dispel the images, at least during dinner.

"How are you doing? I watched your testimony; you were reliving the kidnapping." He left unsaid his concern over her tart remarks that elicited Lyons's outburst in court.

Erin saw his eyes drop to his plate. "I'm OK. Talking about it actually helps because Lyons will be put where she belongs; I'll feel safer with her behind bars. If that sounds callous, well..."

"Not at all. She put you and our baby in danger. But if the 'diminished capacity' defense sails, her sentence may be more lenient, but she'll do enough time to think about her behavior. Savage can't fathom why she'd do something so bizarre—throw away all she's worked for; he thinks she had a mental breakdown. She had no priors."

"People keep saying that. And yet the evidence is solid. You saw the video, found the evidence at the cabin." Erin made a moue of discontent; her face tightened, anticipating sympathy for the criminal.

"Your camcorder's the clincher. I don't doubt the evidence, but..."

"You doubt me."

"You're sure the person in that ninja costume was Alison?"

"And who else would it be? Those sisters were in it together."

"You testified that Abigail was impaired." His eyes matched Shadow's when the pup watched expectantly for Mac's instructions, anticipating her response.

"Not literally. I meant drugged, hypnotized, spaced out —whatever." Erin flicked her wrist in dismissal. She'd stopped eating, her appetite gone. "They're also tied to Mindy Murphy's homicide. I just can't prove it yet." She pushed back from the table. "Be sure to thank your mother for the marina sauce."

"Yet? You're not finished?" he asked.

"No longer hungry. Zach and I need to track down a pink sweater missing a fleur-de-lis button. The Murphy case is five months old! What if they get away with it?" She set her plate in the sink. With a solid kick, the baby knocked her away from the counter. Erin gasped, grasping her distended belly with one hand, her back with another, as a muscle spasm ripped up her back. Behind her instantly, Chris gently rubbed her back, sat down and eased her onto his lap. Working his thumbs in circles at the base of her spine, he massaged slowly, easing up to her shoulders and neck until the tension eased. She leaned against him.

"Sorry, no more shop talk tonight. How about soaking in the tub? Come on; I'll dump in some stress-relief salts and help you climb in. I'll let Shadow out and clean the kitchen. You worked Shadow when you came home, didn't you? You're worn out; I should have noticed." Good as his word, he filled the tub as she undressed and tied her hair up, steadied her while she eased into the scented swirling water, lighted a lavender-scented candle and left. Sliding down into the heat, she tried to shelve work for the moment.

"Know what?" she murmured, "Your and Shadow's eyes are identical." She closed her eyes, laid back and envisioned the deep liquid amber—honey and bourbon eyes. *Be careful, don't let your hormones rule. Get your emotions under control. Or you're in for a long winter of discontent chasing unanswered questions.* In another month, she'd be on maternity leave, so she had to find that pink sweater the killer wore when clubbing Murphy to death.

And when baby makes three, the challenges would multiply. She let the water calm her, buoy her body and soothe the aches and quiet the baby. Water, the metaphor for cleansing and life's journey: "We share the same river of life..." The motor's hum provided enough white noise to distract her; the jets gently pummeled her shoulders and lower back. Cleansing scents of eucalyptus and rosemary exploded as soap bubbles burst in the humid air. By the time Chris reappeared with a warmed towel, she had sponged off. He flicked the drain lever, poured fresh water into a watering can and rinsed her off, wrapped her in a warm cottony cloud, patted her body dry, caressing the soft, rounded sensual parts, and led her to bed, rhapsodizing about the photos he'd taken of her.

4

The landline beside their bed shrilled loudly. Chris grabbed the handset. "Snow. Yes, sir. I'll be there in twenty."

"Whazzit?" Erin squinted her eyes against dawn's early light.

"No need to get up yet. I have to report to HQ. Hotline has a tip on a woman who reported her mother missing and wants to ID the body.

"What time is it?" Drugged by sleep and dreams, she wasn't ready to rise. Her cumbersome body, anchoring her to the mattress, needed the warm nest for a few more minutes while she surfaced mentally.

"Almost seven. "I'll let Shadow out, start the coffee." Chris disappeared. Muffled thumping, grinding, a door opening, Shadow's nails clicking on the back door. Coffee dripping. Returning footsteps. Shifting to her side, she watched her husband shave, the hum of the razor soothing. Then he stepped out of his boxers, into the shower and toggled the lever. The shower spurted to life, blurring the stall doors.

Erin heaved herself into a sitting position, and then pushed off the mattress, trying to clear her head. Poured and doctored coffee into go cups. Pulled yogurt from the fridge and spooned it down. Made peanut-butter toast for Chris and laid a banana beside his plate.

He emerged, buttoning his shirt. Bit off a chunk of toast. "Thanks, babe. Can you come to work later? I've got to motor." He tucked his pistol into a paddle holster in the hollow of his back with his right hand while looping a tie around his neck with his left.

"Yeah. What's the victim's name?" Erin asked as she lathered peanut butter on a granola bar. "Hey, you want a bag for your breakfast?" She watched him juggle the coffee, toast and fruit.

"No, thanks." He slid into a sport coat, stuck the banana under his arm, the toast in his mouth and lifted the coffee as he headed out. "Don't have an ID yet. See you later, babe."

She turned to refill her mug. Stilled when she felt hair lifted off her neck and Chris's lips brushing the nape, up her neck and along her jaw until they found her lips. "Had to have a taste. Love you."

Nails scrabbling at the door demanded her attention. "What did you find out there, girl?" Shadow dropped a field mouse at her foot. "Well, gee, thanks. Leave it!" Erin scooped the rodent onto a dustpan and dumped into the trash bin in the garage. The stainless bowls clanked together. "Yes, Shadow, I know—food." Erin dumped the rest of the bag into the bowl, ran water from the spigot over the laundry tub. "Add dog food to the grocery list." She hopped into the shower to wash her hair.

The landline interrupted her shower. "Hello?" Erin stood dripping, awkwardly drying her hobbit-like body one-handed.

"I wanted to catch you before you left for work. I'll be brief. Would you like to come up this Saturday to help put up apples? Make applesauce, pies and dumplings? Chris can help with the nut harvest. His dad will be harvesting pumpkins. How are you doing?"

"Sure, Erica. We're fine. Getting dressed. Chris left already. Oh, thanks for the marinara sauce and veggies. That's very kind of you."

"Oh, we make batches, and you're welcome. I remember being a working mom, hectic schedules and hurried dinners. Won't hold you, then. Have a good day. See you Saturday."

"Bye." Erin was surprised but pleased her mother-in-law requested help as they ended the call. "I could eat apple dumplings a la mode sprinkled with cinnamon and nutmeg for breakfast!" She admitted to herself, and then replaced the handset and dressed in a flared sweater and cords. Packed turkey sandwiches and apples for lunch in new insulated bags. Lifted Shadow's harness off its hook, clicked her tongue, grabbed her coffee and donned a fleece vest.

At work, she settled Shadow on her cushion, poured water into her pan, and laid a gourmet dog biscuit beside it. The puppy moseyed around the space, nosing the potpourri on Mac's desk. "Leave it." She put the mix on top of her filing cabinet. The dog backed away, sniffed in the corners, at her coat pockets and along the windowsill. The dog nosed the biscuit and then ignored it.

Mac reviewed the evidence left in Mindy's file. Ordinarily it would've been shelved as a cold case, but Mac had time. "Where would I hide an expensive sweater?" she mused aloud when she heard discordant voices in the hallway, one of them Chris's. She listened; the other voice sounded young. "You mean I drove all the way down here and you won't let me see the body?"

Shadow strayed to the hall, cocked her head to one side—brown eyes locked on the stranger. Erin gave her hand signals to sit and stay. She obeyed, but her tail thumped her objection.

"I need some proof of your claim. How do you know she's your mother? We can't just put a body on public display for people to view," Snow said.

"What proof?"

"Driver's license, photos, dental records, x-rays, birth certificate—that sort of thing."

"I have mine." The young lady with straight ebony hair falling nearly to her waist had her back to Mac, who stood in the doorway of her office. Chris looked discomfited, sounded preoccupied. His eyes shifted to his wife's and then back. "Anya Lightfoot." Lightfoot was dressed in an ivory fisherman's sweater and doeskin leggings with matching boots.

"Well, this tells me who you are. Let's go into my office and sort this out." He gestured toward the open door, light spilling out, framing their profiles. He shook his head at Mac, who returned to her office, plucked his lunch off of her desk to deliver to him. "Shadow, come."

"Oh, you're busy. I brought your lunch." She smiled sweetly at him. The young woman turned and faced Mac; her eyes roved over Shadow. Goosebumps crawled along Erin's arms and neck. Except for the dark hair, dusky skin and golden eyes, she could be looking at her own reflection. Each studied the other as the minutes ticked by. Erin took a step and extended her hand. "Hello, I'm Detective Erin McCoy. Shadow, sit." Lightfoot swiveled her head toward Snow, who stood when Mac entered. The women were nonplussed at each other's appearance.

"Anya Lightfoot."

"Please, ladies sit down. Let's sort this out. Are you OK with the dog's presence?" Lightfoot nodded. When everyone had resumed his and her seats, he continued. "Maybe you can give us some background about yourself, your family."

"Of course. I'm at Dickinson Law School. My parents participated in the consecration of the Native burial grounds at the former Carlisle Indian Industrial School last weekend. Perhaps you heard? People from thirty nations attended. They also had a Harvest powwow and dinner at Fort Hunter. We all helped. My brother, a freshman at Dartmouth, is a hoop dancer. At dusk, we conducted the ceremony at the children's burial site to usher their spirits along their journey. So sad, they died of broken hearts, as well as childhood diseases like TB, measles and the flu. Wrenched from their families when Director Pratt relocated Native children and housed them in army barracks, they were lost and homesick! He tore them from their culture, people and language—to be assimilated into your white world."

"Sorry, Miss Lightfoot, could you just give us the basics?" he asked.

Instead, she turned to Mac, and asked, "Are we related? Can you see the similarity between us?"

Mac nodded. "Almost like looking into a mirror. Continue, please. You have my undivided attention." She darted a subtle glance at Snow. "Tell us about your mother." The pup woofed; Erin quieted her by stroking her neck.

"She works for the SRBC." Lightfoot noticed Snow's frown. "She's an agent of the Susquehanna River Basin Commission in charge of policing the waterways, ensuring that companies don't dump toxins in the river or its tributaries. Dad's a national wildlife preservationist and artist.

"When they first met, he arrested mother for sleeping in a National Park without a permit because she grew belligerent. Anyway, that was over twenty years ago. I'm twenty; Pierce is nineteen. Mother was supposed to be canoeing the river, testing for pollutants, water usage and levels—that sort of thing. She parked our little RV along the river and has a cabin at Indian Steps. Dad went home —back to work. When none of us heard from her, we filed a missing persons report."

"Where is home?" Mac asked.

"Near Sayre, Pennsylvania, but my parents are away a lot. So here I am. Is the body one of my people's?"

"Where is your Dad? Shouldn't he be identifying his wife's body?"

"He's upstate shooting wildlife photos, tranqing and tagging animals to track their movements. He has a cell, but the voice mail's full—so it's taking no calls. Who knows? It could be dead or charging. When Jason Lightfoot's prowling and in the zone, he tends to forget other issues temporarily."

"What's your mother's name?" asked Mac.

"We won't call out her name; her restless spirit would return."

"I understand," Mac said. "Write it down."

Snow handed Lightfoot a pad and pen. She wrote and returned the pad to him, laid the pen on his desk. He read the name and looked at his wife for a minute and handed the top sheet to her. "Now we need your dad's phone number and addresses of the Sayre domicile, RV and cabin."

The words read Ahnai Slaughter Lightfoot.

"The RV site doesn't have an address; it's opposite a little place named Winfield between Sunbury and Lewisburg along the river. She keeps the key in a metal tin attached to the frame underneath the steps. For the cabin, key's in a knot hole of a sycamore near the back door." She jotted the address on the pad, plus her dad's.

"Did she ever mention Ethan McCoy to you?" asked Mac.

"Ah, Golden Bear. You must be Red Fox."

"Unless you can provide some verification, I can't show you the body," Snow said. He handed her a card. "You may fax or post records as well."

Mac frowned. "But I can." The dog loped after her handler.

"That's not a good idea—" but he spoke to air, as Mac had vanished. "Please remain seated, Ms. Lightfoot." He picked up the phone and punched in the morgue. "Mac's on her way down to view our Jane Doe."

"She is your wife?" asked Lightfoot. "Carrying your child?"

"You're very observant."

"It's obvious. You both wear rings, she brought you lunch, and she's heavy with child. You are like Dawn in her eyes. Yours are harder to read; you are a serious man with Winter's name and a stern face, but your eyes melt like honey when they watch her. Opposites must attract. And the shepherd?"

"Yes, we're having our first child. Mac is Shadow's handler." Snow smiled with pride, and then frowned. "I should go down with her." He stood. "Support her, if Jane Doe is…"

"Good." She stood. "Let's go together. But Red Fox is stronger than you think. She can handle this task if Cherokee blood runs in her veins. She must favor her father, for Mother said there was none of her in her firstborn. And I agree."

"Do you know Grandmother Slaughter?" asked Snow.

"In Shaconage, place of Blue Smoke, North Carolina? She and Lame Deer live in the Smokies, near—"

"In the Qualla Boundary near the Oconaluftee River. We spent our honeymoon with her. Neither she, Buck or Raven mentioned you or your family. And we saw no photos—"

"Why rub salt in the wound? Though she has never said, Grandmother does not approve of the way Mother left the Boundary, her people, or Golden Bear, but Ahnai doesn't like constraints. Neither does Grandmother speak of Red Fox to us."

"Why do you call her that? Her name is Erin."

"Erin I do not know, but my mother called her first daughter that. Sometimes she described her as Bear Cub too, as a baby. Her hair signifies sun, fire and passion in our culture." Lightfoot glanced at her watch and stood. "I have class soon but shall return when I have proof. You will release her body then. Thanks for your time."

Mac appeared in the doorway with Shadow. "I can't be certain. Our Jane Doe has Native American features, but she's not as tall as I remember and heavier. Of course, that could be—"

"Because you were a child when she left," Lightfoot finished Mac's sentence. "She's gained thirty pounds since then. I shall return as soon as I can obtain some of Mother's records. Understand my parents are nomads, sometimes difficult to reach. One or both could be gone for months at a time. Pierce and I are adults. We're not going to break down because we accept death as part of life. Yes, we're sad, but we must send her spirit on its journey."

"Our policies are meant to protect families' privacy. You understand why we need physical records. We don't want to make a mistake or jump to unwarranted conclusions," Snow said. He glanced from one woman to the other, the resemblance uncanny. Both were the same height, had the same oval face and pointy chin with heads angled slightly, similar stances and body structure. Lightfoot's long dark hair, sharper planes of cheeks, jaw line and cat's eyes set her apart. A living embodiment of a conflicted past was reflected in her attitude.

"I know whites consider my people exotic—They stare at or ignore us. We're revered at times for our lifestyle and our past or dismissed, considered noble or savage. We're anomalies spouting quaint aphorisms, outliers who remind you of America's holocaust. We've survived 500 years of oppression, repression, attempted annihilation, relocation, and assimilation. Now we're reclaiming some of our lands and ways." On the last, she smiled. "I want to claim my mother. Good day."

"You're preaching to the choir here," Mac added. "Let me walk you out."

"No need. I can retrace my steps," Lightfoot said as she turned abruptly and left, her confident footfalls padding down the hall.

"What do you think? How do you feel?" Chris asked.

"I'm not sure. A kaleidoscope of feelings: sad that this young woman lost her mother; uneasy if she's my mother, but I can't grieve 'cause I don't recognize her. I resent that she apparently had a fulfilling life without Dad and me. That she built another family." She parked her hip on the desk beside her husband's chair. "But I can't wallow in that."

He eased her onto his lap and wrapped his arms around her. "Sounds reasonable. We can't know what kind of family life they had. As she said, her parents were often away; the kids might have been on their own a good bit. You're sisters, you know. She described Grandmother and Buck in some detail. She's visited Cherokee. One thing, she has attitude in spades. She'll make one hell of a lawyer."

Erin bussed his lips with her own and stood up, took a deep breath. "I'm OK. Back to work." Snow's intercom buzzed.

"Yes?"

"A courier just dropped a priority package for Mac."

"I'll come out for it. Thanks, Sonja," Mac said.

Snow picked up the receiver and dialed information. "Love you, babe." And into the phone, "Sayre, Pennsylvania." A pause. "Susquehanna River Basin Commission Field Office."

Mac's package held Mindy Miller's husband's taped interview. In her office, she popped it into the recorder and listened to Hunter Woods interrogate the deceased's ex. His irate voice exploded from the machine, "I'm the one who reported her missing! Why would I harm my ex-wife, the mother of my child? We had shared custody!" Hunter calmly questioned him about the couple's history, divorce and Murphy's movements last spring. She pulled the folder; crime scene photos spilled out. Mac took notes, trying to trace the events. No new leads jumped from the tape. "No, don't like the husband for this, unless he's lying, but his reasoning and that passion is hard to fake. Besides no one reported seeing him."

The evidence had burned into her retinas: the pink thread attached to the unique, stamped button, shoe prints, two sets of tire tracks. The vehicle's contents had prints from Luke Flowers, his wife Lindy, and Mindy, plus some unidentified. DNA from the cup and cigarette pack was Mindy's. CPD had found no weapon. Searches of the Flowers, Murphy, Lyons and Benedict domiciles revealed no pink sweater. Her subpoena request to search Abby Benedict and Rye Ralston's Alexandria apartment was denied—no probable cause.

"Until now." Mac dialed Judge Acorn's office and left a message arguing that since the video of her kidnapping had been entered into Evidence, she had probable cause.

"Clearly, Abigail was at that scene. Her home is still the crime scene of an open homicide case. She's obviously complicit in my kidnapping and probably colluded with Lyons on Murphy's demise. She has no alibi for the victim's TOD." Mac left her number for a call back. "Hope she doesn't demand a physical connection because I don't have one." She'd been focused on Lyons so long that she'd let Abby slide. "If only I had a clear trail of evidence."

Her puppy nudged her arm, clicked to the door and whined. Her liquid brown eyes begged. "Okay, let's take a walk. We need a break, don't we, girl?" Erin grabbed a couple of plastic newspaper sleeves, her jacket and Shadow's harness and hustled into the mild, sunshiny October afternoon, huffed around the block and returned to her office fifteen minutes later, sipping water. Shadow lapped noisily from her bowl, flopped down and found the crusty biscuit more inviting.

5

Snow waited in her office, his feet propped on the waste can, index finger tapping his cell phone screen. "Well, well, slacking on the job? Do you want to ride along to Indian Steps with me? We can eat on the way."

"Are you hiding from someone?" Mac asked, peering around. Shadow ambled over and sniffed Chris's Dockers.

"Waiting for you. I sent Savage and Fields north to locate Lightfoot's RV and interview the Sayre Field Office personnel." Lowering his feet to the floor, he pocketed his smart phone and lifted both lunch bags and his wife's backpack. "Let's take the Jeep. Are you really all right?" His pager vibrated. He passed the lunch bags to his wife. He unhooked and glanced at it, picking up Mac's receiver, "What? Uhm, thanks. I'll get it on the way out."

"I'm ambivalent, but biology alone does not a parent make, so I can focus on the job. Shadow, come."

"I meant personally. Wonder what the Chief would say —conflict of interest—if she's your biological mother?"

"There's been no conclusive ID yet," she said, pushing through the side door while her husband turned down the hall to Sonja's desk.

Mac let Shadow attend to business while waiting for Chris to emerge.

He trod across the parking lot. The sun gilded his glossy, brassy hair; he squinted against the sudden glare. "We'll have to detour. Just received a call from a Sandy Ladd about probable evidence at the children's gravesite."

A woman waited inside the black wrought-iron fence, an army officer at ease behind her. Without preamble, she plunged in. "I'm Sandy Ladd, a docent and archivist for the Cumberland County Historical Society. People call from all over the country to visit the former Carlisle

Indian Industrial School site, tracking their ancestors. And I do local tours; today I had a high school group, and one of them noticed the blood." She pointed to the far corner near a line of trees and across some of the grave markers. "I thought it might be connected to that body that Elena Michaels described on the news."

Shadow whined, but Mac kept her at her knee with a sit signal.

Snow blew into the latex gloves and slipped them on while examining brownish maroon drops on the ground and spotting a dozen stone markers. He called a CSU team. "Let the experts test it. But it's blood. Mac." He motioned for her to approach. She stood where he indicated, facing the graves. He came up behind her and pantomimed a possible scenario, "stabbing" her in the heart, following the arc in his mind. "See the minute scallops? Arterial spray." He crouched, shaking his head. "But not as much as I expected. Something blocked the rest."

Ladd blanched at his words.

The officer stepped up. "Afraid any crime committed on Post is a military matter."

"Not if the dump site's in our jurisdiction. Take it up with my boss." He handed over a business card.

Ladd's freckled face paled. "I'll leave you to it." She turned away.

Mac led her from the scene. "Can you answer a few questions?" Ladd nodded tentatively. Mac started the mini recorder. "Did you attend the Native American ceremony here last weekend?"

The woman nodded, turning against the breeze that kicked up; she held her skirt in place. "Yes. I was at Fort Hunter, too. As you know, Native Americans hold powwows during Kipona," an annual festival in Harrisburg, "and travel to various sites instructing us about their culture, history, and language. The Green Corn Festival is usually well attended—nearly a hundred people this year. But this," her hand indicating the cemetery, "was a private, solemn, dignified ceremony for the 192 children buried here."

"So many? Those poor children. That's so tragic. What happened?" Gazing at the rows of simply engraved white gravestones by the side of the road made her heart clinch.

"They died from diseases they had no immunity to fight. And maybe culture shock. Richard Pratt took them from freedom in their tribes and treated them like military recruits. This cemetery is a stark reminder of our own reprehensible treatment of indigenous peoples. Look on my website. In their photos, none of them are smiling. But we do our best to explain his good intentions, which like the Orphan Trains, fell very short of expectations," Ladd's soft voice reported.

"So how many participated in this rite last weekend?"

"Hmm. Maybe twenty-four, though some college students left."

"What did they do here?"

"Formed a semi-circle around." Her arm encompassed the cemetery—a rectangle of ground bordered by a wrought-iron fence along the road. "Said a prayer and chanted in their native tongue. And burned sweet grass and tobacco that wafted across the graves." She pantomimed the gesture. "They sidestepped in harmony with a single drum and chanted—I think it meant good-bye and aided the children's spirits along their path. And the occasion seemed to affirm their people's shared past and a sense of community."

"Did you recognize anyone?"

"Several, yes. Anya Lightfoot volunteers at the historical society on weekends. She introduced me to her family. Another couple, the Dietzes, come every year to visit schools in our area. Another, an Iroquois who sells cars for a living—Littlejohn, I think he said, attended for the first time. Several from the Dakotas, Oklahoma and North Carolina made the long trip." She shrugged. "It was dusk. They dress in full regalia and use their native names and speak in their native tongues. For them, it's also a reunion of sorts, or communion. Coming together in kinship that includes all peoples."

"Impressions?"

"They were quiet, courteous and respectful. Patient and polite, answering questions—educating us all. They ask for nothing, yet give their time freely. The Carlisle Indian Industrial School is like a magnet; people want to know about its history." She shifted her weight, waiting.

"The Lightfoots?" Mac didn't want to ask leading questions, but they needed information. The women backed away as the CSU vehicle pulled in and men unloaded gear.

"Anya's bright and energetic—yet offends easily, quick to defend her people. Pierce and Jason, her brother and father, are quiet. But her mother is stunning and knows it. The family ate together at Fort Hunter, but that was the only time I saw all four of them together. Can't say I noticed much. People were milling around, asking me questions, directions to the base, the War College and Heritage Center, and buying art and artifacts—that sort of thing. I was working, you see."

"What was Mrs. Lightfoot wearing?"

"She goes by Slaughter," Ladd corrected gently. "Ivory doeskin sheath with matching boots and a beautiful, multi-colored shawl that she wore in the fancy dance. The dancers hold them out like wings." She spread her arms straight and bent at the knees to illustrate. "You haven't seen one?" Reading Mac's blank expression, she explained. "A number of women dance in unison, their feet stepping in tune to drums while the men chant. It's quite impressive. The dancers look like they might take flight. It's moving; I even felt my spirits rise." Her eyes fluttered as white-clothed techs fanned out, gathering evidence and stepped back again.

"Did you notice anyone following her? Or any strange behavior?"

She shook her head; her eyes widened. "She's your homicide?"

"We need to verify. Did Jason Lightfoot participate in any way?"

"Oh, yes, at Fort Hunter, he demonstrated weapons, let people shoot his bow and displayed his painting and wildlife photography. I bought a little acrylic of a canoe beside stone steps at a bend in the Susquehanna." Her index fingers and thumbs framed a ten by twelve.

"What was he wearing?"

"A buckskin shirt with leather ties at the neck and blue jeans."

"He didn't drum or dance?"

"No, his son did this complicated dance with ten hoops while Anya narrated how the hoop celebrated the circle and unification of life."

"Anything else you'd like to add?" Mac asked. She released Shadow. Ladd shook her head. "No? Here's my card if you think of anything else."

***

Mac and Snow perched on the Indian Steps at an elbow in the Susquehanna, marveling at the blaze of russet, orange, gold and scarlet leaves shifting and whispering in trees along both banks. The curling current reflected a carnival of colors as leaves parachuted down and sailed downstream. The couple crossed the road and returned to the vehicle. Snow coasted until they found the number on the mailbox, the cabin seven steps down, nearly twenty yards farther. "Ten to one, our vic's murder site's back at the gravesite."

"Did CSU collect anything else?"

He shrugged. "They were still working when we left. I hope they find the Vic's clothes."

"Shit, the door's open!" Mac donned gloves and eased inside without touching the knob. The cabin had been ransacked. Books, maps, and papers dumped from bookcases, cushions and pillows slashed, the fill disgorged. Native artifacts had been dumped on the floor, the paintings turned around, but the perp left a hand-made bow mounted above the fireplace. In the left corner,

41

the galley kitchen's floor was littered with pans, dented cans and spilled dry goods. A similar wreck lay beyond the arch to the bedroom—pillows, blankets and towels strewn about and the adjoining bath, toiletries spilled helter-skelter.

Snow unsnapped his phone, reporting the crime—alerting local police and seeking an assist, requesting a CSU team to the site. He drew on latex and used a pen to lift and turn items. "Please get your camera to document this." They spent the remainder of daylight photographing, perusing contents and looking for clues. He turned one painting around: A lone brave wearing breechclouts squatted beside a birch bark canoe, applying pitch to the seams. The river a silver sliver reflecting greens, gold and rust. In the lower right corner, the initials JL were twigs anchoring three autumn leaves.

"It's the husband's," Mac breathed. "The acrylics make colors jump off the canvas." She knelt and turned another. A nude woman with ebony hair streaming water droplets and hands cupping her a swollen belly stood in a roiling, narrow stream staring back at the viewer. "Ahnai."

Snow sucked in a breath, emitted a low whistle and nudged his wife's elbow. "Man, the guy's talented. Look at the texture." Layered brushstrokes of green tipped in white swirled into a blue stream, rimmed the bank; touches of bronze and gold illuminated her hair and skin, the droplets silver and white. In an ink sketch leaning against the mantle, two Native American children with short spiked hair, enormous dark eyes, and sharply delineated cheeks wore toddler pouts. "At least whoever did this spared the paintings and this sketch."

"Question is: Did he find what he was looking for?"

"What was he—or she—looking for?" asked Mac.

"Wish I knew. Where would she keep a laptop? I don't see a desk."

"I don't know, but I'll look." In the bedroom, she peeked into every crevice, under the mattress, in the curtained recess of a closet: nothing that would predicate a homicide. "Let's look outside." She let Shadow run and sniff the bushes and nose the fallen leaves that blanketed the area. Her eyes panned, seeking what she knew not. Around back, a seasoned canoe was chained upside down to the cabin from protruding hooks. She peered underneath to check the seat, using a sycamore tree to steady her top-heavy torso. "Hey, Chris, I can't reach this knot hole." She glanced around for something to stand on.

"Let's hope nothing in here can bite." On tiptoes, her husband reached in, felt around and withdrew a key and a thumb drive. "Well, well. I think we found what the perp was looking for." His phone chirped; he had a brief conversation with Savage while passing the drive to Mac. "Yeah, same here. Someone tossed the cabin. Did you find a laptop? No, stay there, call for a subpoena for the work PC. Any leads? A body? Where? Damnation, Savage, why didn't you say that first? Any ID? Did you call it in? Say again, you cut out. An arrow? No shit? Notify HQ; call the locals who have jurisdiction. I don't know; try Lewisburg, but have Fields photograph everything. No, I'm on my way."

Mac's iPhone pinged. She checked the TM: subpoena for Benedict's apartment denied. "Rats. Now what'll I do? Shadow, come." The dog hopped in the back seat; then Erin buckled her in.

Chris climbed in the driver's. "Babe, I'm taking you home. I've got to get to the RV site. The guys found a body shot with an arrow. And Savage is not cleared for field duty, so he can't really investigate. I have to go."

"Just take me to HQ for Silver. Please don't tell me the body's the husband."

"The driver's license says Dean Greer. Savage said he's Caucasian. But you can bet he's connected to our case somehow. Would you examine the thumb drive? See what we got?"

"If I get a kiss and dinner out of it."

They leaned together long enough to bruise lips. "Keep the bed warm. I'll be home by eleven."

"Sure you will."

***

At home, Mac booted her computer after throwing navy beans, tomatoes, tomato paste, and pasta in a pot with Italian seasonings to simmer. Changed into stretchy knits. By the time she refreshed her monitor, the drive spewed spreadsheets, data and records of business contacts Slaughter had accumulated over the past five years: a dozen Marcellus Shale drill sites, TMI, an agribusiness named Hamm's Meat and Poultry, a grist mill, lumber yard, a hydroelectric company and others. Luckily, Slaughter had typed asterisks beside those she'd found lacking or questionable. Next to each company, she'd listed the specific violation, date and name of the CEO or rep she dealt with, plus the traits of each person. Plus reference numbers for letters written about the numbers and type of violations.

When the timer buzzed, Erin tossed in spinach leaves to wilt, scooped a bowl of pasta e fagioli, carried it upstairs and read for hours until her eyes crossed and Shadow nosed her arm to go out. They walked into beauty —the night a mosaic of muted colors, a starry navy sky overhead, and a few gauzy clouds flitted across a gibbous moon. The serenity of the moment calmed her senses until Shadow bounded back in. Locking the back door, both turned in.

Dawn spilled golden light into their bedroom; Chris's warm fingers trailed along her body, which was spooned against his. A sudden urge awakened her fully as his hands slowly inched the knit fabric up, touching her slowly, tenderly. Reaching behind, she felt his naked form and turned. Wordlessly, they pleasured each another without bothering baby.

Over breakfast of yogurt, fruit and granola parfaits, they discussed the case. Mac summarized the drive's contents, and Snow brought her up to speed on the

Winfield and Sayre sites. "Tracking this will require every homicide detective on the force. We need to interview all the people she investigated. Savage and Fields already deposed the SRBC Field Office staff and commandeered her PC. Apparently Lightfoot spent most of her time in the field, so staff members displayed no threat," Chris said.

"Ladd said she went by Slaughter. And Dean Greer is on the West Enterprises' payroll, so we'll have to locate his supervisor," she said. "Did you find anything helpful at the RV site connecting Greer and Slaughter?"

Chris gathered their dishes, rinsed and slid them into the dishwasher. Topped off their decaf. "I have to stop at Sheetz for caffeine; this stuff isn't doing anything for me. Still feel groggy. Shall I shower first?"

"Okay, I'll heat soup; you can pick up sandwiches, too. Our fridge is bare, unless you want a cheese sandwich. Oh, and your mom wants our help Saturday, you harvesting nuts, me in the kitchen with apples. Though we could switch, if you prefer. I enjoy nutting." She smiled contentedly, kissed his shoulder as he passed, her hand brushing the topic of conversation.

"You little minx! I don't want you climbing trees until junior is born." He cradled her distended belly.

"Junior? We're not calling him that, are we?"

"No, but I'd like Christopher to be his middle name."

"Ok, then I pick the first."

"You have one in mind?"

"Ethan after Dad, Ian or I'm considering Dylan. I like Elliot, too."

"After the singer?"

"No, the poet: 'Do not go gentle into that good night.'"

"He'd carry both our dads' names. I like them all." Chris disappeared.

Erin heated and ladled the pasta soup into thermoses, and then poured the rest of the coffee into another. "I'd prefer caffeine, too, but mustn't make baby hyper." Showered quickly. She selected green slacks and a heavy, blousy sweater. They slipped out the door half an hour

45

later, puppy in tow and Abby's case study in hand; the car idled at the convenience store while Chris grabbed a turkey sandwich for Erin and roast beef for himself, then they motored on to the CPD headquarters.

On the way, she opened Abby's thesis to the post-it marking her spot:

And though April remained her darling, mother drifted away mentally into a world of her own creation, one that turned out differently. Such breaks with reality were prefaced with terms like, "If only I had married my high-school sweetheart. He's a millionaire, Texas A&M." She'd stare dreamily out the window, mending rips in dresses, braiding hair or the cooking forgotten. Clearly, after the divorce, I was a loadstone around her neck, whereas April was her salvation. She envisioned a modeling contract and comfort for her and her eldest, not realizing that her source of income was about to disappear. With that shock came depression, despair and hardship, alleviated somewhat by her own family's handouts, until her divorce attorney informed her of ways to milk her ex for years. She cried, wailed, kited checks, and worked part-time. But what job can compare to dreams she had spun?

As a result, my dad became a misogynist. He despised her and her tricks, called her a vampire for her battle tactics. After hitting the bottom mentally, financially, physically and psychologically, Dad and I drove to the cold, forbidding north, because he found a job in D.C. and a modest apartment where we stayed for two years, and then he snapped a house off the market on a short sale on the edge of Carlisle in a wooded neighborhood with several acres. Mature fir trees lined the drive for added privacy. Workmen added a security system, steel front and back doors with deadbolts, and a built-in safe in the unfinished basement.

Dad went to work; I went to school. Days unspooled slowly, despite my chores and homework assignments. At 7:30 p.m., when Dad's Dodge swerved into the drive, I set the table. While he fixed dinner, he asked about my day and quizzed me on what I'd accomplished. I was lonely but tried to adjust and avoid doing anything that would call attention to myself because we'd assumed new identities.

"As long as we keep a low profile, we'll be fine. Do you want me to find a sitter? Would that make you more comfortable?" He must have sensed my loneliness in solitude.

I shook my head vehemently. "I'm eleven. I can manage myself, but a dog would be great!" After I wheedled and whined for months, we bought Goldie. And then an Explorer. For a while, the puppy occupied most of our leisure time. We fed, walked and trained the golden retriever day and night in sun, rain and snow. We built her a doghouse and tucked it against the back of the house, where the upstairs deck protected it.

During junior high school, the bullying began. A shy outsider with a Texas drawl and braces, I endured name-calling, tricks and lies that catty girls devised. A loner anyway, I decided I liked the solitude—time to think and plan little devious pranks to amuse myself. I put worms in the ringleader's locker, threw another's wallet into a commode, and scribbled graffiti across another's notebook while she mooned about a JV wrestler.

By the time I entered high school, my studies netted outstanding grades, and my teachers and coaches praised my skills and efforts. As children from the Army War College filtered through, I was no longer considered different. Most accepted me. Of course, by then, the dye was set: I'd learned to plan well ahead for any contingencies. I applied for a dozen scholarships and grants. With waitress tips and assistance from Father, I attended Penn State for my undergrad degree in psychology.

6

Benedict's case study clutched under her arm, Mac arrived at HQ—Shadow patiently waiting at her side—and handed the thumb drive to Sonja. "Would you please print multiple copies of everything on this? Let's start with six, front to back. It may be a lot."

"Sure thing. When do you need them?"

"Sorry for the short notice: for the briefing at nine. Start with the info on Slaughter's business contacts, the ones with violations on the Marcellus Shale companies and CEOs listed. Then the rest as you get them done in the order she has them listed."

"And how are mother and baby doing?"

"Oh, baby's kicking is keeping mother awake at night."

"When's your due date?"

"November 29th."

"Well, you're in the home stretch. The last month is the hardest—the baby's putting pressure on your back, bladder and diaphragm. Good news is that it's almost over. Did you see today's paper?" She walked over to the behemoth copier, turned it on. "I'd better get busy." And then she plugged the drive into her PC port.

"Me, too. See you later. Shadow, come." Mac glanced at *The Patriot's* front-page headline: "Jury Finds Lyons Guilty of Kidnapping." She scanned the article while heading to her office. Sentencing was scheduled for tomorrow. "Finally, I can relax on that score." Erin sighed, since that weight had been removed.

Her computer listed emails from Fields about shelving the Murphy case to focus on their current ones, a summary from Savage about his Sayre findings, and one from Anya about a courier delivering dental records and Dr. Chen about postmortem results: "Deceased had been

stabbed several times with an ice pick or similar weapon
—the first to the heart, piercing the left ventricle, the fatal
blow. I sent semen to the lab for DNA analysis. Nothing
recoverable from fingernails, so perp likely assaulted her
from behind. Letort was the dumpsite; the murder site
would have presented more blood, i.e., arterial spray."

At the CPD briefing, Shadow followed Mac into
Conference One, snuffled around the perimeter and
finally plopped down between her and Snow.
Occasionally, Chris dropped his hand to scratch her
neck. Savage and Fields tried subtly to track the dog's
movements in their peripheral vision.

The Chief assigned Savage and Fields to continue
interviewing along the Northern Tier, Les to work with
locals on the Greer homicide, and Snow and McCoy to
examine Slaughter's connections on the thumb drive. Les
bulleted salient points on the white board as the group
discussed what they'd learned so far.

"This data on her job—any of it helpful?" asked the
Chief. He lifted the collated stack of paper and looked
from Snow to Mac, as if expecting them to summarize the
contents for the team.

"Fresh off the printer, sir," Snow commented. "We
haven't begun to wade through it. It will take some time
to sort out the information, and Sonja is still copying the
spreadsheets of the Marcellus Shale sites in the
Susquehanna River Basin, the companies involved and
the violations cited. Any criminal activity or impropriety
points to a motive to silence her."

"Is there a way to weed out some sites or companies to
a manageable number? Where do you propose to begin?"
asked LT Stuart.

"She's marked the most egregious and numerous
violations of the shale gas/energy companies, noted dates
she met with the reps, names and phone numbers of her
contacts and notations about each person. For example,
the deceased at the RV, one Dean Greer, is listed as Field

Technician for West Enterprises, an active well. The company has the third highest number of citations."

"Les, you can work that angle with the lead—what's his name—on the Greer crime scene?"

"Carl Imhoff," said the LT. "Yes, sir."

The Chief continued. "Find out why Greer was at Lightfoot's RV. Was it business or pleasure? Could be both. Get someone to fax or email us his autopsy results. I want to know where the murder weapon is. Dr. Chen, any other pertinent facts about the autopsy?"

"No, sir. My report is complete, except for the DNA results and tox screen, which, as you know, takes two weeks. When we find the semen donor, we'll have more information, but I wouldn't assume he's the murderer, as there was no trauma to the vaginal area. My conclusion is that sex was consensual. Abrasions on her back and arms could have come from falling or being dragged later."

LT Stuart updated the info on the whiteboard.

"Anyone trying to track down the murder site?" asked March.

"The daughter said she last saw her mother at a Native American ceremony honoring the children who died at the former Carlisle Indian School. Mac and I talked with the historical society's docent, who noticed blood during a high-school tour. The CSU collected evidence, which I sent to the lab while Mac skimmed the thumb drive we found at her cabin at Indian Steps," Snow volunteered.

"All right. Have them search for her clothes. Mac, plow through the paperwork; prioritize possible suspects and give the list to whoever is assigned that area. Stuart, Savage and Fields—the Sayre and RV sites, McCoy and Snow follow-up the Indian Steps site. Track down the husband. Until I hear otherwise, he's our prime suspect. I'll bet he's proficient with a bow.

"Savage, Fields—anything germane to add to our workload or our trove of information?" Chief March asked.

"No leads, if that's what you mean. We're pouring over the office PC but haven't found anything indicating a motive for murder. Slaughter did, however, work out of the Sayre office but spent more time in the field," Savage said. "We're now a kennel?" he asked in an aside to Fields, who shrugged.

A sudden commotion out front brought Shadow to her feet, growling, and trotting out the door—nails clicking on the hall. She charged into the main office—barking and snarling at the raised voices, Mac right behind. The stranger inside the doorway, about six-two, had thick black hair combed back off his forehead and tied behind, a sun-leathered visage, hazel-green eyes and a hawk nose. He wore a v-neck buckskin shirt with leather laces, a rawhide necklace threaded through an old stone arrowhead and jeans.

Shadow caused him to tone down his rhetoric. He spoke to her in his native tongue and gave her the "sit" signal. Though she chomped the air, rumbling deep in her throat, she obeyed. As he dug in his pocket, loaded Glocks trained on him, bullets racked into chambers. His left hand shot up, palm out. "A dog biscuit!" He handed it to Mac, who rewarded her puppy. He put his right hand up as well. "I'm unarmed."

"Good girl. Stay. Jason Lightfoot?" Mac asked.

Anger and trepidation showed in his expression. "Don't tell me I can't see my wife! I drove five hours to get here because Anya tells me you have Ahnai's body! Body! God, she was alive when I left her last Friday." He tossed a folder on the counter. "There's proof: birth and marriage certificates, blood type, and photos—everything you asked for. Now take me to her." His jaw clenched.

Petite Dr. Chen, grey hair feathered forward, stepped to the front and held the gate open. "I shall take you to your wife." She gestured demurely, and then led him down the hallway, Detective Snow trailing in their wake.

Frozen while staring at the past resurrected in the flesh, CPD personnel blinked as from dream-waking and returned to their duties. March pulled Mac aside. "Get him in an interview room," he ordered between clenched teeth. "I want Lightfoot's every second accounted for since last Friday."

Mac waited several steps behind Snow and Lightfoot at the morgue's viewing window. The man smelled of sun and rain, of leather and earth, like her uncle. A rawhide strip anchored a single braid of hair at the nape of his neck. Head down, his taut shoulders heaved. Before anyone could blink, he shouldered his way into the morgue and gathered the body into his arms. His tears dripped onto her face, and then he laid her down gently. "I'm taking her with me. Do you have any winding sheets?" He asked the coroner.

"Why don't we wait until you've finalized your plans?" Dr. Chen asked.

Snow interjected. "Not just yet, sir. We need to ask you a few questions, clarify some of our concerns." Calm and clear, his voice allowed no equivocation. Lightfoot nodded reluctantly and followed them upstairs. Once settled with mugs of coffee, the detectives sat opposite him. Snow placed the recorder on the table and identified participants and case information.

"We're really sorry for your loss and hate to intrude on your sorrow at this time, but can you tell us where and when you last saw your wife? And where you've been? We really need a timeline here," Mac said. Lightfoot's eyes leveled on hers, reading her expression.

"All right. We had a powwow at Kipona, then at Fort Hunter—our Green Corn Festival, giving thanks for Nature's bountiful gifts. We demonstrated how our ancestors prepared foods and shared them with the people attending. On the former Carlisle Indian Industrial School grounds, we held a brief ceremony. The women burned tobacco, sweet grass and sage over the children's graves to ease their spirits on their journey. My guide and I left immediately after I bid my family goodbye; we had to track, photograph and tag wildlife crossing the New York state border into Pennsylvania."

"How can we reach this guide to verify?"

"My alibi? He's a professional Seneca guide—leads hunting parties up north, into Canada, usually for two weeks at a time." He reached for his wallet, revealing a knife sheathed in worn leather strapped to his belt. He paged through several business cards, laid the guide's on the table and then his.

Snow picked up both, noticed the professional quality and handed them to Mac. "Okay, then what?"

Lightfoot summarized his movements, reported that his children headed back to Dickinson Law School and Dartmouth College. "Pierce caught a ride with Oneida drummers headed there for a symposium. Dartmouth has a Native American Studies started by the late Professor Michael Dorris. He was also a novelist."

"*Yellow Raft in Blue Water,*" Mac supplied. "He was married to Louise Erdrich."

The man's eyes studied her. "Anya tells me you're my wife's firstborn. I'm truly sorry that she left you and your father."

"Thank you. Do you know what Slaughter planned to do after the ceremony at the cemetery?" She used the surname purposely.

"Get her canoe, take water samples from the Susquehanna near one of the Marcellus Shale well sites, then drive to the RV." He shrugged, his lips thinned. "She doesn't give me her itinerary."

"I hope you won't take offense, but we need to know if you and your wife are living together."

The man smiled ruefully, considered the question. "Not in the sense you imply. Our jobs carry us apart. Her work is tedious; she has 444 miles of river to monitor, investigate and test, and I don't know how many businesses to deal with. Meeting irate Shale Field Technicians and CEOs demands patience. I work for the Commonwealth, Department of Forestry, Northern Tier."

"Is it possible she was having an affair? That someone retaliated? For not revealing that she was married?"

"Anything's possible." The hazel-green eyes hardened.

"Are you seeing other women?"

"No." Lightfoot clenched his hands, dropped them to his lap.

"What's your wife's background? And yours?"

"At first, she majored in chemistry, then switched to geology; my degree's in wildlife management. Surprised?"

"Just acquiring information, sir," Snow answered calmly. Do you know if your wife had arguments, threats, or concerns about her work or any of the people she dealt with?"

"Detective, we spend little time together under one roof."

"So you're separated."

"No."

"Where do you spend most of your time?"

"On the road. My family home's just south of Sayre, as Anya told you. I have a studio in the barn there—like Andrew Wythe. I bunk in the loft when I'm there. I own the Pace Arrow at Winfield; the Indian Steps Cabin is Ahnai's." He emphasized, elongated each syllable: Ah-nah-ee's.

"Do you display or sell your work? You're extremely talented," Mac said to lighten the exchange. Lightfoot glanced at her. "We saw several at the Indian Steps cabin. Have you been there since last Friday?"

"Sometimes to the first question, no to the second. And thank you."

"The cabin had been ransacked. Know anything about that?" asked Snow.

"But whoever did it left your paintings and the ink sketch of the kids intact," Mac added.

Again the man made eye contact with both detectives. "No."

"Any idea who or what might steal valuables from your wife?"

He shook his head and shrugged. "She handled lots of sensitive information regarding her work, but why kill her for that?"

"Good question," Snow said.

After they'd exhausted their queries, the detectives stood. Snow offered his hand, which Lightfoot shook. "Thanks for your time. Where can we reach you if we have more questions?"

Lightfoot pointed his chin toward the cards.

"I assume you can shoot a bow?" Mac asked.

He nodded, angling toward her. "Of course. And a rifle, shotgun and camera. I can paddle a canoe, kayak, track game, and gut a deer as well. I cook, paint, carve, and ride. Why do you ask?"

"Do you own a bow?" Mac persisted.

"Several, yes, one's in the truck. I use it for hunting."

"That seems cruel." She frowned. When Shadow scratched at the door, Mac let her in, signaled her to sit. The dog's amber eyes roved among the speakers, resting on Lightfoot, assessing the situation.

"Why? Don't you shoot rifles? We eat my game. Someone butchers those animals you buy at the grocery. I also tranq and tag wildlife—bears especially to relocate them to safer areas. We humans are encroaching on their habitat, but *we* move *them*, just as the Europeans did to us." His tone relaxed. "Well, if that's all..."

The door banged open, Shadow yelping her surprise and skittered sideways. In walked FBI Special Agent Lionel Howard from the D.C. office. "In that case, you're under arrest. Top o' the day to you, detectives."

Lightfoot frowned as if trying to recollect the stranger's face.

"On what grounds?" Snow's voice hardened.

"Murdering a federal agent."

"No, his wife worked for SRBC," Mac corrected.

"Dean Greer—shot through the heart with one of Lightfoot's arrows."

"Greer's body was found in Winfield along the river, propped against your wife's RV," Snow explained to Lightfoot. "He was a Field Tech at West Enterprises, a Marcellus Shale company."

"That's his day job. He was an undercover DEP agent investigating which Susquehanna River Basin companies are dumping illegal effluence into the river, which runs into the Chesapeake. He and Ahnai Lightfoot reported a host of the Marcellus Shale industry's environmental violations. The graft, drug use and kickbacks are legion," Howard reported.

"She goes by Slaughter," Lightfoot said.

"Why now?" Snow asked. "The EPA has been asleep at the wheel every since Dick Cheney created the Halliburton loophole, exempting the gas and oil industries from most environmental laws."

Howard shot him a poisonous glance without responding.

"Why do you think I am responsible?" asked Lightfoot. "I need to collect my wife's body, plan her funeral."

"Your fingerprints were found on the murder weapon at the crime scene. Someone else can make the arrangements." Howard nodded his head toward Lightfoot; two suits emerged from the hall to shackle his hands behind his back. One intoned the Miranda rights while Shadow voiced her displeasure.

Lightfoot did not resist. "I don't delegate my responsibilities to others. The RV belongs to me. I'm innocent of this charge. I do not shoot people."

"Not even your wife's lover?" Howard said. "Cheerio, chaps." The agent aimed the last at Snow and Mac as the agents ushered Lightfoot down the hall.

"I want a lawyer," Lightfoot asserted.

"That was sudden." Snow turned to Mac. "Did you see that coming?"

"Hell, no. We don't know much about the RV site. How did they get his prints verified so fast?" she asked.

"They were probably in a state government database."

"Anya's in law school. Perhaps she'll know a criminal lawyer."

"My money's on Greeks bearing gifts." He kneeled to pet the puppy. Shadow rolled belly up, which he obligingly rubbed. "Good dog."

"She's a working dog, you know." Mac watched Chris stroke the dog's fur thoughtfully.

"So? You're a working girl, er, woman, and you like to be petted."

Mac smiled, rubbing her lower back; the baby shifted. She felt a heel in her rib. "I can't argue with that. Karagianis? Of course! This case has media frenzy written all over it—it's right up his alley."

"Nothing we can do tonight. Lawyers' offices are closed. Let's go home and hope no additional homicides occur tonight."

After leaving a brief message on the charismatic lawyer's voice mail, Erin washed, brushed her hair and changed into stretchy loungewear while Chris heated clam chowder and tossed a salad together, adding apples, dried cranberries and chopped walnuts to the vegetables. Done for the day, Erin turned in after letting the dog out; Chris updated his files.

***

The Homicide team moved to Conference One to spread out files, photos, add to the white boards and make room for the recorders, tapes, and boxes of accumulating data. Huddleston brought in a PC and hooked it up in the corner with an all-in-one printer/scanner/fax.

During the remainder of the week, Savage and Fields interviewed personnel at Shale sites in the Basin, trying to ascertain Ahnai Slaughter's movements until her death. "The SRBC team evaluates the impact of the wells and possible contamination on forest, streams and aquatic life; the runoff into roads and tributaries, disposal of 'flowback'—fluids returning to the surface after fracking—and gas migration into wells," explained a person from the Field Office. They listened to the Sayre interviews, seeking any clues to explain the murders.

It was a tedious, time-consuming task. Slaughter had interacted with Field and lab Techs, CEOs, secretaries, design and mechanical engineers, drill-site managers, roustabouts, wastewater truck drivers, geologists and DEP inspectors. She monitored water levels and usage of the active wells in the Susquehanna Basin. The time frame had gaping holes when she'd threaded her way along the sparkling waters to the next site. She'd starred Hamm's Meat and Poultry. The detectives combed through copious meetings notes, reports, consultations, and a pile of correspondence.

Fields' reports were peppered with statistics like "active wells use on average four to five millions gallons of water to release the natural gas. And hundreds of trucks are needed to haul fresh water in, wastewater out." Whether in an effort to be thorough, educate himself or inform others, he didn't say.

"Did any of you guys find a written notebook or a journal? Or a camera?" Mac asked no one in particular. "She wouldn't have taken electronics like those or her laptop in a canoe." No one answered, each occupied with his own task. She walked to the break room for a bottle of water while mulling over the possibilities that any number of people had a motive for murder, including Jason Lightfoot. If Agent Howard were right, a host of people at West Enterprises, and how many as yet unidentified personnel connected to SRBC and Marcellus Shale and other industries along the Susquehanna had means, motive, opportunity and the nerve to cross that boundary from rage to murder?

7

A mild sunny Saturday lured the Snows outdoors early. Chris tromped off in jeans, flannel shirt and boots, carrying five-gallon pails to gather nuts while Erin clocked Shadow's run through the obstacle course. She thumbed the stopwatch tab. "Three minutes! That's good, but is it good enough?" Then she pulled a baggie from her jean pocket, opened it, let her sniff it. "Find, Shadow." Erin hiked the trail, waiting until she heard the dog's single "Woof!" The dog sat beside the tree where Mac had stashed a joint. "Well done!" and gave her a treat. "Let's try again." She moved "the evidence" while Shadow bounded back to the starting point. After the workout, Mac said, "OK. Let's find Chris." They followed the plunking sounds until they found him standing near the top of a ladder, head buried among the branches, hidden by leaves.

"Need some help?" She offered. "This is like 'After Apple Picking,' by Robert Frost: 'My long, two-pointed ladder's sticking through a tree Toward Heaven still, And there's a barrel I didn't fill/Beside it.' "

"Frost again? He sounds gloomy, and I'm filling these."

"He's a kindred spirit. I'm glad those who feel deeply share their insights with the rest of us, so we know suffering's shared."

"Introspection's a fine thing if you engage in other pursuits too. I'm glad you're not gloomy. Here, I'll pass the nuts down to you." He used a gallon bucket to hold the walnuts as he picked, then lowered it to Erin, who emptied them into the larger containers on the ground. The air carried spicy scents of cinnamon, dried leaves and smoke. A harvester droned in the distance. The breeze spun leaves from trees; dried claws scuttled across the ground. They worked until they filled three pails while Shadow explored, amusing herself with fetching or chewing sticks.

"Want some coffee? And a sandwich?" she asked. She slapped her thigh. "Shadow, leave it. Come." The dog meandered over and inspected the nuts, considering. One disappeared into the puppy's mouth with one crunch and a gulp.

"Leave it, Shadow!" Erin yelled, grabbing the dog's halter. "Come."

"Sure. Be down in fifteen."

After lunch, she walked up to the farmhouse when Chris returned to nutting. She pressed the doorbell and waited. Erica threw open the door and called, "Surprise!" Women popped up from their hiding places. The living room was festooned with baby blue crepe streamers. Mylar balloons hovered over the dining room table anchored by ribbons to gaily-wrapped gifts. Danelle hugged her; Sonja smiled, daughter Olivia by her side. Her stepmother Janelle held a basket with slips of paper. Kayla jiggled in front of her mother, Jack's wife Dreena, hugging an adorable blue corduroy teddy. Debra Stone stood shyly to one side, her hands behind her back. Even the new DARE Officer Lee Jeffers, her blond mane pulled back in a low tail, clapped excitedly.

Erin, rooted to the stoop, clapped her hands to her face. "I had no idea. I thought I was helping with apples!" She stepped into the house as Erica pressed a warm punch cup into her hands. "Sorry, your cider is spiced but not spiked." She smiled, pleased. "Come on, everyone, let's start the games." The first icebreaker involved introductions, followed by a timed contest of making words from "Expecting a Boy." Erica awarded game winners with small prizes. Soon the ladies were talking and joking about their own pregnancies, laughing at their cramps, pain and episiotomies. Dreena mentioned her husband's panic, Danelle, her husband's absence.

"What's in everyone else's punch?" Erin asked.

"Apple wine. It's tasty," Sonja said, tipping her cup to her lips.

After the games, the women commented on each gift as Erin opened it: blue crib bumpers and linen printed with little bears plus waterproof mattress pads from Sonja and Ozzie; onesies, little rompers and a baby book from Debra; a light that projected stars on the ceiling from her stepmother; Janelle had also knitted a blanket and a soft powder blue outfit with cap and booties for bringing baby home. Dreena and Jeff gave baby monitors and a collection of small foam balls for little hands. Kayla surrendered the blue teddy with some reluctance; Olivia handed Erin a bouquet of baby rattles tied with blue ribbon. Jack sent a box of board books with stuffed animals that complemented each story. Gift cards were tucked into a car seat from her in-laws. Danelle, snapping photos unobtrusively, gave the baby a wooden rocking horse.

"Did Chris know about this?" Erin shed tears at everyone's generosity. "I had no idea. He didn't tell me. We thank you so much for coming and giving us these wonderful gifts. Actually, we haven't even had time to talk much about the big event. Let alone buy anything."

"The nursery's not ready?" asked Lee. Erin shook her head slowly.

"He'll change your life," Debra said.

"How's Tamara?" Erin folded the wrapping paper while Dreena wrote on each envelope what everyone gave and then stacked the gift cards into a basket for Erin to take home for the thank-you notes.

"She's in all-day kindergarten now. I wanted to thank you all..." Her glance took in Sonja as well, "for the Easter Basket. She sleeps with the pink bunny. That was so thoughtful." Sonja winked and Erin hugged the woman. "Tyrone has her through the week; I have her on weekends. I'm working at Giant full-time. We'll be fine."

"Get ready for the diaper changing," Sonja said to Erin.

"And pacing the floor during long, sleepless nights," Danelle laughed.

"And baby spit-up on your clothes," Olivia added. The adults gave her a strange look. "I have a good memory, and I babysit."

"Cake and ice cream anyone?" Erica refilled drinks. The women shifted to the dining table, chatting about little moments. "Help yourself to the party favors." A small basket brimming with diminutive decorative gourds and pumpkins, shiny apples and nuts graced each place. Janelle sliced cake and Christopher Snow, Sr. dipped ice cream. "Anyone want coffee?" A chorus of yeses responded, so he returned to the kitchen to prepare them.

When finished with coffee and cake, Erin thanked everyone again as the women clustered around the door. Erica opened it and indicated the walkway lined with round, fat pumpkins. "And please take a pumpkin home for a jack-o-lantern."

"Why didn't you tell me?" Erin whispered to Janelle.

"Spoil the surprise and miss the shock on your face? No way. It'll be OK, darling. You and Chris will be prepared next month. I have no advice, other than to say take it a day at a time. You'll love parenthood, but it's challenging too. And you can always call us."

"And if you're not ready, so what? The baby won't know or care. Just enjoy him. He won't be a baby long," Sonja added.

"Says the voice of experience, though I feel as if I've been carrying him for a year!" returned Erin, smiling and squeezing her admin's arm and added. "Thanks, Olivia, for the rattles. He'll love them."

"Say hi to Dad and Liam." She kissed her stepmother, who stepped outside, waving goodbye as she climbed into her sedan.

"This is the kindest gesture I could imagine. Thanks, Erica." Erin hugged her mother-in-law and roped her niece into her arms. "Thanks for the blue teddy bear, Kayla; it's so soft and cuddly. We'll put it in his crib."

Professor Snow appeared at the kitchen door, a mug of coffee in hand, and his namesake directly behind with his own mug stepped into the living room. Erin added, "I appreciate you and Mommy coming all this way."

"We rode the train and rented the car in Middletown. It was fun—a ladies day out." Dreena smiled at her sister-in-law.

"I picked the bear out myself," Kayla offered. "Now can I help Granddad and Uncle Chris carry the presents to your house? And meet Shadow?"

"Sure, pumpkin, but let's load them in the Jeep first: fewer trips that way." Chris smiled and started for the table.

"Wait, Chris. I'd like you to meet Danelle, my best friend and college roommate." Danelle, last in line, held out her hand to Chris, who took it, smiled and tilted his head to study her.

"Erin described you exactly, though you're younger than I imagined," Danelle observed.

"I could say the same. She said you're petite, dress stylishly and had a designer pixie haircut. I'd add that you remind me of Audrey Hepburn. You and Erin both look about twenty-one. It's good to finally meet you."

"OMG!" Danelle threw herself into his arms and hugged him. "You just made my day." She stepped back, blushing and turned to Erin and whispered, "He's stone solid!" Her hands rearranged her blue and green silk scarf loosely around her thin neck.

"Kayla, let's go; grab a few packages. Then we'll come back here to help with apples and dinner. Later, we can carve a jack-o-lantern for you to take home." He scooped up an armload of gifts. "You can hide it in a shopping bag on the train."

"OK, but I'd rather have the baby when he gets here. He'd be more fun." Kayla skipped off alongside Chris, the bear stacked on a gift box she carried. He laughed at her frankness.

Erin thanked Danelle for coming so far when she had much to do buying a condo, settling into a new community and adjusting to a new job. "Where's Sydney?"

"With Grandma. Wouldn't dream of missing your big event. I'll even take photos for Christmas cards, if you'd like, in a few weeks." She waved her manicured nails and stepped nimbly into her sporty blue Camero.

"Aren't you glad she returned to the states? You'll see more of each other now. You're not too tired to help with the apples? They're waiting in the solarium." Erica turned energetically toward her next project, her dark brown pageboy swinging with her.

"Even though a decade has passed, we just picked up where we left off," Erin answered. "Absolutely I'll help. I've been thinking about apple pies, sauce and dumplings all day. And smelling the mulled cider from the walnut trees where Shadow and I were helping Chris."

"Oh, the scent carried all that way! That's surprising," Erica said.

"I'll gather up the decorations; I'll join you then," Dreena added as she cleared the table with familiar ease, pulling the ribbon and bows through cardboard with the gifts to send along to the bungalow on the next trip.

"Don't you just love Harvest time? Life is so bountiful, and we're so thankful for you all. And grandchildren are the best blessings! They're the reasons I had children! Now, here." Erica thrust a colander and peeler loaded with McIntosh, Courtland, Gala and Golden Delicious at Erin, set another down for Dreena beside a nutcracker with a bowl of pecans and walnuts, then settled one in her own lap. "We can freeze Dreena's until Thanksgiving to take back when her family drives down."

When Dreena and Kayla joined them, Erica said, "Now tell us how your design business is faring. Any exciting new projects?" Kayla sat beside her mother to shell nuts. She giggled at the crack and crunch as the white-whiskered wooden nutcracker's jaws clacked shut. "He's in the Christmas ballet, too!" Her mother picked out the shells and sealed the nutmeats into quart freezer bags.

"Yes. I just signed a contract to redecorate a three-story brownstone supposedly for a well-known model, whom I've yet to meet, but her agent said she prefers earth tones with splashes of color!" Dreena launched into a description of her plans.

In the kitchen, the men clattered and prepped pans, rolled out dough and fitted it into pie plates, crimping the edges. Chris and his dad mixed the spices, setting each portion in shot glasses behind tins lining the island to streamline the process. Mac peeled apples, trying for a long continuous strip. The women chatted over the baby gifts—all practical selections. "And not one a duplicate!" When Erica smiled, her crow's feet looked like eyelashes. A true sun-worshipper, her skin still retained some summer tan, plus the dark freckles that signaled skin damage.

Warmth from food, family and festivity engulfed the group engaged in their annual autumn ritual. Bringing in the food from the garden and orchard, preserving it and preparing for winter, Erin felt accepted. A rare joy suffused her, enveloped in their midst, the family looking forward to Thanksgiving—the only time during the year that the Snow family was united. And a baby on his way!

8

At work, the mood was frenetic. Elena Michaels, her cameraman on her heels, burst into the precinct, waving her mic. Phones jangled insistently. "Is it true that your Jane Doe is a Native American from the Carlisle Indian School ceremony? Is her death connected to the powwow? Can you tell us how she died? Certainly the CPD has some information you can share with the public. Chris, if you have no comment, let me see Reese."

Mac halted and pivoted at the reporter's words; Shadow hugged her thigh, a hum in her throat. Detective Snow turned as well, shrugged. "Yes, Elena, our Jane Doe is Cherokee, formerly employed by the SRBC, the organization that regulates the Susquehanna's water consumption, levels and quality by monitoring the businesses that use it. Her husband, Jason Lightfoot, positively identified her body late last night."

"SRBC stands for..."

"Google it." His brusque tone conveyed a message that CPD wasn't doing her legwork.

She snapped the mic under her chin. "Is her death related to Marcellus Shale production? Do you have any leads?" And then aimed the mic at Snow, who arched a brow in her direction.

"All homicide detectives are involved in the on-going investigation."

"Do the police suspect the husband of foul play?"

"You know I can't reveal the specifics of our investigation." He stepped back and consulted his watch. "Now, if you'll excuse me, you can attend Chief March's press conference with all the other reporters."

"What's the victim's name? How was she murdered?"

"You'll be briefed this afternoon. Excuse us, we have business to attend to." He turned his back to her.

"I'll talk to Reese." Her voice rose insistently.

"He's on assignment." Snow disappeared down the hall.

Mac waited at her office door, handing him a mug of java. "And you're on a first-name basis with her?"

"She's Savage's ex wife."

"Ah, that explains it." As she turned into her office to tackle her work, her husband detoured into the Chief's office. Phones rang, footsteps clomped along the hall, and conversation spilled from the break room—the usual sounds of a typical day at Carlisle Police Headquarters.

Defense counselor Karagianis materialized in her doorway and leaned against the jam, one hip cocked, arms crossed, smiling like a benevolent god. "Thank you for the tip, Detective McCoy or should I address you as Snow?" Shadow perked up and trotted over to check out the visitor. Mac motioned for her to sit. "Friend, Shadow." The puppy sat directly in front of the lawyer, watching and waiting expectantly.

Mac smiled in spite of wishing she weren't. "McCoy's fine. Are you representing Lightfoot?"

"I couldn't pass up such a glowing opportunity." His blue eyes actually crinkled gleefully. "May I sit down?" He parked his body in the visitor's chair and stretched his legs out. An impeccably crisp striped grey suit, a triangle of white handkerchief peeking from his breast pocket matched his blindingly white shirt, and the red power tie completed the effect.

"Can I help you further, counselor?" Mac asked equably.

He extracted a spiral-bound notebook from an inside pocket.

"You can tell me where he is." He waited patiently, pen suspended.

"And give me his cell number, for starters. Plus I'd appreciate any pertinent background information you can provide."

"FBI Special Agent Howard took Lightfoot into custody last night for the alleged murder of Dean Greer, a Field Tech for West Enterprises, a Marcellus Shale company. And he's a suspect in his wife's homicide. I assume they went to D.C." She spread her palms out. She checked her file and recited the numbers he'd requested. "Now you know what I know."

He laughed. "I doubt that, but it's a start. Was he arrested or just detained for questioning? Wait, you said wife's—Lightfoot was married to your homicide victim?"

"They Mirandized him. Yes, Ahnai Slaughter."

"Because?"

"Apparently his fingerprints are on the murder weapon."

"Well, that's serious. Where did the Greer homicide occur? I assume it's related to yours."

"And I assume you heard the reporter. It occurred near Winfield on R 15 between Sunbury and Lewisburg at an RV belonging to the suspect and the deceased."

He grinned at her. "Ah, there's the answer. Thanks for your time. Please let me know how I can return the favor." He gestured at her abdomen. "When are you due?"

"Oh, I will." She smiled coyly. "Next month."

Snow rounded Mac's office jamb and drew up sharply to avoid colliding with her guest. "Hello, counselor. How are you?"

"Well, thank you." He stood and bowed in Mac's direction. "Good day. If you'll excuse me...work calls." He angled his body past Snow and Shadow.

"I take it he's representing Lightfoot. You like him, don't you? Let's motor. We have a lead. Someone just called in a tip about an argument between Slaughter and the farmer who owns Hamm's Meat and Poultry. He threatened her."

"Please. Karagianis is old enough to be my father." She gathered her belongings, tucked her Glock into its holster and followed him to the Jeep. Shadow obligingly followed, but Erin snapped the leash on her halter anyway.

"I meant Lightfoot," Snow clarified. He waved away her protest.

"Really, Christopher! He's my stepfather."

***

The agri-business stretched to the west, spread out over a hundred acres, if the corn in the background belonged to him. Barnyard odors assailed their nostrils as they trekked up the long gravel drive to the sprawling barn on the left. Another long barn sprouting shiny aluminum fans topped the small rise on the hill to the right. Nearly empty twin silos flanked the barns. Oinking to the left, clucking to the right. They waded through tall grasses around to the rear where sows wallowed; one too heavy to move snored laboriously in the corner.

A stocky, beefy man wearing overalls over a plaid flannel shirt was dumping slop into a long trough inside the fence. His red face sported a network of broken capillaries. His rheumy eyes had drooping lids; ears stuck out from matted, unwashed white hair, but he smiled affably enough when he saw the detectives. "Howdy, what can I do ya for?" He wiped his handed against his thighs and approached, hand extended. Until he saw the shields displayed. He dropped his hand.

"Are you Johann Hamm?" His head bobbed. "We're Carlisle Police Detectives Christopher Snow and Erin McCoy here to ask you a few questions about your altercation with a Susquehanna River Basin employee." His thumb depressed the record button, and he listed the requisite information.

"Pretty far from your jurisdiction, aren't you, sonny?" They felt the change in attitude with the chill in the air.

"We're investigating the murder of Ahnai Slaughter Lightfoot, whose body was found dumped in Letort in

Carlisle. We heard you had heated words with her. What brought about the argument?"

"That Indian? She cited me again for run-off. Claimed I was using DDT, which any fool knows is outlawed. Can't even buy it nowadays."

"Why did the discussion escalate into an argument?" asked Mac.

"'Cause I called her a liar. She slapped three citations on me. Said she'd be back to test the water again, would withdraw my permit to use river water. Threatened to bring agents to shut me down. I shooed her off my property at the point of my shotgun. I got the right to defend myself."

"How exactly did you threaten her?" Snow asked.

"Who tole you that?"

"I'm not a liberty to say."

"I told her to git off my land or I'd shoot!" he shouted, and then rubbed a large chafed hand across his forehead. "You don't really think I got time to chase her tail across the state, do ya? Seems others were doin' that." He nodded as Mac and Snow exchanged a glance.

"What do you mean?" Snow tried to keep his face blank.

"Do you have an alibi for October fifth and sixth?" Mac let the man's coarse comment ride, shifted her gaze to check Shadow, sniffing the air curiously; they'd left her in the vehicle with the windows cracked, but her occasional barks served as a warning for Hamm to tone down.

"Reckon I was here. Ya kin ask my wife up at the house or the farm hands. Ricardo's feedin' chickens. Zeke's balin' hay. Take my word for it, I dint shoot any Indian squaw."

Mac had turned on her heel at the insult to huff away but stopped and wheeled back, her finger pointing at his chest. "You could've hired it done, old man. Don't play with us; we'll be back if your alibi doesn't hold." He made a move toward her.

"Don't," she warned. "I'd love an excuse to restrain and drag you back to CPD for questioning. Don't follow us. You need to sit tight; we need independent collaboration." And then she stalked off. Snow followed Mac, as she marched to the car. Their sentry barked furiously at Hamm—her hackles up.

"Let's talk to the field hands in the coop first. I hope he doesn't have a cell phone to warn them," she said.

Snow cocked his head at her quizzically. "You like him for this?"

"Hell, no, I don't like him at all. The 'ole coot's just blowing hot air."

He accelerated up the drive and stopped outside the sliding doors at the end of the barn. Sliding the door open a crack, Snow yelled, "Ricardo?" The stench of chicken shit assailed their nostrils; feathers flew thickly in the fetid air. Stacks of wire cages held thousands of squawking poultry. Mac backed out holding her nose, fighting back the nausea as Shadow squeezed out of the open passenger's door.

A tanned man with a round weathered face, dark wavy hair, furry brows and handlebar mustache stepped out into the afternoon sunshine, his hand shading his eyes. "Buenas tardes."

Snow introduced Mac and himself and asked the questions he'd put to the owner. Yes, he knew the Indian inspector, Ricardo said. "She asked many questions. Left angry."

"Why?" Mac said.

"Mr. Hamm muy loco. He aim gun at her. 'You leave,'" he said, pantomiming holding a shotgun at his waist. "She left."

"When did this argument occur?" Snow asked.

"Maybe three weeks ago."

"Did she return?"

"No, sir. But she and her company sent citations and fines on papers."

"Where were you last weekend?"

"Here. I work every day."

"What about Mr. Hamm?"

"He here, too. Busy season."

"Seven days a week?" Snow checked.

"Yes, sir. The crops and animals, they don't wait."

They struck out at the farm. Zeke and Mrs. Hamm relayed similar responses. She handed Snow the SRBC citation letter, a warning "to develop and implement a proper waste management and pollution prevention plan and submit it to the SRBC by the end of the month."

Glancing at the top, he noted the date, September fourteenth.

"May we copy this letter and return—"

The woman waved her hand in dismissal. "Keep it. We have more."

Mac found Shadow drinking water from a bucket under the downspout at the corner of the house. "Well, at least rain water is safe to drink, I think." She peered into it as she pulled the dog away.

The couple and Shadow headed south, too tired and hungry for conversation or analysis. Clearly farmer Hamm was too occupied with his work to follow Ahnai down the Susquehanna. No boat on the premises that they could see.

On impulse, Snow pulled into the Red Rabbit for burgers, fries and milkshakes.

9

Shadow's test day dawned cloudy and raw—the first hint that winter waited. Erin showered, ate and fed Shadow. Chris was shaving as his wife let the puppy out and jogged to the obstacle course. They ran through it three times. Then Mac pulled out a blood-dotted piece of hanky, let the dog sniff, and said, "Shadow, find." Again, within three minutes the dog found the other half, voiced her discovery and sat. Mac ran her through all voice commands, the dog hesitating only on "leave it." Erin repeated the exercises, using only hand signals this time.

"I don't know what else we can do," she told her shepherd. "Just don't let those male dogs intimidate you. You're still young, so they might be faster, if that matters so much, but you're lighter."

Shadow danced nervously around, expecting more. Erin gave her a Milkbone. "Okay, we can play catch, but I don't want to tire you." She pulled a Frisbee from Shadow's toy box in the garage.

When they were ready to go, Erin ran through a last-minute check: bottled water, dog biscuits, sandwich and Shadow's water bowl.

At the K9 site, dew slicked every glass blade; fog ghosted from the Yellow Breeches. Except for the Scarlet Oaks, leaves had dropped from the trees. Dogs on leashes paced or sat quietly alongside their handlers. One officer was walking his dog along the fence. Erin counted ten, including Shadow, as Corey moved through the group, greeting each officer—human and canine. The men shuffled around the clearing, shaking hands with ones they knew. Eyes slid over Mac and Shadow, the men keeping their distance. She and Shadow strode to the closest—a seasoned vet with a shaved head with

73

pinpricks of grey showing, eyes like pecans and a slight limp. The dogs nosed each other. He extended his hand and shook Mac's. "Greg Vincent, State College."

"Erin McCoy, Carlisle."

"Your first time?" Vincent asked.

"For both of us." She nodded toward Shadow. "Any advice for the newbies?"

"Let your dog do the work. Stay calm and she will, too. She looks young."

"Shadow's not a year old yet."

"Coffee and donuts in the building. Help yourselves." Corey toasted them with his lidded cup. "Let's go around the circle, introduce ourselves for the sake of our newcomers." When the group had, he said, "Here's how we're going to proceed." He outlined each contest. "Officers will go alphabetically, by the canine officer's name. I'll announce each. You'll go to the starting line, unleash your dog. Handlers can give voice or hand signals and encourage his, and her, partner through the obstacle course, but you may not touch the shepherd. Be alert; the course has changed. I'll time." He indicated the stopwatch. "After that, we'll do the 'seek and find' drills. I've hidden one half of a common item—all different items —and I'll hand the other to each officer. Then we'll break for lunch. Up first, Brutus."

Vincent and Brutus approached the course.

Mac relaxed somewhat, though her mouth was dry and palms clammy despite the chill. Shadow's alert eyes tracked Brutus's movements. Her hind legs shifted restlessly. "Steady, girl. We have to wait our turn." She ran her fingers along her puppy's neck to settle her but didn't request that she sit.

"Next, Cain." Both handler and dog with silver muzzles lined up.

Kauffman had elongated the course, placing some equipment in the woods, like hers. She smiled at that change.

As a handler ambled by, his dog turned and growled threateningly, lips curled back, showing teeth. He lunged at Shadow, hackles up, so Mac threw her water in the dog's face as the handler jerked back and shortened his leash. "Heel, Leo! Sorry about that."

Mac waited a tick. "We'll let it slide this time." The man had already sauntered into the building. "Next time I'll kick him in the face or mace him." She took a second to remove keys from her jeans and loop them onto her belt, a slender container of pepper spray attached. "You, okay, girl?"

Mac and Shadow went second to last. Feeling ungainly and top-heavy, she grunted as she unleashed Shadow, who took off, running ahead through tires, then the concrete pipe, leaped the pile of broken rock, bypassed the slide at the far left, camouflaged by bushes. Mac didn't stop her because Corey was timing. Shadow jumped a broken gate and completed the course, bounding over to Mac, who was standing midway between the start and finish block, expecting a treat. "To the finish, Shadow." Mac jogged along beside her dog for the final stretch. "Good girl." She produced a biscuit from her jacket pocket.

"Zeke."

Mac took Shadow inside for water and poured herself coffee. She plucked a cider donut out of the box and fed half of it to Shadow. "Don't know, girl, but I think skipping the slide will cost us both." Her puppy redeemed herself with the next drill—finding a blood-soaked doll in ninety seconds.

When they broke for lunch, and men and dogs climbed into white SUVs to form a caravan to their favorite restaurants, Corey pulled Mac aside. "Shadow did well on seeking and finding. Sorry, she leaped over the rocks and skipped the slide and then went to you instead of returning to the finish line. What if a body had been under those rocks?"

"She thought she was done. I always reward her when she completes the course."

"But she didn't complete it. I have to disqualify her."

"Does that mean she won't be certified for fieldwork?" she asked.

He nodded. "I think she's too young yet. We'll keep working her."

"When does she get to try again? And how do I warn her? Should I have called her back to do the slide? She can do that: We have one at home."

"I know. You should have corrected her, but it would've still taken time. We have another round of skill sets in March. I'll test her again then. Meanwhile, take her to as many locales where she'll be exposed to various situations. Schools would be good. When she's actually working, she can't be distracted and miss what she's looking for."

"That's not fair. Who of us gets 100% of anything? Don't penalize her because I didn't know what to expect. She would've done the slide if I'd called her back."

"I'm penalizing both of you. Better luck next time. And you don't have to return after lunch. You're done today."

Mac wrestled the passenger door open for Shadow. Driving home, she blinked away tears of frustration. "We'll nail it next time, girl, because I'll have three months off when this little dude is born. We'll work every day, and we'll go to schools, malls, the Farm Show, the Ragged Edge, King's Gap and everywhere we can. We'll seek and find! We'll show all those men! Even and especially Mr. Perfection Kauffman." Shadow's brown soulful eyes watched Erin's earnestly, as though she shared her disappointment and understood that they'd failed.

"It's OK, girl. It was legit—I can't claim discrimination because you did skip the slide altogether. All we can do is practice. Maybe Kauffman's right; once you're older, you will focus better. Next time, you'll beat them all!" She turned onto R 174 and headed home, tired and discouraged but determined to improve.

10

Next morning, Lightfoot was leaning against his truck parked in the CPD lot, the sun glinting off his black hair like rain when Mac drove up beside him. She climbed out of Silver and let Shadow out. The pup sniffed at his knees and boots, his jeans and crotch. He knelt down to run his hands over her ears, neck, and down her back; in sunlight, his skin radiated a pale golden copper. "She's a beauty."

"She sure is," Snow appeared, touching Mac's shoulder with his. "She's the most beautiful woman I know." He winked at his wife.

Lightfoot stood. "I meant the dog. Shadow's an interesting name. I wanted to thank Mac personally for finding me a good lawyer pronto."

She smiled up at him. "Glad to help." Lightfoot's eyes noted Snow's brows rise in mild surprise.

"So you don't believe I'm guilty," he said to Mac.

"I don't know, but you have the right to a lawyer and due process," Mac answered.

The Native American pushed off from the fender. "So what's next?"

"Not sure what you mean," Snow responded.

"I'm going to help. I can track. I'll find clues no one else will."

"You're a civilian; you can't interfere with or impede an on-going police investigation."

"No, I'm a state officer; I can make arrests. I'll do it with or without you." The man sounded determined. "Look, did you take anything from the cabin?"

"Fingerprints." Snow withheld the thumb drive discovery.

"What was missing?" Lightfoot asked.

Mac mentally reviewed the paintings, ransacked kitchen, piles of books and papers, bow over the fireplace... "The arrows."

"Yes. Ahnai's arrows and quiver were gone. And her purse." He let that sink in. "Would I shoot anyone with arrows I'd made? The trail would lead directly to me. No one's that stupid. Someone's trying to frame me to cover his crime. And did anyone see me argue with my wife?"

Mac bided her time, as Shadow sniffed Lightfoot's Ram, knowing her husband had to make this decision because he was being proprietary again. She was determined to use Lightfoot's expertise regardless. He raised excellent points; he probably knew some answers as well.

Snow gestured to HQ. "Let's get started. We have more questions. Did you know Dean Greer?"

"I did. He worked with Ahnai. They canoed the river together, did similar tests, coauthored reports. I was glad she had company. The Susquehanna can be a deceiving, dangerous witch as well as life-giver and home to a host of fish, flora, insects and amphibians." The three entered the side entrance of the building and ducked into Snow's office.

Snow went for coffee while the other two settled, Lightfoot lifting the backpack from Mac's shoulder to the floor. When Snow joined them, he asked Lightfoot, "Did you argue with you wife?" Shadow ambled off, probably in search of her water dish in Mac's office.

"No. Our family's not together often now the kids are in college. The powwows are our time of fellowship and community. We seek harmony and share our way of living. At this stage, arguing would be pointless."

"Why?" asked Snow.

"The wrinkles in time form folds that hide crevices. In the gaps are the meanings we make. Our culture is very different from yours; many tribes were originally matriarchal. Memories, experiences and perspectives differ, yet our peoples' histories outweigh our individual differences. I can't live in the past or waste my life on anger and regret. It saps one's energy."

The detectives exchanged glances.

"What exactly do you mean?" asked Snow. "That you drifted apart?"

"That and more. Ahnai honored most of our customs but welcomed the attention she garnered and capitalized on that whenever she could, wherever she was," Lightfoot explained. "She's a powerful and attractive woman who enjoys her independence."

"We could say the same about you—a foot in both worlds."

"You could."

"You said that you had information," Mac prodded.

"There's a Gathering in Gettysburg November third."

"A powwow?"

"No, more like a seminar: storytelling, dancing, sharing our rituals and demonstrating our crafts at the college."

"That's good news. Will the same participants who attended the Carlisle Indian Industrial School ceremony be there?" asked Mac. "Will you participate?"

"Yes. If the gods are willing, the creek doesn't rise and that FBI agent doesn't arrest me again."

Mac frowned. "Gods?"

"Is not the Christian God a triumvirate?" Lightfoot stated.

"They're three facets of the same entity."

"Aren't we all? We honor our collective heritage, including Spiderwoman, Iyatiku and Irriaku, Coyote the Trickster, Father Sky and the Twins of Good and Evil. Our stories tell our children about our past, present and future, as well as their place on and duty to Earth."

"How did Karagianis get you released so soon?" Snow steered the conversation in another direction.

"The Pace Arrow at Winfield belongs to me. He argued that my prints would be on the arrows because I made them. And I was upstate at the time of her death. Besides, there's another possibility."

Snow's intercom buzzed. He ignored it. "That would be?"

"A saboteur at work. What if people associated with Marcellus Shale are being picked off because environmentalists want the industry shut down? Or if some are involved in illegal activities?"

"That could be Native Americans," countered Snow.

"Or a dozen other groups. Look what the natural gas and petroleum industries have done out West. The grass around those sites died from the by-products of drilling with chemicals. Little grows in salt and sand."

"You've been at these sites?" asked Mac.

"Out West? No. But I've seen photos. Read Nicholas Evan's *The Divide*; you'll get the idea. Here, yes. I come across wells when I tag and track animals. Can't miss 'em. Well rigs are mammoth monoliths that bore into the Earth. Horizontal drills pump millions of gallons of water, sand and chemicals that fracture the shale, releasing trapped gas." He shrugged. "I'm not an expert. You should see for yourself."

The intercom buzzed again. Snow answered and listened.

"The Chief says we have another body. Williamsport Police and Sunbury's Detective Imhoff are on the scene. Apparently, he sees a connection to his homicide. Come on, Mac, we're going to see a well site first hand." Shadow's nails clicked along the hall; she sensed they were going someplace.

"I guess I'm on my own recognizance," Lightfoot said, standing and striding out the door with them.

Snow nodded. "Where will you be?"

"Indian Steps. I took two weeks vacation when I was arrested. Didn't want cops dogging me at work. I must arrange my wife's funeral."

"When will that occur?" asked Mac. "Has Dr. Chen released her body?"

"Yes. Saturday."

"We'd like to come. Where will it be held?" Snow asked.

"On the bank of the Susquehanna at Indian Steps at dusk."

Lightfoot climbed into his vehicle and pulled out ahead of the Jeep. Snow called Sonja to request an alert on anyone using bank or credit cards belonged to Ahnai Slaughter/Lightfoot. He glanced at Mac, who was staring out the window.

"I know what you're thinking," he said without preamble.

"You have no idea what I'm thinking," Mac shot back.

"Then tell me." He tried for an even tone despite anger crawling up this throat.

"I was wondering what he has that my Dad didn't have."

"Oh. Well, apparently he couldn't keep her either. Some women are like that—scouting for a better landing spot. Greener money."

"You're mixing metaphors. I don't know any women like that. He's right, you know. No one's mentioned sabotage," Mac said. "He can help."

He let the topic of Jason Lightfoot go. "What's the most likely scenario?"

"I'd say jealously, greed, revenge—not necessarily in that order."

"If it's the first, the husband's the best candidate for his wife's murder. See if you can locate West Enterprises on your GPS."

"And if it's work-related: sabotage, blackmail or kickbacks?"

"We shall see."

***

At West Enterprises outside Williamsport, the Jeep rolled past a pond of relatively clear water, up an incline where topsoil and tons of earth had been gouged out to level the site. They passed a mountain of sand and twenty-foot wall of dirt and debris embedded with rock. Drilling equipment and trucks spread across several acres of the drill site. They bumped past police cars and a coroner's van. At the top of the hill lay a much wider pool of polluted brackish, muddy-colored water, odors in its chemical stew spilling off and oils slithering on the surface. Mac leashed Shadow, dug the Canon from her backpack, and then exited the Jeep, following Snow to the edge of the tarp-lined impoundment pond.

Police milled around the pond where a body floated—an arrow protruding from his back pinned with a paper labeled MYOB. Work had stopped; men loitered along the perimeter, taking advantage of the loll in activity. Some smoked; others spoke quietly to one another. Hardhats dotted the hoods of numerous pick-ups. In the center of the pad, a vertical red frame housing the drill thrust at least a hundred feet into the air. Several acres had been cleared of all vegetation—a scar that had formerly been a forest. Ugly black machinery like giant capped spigots, huge drums, spools of wire and hose, pipes and a crane hovered around the base. A dozen tankers were parked idling, waiting. At the back sat a trailer that looked like an office.

They introduced themselves to the local police. Carl Imhoff paced, his short blond hair stiff as dried grass. Another man stood to his left, arms akimbo, while a small CAT hooked the body by its belt to the lip of the pond's liner. Uniformed Hazmat officers waded in and lifted the body onto land. Mac gave her dog a "stay" signal. Slid her camera out of her pocket and shot the corpse from varying angles. A crime scene photographer frowned but said nothing.

"This is Otto Kraus, site manager." Imhoff gestured to the man beside him. "Detectives Snow and McCoy, Carlisle Homicide."

The portly manager frowned, his florid face a mask of frustration and confusion—his lips a grim slash below a trimmed mustache, a dash of mustard clinging to it. "Damn it to hell. What's your interest here?" He aimed his question at Snow.

Shadow jingled her harness, restive, her nose sniffing the air.

"This homicide matches the MO of one related to ours," Snow said.

"Imhoff?" Kraus apparently wanted to know why a Sunbury detective was interested.

"Murder in Winfield—an arrow through the heart: Dean Greer."

"No shit?" The man's eyebrows shot up. "He's our Field Tech."

"And who's this?" Snow indicated the dripping body at their feet.

"He's our Safety Coordinator, Gary Hauck."

"Did he know Greer?" asked Mac. Kraus looked at Mac with a start as if just noticing her. His eyes lowered to Shadow. He hiked up his pants over a protruding beer belly. "Of course; they worked and bunked together back at the West Enterprises' RV Park, number twelve." His head indicated the direction they'd come.

Marcellus Shale hired thousands to work the Northern Tier and Western Pennsylvania to clear land, build and process the wells, pads and rigs, drilling and setting pipe to harness and move gas once the drill had fractured the shale beneath with pressurized water, sand and chemicals. They needed engineers to build the roads, truck drivers to haul millions of gallons of fresh water in and wastewater out. Roustabouts handled the grunt work, throwing their hands to jobs they were able to do.

Casually dressed in khakis and a long-sleeve sweater, shield glittering on his belt, Imhoff raked his blond hair off this forehead. Sunglasses hid hooded blue eyes, which panned the scene. The Williamsport coroner looked near retirement. His grey hair thinning, his gloved hands shaking slightly as he sawed the exposed arrow off, handed it to a CSU member, who bagged it.

"What's that print on the back?" inquired Mac.

"It's all run together," answered the coroner; he peeled it off and handed it to an assistant who paper bagged it.

"Maybe the lab guys can work wonders," Snow commented, squinting against the glare off the polluted pool—a noxious and nauseas miasma. He stepped away to give Imhoff space to confer and instruct his deputy, waving Mac back as well. Interviewing well-site employees should be a priority, since many potential eyewitnesses were on the scene.

The coroner, with an assist from the CAT operator, turned the body. On-lookers gasped; the dead man's face and hands were covered with chemical burns: his eyebrows had disintegrated, and eyes were grey, glassy orbs with no distinguishable pupils.

"What's in this water?" Mac said.

"What isn't?" the site manager waved his hand. "Brine, sand solvents, biocides, alcohols, foaming and anti-foam agents, corrosion inhibitors, and about 500 other corrosive chemicals."

"When was he discovered?" Imhoff pulled out a notebook.

"Couple hours ago. We called the authorities." Kraus sounded defensive and worried. "How long will you tie up my site?"

"Until further notice. Once my men and Williamsport police finish interviewing, you can dismiss your people for the rest of the week. We'll have to comb the crime scene for prints, evidence. I need someone—Snow will you head the RV investigation? Take a tech along. Seal it when you're done." He unlatched his cell, then changed his mind, anchored it to his belt and motioned another man over. "Sid, your truck's got a trailer hitch?" Sid nodded. "Go along with Snow to the RV Park, which is outside Williamsport's jurisdiction. When the Carlisle detectives seal it, haul it to Sunbury HQ. Thanks, man." Slapped him on the back.

"I need interviews of Kraus and everyone else present on tape. Find out about any laid-off workers, anyone with a gripe or a grudge, any hotheads. Can you fax me phone records, financials and any info you deem pertinent?

Postmortem, too, with prints, especially from that arrow." Snow returned, willing to cooperate but refusing to take orders from the younger man. "And what about Greer's autopsy?"

"I'll do that report myself. Hell, Snow, are you hiring me?" Imhoff said facetiously. "Yes, I'll see that you get copies of everything. Think this is connected to your homicide?"

"Slaughter? I know it is. I want to know about those connections. If we can find what we're dealing with, then we'll know which leads to pursue. Now it's a hydra. We have to narrow the field if we're to get to the bottom of this. Somebody here knows, saw or overheard something."

Snow waved Mac over as he hiked back to the Jeep. She poured water for Shadow and pocketed granola bars and apples to eat on the way.

"I can't make heads or tails of all this." Mac gestured toward the site. "Someone is picking off Shale employees, pointing us to Native Americans. The arrow's identical to the one that shot Greer. I can't tell if the message is personal or political, an attempt to shut down operations here. One well won't make much of a difference to the industry in a state with nearly 1,600 active wells."

Snow navigated the two-lane road to the RV Park where twenty-four campers were parked on either side of a graveled drive. "One way to solve a housing shortage, but not ideal." Number twelve was last in the row to the right. They got out, gloved up and left Shadow in the back seat, the Jeep under a Sycamore, window cracked. "The lock's busted."

Inside, the cramped quarters had been searched but not trashed like Slaughter's cabin. "Once all the data is collected, we can sift through it." They systematically combed through clothes, under mattresses and in cubbies. Dirty dishes were stacked in the tiny sink. Some canned goods, crackers, instant oatmeal packets in the overhead cabinet. Dishes and glasses in the next.

"Nothing's jumping out at me." She stopped to stretch her back, opened the fridge and peered in. "The men left a six-pack, an OJ carton, cinnamon bagels, butter and bottled water. Want a beer?" she asked as she lifted the OJ carton and shook it, frowning.

"No, and you don't either," Snow said as he searched the bed over the cab, and then unfolded the bench to check under mattresses. He kissed the top of her head. "How are you and our little hitchhiker doing?" He patted her round, tight mound.

"A bit crowded in here." She shook the carton. "Why would you put an empty carton back inside?" Squeezed it open. Dumped out wads of hundreds, one wrapped in paper. "Well, well, well."

"Pun intended?" Snow deftly teased the paper off and opened it.

"A list of names, well sites—similar to Ahnai's thumb drive." The spreadsheet listed the violations with monetary notations by some names. It was wrapped around a Franklin with a smear of dried blood.

Mac leaned over his arm. "And blood. Let's keep this one to type and check for prints. Look at various dollar amounts beside some of the names and violations crossed off. Look, Kraus is listed. And Hauk. Is it some kind of payoff or kickback? I'm going to let Shadow out."

Snow unsnapped his cell, thumbed through numbers and pushed call.

"Yeah, we got a roll of Franklins and a list with a $700 notation by Kraus' name, $1,000 by the Safety Director's. Ask Kraus about that. Neighborhood of ten thousand, I'd guess." Sharp barks assailed his ears. He thumped out of the camper. Shadow's head ducked under the camper, digging furiously; dirt flew out between pumping paws, her nose to the ground. The quivering dog withdrew, sat and woofed once. Mac gave her a treat. "Good girl! A find! Something's under here."

"I'll get it." Snow scrabbled on all fours. "It's an insulated pizza box."

He shook off excess dirt into an evidence bag and opened the box; the stomach-curdling odor of dried copper and iron spilled out. He slowly extracted a scarlet shawl stamped with sun symbols with six-inch fringe matted with blood.

"Clothes Ahnai wore the last day of her life." Mac winced.

"I'll take those," Sid materialized behind them. "If you'd just put them back in—" He motioned to the insulated bag and covered his nose. "Did you find anything else?"

"No, we'll take this for our homicide investigation—our vic's clothes. Yeah, we left a juice carton filled with Franklins inside for you. Can you track the serial numbers?" Her husband didn't mention the spreadsheet, so Mac kept mum about the bill in an envelope with blood obliterating Ben's face, but her heart tripped in her chest. Baby squirmed.

"I'll dust for prints." Sid disappeared into the camper. When the tech reappeared twenty minutes later, they locked windows and sealed the Pace Arrow with crime scene tape. "Time to go home. And we're going out for dinner. It's too late to cook." He watched Erin slowly executing her Tai Chi movements. When she finished, she gave him a tired smile, snuggled against him for a minute.

"No argument here." She slapped her thigh, her "Let's go" signal to Shadow, who hopped in the back of the Jeep.

By the time they arrived home, darkness had chased dusk away. Clear but chilly, the night's crisp air was a cleansing antidote to the day's events. They noticed jack-o-lanterns glowing on stoops, sheeted ghosts hanging from trees and life-sized Halloween blow-ups bobbing in the wind like tipsy drunks.

After stopping for dinner at a diner, they journeyed home, bone weary from the long drive to Williamsport and the day's exhausting, frustrating work. Neither brought up Shadow's find; this was a day to bury and banish from their conversation.

After showers and changing, they collapsed into bed.

"What are you planning tomorrow?" Chris asked her while massaging her feet, smiling, running his thumb up her instep, which elicited a little gurgling in the back of her throat. His left hand kneaded her calves. Both hands inched up her thighs and stopped when they met no resistance.

"I'm meeting Danelle for lunch at the Ragged Edge and telling my parents that we won't be down for Thanksgiving, for the first time in my life. But we'll spend Christmas with them. What about you? Don't stop now."

"Savage is coming over for the Eagles football game." He shrugged, leaning over her. "Then we'll probably work the case or finish the sunroom." Their conversation ceased.

11

Erin arrived early for her luncheon, parking Silver in front of the McCoy house. She and Shadow mounted the steps and rang the bell. No answer. "Must be at work. Let's go get a sandwich, girl." They ambled down the block, turned the corner, and climbed the steps. Entering the warmth and bustle of the coffee shop calmed and comforted her. She glanced at the chalkboard while waiting in line. Four college kids hustled behind the glass display case. The cappuccino machines gurgled, spit and frothed milk. In the back, others were making sandwiches. Brownies, fruit tarts, several types of super-sized cookies and various pies in refrigerated case tempted patrons.

College students, professors and tourists milled around and sat in the salmon-tinted room eating, drinking and conversing. Local artists' paintings adorned the walls, price tags beneath each. A wall of mugs on wooden pegs faced the one-time living room. Customers who preferred mugs could take one and hand it to the clerk taking orders.

"Are dogs allowed in here?" the man in front turned to ask.

"She's a K-9 officer, sir. And we're going out to the patio."

"Erin! Come around here and give your dad a hug!" Ethan's voice boomed as he ambled out of the workspace, stripping off his apron, tossing it on the counter. He hugged her and dropped to ruffle Shadow's fur. "And this is Shadow; what a beautiful animal. Such a shiny coat. Why didn't you tell us you were coming?"

"To surprise you. Really? I'm meeting Danelle for lunch."

"Danelle? I thought she was abroad."

"She was. She's now divorced and has a three-year old daughter. We're meeting to catch up. Shadow's still in training. The K-9 instructor said to take her out in public, get her accustomed to being around people."

"Hey, Jake. Got a minute?" One of the college students materialized in the doorway. Tall, lean, clean-cut, and cute with brown wavy hair, he smiled down at her, casual and friendly.

"Meet my assistant manager, soon to be partner. This is my daughter, Erin Snow and K-9 trainee, Shadow."

"What can I get you?" Jake asked after exchanging pleasantries.

"I'll have your turkey special and a decaf pumpkin latte—the best I've ever tasted. Oh, the cranberry sauce on the side, please. I'll be on the patio waiting for my friend. She'll order when she arrives. Nice meeting you, Jake. And thanks."

"Likewise. It'll be out in a few."

Her dad walked her out into an Indian summer day and wiped off a table for her. She lowered her awkward bulk onto a wrought iron chair, signaling Shadow to sit.

"How are you and my grandson faring, lass?"

"Oh, well enough, I suppose. He's lively, but I'm ready for him to arrive." She sighed. "Dad, you know we're working on a homicide."

He nodded sadly and sat heavily onto a wrought-iron chair. "I saw the photo. I'm sorry, of course, but Ahnai and I were a lifetime ago. If you grieve..."

"Oh, I know that. It's just that I don't know how to feel. She had another family, you know—a boy and a girl, both in college."

"Don't let it get you down; she was a free spirit. Look how well you've coped! Now you have Chris, a baby on the way and us." He smiled ruefully. He looked up and stood. "Danelle! You haven't changed a day in a decade! And who's this little beauty?"

Danelle said, "This is Sydney. Sydney, this is my best friend's daddy, Mr. McCoy." She pointed to Erin. "And this is my best friend from college, Mrs. Snow."

"Hello, sir. Mrs. Snow. This is Eeyore." Wearing a toddler-sized knapsack, she held up the sad, floppy donkey and then tucked him back into the crook of her arm. She had chin-length caramel-colored, wispy hair, and pale blue eyes. Her pink tunic over purple leggings mimicked Danelle's outfit except her black hair was cut in a stylish long pixie paired with black leggings and a white top.

"Pleased to met you, Sydney. And Eeyore." He bowed and took her wee one in his big paw. He straightened. "Well, I'll let you three catch up. What would you ladies like for lunch?"

"You look fit and healthy, Mr. McCoy. Please say hello to Janelle and Liam for me. He must be in college by now," Danelle observed. "I'll have your Mediterranean salad with the house dressing. Perrier to drink. What would you like, honey?"

"Mac 'n cheese."

"Oh, I don't know if they have that," Danelle glanced dubiously at Ethan.

"Oh, we can fix that for the little lady. Nice to see you again, Danelle. Welcome, back and call me Ethan. And milk to drink for Sydney?"

"Choc' late shake, please." Sydney noticed Shadow lying at Erin's feet and dropped to a crouch to pet her. "Doggie."

"Child-sized, please. Thanks." Danelle turned quickly to her daughter. "Careful, Syd. The puppy doesn't know you. Be slow and gentle."

Ethan turned to the back door, took Erin's sandwich from the Jake, wheeled around and set it before his daughter, who smiled her thanks while keeping her eyes on Shadow and Sydney. Her puppy had no experience with a child this young.

"Make a fist and put out your hand. Let her sniff it. You can pet her, just not on top of her head." Erin wasn't sure the toddler would understand dominance, so she refrained. Sydney squatted to the dog's level and did as Erin instructed and then stroked the puppy's back gingerly. "Her coat is shiny. Puppy's eyes are honey-brown, but not like Mummy's. Hers are like coffee."

"OK. Sit up to the table like a big girl. We don't want to disturb the other diners." She gave Erin a quick, solid hug. "No, don't get up." And took the chair beside her. Danelle slid Sydney's Disney backpack off, unzipping it and lifting her daughter into a chair. "How about coloring?" she asked, pulling sanitizer from her Louis Vitton bag, rubbing it into her and her daughter's palms.

"I can do it myself." Sydney reached for the pack and dug into it for a box of fat crayons and a book.

A shadow shaded their table. A brunette with copper highlights waited a second, and then launched. "Hello, I'm Elena Michaels with WHTM news." She indicated a table several yards away. "And my cameraman, Tom Dillon." A bulky video camera, the station logo on its weatherproof cover, squatted on the table. "I'd like to know if I could schedule an interview with you, Detective McCoy. I have questions about the Lightfoot case, and I'd like accurate information."

"No, sorry. This is not the time or place. Besides, CPD has a media spokesperson. If you'll contact him, I'm sure he can answer some of your questions. This is my lunch hour."

Jake delivered the salad, child's plate and shake and withdrew.

"Thank you," Danelle and Sydney said in unison.

"Yes, I know. But I'd like to speak to you, the only female in Homicide. Get a woman's perspective and insights."

"I'm not at liberty to discuss an on-going investigation. Please call the station."

The woman frowned. "Reese said you were a hard case." And she stomped back to her table.

"Well, the nerve," Danelle whispered. "Who's Reese?"

"Her ex and Chris's partner. Remember, the one who recently returned from Iraq and Afghanistan?"

"Oh. Well, you look great. You are literally glowing. Marriage and motherhood apparently suit you."

Erin smiled. "Yes, Chris amazes me. He treats me like an equal on the job; at home, he cooks and does laundry as much as I do. He's thoughtful and considerate and sexy as—well, he could be a male model. I think he favors Bono—a younger version, but when he smiles, it changes his entire face... his bourbon eyes alight! Oh, excuse me. Too much information?"

"Not at all. I'm glad you're so enthused. He *should* treat you well; you're a gem and you're still newlyweds." Danelle laughed. "Let's hope it lasts. Mine didn't." She sighed wistfully. "But I have Sydney."

They spent several minutes eating. Danelle scooped a small helping of salad onto her daughter's plate. "I'd like you to eat some greens, too, Syd." Though awkward with the large fork, the little girl was managing well. She obligingly speared some greens and shoved them in her mouth.

"Tell me about your job," Erin said, enjoying the turkey sandwich. She glanced at Shadow, head resting on paws, her eyes tracking dried, brittle leaves scuttling across the slate patio.

Danelle popped a cherry tomato into her mouth, chewed and swallowed. "Well, I like studio work. When the models come to me, they take instruction well, but on location, the teens are easily distracted. When spectators who happen on the shoot realize what we're doing, they tend to stand around and gawk. Makes some girls uneasy. So, when schedules allow, we start at dawn to avoid crowds."

"And who are your clients? Your job sounds so glamorous."

"You're kidding! Yours sounds so adventurous. Work's work—lugging equipment, like extra battery packs, a back-up camera, case, and tripod. Dealing with prima donnas. My clients are mainly the big-box department stores; their advertising booklets appear in the Sunday supplements. I'm thinking about doing studio portraits, too, but Tony gives me a generous alimony and child support."

"May I be excused?" Sydney asked, laying Eeyore on the table.

"You haven't finished your lunch," her mother said.

Sydney rubbed her belly. "I'm full. I ate salad."

"Well, the adults haven't finished. Why don't you find your Etch-a-Sketch or learning laptop?" Sydney hunted idly through the backpack. "How's your job? I heard about your homicide on the news. I'm so sorry." She laid a hand over Erin's, paused and glanced toward the news people. "Never mind. I think she's eavesdropping. The camera's aimed this way."

"They're not recording?" Erin whipped around, stood up and approached the table, Shadow at her thigh. "Please respect my privacy and shut that camera off. I'm not going to discuss work. If you do not, I'll ask the owner to escort you from the premises."

"We're done anyway. You know, bitchiness doesn't become you. The men always work with me." Michaels gave Tom a "wrap it up" signal.

A commotion ensued behind her. Erin turned to find Danelle hurrying along the sidewalk, calling her daughter's name, her head swiveling in every direction. Erin grabbed the blue donkey and held it in front of Shadow's nose. She unhooked the leash. "Shadow, find Sydney." The dog jumped a row of yellow mums, following the scent into the parking lot adjacent to the coffeehouse —in the opposite direction that Danelle took. Erin followed Shadow at a slower pace. She stopped in the alley, scanning. Several minutes passed while anxiety gripped her stomach. As she rounded the corner, Shadow stood between Sydney and an elderly African-American woman, hair and neck totally wrapped in a maroon scarf, her body covered by a matching long, thin dress. "Will the dog bite?" the woman asked tightly, her body stiff.

Erin approached, gave her puppy a Milkbone and a pat, and then took Sydney's hand. "Good girl, it's okay now. She might if she perceives that you're a threat. It was good that you stood still."

"Is the little girl lost?"

"Not now, but thank you for watching over her." Erin handed Eeyore to the little girl.

"Is she your daughter?" The woman seemed genuinely concerned.

"No, ma'am, she isn't. Thanks again." She snapped the leash to the halter. "Shadow, heel."

By the time Erin and Sydney approached the patio, Danelle had caught up to them. Visibly shaken, she stopped, wicked away tears, and took a deep breath. She crouched down in front of her daughter, hands gripping the girl's arms. Sydney stared at the sidewalk. Danelle asked quietly, "Sydney, look at me. Where were you going just now?"

"Exploring." She clutched her stuffed animal to her chest, her chin on its head, pouting.

"You must not take off like that ever again. You don't know the people here. While most may be kind, some strangers would take you."

"Why?"

"Because you are so pretty, and maybe they don't have a little girl of their own." Shaking, Danelle stood and took the little hand. "And now we're going home for a time out. Say thank you to Mrs. Snow and Shadow."

After hugs and promises to keep in touch, Erin and Shadow went back to their table. Her dad was waiting. "I boxed up the other half of your sandwich. "I heard the commotion. Did the newswoman catch you? Did Sydney wander away?"

Erin nodded, picked up her purse. "Do you have a minute to talk?" Father and daughter sat down.

"Shadow found her. Did you talk to the newswoman?" Ethan shook his head no. Erin sketched what she could about their homicide investigation, identifying the reporter and her former connection to the squad. Then she explained that she and Chris would not be home for Thanksgiving because of her due date. "But his mother asked me to invite you to their house for Thanksgiving dinner. We'll come to Gettysburg for Christmas."

He considered her words. "Well, I'll have to check with Janelle and Liam. I suppose we could." He smiled warmly. "We will if that baby decides to make an early appearance." He took her hands in his. "In the meantime, take care. Drive carefully. Love you. When does your maternity leave start?"

"Whenever the baby's born." She hugged and kissed her dad's cheek and waved as he returned to work. "Shadow, come. Good girl! Good find!" She sighed, worrying about watching children 24/7 as she wended her way to her vehicle and drove by Gettysburg College to inquire about the Native American seminar. The events coordinator gave her a brochure, which she paged through, glancing at the colorful photos and scanning the schedule of activities and demonstrations.

Driving half way around the square and up R 34 towards Mt. Holly, she touched her dog, wanting to emphasize the importance of locating Sydney. "Good job today, Shadow." Harnessed in the passenger's seat, the dog turned her eyes from the road and connected with Erin's. "We'll pass the test next time."

On the way home, she stopped at Sandoe's market to pick up a few vegetables, honey, pasta and Gettysburg pretzels.

12

Arriving at Indian Steps at dusk, Snow, Mac and
Shadow stood on the opposite side of the road, as
Lightfoot's friends and family had squeezed onto the
isthmus of land between road and river. The wind carried
the hint of winter—the sharp chill rustled the pine
needles. The outsiders observed, quietly scanning each
face—eerie in this half-light—to identify those who
attended. Jason, Anya and Pierce Lightfoot stood lower on
the stone steps—just their heads visible. Others clustered
behind the trio and along the bank, waiting. Drumming
started first, followed by men's chanting. This time, Jason
lit the ceremonial offering; the scent of tobacco and
something sharper that Mac couldn't place wafted back.
Shadow sniffed the air curiously, her nose panned one-
eighty; her hind legs shifted; she pawed the gravel. Mac
signaled her to sit.

Snow walked about fifteen feet up the road and back,
his eyes roving among the denuded trees, seeking any
bystanders who didn't belong, but the pines made the
task difficult. He crossed the road and disappeared
among the stand of trees along the banks.

Mac listened to this burial ritual, a first for her—not
knowing whether it was traditional or a nod to Ahnai's
business on the water, or perhaps her wishes, though
that was doubtful given that murderer took her unaware.
Mac crossed the road to better see as Anya pushed off the
canoe carrying her mother's body wrapped snugly in
winding sheets lying on branches; only Ahnai's face and
black hair were visible.

Jason's words drifted on the wind as the volume of
chanting rose to a crescendo—a unified wail of mourning.
Suddenly voices and drums fell silent. The acrid odor of

gasoline flared Mac's nostrils. Pierce held the torch overhead while his father strung a bow, notched an arrow, its tip turbaned in wet cloth, touched it to the flame. He sent the flaming arrow arcing in the air, landing in the canoe. Flames licked the night and black smoke curled and climbed higher as the canoe drifted downriver and engulfed the body, then the birch bark.

Snow quietly materialized by Mac's side, as they crossed back over the road, a concrete division of culture and history that wasn't part of hers. So dramatic and final, the cremation distressed her as nothing else had done. Tears pooled in the corners of her eyes for their family's loss, but her own had happened years ago; she, like the river, had moved on—their ripples buried in the past, her footsteps in the current.

***

Next morning at their daily briefing, the coroner reviewed the results of their Vic's tox screen. Slaughter's blood tested positive for marijuana and alcohol. "Semen tests indicate two different donors. I requested tissue samples from both murder victims and sent them to the DNA lab." Dr. Chen laid the results in front of Snow and McCoy. "Two matches: Dean Greer and Jason Lightfoot."

"Well, well, he didn't tell us that." Snow glanced to see Mac's reaction.

"She was his wife; I don't see how that changes anything," she said.

"Perhaps he was the last person to see her alive," he suggested.

"I doubt that. He said he left before she did. I think Sandy Ladd—the Cumberland County Historical Society's archivist—told us that too."

"They obviously connected at some point," Savage commented.

"Oh, Snow, I signed off on your request to hire Imhoff as a consultant in this case; now communication can flow both ways. OK, what else do we have?" asked Chief March to move the meeting along.

Mac and Snow noted highlights of their investigation at the West Enterprises drill and RV sites, including the money discovery. "I kept our Vic's clothes and gave them to Dr. Chen for testing. Have you had time to examine them?"

"I did. They match her blood type. The pinpoint hole in her shift corresponds with the fatal wound to the heart. Blood pattern on the front and neck bruising are consistent with the assailant grabbing her from behind with a chokehold and stabbing her heart. It would have sprayed onto anything directly in front of her. The boots are unique—handmade and match her shoe size. I removed the sole; the imprint of her heel and toes aligned perfectly; she wore them without socks. The fibers I took from her wounds match the shawl, which is also covered with her blood. I also found hair and a blood sample that were not hers on the wrap. I shall send that off to be tested as well."

"Thank you. Now we know that we're on the right track. Greer's semen signifies a lead we need to explore—and a motive for the husband to avenge her honor or his wounded ego," Snow said.

"So we're looking at the husband again?" asked LT Stuart from the white board.

"The fact that he wasn't forthcoming about intercourse with her means we need to look at him more closely. After all, his prints were on the arrow that killed Greer as well. We need to search his place."

"He told us he made them. That's easy to verify. He also said he was glad Greer worked with his wife because the river is treacherous. That in itself, however," Mac said, "doesn't prove anything. Karagianis got him released from FBI custody. His lawyer will shred anyone in court who contradicts him or the facts."

Snow shifted uncomfortably in the seat beside her at her defensive tone. "I'll order the subpoena for his Sayre loft and studio," he said.

"But the barn only. The house belongs to his parents," Mac added.

"Make any hay with interviews in Sayre and at the drill murder site?" Chief asked Savage and Fields. "Did Imhoff send us anything?"

"Nothing conclusive. The Field Office super knew that Lightfoot and Greer worked together. Said his agent did good work, kept on top of the paper work, and considered her citations appropriate. One complaint—a man named Hamm, but he claimed the imbroglio had been solved; Lightfoot extended his deadline for rectifying improper waste disposal. The tapes are in my office if anyone wants to listen to them. Zach?"

"Let's use her maiden name—Slaughter," Mac interjected. "It avoids confusion with the husband," she added as all eyes had turned to her.

"Where's your pooch?" Savage asked Mac.

"Kraus's secretary hinted at a liaison between Greer and Ahnai. And the company with the most citations sent the SRBC a letter complaining of her aggressive tendencies," Zach added.

"Any threats from that quarter?" asked the LT.

"No, sir. We weren't at the West Enterprises drill site, so..." Fields' sentence trailed as he refilled his mug.

"Where does the money trail lead?" Chief wondered. His detectives mulled that over for a few minutes.

"Well, it points toward bribery or blackmail, so either Hauck—the vic at the Williamsport site—or Greer were involved in something illegal."

"But we haven't followed up on that. I asked Imhoff to interview the drill site manager—Kraus—about any improprieties and requested the company's phone and financial records. Said he'd send them along. Also requested the Vic's credit card and bank records. The husband reported his wife's arrows, quiver and purse were missing from the Indian Steps cabin."

"Mac, did you shoot the West Enterprises homicide site?"

"Yes, sir, nearly a hundred photos. One of Lightfoot's arrows in Hauck's back is identical to the one left in Greer's chest; a note pinned to him said, 'MYOB.' That tells me their Safety Officer must've found discrepancies or was involved in illegal activity, covering up the worst violations. Greer and Hauck's deaths suggest they were eliminated because one or both witnessed, did something, or stumbled on incriminating evidence. Because the men roomed together, we don't yet know who handled the money."

"All right. Sit tight on that until you get Imhoff's reports. Search Lightfoot's place when you have subpoena in hand. And bring him in again for questioning. He's still a common element in the murders. How do you know he made all the arrows? Find out what and why he's withholding info."

"They're a distinctive shade of green—like untreated wood and docked with real bird feathers. For example, Slaughter's had trimmed raven feathers. One more thing, sir," Mac said. "We need to go to Gettysburg College next weekend to interview the Native Americans who attended the Carlisle Indian School ceremony. Might be able to pry information from them about Slaughter's last movements." She held up the brochure.

Chris raised an eyebrow in query. They'd discuss that later because he expected her to apprise him of any new developments.

"Sounds like a sensible plan. Something's bound to shake loose soon. Stay focused, people and follow the evidence. Dismissed. Mac, you stay."

He flipped the local newspaper over. She saw a photo of her, Shadow sheltering Sydney and the African-American woman with a headline: "Dog Finds Tot!" and a caption beneath identifying her and Shadow, but no article. She breathed deeply and blew it out. "Did your dog get certification? Was this an official police action?"

"No, sir. Good Samaritan. Shadow skipped the slide on the obstacle course. She'll pass in March; I work her every day. Kauffman told me to expose her to the public, so she won't be distracted from her task. And no, I was lunching with a friend. Her daughter wandered away. Matter of fact, I asked Michaels to leave the premises because she was filming our private conversation."

"About?"

"It was private, but Michaels accosted me about the Slaughter homicide. Thought her connection to Savage entitled her. I declined and referred her to PR or you, sir."

"Did I miss something?" the Chief asked.

"About what, sir?" Mac seemed puzzled.

"Assignments. Snow and Savage are partners. You and Fields."

Mac's cheeks colored. "Has Savage been cleared for field duty? I thought I was to partner with Snow until then."

"Yes, he has. But as we're in so deep, you and Snow can finish what you started. And I hear that our Vic is your mother?"

"Biological, yes sir. But I haven't seen her for twenty-three years. Couldn't even ID her, she'd changed so."

"And you didn't think to inform me of this?"

"I didn't think it germane. I can still perform my job."

"Are you biased in any way toward your stepfather?"

"Stepfather?" she croaked.

"Jason Lightfoot."

"No, sir. I'd never met the man before this case. I consider my Dad and stepmother my parents."

"Tread carefully. Do everything by the book. Keep me informed. I won't tolerate anything from my squad that could be misconstrued or sabotaged in court by a wily defense attorney. Finally, your maternity will run from Thanksgiving to March seventeenth, unless you deliver early, if so, from the delivery date. Dismissed."

"Whew," Mac brushed hair off her brow on the way to her office. Chris sat at her desk, talking on his cell. Shadow moseyed over and nosed his hand. Chris hopped up and perched on her desk as she rounded it. He'd bought her a cushion, still warm from his behind. She planted a quiet kiss on his mouth, which he returned, and pointed to the memory foam cushion while the other party talked.

"Chief signed off on your consulting. Great." He peered at her desk calendar. "Yes, Monday's good. And you'll bring the records?" He disconnected and turned to his wife. "You don't fool me," Chris said. "That kiss was to soothe my ire about springing the seminar brochure!"

"Ire? Nah, the kiss was because I love you. Were your ears burning yesterday? I was talking about you." She hugged him.

"I won't hear about it on the six o'clock news will I?"

"You just might, smart ass." Mac pushed away.

"What, bragging about my prowess?" he teased.

"Your ego. I can't help what Michaels did. I carefully steered clear of any talk about our current case, even though she inquired. I asked her to leave the Ragged Edge when I caught her filming our conversation," she said indignantly.

He smiled at her stern expression. "You know, it's OK to feed Michaels tidbits now and then, especially when facts can be verified elsewhere. Just avoid conjecture or theories."

"Let her work for it; I'm not the CPD spokesperson. Let's eat lunch out. I want to discuss this," waving the brochure, "and report on the Chief's last dictum. Thanks for the warm seat."

"Sure. As long as it's close, we need to get back and look over that spreadsheet you found with the Franklin. We'll print the drill site photos while we're out. Did you get a shot of the money?" He eased her out of the chair. "You're welcome for the cushion; I don't want you to have a sore behind. And I want payment in trade."

"Yes, sir, I did. You're so thoughtful. The memory stick's in my purse." She ignored the last statement. "I also kept and sent that hundred off to ID the bloody print."

"Erin, I need to know these things. You withheld evidence?"

"Must I remind you of the spreadsheet you purloined?"

"OK. I'll mention it in our next briefing."

"But let's withhold news of the bill until the lab gets back to us," she said. Over soup and salad at Scales, Erin told Chris about the seminar and her luncheon with Danelle and Sydney's escapade. He munched on barbeque on a bun with his salad.

"Well, I saw that something transpired involving Shadow."

"Oh, Michaels did that." She brushed that topic aside and shared the Chief's mild rebuke and his marching orders about her leave.

In the time remaining, Chris revealed Imhoff's conversation and changed the subject. "What are we doing for Halloween?"

"I don't know. Do you have a parade or party in mind? I can go dressed as a pumpkin."

He laughed. "I meant making a jack-o-lantern, but we usually don't get any trick-or-treaters; we're so far out, no other houses around. And that intersection is dangerous."

"Let's take Shadow home first. I forgot to feed her this morning. Matter of fact, I'll stay home and give her a workout. I can type reports on my laptop, email them. Chief wants one on Shadow's progress anyway."

At the bungalow, Mac fed Shadow and then put her through her paces. They meandered a couple of miles along the trail in the woods. "You know, we can expand the course to introduce you to other scenarios. Perhaps arrange a mock bomb threat at the high school, simulate a shooting at a mall or a drug search. We need to consult other people about that."

The last vestiges of Autumn thrilled her senses: crumpled leaves bereft of their glory still exuded a warm muskiness; dry, frost-blasted grasses crunched underfoot, "bare ruined choirs where late the sweet birds sang," and air laden wood smoke reminiscent of camp fires wafted in her direction. This season marked apple festivals, county fairs, football games and little masqueraders begging for candy, a time when high schools and colleges held alumni reunions and homecoming games. Native Americans also celebrated the Green Corn Festival. "And we'll celebrate Thanksgiving with the Snows, Christmas with the McCoys.

"Sorry, girl, tomorrow morning you have to stay home."

13

Snow and Mac shouldered their way through the students clustered at the gym's entrance and found the arena. The perimeter was divided into spaces with hunter green pipe and drape. Most tables were laden with artifacts, art, photos, leather goods, carved animals, drums, dream catchers, turquoise on silver jewelry, note cards and calendars, and baskets of every size. Native Americans monitored each booth, working on their wares. In the center, Anya Lightfoot was talking to a youth dressed only in a loincloth. His cocoa hair was thinly braided along his temples and the rest—razor cut like a lion's mane—brushed his shoulders. Beside him a full warrior's regalia—including a bonnet of eagle feathers stood on a wooden valet. Beneath sat a pair of moccasins. Rows of chairs formed a semi-circle before them, many already occupied.

The detectives' first pick stood before a wide corner booth near the outside exit arrayed with bows, war clubs, tomahawks, sling shots, and blow guns. The other side displayed large paintings on easels, smaller ones on a table in front, and prints in plastic sleeves in an x-shaped cradle. Rays slanting through the glass highlighted golden copper skin as he arranged wildlife photos in display racks at the right. One, a close-up of a bald eagle perched on her nest feeding two downy chicks, beaks open, caught Mac's attention. The same photo covered a 2008 calendar.

"Lightfoot? Do you have a few minutes?" Snow began. The man's ready smile faded to an expression of wariness. He nodded and motioned toward the exit door. Though the morning was chilly, the sun warmed the brick behind them. Lightfoot eyed his booth.

"Your wife's tox screen and DNA tests came back," Mac paused to see if he anticipated her next sentence.

He hunched athletic shoulders. "You found my DNA. Yes, I had sex with my wife. Obviously so do you. That's not a crime."

"You didn't tell us you were probably the last to see her alive," Snow said.

"I told you that. We ate lunch together. I hadn't seen her for two months. I wanted her; surely you understand that. And do you tell everyone what happens in the privacy of your bed?"

"No, of course not, but omitting that makes you look suspicious, like you murdered her for revenge," Mac said.

"Why would I do that? Oh, you found something else."

"Sorry, yes," Snow reported.

"Dean Greer's," Lightfoot said with certainty.

"You see why that gives you a motive to murder?" Mac said quietly.

"But I didn't." Hazel-green eyes bored into hers. "Are you here to arrest me?"

"And make a spectacle? Not on your life. We know where to find you." Snow motioned toward the door. "Is your son here?"

"Yes, he's in the locker room practicing."

Music greeted their ears as they entered. Pierce Lightfoot, a younger version of his dad, his espresso hair hobbled back out of his way, wore buckskin breechclouts, whirled five hoops around his waist, knees and arm while bending for another from a pile beside him. The hoops stilled and were set aside; he shut off the boom box and stood—a look of sullen insouciance on his features. His brown, hooded eyes roved to their detective shields. "Can I help you?"

"We hope so. We're investigating your mother's death," Snow said.

"Would you recount that last day at the Carlisle Indian Industrial School Ceremony, especially anything unusual?"

He described a scenario similar to his father's and Ladd's accounts. "That's it. After the cemetery ceremony, I bid my family farewell and returned to Dartmouth with Dakota Burns and Ryan Riley."

"Are they here today?" Mac asked.

"Dakota's modeling regalia in the middle of the gym," his head angled right. "He goes first this morning. Anya describes the regalia and answers questions as he puts each piece on."

"And Riley? What's his role?"

"Her role. Helps man the booths. She stayed on campus to study. We have midterms coming up, and she has a paper due."

"Do you have a phone number for her?" Mac pulled out her spiral notepad and wrote it down as he reeled numbers off. He hadn't answered the first question.

"So nothing untoward happened? No arguments or altercations?" Snow probed. Lines furrowed his brow as he shifted his weight, sat down on a bench, motioning the others to sit. Two seminar participants pushed through the door, "Hey, the frame's up," but backed out when they saw the detectives with Pierce.

He paused. "We were absorbed in what we were doing." His eyes narrowed, slid to the door. He picked up the sweatshirt beside him and slid it over his head, his face a mask of indifference.

"Can you identify anyone else in Carlisle who is also here?" Snow asked.

"Uh, yeah, almost everybody except Sara Wolf, the storyteller and Tory Haller, the author." Lightfoot slipped into moccasins.

"Why did you leave early? Did your mother and father have words—an argument?" Mac asked.

He finally smiled. "My mother always has words, sister. They talked, not argued." His eyes alighted on her auburn hair and slid away.

It was Mac's turn to be startled. "You know your father is the FBI's prime suspect?"

The younger Lightfoot shrugged. "He didn't kill my mother. Look, I have to help build a sweat lodge outside."

Snow handed him a card. "If you think of anything, call the station or my cell anytime."

They circulated among the booths, asking questions and taking notes. Too much background noise rendered the recorder worthless. Mac asked the basket weaver if she could weave; the silver-haired woman surrendered it wordlessly, strips of damp willow trailing. Erin worked a half row, and then returned it. "Thank you."

The lady smiled. "You've done this before."

"Grandmother taught me." Visions of the Smokies crossed her mind.

In the center, spectators seated, Anya tested the mic, introduced herself and Dakota Burns, explaining the purpose and significance of each garment as he donned it. She passed a patch of buckskin for them to feel. Then he stepped into fringed leggings and added a wampum belt. Next, the beaded chest plate. Finally, she held the war bonnet in her hand and told the significance of the warrior's eagle feathers to many tribes.

Jason Lightfoot approached the group with bow and arrow in hand. At the end of the room stood a deer target, a bale of hay behind it.

Anya backed out of the way. "Now my father will explain our weapons."

Lightfoot handed the young man an unstrung bow and quiver of arrows. The daughter surrendered the mic to her father. He said, "Thank you all for coming today to learn of our heritage. I'd like you to welcome my wife's firstborn, Detective Erin McCoy and her husband Christopher Snow." Foot tapping and a spate of drumming followed. Mac turned toward Lightfoot speechless, nodding, blood rushing up her neck and face and turned away from the crowd to examine some wares.

Lightfoot then explained the bow-stringing process as Dakota demonstrated, notching the arrow, the purpose of the feathers and the profile aiming stance. Finally, the young man released the arrow, which arced and homed on the deer's midsection, thunking dead center. The youth also threw a tomahawk, knife, war club and spear, but stepped aside for Lightfoot. Needing both hands, father surrendered the mic to daughter; he rubbed the flint against a dowel until spark ignited the wood and sent up a smoke spiral. College officials eyed the smoke nervously, but he dropped the dowel into a cup of water and returned to his booth, thanking the crowd for their attention.

Introducing her brother next, Anya said, "The hoop is sacred to our people because the turning circles encompass all Nature; all are included within the circles, which embrace and transcend clock and calendar time. The hoops celebrate our unity and pays homage to all."

The drumming started slowly, the rhythm and slow chanting mesmerizing. Stepping in tune, Pierce emerged in breechclouts carrying his hoops; he slipped one hoop over his head; it fell to his knees as his hips gyrated to set it spinning. Then he bent for another that orbited his waist. The third twirled around his neck. He looped one over an extended leg and then, each arm. He kept them moving, then corralled them one by one, his body twisting and twirling. Then he whirled them in concert. Erin was moved to tears, reminded of universal time unbounded by daily routine: eternal time high and wide, a concept hard to grasp. The music, hoops spinning like W. B. Yeats's gyre caught her in a ceremonial timelessness that soothed and connected. When the music stopped, Erin suddenly snapped back to the moment.

Stopping at the last booth, she bought fry bead and handed Chris a hunk to taste. "Let's enjoy the moment."

"So nothing occurred at the ceremony in Carlisle that struck you as odd?" Snow asked the woman frying bread. He bit into the warm bread and chewed.

"Young Lightfoot usually prepares the tobacco for the ceremonial pipe, that day—an offering for the little ones' spirits. In Carlisle, his sister mixed the herbs in a gourd for her mother." A chef's apron covered her ample bosom and wide hips. Her arms jiggled as she deftly removed a batch of fry bread one by one from an electric skillet onto paper towels to drain.

"Ahnai Slaughter led the ceremony?" Snow asked, surprised.

"She's the elder for the tribe of Eastern Band of Cherokee, but any mother in the tribe can stand in for Corn Woman."

"Did she seem upset her son wasn't there?" asked Mac.

"Not really. He was with his father demonstrating weapons." She dropped four mounds of dough into the oil; they spread and puffed, turning golden. The woman expertly flipped each one. "And some of the young people do not share the old ways."

"But can he shoot a bow?" Mac wondered.

"Of course. All the men can—and a number of women, too."

The detectives put away their notebooks and mingled. Chris bought Erin silver filigree dream-catcher earrings and a slingshot for himself. She returned to Lightfoot's booth to buy the eagle photo calendar, and also bought Christmas presents: turquoise nuggets on posts for Danelle; silver circles with three thin tinsels dangling from the bottom for Erica and Janelle, and soft, stuffed polar bear cubs for Sydney and Kayla; a sweet fat hedgehog for her baby, and a Husky pup for Tamara. Another find—a set of basal wood airplane models for Kyle. Erin pulled a tomato from her purse, snapped open the plastic tote, placing her purchases inside, the plane kit first. By the time she straightened, Pierce was inches from her.

"Stay away from my father. Quit asking questions. You don't belong."

"Excuse me?" Mac was taken aback by the resentment radiating off the young man. His eyes darted dislike into hers.

"You whites waltz in here like you own the place and interrupt our ceremonies. I see your eyes on him while you carry another's child. You are your mother's daughter, after all." His vitriol caught her off guard.

"I didn't claim tribal affiliation—never have. I don't know enough about your traditions because my father reared me. *Your* mother abandoned us when I was a toddler." She spat out, knowing she'd lost control. "Calling me 'white' is like my calling you 'Indian.' I have many roles. I'm a homicide detective trying to find your mother's killer. You and your father are suspects. Our job is to question you. So piss off." She tried to pass.

Instead, his hand latched onto her neck; a knife materialized, the point piercing her chin while he backed her against the glass exit door. A voice, low and threatening, uttered a command in their native tongue. She recognized "chiluk-ki," cave people or Cherokee. A large hand gripped Pierce's—applying pressure on the scaphoid bone until his son released the knife and dropped his left hand from her throat. Erin stilled. Pierce's father turned her face aside to examine her neck where the knife had pricked her skin. Blood drops stippled there. Lightfoot whipped a handkerchief from his back pocket, applying gentle pressure to her wound.

"Are you OK?" His eyes filled with concern.

Then she heard her husband's voice.

"You are under arrest for assaulting a police detective with a deadly weapon," Snow said to Pierce. He turned him roughly and clamped on metal cuffs behind his back. He lugged him backwards into the locker room and sat him down hard on a bench. He flipped his cell open and called for an assist from Adams County police to transport a prisoner to Carlisle. When they reentered the gym, whispers of discontent circled. All other activity ceased as eyes watched them leave. The good will had evaporated. After an officer collected Pierce, Chris drove to the Ragged Edge for lunch. "What caused that altercation?" he asked.

Erin described the incident, trying to remain calm, though she wanted to ask him if he had any idea the damage he had done. "It wasn't dire. I could have peppered him, but I chose not to make a scene."

"It's not what it looked like from where I stood. Christ, Erin, he had a knife at your throat. You were bleeding. You should have stopped him."

She shook her head. "Then he would have lost face in front of his people. His dad disarmed him."

"Yes, I saw the tender scene that followed."

"He was just concerned." She stared out of the windshield.

"Yeah, I'll bet he was."

"Pierce won't be helpful in jail." She steered away from that topic.

"We'll see. He'll quit lying once I have him in the box. For all we know, maybe he killed his mother and the others. Seems angry enough. And don't change the subject."

Erin gritted her teeth. "Sorry. Is that you or your dick talking?"

Snow didn't say another word until he ordered sandwiches at Ragged Edge. Nor did Erin speak, as her edges were ragged as well.

"What brings you two to Gettysburg?" Ethan sat with them after they ordered, ignoring the tension. They told him about the seminars at the college, as Erin tried to regain her equanimity. Chris described the various booths and wares for sale. A coed brought their sandwiches and returned with a cappuccino and a decaf pumpkin latte.

"Where's your shadow?" her dad asked. Other patrons settled down around square tables packed closely in the back room. Conversations from the front room filtered back to them, often interrupted by ripples of laughter and bonhomie. Coeds shifted, switched tables and chatted about upcoming midterms, unfinished essays, books and selling texts.

"We left her at home," Mac said, checking her watch. "I knew the seminar would be crowded, and I wasn't sure I could control her and ask questions too. Jam-packed here as well."

"Always, on weekends. The lunch crowd doesn't thin out until three because they tarry over coffee and dessert." Other servers shuttled back and forth from the steamy kitchen, laden with plates and drinks. "Aren't you going to eat that other half?" he asked his daughter.

"I'm full." Nevertheless, she scooped the last spoonful of cranberry sauce from the condiment cup just to keep her hands occupied.

So Ethan picked up the turkey sandwich and bit off half. He borrowed her napkin to catch the drips of mayo that escaped and shared some of Jake's new ideas—evening poetry readings and adding a coffee bar at HACC's Gettysburg campus. As they bid goodbyes, Erin tried to sound enthusiastic. "Please come for Thanksgiving dinner!"

Back in Carlisle, Snow dropped Erin at home, while he drove on to HQ to interrogate Pierce Lightfoot. Since she refused to press charges, he could only hold the boy overnight after he bled him for information.

She deposited the Christmas presents in the spare bedroom closet.

Then led Shadow through a workout and a search/find session, changing the routine. Each time they approached an obstacle, she laid her hand on it and said, "Pipe. Ladder. Tires. Hunting blind." When Kauffman retested her dog, Mac would quickly name each piece to ensure that Shadow missed none. Words and signals gave Shadow both audio and visual clues. Satisfied on that score, Erin went inside to feed the dog.

The workout had settled her enough to eat a tossed salad, adding sliced apples, feta, dried cranberries and walnuts with a steaming cup of chamomile tea. And then rewarded herself with two dips of rocky road topped with hot fudge. She took a leisurely shower, the steam clearing her sinuses and the pounding rivulets easing the day's tension from her shoulders. Pulling on warm, roomy knit pajamas, Erin heated her rice snake in the microwave for her cold feet and crawled into bed.

14

The Snows awoke Monday to an iceberg house. Cursing, Chris checked the furnace and called their HVAC repairman. Erin let Shadow out, hopping up and down until the dog finished and hightailed it back inside. She showered and filled the coffee filter, pushed it back in position and then pushed start. The top flew out, spewed coffee grounds on her robe, the floor and the counter. "Son of a bitch!" Erin tried it again but held the top shut. Luckily, she hadn't dressed. She was sopping up wet grounds when her husband returned to the kitchen.

He shook his head. "Let it go. We can stop at Sheetz for breakfast." Lumbering into bathroom to shower and shave, he emerged dressed in suit and tie to find the mess vanquished and his wife sipping coffee.

"I need caffeine this morning," she said. "Whatever holds the filter in place broke off."

"It's plastic. We'll buy a new one." He shrugged, a vein pulsing at his temple. "Let's go. It's too damn cold to stay here." And marched out to the Jeep. "Leave Shadow. You can get her at lunchtime."

Erin didn't argue. "Stay, Shadow. I'll be back soon," touched the puppy's shoulder in farewell and silently followed him to the Jeep.

Stopping at Sheetz, he glanced at her. "Egg and cheese muffin? Decaf mocha?" She nodded. Returning, he handed her the bag, placed the drinks in the console between them. Slammed the driver's door, reversed and aimed the vehicle toward town. "I'm removing you from this case."

"Like hell. You can't do that," Mac objected. "Why?"

"I think I just did. I'm the primary."

She fought for control, guessing this to be an extension of yesterday's incident. "May I ask why?" She couldn't keep the acidity hidden.

"You have no objectivity, a conflict of interest, the Vic's your biological mother, and you apparently have a thing for your stepfather."

"What are you talking about?" she asked.

"Oh, I don't know, little things: Yesterday, Lightfoot's hands on you. Your snide reaction to my objection."

"I reacted to your tone of propriety," she argued.

"Think I'm entitled; you're my wife."

"But not your property. Does acting like a complete asshole come naturally, or do you have to work at it?" Erin challenged, too late noting the hurt in his eyes, but she was pissed: he was using his authority to punish her for a personal issue. She bit her lip, staring ahead, vowing to say no more. She didn't have to see him to know he was internalizing his anger to be civil.

"Why do you take everything I say the wrong way? Listen, I'm willing to keep this between us if you will remain at HQ to run the briefing room in my absence. Imhoff and I are going to Williamsport to question Kraus and the workers on site again. You will assess the situation daily, keep us in the field informed, write reports, and notify us of in-coming leads, new evidence, or anything you deem notable."

She fought her own need to speak, waiting for an "or else."

In absence of a response, Chris wagged his index finger between them. "As long as you're my wife, the only hands laid on you are mine, unless he's an M.D., relative or confessor. Understood?"

"He's my stepfather. He was seeing if I were hurt." Erin seethed and crossed her arms over her chest. The baby jerked within her, shifting her sidewise; she bumped her head on the window, and nausea washed over her like the chills. "And for your information, I'm not Catholic."

"At least nod or shake your head at my terms."

"And if I won't?" She resented his mingling a personal issue with work. But he was her immediate supervisor; she had no choice.

"I'll make it formal with a visit to the Chief to remove you."

She nodded once.

"Then we'll let it go until the baby is born. This stress is hard on all of us; we don't need the extra aggravation of arguing."

And when what? She kept her silence, stalking into her office ahead of him and leaving breakfast in the Jeep. Her phone flashed: voice mail.

A first: Elena Michaels requesting an on-air interview with her and Savage. "We're doing a segment on crime in Carlisle." The second: Sonja telling her that Michaels called again. Third from Lightfoot: "I apologize for my son's behavior. He knows better. The Greers' home is near Raccoon Mountain. I can take you if you wish."

Good. Finally someone who can move this case along, thought Mac.

At HQ, the squad met in Conference One as data accumulated. Surprised to find Imhoff already ensconced in a cushy conference chair, unloading files, photos, records, and taped interviews from a carton. Mac brought her photos; Snow had copied the spreadsheet with the sums of money listed. Once all pertinent paperwork lay before them with Stuart at the white boards, March conducted the briefing, introducing Imhoff and explaining his role at CPD.

LT Stuart summarized the bulleted notes on the boards; Snow reported the latest on finding Slaughter's clothes, giving all credit to Shadow, and Mac updated the others on the Native American seminars. Next Savage reviewed West Enterprise's Field Tech Dean Greer's homicide at Slaughter/Lightfoot's RV.

Finally, Imhoff weighed in, raking fingers through two-toned blond hair. He nodded at the pile of tapes. "What we've learned from W.E. interviews: someone in the company is paying employees to doctor data, specifically the number and types of environmental violations and the steps taken, or lack thereof, to rectify the situation. Whether Greer and Hauck—the drill site victim found in the impoundment pond—were both dirty, or a third silenced them and killed your Vic is uncertain at this point.

"The state police and Williamsport are assisting, but I'm at a loss as to why your Vic was stabbed and the others shot with arrows. It's unusual for a spree or serial killer, if that's what we're looking at, to change his MO. Or we could have two killers, as shoe prints found at two sites differ in size and imprint. One is a hiking boot, the other an athletic shoe. Did you have different footprints at Letort?"

"We retrieved no clear prints; the killer must have worn protective covers," Savage stated. "And there were too many to catalogue at the murder scene: moccasins, boots, sneakers among them. Some we cast; others were too trampled."

"Well, where does that leave us?" asked Chief March.

"Shit up the creek without a paddle," offered Fields.

"Not quite," Snow said, smiling sheepishly. "I have a list of who took money, for what we don't know. Could be payoffs that Carl mentioned, or could be blackmail, kickbacks of funds siphoned off the gas royalties. Looks like the original was stapled, so let's have Huddleston go over the drive's files." He passed the sheet around. "Does this list correspond in any way to what you learned from the drill site interviews?" he asked Imhoff.

"Where did you find this?" the Chief asked.

"At the RV with about ten grand Mac found in an empty juice carton in back of the fridge."

"You took evidence from a crime scene?" Imhoff chewed on his lip, looking perturbed and preoccupied with his own thoughts.

"I'm sharing our evidence from our vic's thumb drive, which the murderer failed to find when tossing

Slaughter's cabin. Perhaps she found the money and confronted Greer, which led to her death. Or they both took it to Hauck, endangering them all," Snow said.

"Or she's dirty, too," Savage said.

"What's on that drive?" Imhoff asked sharply, his deep, wide eyebrows shadowing his eyes, but his knee jigged nervously.

Mac stirred, defending Ahnai. "Doesn't fit her SRBC work profile, which is impeccable considering her twelve years of service. She had excellent evaluations, timely reports and follow-ups with companies re compliance." She arranged her drill-site photos in order, cringing internally at Hauck's chemical burns and cloudy colorless orbs. "Besides, the MYOB on Hauck's back connotes more. As the Safety Officer, maybe he found irregularities, pursued them or witnessed something illegal and got killed for his efforts. Or pissed off somebody who retaliated with a bow and arrow to frame Lightfoot."

The Chief shook his head at the possibilities. "All right, men and Mac. Let's examine the evidence in front of us first. Take notes. Listen to the interviews. Cross reference CPD info with Imhoff's. See what shakes out. Then we'll take fifteen at eleven. Lunch is being catered, delivered at noon, so we can make the most of our consultant's time here. Afterward, I have to inform city leaders and mayors and confer with the press. Snow will make assignments, since LT Stuart is going with me, but Les will be available tomorrow. So let's get to it." He lowered his weight to his chair, knees cracking, corralled some tapes, recorder and headphones and bent to his task. Each tackled the project before him. Mac studied each eight by ten under her magnifying glass. By the time they broke for various wraps, chips and crudités with ranch and humus, capped by a plate of chewy brownies, the squad decided they didn't have the information or evidence to make an arrest.

"We'll have to return to the murder sites, canvass them again; get something concrete to nail this perp. Surely he left something somewhere. Find it before the feds muscle in. Agent Howard's already arrested our vic's husband once," Snow commented. "Mac—with me to the Indian School grounds, Savage and Fields, to Fort Hunter. Tomorrow, we switch personnel. I'll ask Stuart, Imhoff and Fields to assist me with Williamsport interviews. Savage, you and Mac stay here to cover and disseminate in-coming and out-going data. You're out of here; bring me something concrete. Lean on people this time if you have to."

Mac went home to take Shadow out and refill her water dish. "Come on, girl, let's motor. Can't leave you in this cold house." AT HQ, she grabbed bottled water from the break room fridge. Chris stopped by her office, shouldered her backpack. They walked out together, climbed aboard the Jeep; she told him about Michaels' calls. He palmed the steering wheel and aimed the vehicle towards Letort and the former Carlisle Indian Industrial School and then Cumberland County Historical Office to find Ladd, if need be.

"You and Savage? OK, just clear it with PR."

The couple put aside their personal differences on the job.

At the site, noting their shields, the guard acquiesced. "Permission granted." Another Indian summer afternoon embraced them as they combed through the grounds while the sun dropped. Clouds ambled overhead against a vivid blue sky. Mac didn't expect to find much, as three weeks had elapsed, then wandered over to the trees opposite the graves and looked up. "If someone didn't belong here or didn't want to be seen, the only places to hide are inside the buildings or in the trees." After locating a ladder, Chris clambered up with a sigh, obliging. "Well, I'll be damned." He fished a glassine from his pocket. "Do you have tweezers in your backpack?"

She retrieved them, handed them up, while Shadow wandered behind a clapboard building where Native American children aged seven to eighteen had been housed from 1879—1918. During those thirty-nine years, about 120,000 Native American children studied academics in the mornings and vocational skills in the afternoons in another building. Thinking, Erin shook her head sadly that misguided intentions did more harm than good to the children who resented Pratt's military regimentation and the alien culture forced upon them.

Chris backed down the ladder, handing her a scrap of grey cloth that'd snagged on a limb to label and date. "Looks like a scrap of sweats. Please hold the ladder. I have to climb into the tree." It wobbled until his feet disappeared, finally reemerging, a bird's nest in one hand.

"What the hell?" Mac asked, until he placed it in her gloved hand. She peered closely at the discrete materials. "Human hair."

"Good call. Who hides in trees besides you?"

"Those who look up: Native Americans, children, teens, animals and apple pickers." But she accepted his praise as a kind of truce that eased her anger but not her bruised feelings. From behind a clapboard building, Shadow gave one "woof," signaling a find.

"Good girl." Mac gave her a triangular treat. "I can't kneel down."

"Oh, right, but I'm the eldest." He tweezed the joint butt, dropped it into another evidence bag, and labeled it. "DNA." They perused the rear of every building, picking through brittle leaves and dry grass. They gathered shards of amber glass, bird feathers, and a matchbook cover from the Seafood Shack in Boston. Canvassing the interiors revealed nothing; CSU had apparently excavated everything worthwhile. They drew a blank at the creek. Then Snow pulled off his shoes and waded into the frigid water, examining the bed inch by inch. He found a penny, broken shells and a fishhook with filament attached. Again Shadow, sitting on the bridge, signaled a find.

"I don't see anything, girl." But the dog smelled something. Back to the backpack, Erin retrieved her magnifying glass, pouring over the lichen-laden bridge. A shiny point winked in the sunlight. Using tweezers, she teased it from a crevice where mortar had disintegrated. Carefully, she extracted a long, slender shaft of metal with a rusty point. "The murder weapon! Ice pick! Well, the handle's missing, but it's stained with dried blood, I bet." She bagged the wickedly sharp projectile. "Anything else in the water?" He climbed out onto the bank, pocketing the penny.

"Brown trout. If our killer threw the handle in here, it's downstream by now—long gone. Let's go home. I'm wet and tired." He stuffed his socks into his loafers, picked them up and minced his way over the gravel toward the Jeep as Erin loaded Shadow.

"Well, we could wade downstream and check," she suggested. He threw her a disgruntled look. "I'm kidding. I'm famished, my back aches, my ankles are swollen and these boots are pinching by toes. What's for dinner?" she asked.

Chris hunched his shoulders. "Won't know until we see what we've got. But you got groceries recently?" She nodded. "We'll throw omelets together if all the meat's frozen. You didn't thaw anything?"

She shook her head. "I was too busy mopping up coffee grounds. Oh, we need to stop for a new coffeepot."

Chris nodded wearily, pulling into the nearest strip mall, parked the Jeep and stopped, realizing he was barefoot. "Can you pick one out?"

She nodded and trudged into the department store, fished in her purse for a coupon. Habitually, she carried current coupons from their local stores in her purse, so she'd save their hard-earned dollars. "Ah, twenty percent off! Let's see. Uhm." She perused the models displayed. "Nice, but it's too pricey. Oh, a cappuccino machine! YIKES! A thousand dollars?" She selected a Cuisinart drip, moved through the checkout line, paid with plastic and scrambled—insofar as her bulk allowed—to the Jeep. "And you want dinner too, don'tcha puppy?" Erin reached back to riffle her ruff as she climbed in, ignoring Chris's exasperated look.

Dinner was a somber affair, with neither of them initiating any conversation or volunteering any information instead of combing over the case as they usually did. For her part, Erin was still smarting from Chris's ambiguous threat and removing her from the case unofficially. *What happens after the baby's born*, she wondered, but hurt pride kept her tongue still. Chris was hurting, too, but she felt disinclined to comfort him.

15

Next morning, Erin led her dog outside as wan peach light rimmed the horizon and maneuvered Shadow through the obstacles in reverse order. Erin identified each item along the course and walked her back to the usual starting point. "Find the slide, Shadow!" Signals accompanied the verbal commands. The dog hustled to the slide, barked, and sat, waiting. Her soft brown eyes studied her handler, seeking praise. "Good girl! I'm trying to prepare you for all contingencies," she told her. "Up and over." The dog climbed the ladder and slid down gingerly. She awarded her with a treat, slapped her thigh and waddled after her into the bungalow after the Jeep's taillight disappeared from view. "Need to approach that slide more aggressively next time."

She washed and dumped plump blueberries over a heated waffle, drizzling a teaspoon of honey over, and indulged in the sumptuous treat. She showered, dressed, and then fed and watered Shadow. Drove to work, stopping for a decaf pumpkin latte at Sheetz to compensate for yesterday morning's fast. "To fast from fast food!" She laughed, while Shadow watched the road from her rare vantage point in passenger's seat.

First thing at work, she called Michaels and begrudgingly agreed to appear on TV. "Why me? Why not Detective Snow?"

"Chief March said he's too busy with triple homicides. Look, we'll tape it Friday morning, run it Saturday and Sunday prime time. Besides, Reese can probably relay what Snow would; he has an eye for detail and a good memory. You'll relate a woman's perspective. And thanks."

"I won't answer any personal questions."

"I won't ask any," Michaels assured her.

Settling into a comfy chair in Conference One, she organized the paper, scrutinizing the white boards, pacing the perimeter. She heard staff entering the office, the conversations a polite background buzz. The conference door smacked open; in backed Savage with coffee in one hand, plated pastries in the other. "High Street Bakery." He made a show of removing the clear plastic cover, offering the plate one-handed, bowing like a butler.

"I had breakfast, but thanks," Mac said.

He selected a fat croissant. "Raspberry and Bavarian crème. if you change your mind, there's a Boston crème glazed with chocolate frosting." Knowing her chocolate craving, he put the plate in front of her and sat down to enjoy his pastry. "Trouble in Paradise?" He leveled his eyes at hers until she sat too.

"Excuse me?" she asked.

"Don't play dumb. It doesn't suit you. What's going on?"

"What makes you think that anything's going on?"

"One: you didn't arrive together. Two: you haven't made that adoring eye contact lately. What... 'You've lost that loving feeling'?"

"How's that any of your concern?" Erin wanted to know.

"And three: he left me to guard you." Savage winked.

"The fox watching the hen house?" she quipped.

"No, just the hen." His eyes travelled over her.

"I'm not going to discuss my personal life with you."

"Well, I'll try to understand. But frankly you should—"

"Really? And how did that work for you and Elena?" Mac snapped.

"Not well, though we had three fine years when she showed some interest." He sighed, his dark eyes reflective.

"What was the problem? You have a roving eye?"

"Nah. It was mainly my fault—a cop's life. She just couldn't housebreak me. I don't mean I pissed in the corners—"

"I know what you mean." She shook her head. "Let's get to work."

"Don't cross him, Erin. And don't trivialize or hurt his feelings. He's more sensitive than he lets on."

She looked up in surprise at his use of her first name. "What do you mean?"

"You know what I mean. He will eviscerate any rival."

"Then beware his 'vorpal sword/The vorpal blade goes snicker-snak!'" Mac quoted, weary of verbal jousting. "He has no rival."

"Then why do you stare at Lightfoot?" Savage asked.

"Reading body language tells me when people lie, pause, omit or provide too much info, plus tone of voice and the vibes they emanate translate mood, levels of anxiety and evasion—to name a few. I look for criminal earmarks. Why?"

Savage shook his head in disagreement. "No. It appears you're coming on to them. Extended eye contact means you're available. You may be unaware, but you radiate sex. That auburn hair, those artfully mussed curls draping over bare, milky skin that a guy wants to lap up like a puppy, those heavily fringed sea-foam eyes, and those long legs a man could slide his hand up, and swollen belly—proof that you've been fu—"

"Stop that! Don't make me something I'm not. Quit even thinking that way. Chris is jealous enough without you fueling the flames. Are you trying to put a wedge between us? Because not in this lifetime would I—"

"Don't twist your panties. I'm trying to give you advice to save your marriage. Find a way to get back to the honeymoon stage."

"Kiss my ass! MYOB. We *are* working on it. Can we get to work here? Speaking of Elena, we meet her Friday to tape an interview for WHTM's Carlisle Crime Forum." Just the thought engendered a wave of nausea.

"Make it bare. I have a lead for you on the Murphy case." He smiled conspiratorially.

"Well, give it up, Reese," she said impatiently, trying to ride out the queasiness she felt being around him, the acid climbing her esophagus.

"First, the lab sent DNA results from the water bottle."

"Five months have passed since her case. Which water bottle?"

"The one Abby Benedict drank from when Snow and I interviewed her at the Adams County Police station."

"And?" She sat up, as did Shadow, anticipating travel.

"It matches the epidermis samples under Murphy's fingernails. And two," he waggled a folded paper, "an arrest warrant."

She rose to her feet. Shadow jumped to attention. "Let's go. Know the suspect's whereabouts?" She shouldered her purse, dumped the empty latte cup in the trash. Erin followed Savage's dubious gaze to the dog. "She goes where I go. I'll drive."

"The hell you will. We'll take the Bronco." Savage filled her in on Benedict's movements at University of Maryland. The tail CPD put on her car, recording her packing and hauling boxes to the post office. "Mailed them to Edinburgh, Scotland. Once she books, we won't get another shot at her for a year, if ever."

She motioned for him to continue.

"Her fiancé's residency."

"Yes, and now? She's booked a flight out of BWI?" she guessed.

"Right."

"She's on the way to the airport?" Mac practically screeched.

"Not yet." He laid the bubble on the dash, flipped it on, turned south and floored the accelerator, "Buckle up," even though they already were.

She peppered him with questions in an attempt to get up to speed.

"Will the DNA sample match be enough to convict in the first degree?"

"Depends on the jury, but I doubt it. What else have you got?"

"Well, I don't have it yet, but I'm hunting a pink sweater that matches the thread and button I found at the scene. The lipstick on the mirror matched Mindy's DNA, but it's a popular color, so maybe she found it—stole it. Benedict caught her in the act, but Murphy ran—almost made it to her car."

"You never found the sweater?" He levered the siren, whipped into the passing lane and booked. Cars pulled out of the way, leaving them an open concrete ribbon. Shadow howled from the back.

"The siren hurts her ears. Is it necessary?" Mac asked. "Not a scrap, and CSU tore their Michaux cabin apart, even gathered the ashes from the fireplace and woodstove."

He turned the siren off, but the lights continued to flash and rotate, which was just as effective in traffic. "Spoilsport."

"Does the warrant cover her apartment?" She sat up.

"It does. CSU is en route but has orders to stand by until the couple leaves for the airport."

She slumped back into the seat. "On second thought, the sweater won't be there. Too much time has passed."

"She got rid of it?" Savage speculated.

"I don't think so. It's an expensive sweater—not one I'd destroy. Benedict's clever; she's slick—slipped out of every tight spot. But that sweater's somewhere. My gut knows it."

Reese shook his head. "Find it, but it sounds like a long shot."

"OMG, that's it! She mailed it! That's the perfect, long-term solution. Goodbye incriminating evidence, hello freedom. Did you seize the packages?"

"Your fed admirer Howard did. They're waiting at Baltimore Post Office for our inspection."

"That's great, but that sweater wouldn't be going with her. It's solid evidence connecting her to the crime scene. She'll want it gone forever. We didn't find it burned or buried at the cabin, in any closets, crawlspace or attic."

She turned to the back seat; Shadow was sleeping, head on paws, her lean body stretched out fully, and hind legs splayed behind her instead of sitting on her haunches as she usually did in the Jeep or Silver.

Miles whizzed by at a dizzying speed, Savage pushing the Bronco hard as they passed the "Welcome to Maryland" sign. "What would you do in that situation if you were Abby?" he asked.

"Mail it to my best friend or relative, donate it to Goodwill or Salvation Army, or remove those unique buttons and dye it a darker color."

"Luminol would still show up any blood splatter."

"Yes, that's the reason it can't come to light. Hey, she has a cousin—two, actually, Dana Flowers and Dale Evan." She unearthed her iPhone, called Hunter, requested a search warrant for both cousins' domiciles. "We're looking for a pale pink, rabbit soft sweater with silver buttons with a fleur de lis stamped on them. Women's size ten, perhaps a mixture of mohair and cotton or cashmere." She listened to his comments. "Thanks. Let me know what surfaces at either place."

Next call. "Agent Howard, yes, thanks, I'm fine. We're in route to detain our killer in the Murphy homicide last May." His good-natured voice hummed through space, bonhomie clearly evident. "Can you spare Perez or someone to search luggage and packages you held at the post office in Baltimore?"

The FBI agent spoke at length about a three-pronged approach.

"What? A package at the D.C. post office, too? Did you search it?"

She paused while listening to his response.

"We're looking for a pale pink sweater worn during the fatal attack on Mindy Murphy. Finding the murder weapon would also clinch it. Look for a small bat—like teams give away as a souvenir on opening day or kids' days—whatever. Preferably with blood stains. Or anything similar that could deliver blunt force trauma," Mac said.

She paused to listen. "No, Snow went to Williamsport to work the current case. Thanks. Savage is with me."

"Don't thank me yet; I haven't found anything," said Howard. "If I do, love, you owe me one."

She laughed nervously. "We'll see what kicks out."

Savage wheeled the SUV into temp parking at BWI. The doors echoed in the cold cavernous space. They hustled to the concourse, examined the monitors for the flights to Edinburgh departure times. "There's one at 2:00 p.m." Mac checked her watch, but Savage bounded forward; they displayed ID to federal screeners, squeezed around detectors, disgruntled passengers mumbling, "Hey, watch out, wait you turn; we're in line first," and similar complaints, which they ignored. Shadow, wearing the K-9 vest, parted the waves before them. She trotted along, nose in the air, alert for any suspicious or sudden movements. Mac wagged her head to and fro across the aisles, scanning people waiting to board, their wheelies, totes and oversized handbags parked beside or in front.

Children loitered about, mesmerized by hand-held video games, comics, chapter books or ear buds plugged in with tinny music leaking out. Others pestered their harried parents or pasted their hands and face against the glass, watching great silver birds land or take off. Outside, workers wearing fluorescent vests flagged the planes next to the umbilical cord connecting them to the airport. They walked past people wearing turbans, saris, burkas—Mac glancing closely at faces to assure herself the passenger was female, not that that was any consolation lately. Men wearing suits, jeans, sweats and uniforms strolled along, thumbing messages, cell phones plastered to their ears. Porters in beeping carts carried those needing assistance down the middle of the aisle, herding the masses aside against the inside wall. They skirted seats filled with people snacking on trail mix, popcorn, apples, or eating sandwiches bought along the concourse. A bedraggled woman pushed a stroller loaded with baggage, a toddler walking along beside, one hand on his ride while the father carried a sleeping infant in a sling strapped to his chest. Pilots and flight attendants wheeling smart, compact luggage clipped confidently along to their next flight—spotless and stylish in snug black or blue uniforms decorated with pins.

Finally, Mac saw the couple in the queue that trailed into the aisle waiting to board the flight to Scotland, their heads tilted together, shadowed profiles revealing her distinctive rounded face, his dark wavy hair and leaner, taller frame. The airport attendant at the podium picked up the mic. "The first class passengers and those needing assistance are welcome to board at this time."

Mac gave Shadow a silent signal; the trio moved closer, walking along the queue. When parallel to the couple, Savage gripped Benedict's arm and yanked her out of line. She stumbled sideways.

She started and tried to pull her arm away. "Rye! Do something. These cops are trying to detain me. I'll miss our flight."

"You are under arrest for the murder of Mindy Murphy last May at your domicile. You have the right to remain silent; if you give up that right, anything you say—" Mac intoned.

"Stop that. Everyone knows the Miranda rights. Let me go. You have no proof that I did anything illegal. I gave you my alibi ten times. Why would I kill a woman I didn't even know, had never met? Let me go; you're making a scene." Color flushed up her neck.

"Then come peacefully because you're coming with us to be arraigned at the Cumberland County Courthouse in Carlisle for first-degree murder, an egregious and unnecessary act on a woman who had no weapon and posed no threat." Savage restrained her hands behind her back again.

Abby turned to her fiancé and wailed, "Rye, do something."

He shook his head sadly, nervously toying with the strap to his laptop and chewing his lip. "I'm getting on this plane, I have to. Abby, call your lawyer."

"I didn't do this," she struggled, wrenching left and right.

"Then call Denise." Rye smiled ruefully. "You can catch a later flight. Here." He reached over Mac's head to hand Abby her ticket. "Good luck, babe. Call me and let me know how you make out."

"Rows one and two may board at this time," called the voice.

Ralston turned his back and walked up to the podium until his ticket was scanned, and he practically ran, trundling his wheelie down the walkway.

Benedict renewed her onslaught. "You asshole dicks never give up, harassing innocent civilians, do you? Why are you here now? How dare you disrupt my life? I demand to call my lawyer before you confiscate my personal belongings. What makes you think you can charge me? Where's your proof? I'll sue you for false arrest! And slander for damaging my good name. And harassment. Denise will bury you in lawsuits."

They ignored her until they reached the Bronco, pushed her into the back seat. Savage restrained her ankles and buckled her in. "What about my luggage? All my new clothes, make-up and other stuff are still sitting in the airport! Let me go back for it."

"Shadow, up." The shepherd hopped in back beside Benedict. Savage folded himself behind the wheel, and Mac settled heavily into the passenger seat, buckling her seat belt, wincing when the baby kicked against the restraint. She looked up the British Airways number, called and requested them to pull Ms. Abigail Benedict's luggage from the two o-clock Edinburg Flight and hold it in their office until FBI Agents Howard or Perez could collect it.

That silenced the coed for five minutes, until she noticed her case study sticking from Mac's CPD tote. "You're still reading my case study? Why? There's nothing in it about Murphy's death because there's nothing there; this charge is bogus. I want to call Denise."

"You can call her when we get to HQ. You want answers to your questions? One, your DNA is a match to the epidermis the coroner scraped from the deceased's fingernails. Two, we have warrant to search for the pink sweater you wore that night. Will Luminol reveal her blood splatter on it? Your fingerprints were found on the hypos CSU found buried at the cabin. Apparently the chemicals leeched into the soil, killing the grass above the spot. You might as well have painted a bull's-eye over them. At your D.C. apartment, we found Belladonna plants, traces of which were in the syringes used to kill your father and attack Elizabeth Selfe. Shall I continue or are you going to tell us what happened?" Mac asked.

Only the sound of angry breathing huffed from the rear.

"OK, it appears you came upon Murphy in your house. Maybe you caught her writing 'bastard' on the mirror with your tube of red rum lipstick. Must've been her second trip because we found a stack of bills in her vehicle. She ran with whatever contraband she'd found in the home. She turned to fight, clawing your skin, ripping off a button and thread from your expensive pink sweater. You or Alison clobbered her from behind. Trying to ward off the blows, she collapses, her brain bleeding. You let her die, when a call to 911 might have saved her. She left a thirteen-year old daughter." Savage summarized the scenario.

Back at the station, the two perp-walked Benedict along the street in full view of cameras and TV stations' monstrous video cameras. Elena Michaels blocked their path. "Detectives Savage and McCoy, what can you tell our viewers? Are you arresting Abigail Benedict? Can you give us any details?" Her bluish greys tracked between the two, ready to thrust the mic under either detective's chin.

Mac nodded to Savage; it was his collar.

"We're arresting Abigail Benedict for the murder of Mindy Murphy last May at her domicile. We tracked her to BWI where she and her fiancé were boarding a flight to Edinburgh, Scotland. Benedict will be detained, arraigned and bound over for trial—probably sometime after the first of the year. Her attorney, Denise Wilhelm, also represented her sister Alison Lyons in Detective McCoy's kidnapping last summer. This arrest concludes the media-dubbed 'needle pricker' case." Then they marched Benedict into HQ, while cameras clicked and video recorded.

Michaels turned to the camera, mic ready. "Folks, you heard it here first! Abigail Benedict has been arrested, will be arraigned and held without bail, since she's a flight risk. This gruesome murder was a senseless bludgeoning of an Ohio woman allegedly guilty of retrieving money stolen from her sister's family estate. The victim was caught in the web of scheming sisters determined to avenge their father's death and keep his purloined wealth. April Alison Lyons and Abigail Benedict will go down in the history of Carlisle jurisprudence as 'black widows.'

"I'll report more at seven and eleven when we have more details. Thanks to Detectives Reese Savage and Erin McCoy, Carlisle is now a safer town. This is Elena Michaels, now back to you." She made a cut signal and relaxed her tense shoulders, pleased that Savage had given her so much, a rare gesture from her ex. She wanted an exclusive interview with the prisoner. She backed away from the press throng.

Mac and Shadow circled the building so the dog could relieve herself. "I thought a black widow was a trophy wife who killed her wealthy husband for his money," she said.

"Same idea. Come on into HQ; we got a couple of hours to monitor in-coming calls in Conference One. Let's see what's up." He held the side door open as he shivered in a lined jacket too light for November weather. "Your immediate superior has placed four calls to the landline."

"Why didn't he call my cell?" Erin refilled Shadow's water dish and gave her a marrowbone to gnaw on; the shepherd immediately settled down to business. Mac smiled; dogs are so easily satisfied with life's simple treats. She dug her iPhone from her purse and listened to her calls. First, Snow, requesting a background check on Dean Greer's estranged wife, Sienna, a West Enterprises' employee at the Williamsport site. Ten minutes later, another call, asking if she could TM the information. "I interviewed her, but her answers were skewed. Just sketch her background. I want to know what she's up to, if she has a record."

She eased her body into a padded chair and picked up a blinking landline to listen to messages. Her husband's irate voice: "This is important; neither you nor Savage are at HQ working this case? Where the hell are you?"

She ran a Google search on West's employees and found a statuesque woman with broad shoulders, windblown hair the color of brown sugar, a sun-drenched wide face blinking in the harsh light standing by her rig, one steel-toed boot resting on the running board. Broad smile, white teeth, she looked like a throwback to the 1940's. Mac scanned her profile, reached for the phone, but Savage connected first. Standing behind her, his hand grazed her shoulder and brushed against her breast as he slid her laptop across in front of him, then sat down.

"Yes, Mac found her job profile; it lists her as a former roustabout, now a waste-water truck driver. How'd we miss her the first time around?" He put Chris on speaker while he rang his finger along her arm. She shook it off impatiently.

"Who knows? She could've been absent or lying low. She was not happy that I pulled her out of truck line to question her. She and her husband were estranged because he was having an affair with our homicide victim.

I taped the interview, and I'm on my way home because I couldn't raise either of you on the phone. Is her address on the profile?"

"No," Mac answered.

"Where in the hell have you two been? I couldn't raise anybody at HQ. I gave you both a direct order to handle in-coming data and field assist. Imhoff interviewed the site manager while Les gathered the roustabouts together to get a handle on their movements, connections."

"Savage and I had to go to Baltimore to pluck Abby Benedict out of the queue for an Edinburg flight. We arrested her for Mindy Murphy's murder and brought her back to Carlisle for arraignment."

"On what grounds?"

"DNA match from a water bottle and epidermis under Murphy's fingernails."

"Afraid that's not enough. I need your help on *this* case." Impatience thinned his voice; the Jeep engine's hum interfered at times and blurred his speech, or his cell was fading out over the mountains.

"We have other evidence; it's solid, Chris, really."

"This is an order: a killer's roaming around at this site hell bent on eliminating anyone he or she doesn't like." Air rushed through the cell, its sibilant hiss interfering. "Hell, she's nearly as big as I am."

"Wicked smile though. On the rough side but seems friendly enough. Hey, Hauck was dumped in wastewater and then shot; he went in face first. Might there be a connection?" Savage asked while taking notes.

"Any priors?" Chris said.

Mac wrested control of her laptop from Savage and rolled away from him. "Several: assaulted her husband; he refused to press charges. Two DUIs, and a citation for a road rage incident; three speeding tickets with her tanker and an arrest in a bar fight with Greer. So she's not afraid to tangle." Mac felt Savage's breath on her neck, swerved to face him as she drew her weapon, and held him at gunpoint. "Chris, where are you exactly?"

"About twelve miles south of Lewisburg." His eyes strayed to the river—a glistening, roiling silvery-gold ribbon. The fog had lifted; tiny crosses of light danced on the ripples. Suddenly they heard squealing breaks followed by metal smacking metal, and what sounded like dragging.

"Describe your Location! Savage, put out a BOLO on the Jeep—NOW!" She racked a bullet into the chamber; Shadow growled a warning at the man's elbow. He did as he was told.

"Son of a bitch. That bitch is pushing me into the river."

They heard gears ripping, a crash and then a low rumbling—like a car going over an embankment. Mac looked at Savage. "Can you get a chopper?" She holstered her weapon, slapped her thigh; Shadow jumped to her side. She ran to her husband's office and found his navy workout sweats he used to throttle the punching bag in the CPD gym. Grabbed the sweatshirt too. "Let's go, girl."

"Probably." His insouciant smirk was infuriating. He stood, flipped open his cell and spoke for a few minutes. "There's one at the Post now. Let's go." He jerked on his jacket, grabbed the Bronco's keys and waited for Shadow and Erin to exit. He scurried to the vehicle. Savage brought the Bronco to the door; the minute the girls ducked inside, he swung the SUV around and tore out of the parking lot, aimed for the Post, flicking the switch for the lights and siren.

The bird sat fueled and waiting with a flight navigator in the co-pilot's seat. The whirling blades whipped Mac's hair across her face, scattered desiccated leaves and flattened the zebra grass—the sound beating down all others. The rotors' roar hurt her teeth and ears. Shadow jumped in first. Savage ducked and ran. His foot anchored on the pontoon, he turned to lift Erin but first planted a kiss on her lips. "Payment," he whispered in her crimson ear and climbed into the pilot's seat.

The noise level allowed no conversation. Within minutes, they were airborne, traveling north, then west following 322 and then traced the Susquehanna north toward Sunbury. They could see the skid marks as they hovered—the Jeep on the bank. Trees blocked their vision of the road. Savage banked over the water to get a better view, hovering near the Jeep, water lapping the vehicle's front tires. Because the sun's glare off the water blinded them, they couldn't see Snow. Again the pilot circled slowly, spotting a man in the water, face down, tangled in driftwood. Savage eased closer until they were six feet over the body. Erin let Shadow sniff the sweatshirt. "Find Chris, Shadow. Fetch."

The dog sailed out of the open cockpit—her body arched over the water, splashing and paddling while Savage set the chopper down. He leaped in, rolled Snow over and helped the dog haul him into the back. He boosted a shivering dog next to Mac, who found a towel to rub her down. Chris's body was cold. "Blankets!" she yelled. A wool army blanket materialized. Mac cleared debris from her husband's airways, blew her breath into his mouth, alternating with CPR compressions. "Staying alive, staying alive. Huh, huh, huh," puffing over her distended abdomen. Snow gagged and choked; Mac rolled him onto his side. River water spewed from his mouth. "Get him out of these clothes." It was difficult to work in the four feet of space in back, but Savage helped rotate him while she stripped Chris and wrapped him in the blanket. "Shadow, down by Chris." The pup obeyed, lending him her warmth. Mac gave her two treats. "Good girl."

His complexion like clay, his fingers wrinkled, he looked to have been in the water awhile. A sideways "V" branded his cheek. His eyes were closed, lips blue. Rivulets ran into his face; she brushed them away. "Get us to the nearest hospital! Hypothermia has set in." The navigator got them a flight path; Savage started the rotors; the bird climbed and landed at the Sunbury

Community Hospital within minutes, where attendants met them on the helipad, transferred the patient to a gurney and whisked him into the ER.

Trembling with shock and fear, Mac chastised herself mentally for chasing Benedict while Chris needed her to feed him information. She and Shadow hurried along after the gurney. She fished for her shield holding it up for people to see. A guy blocked their path. Shadow growled—a low throaty rumble. Mac let her. The white-clad attendant backed up but said, "Sorry you can't go in there." The gurney rolled through automatic doors.

"Shadow, guard," Mac responded. The shepherd jumped against the startled orderly and knocked him down, her jaws locking around his considerable bicep. "Be very still, or my K-9 officer will shred your arm to ribbons. I am that man's wife, and I am going back there with him, and every available doctor had better resuscitate him now. We're Carlisle Police Department Homicide detectives. I'm going to release my shepherd, but you sit tight. Savage, we need an APB on Sienna Greer. Have locals arrest her for attempted vehicular manslaughter. Shadow, release." The dog let go but sat close by.

Savage nodded, noting Mac's pupils, shocked wide, rapid shallow breathing, and tears pooling in her eyes. Anger spooled off her in waves—at herself, at him and especially that Greer woman. He spoke low into his cell, giving rapid-fire orders at HQ, told Sonja to get the word out to Sunbury, Williamsport and all communities along the Susquehanna from Williamsport to Sunbury and Carlisle. "Get Greer's photo from the West Enterprises website, print and wire it across the Susquehanna Valley. He described her blue rig, relayed the plate numbers. Called Imhoff, and then Williamsport police with similar instructions. "Send a cruiser around to her house; arrest her on sight. Call a local magistrate for an arrest warrant and a subpoena for her residence. Check the local bars, too, where drill–site workers hang out. She's about six feet, 175, light brown hair. Wears plaid flannels, jeans and steel-toed boots. Consider her armed and dangerous. We're sending out the woman's photo over the wires and computers." He paused for breath while the cop asked questions. "She rammed our senior detective's vehicle off the road, dumping him into the Susquehanna. Better get her under lock and key, or McCoy will shoot first, ask questions later." Finally, he phoned Chief March with their ten-twenty.

"Yes, he's alive, breathing but unconscious. Don't know his status. McCoy and Shadow are with him. She's a feisty fox. She sicced her shepherd on an orderly who wouldn't let her go back to ER with Snow. Yes, sir." He smiled into the phone.

Savage sat in the ER lobby until McCoy blew through the doors. "Did you get out a BOLO and APB with orders to shoot on sight? Call HQ? Get the bitch's mug out? Her plates? If she runs, she'll abandon her rig. If we don't catch her, she'll run to ground. She knows Chris is a Homicide detective. He must have learned something damning for her to attack him in broad daylight like that."

"So he's going to be OK?" Savage let her emote. On top of the crisis, she was also furious about his kiss.

"Yeah, he's breathing on his own; doctor's bringing his body temp up slowly. Can you get somebody to retrieve and tow the Jeep back to Carlisle?" She toweled Shadow vigorously and bought her water from a vending machine in the lobby.

"I have to fly the bird back to Post, but local cops may impound the Jeep—evidence in a crime scene. Except for the rear bumper and fenders, it didn't look damaged. But we want paint samples sent to the lab. Are you OK?"

"I am now. And I'm willing to forget that contact at HQ and at the chopper, since you helped save Chris's life."

He stood and hunched his shoulders. "S'what friends are for." He smiled sadly. "I'm glad he'll recover, but I'm not sorry for the kiss. Just don't tell him."

She glared at him. "Go back to Elena or find someone new. If you ever pull a trick like that again, I will tell him."

Inside the ER room, a physician's assistant was checking Chris's monitors. The numbers were nearing normal levels. An overhead spotlight hovered on her husband like an alien eye. Chris's coloring had improved slightly. His hair had been shorn and several staples held an angry red scalp shut. Blood had dried and clotted around the wound.

"What are his chances for recovery?" Erin asked. Tears leaked but she wicked them away.

"And you are?" The man swung around facing her, his salt and pepper hair looking snipped with pinking shears; uneven bangs hid his forehead. And noticed Shadow. "That dog can't be in here."

"I'm that detective's wife. Shadow's a K-9 officer. She goes where I go." Flashed her badge. She laid a hand on her husband's leg; the blanket was warm. Along the end wall, clear plastic bags held nasal oxygen cannulas, HYGIA BP cuffs, foam electrodes and adhesive sensors in wire baskets. Black diagnostic equipment was mounted on the wall.

The assistant complied. "Vitals look good. We stapled his scalp wound. The cold water actually kept him alive by slowing down his body's systems, lessening his need for oxygen. How long was he in the water?"

"I don't know, maybe ten, fifteen minutes? But face down. We were on the phone when it happened." She swallowed her fear. "Brain damage?"

"Now that's the question. Won't know until he wakes up. EKG is picture perfect. Lungs are clear; must have found an air pocket. We're getting ready to move him into a room."

"He was draped over a branch. If he can travel, I'd like to fly him home." She wanted to hide him away until they had a lock on Greer.

The man shook his head. "Not until he wakes up; then we can assess his condition. He's scheduled for a CT scan and MRI later, though nothing else seems damaged, we can't know about internal bleeding. May have to keep him overnight."

"Then I'll stay with him." In the hallway, Erin called Sunbury police for a guard to be posted outside, alerting them to the attempted homicide.

A technician came for the tests; Erin and Shadow followed, her shield on display and watched while the attendant moved him into position and booted up a computer. A wide white arm panned over Chris, humming up and down his body. By the time they had completed the scans, Chris's room was ready. After another wait, PAs transferred him to a bed, added another layer of warmed blankets and performed other tasks. When they left, his dinner arrived, but the patient slept. She was famished and ate his soup, some bland chicken with yellow gravy and carrots. The rest she gave to Shadow, and then rode the elevator down to take the dog out. Back in Chris's room, she bunched up a blanket into a nest in the corner. "Shadow, bed." The dog curled into a comma and sank onto the warm blankets.

Outside, darkness engulfed the city. Erin undressed, hid her pistol under the pillow and crawled in beside him, backing until their bodies touched, sharing her warmth. She closed her eyes, listened to the humming and buzzing sounds, the steps in the hallway, and her husband's even breathing, then descended into sleep.

Next morning, her eyes flew open, took in her surroundings. Chris's arm was wrapped under her breasts, his breath warming her ear, his body responding to hers. Thankful tears welled from her soul; she carefully turned to face him. His eyes studied her expression, puzzled. "Oh, Chris. I'm so sorry. You could've been killed... thought I'd lost you. You were facedown in the river! Forgive me. Don't be angry. I love you with every fiber of my being." Tears flowed in earnest. He wiped them away with his thumb and then stemmed the flow with the edge of the thin, cotton blanket.

"I'm not angry." He leaned in to kiss her, cupping her neck with his hand. The baby shifted; Chris moved his hand down, splayed his palm over her abdomen, tracking his son's movement. "Well, I was, but I can't stay angry at you for long."

She traced his jaw, neck and shoulder with her forefinger, ran her hand over his arm, down his torso. Hugged him gently. "I love everything about you. I'll do anything to keep you."

One corner of his mouth kicked up. "I doubt that, but thanks for the sentiment. What's wrong?"

"You said, 'wait until after the baby is born.' I don't know what to think—that you'd leave? I'm truly sorry we fought, but I wasn't inviting anything. I always study suspects' body language and tone while questioning persons—"

He put his lips against hers, kissing until she quieted, settled.

Footfalls echoed down the hall. Shadow leaped to attention, body alert and eyes on the door. Mac rolled, slipped into jeans and sweater, and slid her weapon from beneath the pillow, hiding it against her side. She perched on the visitor's chair as the door opened. LT Les Stuart strode in—his six-three frame a commanding presence. "Ah, you're awake. No worse for the dip in the river. You can thank your wife that you're still breathing. She and Savage got a chopper in the air. Shadow plucked you out."

"That's the second time my wife saved my life," Chris said. He cranked the bed up slightly. "You're just coming from Williamsport?"

Stuart nodded and then shook his head no. "I caught Mac's call about a watch on your door. Seems your assailant's still at large."

"If I were she, I'd have ditched the rig and crossed the border by now," Mac observed. She finger-combed her hair, eyes roving for her purse, aware she must look rumpled and disheveled.

"Border Patrol would have stopped and detained her," the LT said.

Ah, she'd dropped it beside Shadow's bed blanket. "I'd better take Shadow out." She slapped her thigh and snagged the loop of her purse.

Upon their return to the room, the LT had left. "Where's Stuart?"

"Getting his vehicle. He's been up all night. We're going home with him. Would you find a doctor who can discharge me? And locate my Jeep?"

On the ride home, Stuart updated the pair on the squad's movements. "Imhoff, Savage and Fields were on the road yesterday." A call interrupted him. He listened, told the caller to impound and tow it.

"They found the rig near the New York State border. Savage and Fields interviewed area diners, businesses and residents along the highway yesterday. The search warrant on Greer's domicile came through."

Mac's iPhone pinged as Shadow shifted against her, whimpering in her sleep. "McCoy." It was Savage. "It's for you." She handed Chris her cell and listened.

"Thanks, man, appreciate it. For yesterday, too—the chopper. No, I'll take care of that. Ten four." Snow pushed end and returned the phone.

"Reese drove the Jeep to Fine Line," an auto body shop on Trindle. "He's at HQ, writing his report on yesterday's incident." Snow frowned and rubbed his forehead. He coughed and cleared his throat. "And thank you too," his eyes cast back to his wife, "For staying on top of things yesterday. I didn't even notice Greer until impact."

"It's just lucky you two were on the phone. Savage said the cell coordinates were easy to pinpoint," Stuart said.

Mac said nothing. Chris wouldn't have been in danger had she or Savage ferried him information, alerted Snow to Greer's rap sheet so he'd be forewarned. "Why were you alone?" she asked Chris, an infraction of CPD regs.

"I stayed to complete interviews," Les offered, patting the nylon case on the seat beside him. "That won't happen again. No one goes on a call or into the field without a partner. We're currently short-staffed, but that will soon be corrected. Chief's hiring three new recruits— to start training immediately." He sighed. "Sorry, man, that was close." He grasped Snow's arm, shook it gently and released it. "Take what time you need to recoup." Snow nodded.

At home, Mac heated chili, opened crackers and filled two glasses with cold water. She fed and watered Shadow, then let her out briefly. "No obstacle course today." Her adrenaline spent, exhaustion tugged Erin's limbs. Her head, neck and lower back ached from the stress and strain. The couple crawled into bed and slept.

Next morning, a warm, wet nose bumped Erin's hand, then buried into her armpit. She groggily lumbered out of bed to let Shadow out and started coffee. Let the dog back in, dumped food and water in her bowls. She eased the bathroom door to and showered quickly. Toweled off, donned her robe. Slid out to the kitchen. From the bedroom, she heard strangled coughing and poured a glass of water for Chris. Sitting on the bed—head in hand like Rodin's statue—he hacked away. "You're burning up. I'll call the doctor." She whirled around, but his hand gripped her arm, halting her momentum.

He shook his head and took the water, sipped slowly and then his hand went to his throat. "Do we have any cold medicine?" His voice hoarse.

"I'll check. And make you some hot tea with honey." Erin rummaged through the medicine cabinet and found Sudafed and some prescription-strength cough syrup with codeine. He took two little red pills and downed the syrup. "Just coffee, please."

She poured coffee and doctored them with creamer and sweetener. Popped frozen waffles in to toast, took peanut butter and jelly from the cabinet for Chris's, and honey and blueberries for hers. She carried their mugs back to bedroom to dress and handed him one.

Chris hadn't moved, so she sat the tray on the nightstand, felt his forehead. "Baby, you're burning up. You can't go to work like that."

He took a few sips, set the mug aside and crawled back under the duvet. "Calling in sick."

Dressing in maternity cords—the elastic fully-stretched—and a crocheted cardigan over a turtleneck, Erin dashed to the kitchen, yanked a sinus mask from the freezer, doubled back and laid it on his feverish forehead. She bent over him, but his hand stopped her. "No kisses. Don't want you sick," he rasped.

"Do you want your breakfast?" she asked.

He shook his head, so she removed his tray.

"I'll put your waffle in the toaster oven if you want it later. Shall I leave Shadow with you?"

His hand signaled OK.

"Call if you need me. I'll be home at noon to let her out. I'll bring you some soup. Love you." Despite his discomfort, his lips quirked up slightly. Back in the kitchen, she gobbled her waffle. Shadow licked up the blueberry Erin had dropped, her face a grimace of surprise. Erin laid a hand on her dog's neck. "Don't like blueberries? Drop it. You stay home with Chris, today." Filled her go mug with a second cup, popped on the lid. She gathered her things and then stepped into the garage to get her car.

She stopped. No Jeep. "It's at the shop. Well, Chris won't be going anywhere today. That's good."

When Erin entered Conference One, LT Stuart raised his brows looking behind her.

"Chris is hacking his head off. He called in sick," Mac explained.

Stuart groused about the screw-up yesterday during briefing. "The Chief wants reports from each of you. Savage is the only one who submitted something. As soon as we're done here, the rest of you will complete yours before you leave the station this morning.

"Bring me up to speed. What's our progress? Do we have all the well site interviews? And what were you two doing before Snow's assault?" He directed that to Savage and Mac.

"Arrested Ms. Benedict for Mindy Murphy's murder."

"Good work. I suppose you have solid evidence?"

"Yes, sir. It's in my report, sir," Savage answered.

"We're missing the killer's pink sweater," Mac admitted.

"Find it," Chief March said. "Put this old case to bed; we have three current ones that need our undivided attention."

"Did you get Snow's interview with the Greer woman? We have a manhunt out searching for her from here to Williamsport. Did Snow definitely ID her as his assailant?" Les looked at Mac.

She scrolled back her memory re the recorder and nodded. "Affirmative, sir, on the ID." Paused. "The interview must still be in the Jeep. He said he had it with him. The Jeep's at the auto body shop."

"Savage, get on that now. We need clues. Greer might have told him something to lead us to her. I won't bother Snow now. Mac, summarize what happened, starting with the phone call."

Reese hurried out to retrieve the taped interview.

When she'd updated everyone on their activities, Les turned to Imhoff.

"OK, Sunbury. Point us in the right direction. Who are the usual suspects? Narrow it down to a manageable number."

"Hmm. The boss Kraus—well-site super's not talking. Greer had been chummy with Hauk. Not much help there. CEO at SRBC's field office knows more than he's telling. How about Jason Lightfoot? His motive is strongest. Maybe both secretaries—at Sayre and

Williamsport know more." Imhoff shrugged, his heavy eyebrows wagging as he spoke.

"Three murders and no hard suspects? Arrest those who won't cooperate for obstructing justice and haul them into your respective headquarters for heavy questioning," Les insisted.

"Anything to add, Fields?" asked the Chief.

"We've been playing zone, but Hauk's wife witnessed a knock-down argument between Hauk and Dean Greer about Slaughter when she brought her husband's lunch one day. Her remark is on the tapes," Zach said. "Ms. Benedict's been arraigned. Bail denied—flight risk. She's suing us for false arrest, insists on seeing Snow. Court date's set first week in January. Wilhelm said she'd subpoena a number of us to testify."

"Duly noted. Drum up some eyewitnesses and recover some hard evidence on these current cases," The Chief huffed. "But reports first. Listen to interviews second. Scour third. And anyone who brings me info on the Greer woman can take a comp day afterward. Any legwork," waving his hand across the sea of paper on the table before them, "handoff to whoever can expedite it quickly. Dismissed."

Mac scurried off to her office to call Agent Isola Perez and explained her theory about Abby Benedict mailing the sweater she wore when she or her sister bludgeoned Mindy Murphy to death. "Can your agents canvass the Alexandria, VA, Baltimore, MD and D.C. post offices for any packages left or returned from Benedict to either Dana Flowers or Dale Evan?" She listed their addresses. "I'll take Frederick, Hagerstown, Carlisle and others she may have chosen when she shipped her trunk and boxes to Edinburgh."

"You have in her in custody?"

"Yes, thank Howard for the airline tip. We pulled Benedict out of the boarding queue; she's cooling her heels in jail until her trial. But our other cases are front burners. Yesterday a suspect Snow interviewed ran him into the river with her rig." Mac hiccupped but swallowed her sob. "We almost lost him. I really appreciate the FBI's help 'cause we're spread a little thin now, even with help from the Sunbury and Williamsport police."

"That's our job. Sure, I'll put someone on this today, but it's a long shot. What makes you think that package didn't make its destination?"

"Don't think she wanted us to find it, but she doesn't want anyone else to have the sweater either. It ties her to the murder. Just a hunch."

"Huh. Most criminals don't think that far ahead."

"She's not like most criminals. If you like, I'll mail you her case study; read it or hand it off to Howard for BSU training. It's very intriguing."

"Don't be coy, McCoy. Just tell me what you've got."

Mac sketched their case thus far but reiterated that she needed a clincher. Then she wrote and filed her report on the previous day's events. Stopped to get a carton of chicken noodle soup, cough drops and two liters of ginger ale. Hurried home to let Shadow out and nuked the soup. Whistled Shadow in and carried the soup to Chris, helped herself to a cup. He sat up, took the tray and settled it on his lap. He dipped the spoon in and carefully tested the temp against his lips and then swallowed.

Eyes rimmed in red, sinuses puffy and nose clogged, he looked miserable. His shaved head was marred with ugly staples and cheeks bore scratches from the branch in the river. He crumbled crackers into the broth and spooned soup into his mouth. "Chief pissed?"

"No, but Les is. Claimed we dropped the ball. Maybe he's feeling guilty for leaving you alone with the Amazon who ran you down. What happened—interview go south?"

He shook his head. "Not really. At first she seemed concerned about the work stoppage. Two deaths connected to the job site. Didn't seem interested in our vic. Just listen to the tape; I'd like your feedback."

"Savage went to the auto body shop to get the tape from the Jeep. He hadn't returned by lunchtime. And I wanted to come home to check on you. You were burning up this morning." The soup contained generous cubes of chicken swimming in a hearty broth with noodles, bits of celery, onion and carrots—and parsley. "Do you still have a fever? How do you feel?"

He shrugged.

"Should I call the doctor or your mom? Schedule an appointment?"

He glared at her for a minute and shook his head.

Erin finished her soup. She approached the bed and laid her hand on his forehead. "Still hot. I'm going to take your temperature. You must've picked up a nasty bug from the river." Found the thermometer, hustled to the bed, waited until he finished his ginger ale. "Open."

He looked up at her, an argument in his eyes but sighed resignedly and opened his mouth. Erin levered it under his tongue. Sat on the bed's edge and rubbed her husband's arm in empathy. "Sorry you feel rotten. Shall I update you?" Chris nodded, his eyes on hers. So she summarized the morning briefing and explained her mission about locating the sweater. "Do you want more soup?"

He nodded and passed her the tray. Shadow paraded around her as Erin zapped the second helping. Poured more ginger ale and retraced her steps. Extracted the thermometer: 101 degrees. "Where's the sinus mask? I'll refreeze it." Chris picked up the warm, limp mask and handed it to her. He lifted her hand and rubbed it along his cheek, held it to his swollen nose. "What are you wearing today?" He liked to whiff scents emanating from her hair and skin from the shampoo, shower gel or lotion she wore and guess the scents.

"Rain-Kissed Leaves. Shall I stay home with you?" His eyes grew watery; he kissed her knuckles, opened her fingers, rubbing his thumb on her palm, and then let her go. She replaced the thermometer and stuck the sinus mask in the freezer. Back in the bedroom with more Sudafed and a packet of Alka-Seltzer to give him a choice, he took the pills. "About yesterday," his voice husky.

Erin waited but really didn't want to revisit that harrowing scene, seeing his inert body floating, perhaps minutes from drowning. *If Savage wasn't a pilot, if he couldn't have snared a chopper, if she hadn't been on the phone then... if he hadn't worn that puffy vest... If Shadow hadn't leaped and grabbed the scruff of his collar...* She nodded at him to continue.

"I slammed my head against the grab bar or maybe the frame. The Jeep stopped at the water's edge. Dizzy. Bleeding. Thought cold water would stop the bleeding. Felt heat on my back. Falling in and flailing around, I hooked my arm around a dead branch floating... Vest held me up. Tried to keep head above water, but dizziness..."

Erin let her tears fall unabated and laid her head against his bare chest; his heart beat soundly, steadily drumming reassuringly, but she could also hear wheezing. His chin rested on the top of her head. "I'm not afraid to die."

"Chris, don't—"

"I was floating through an arch in warm, slanted light toward a figure of a young man dressed in a robe, too far away to see clearly. Behind me, I saw your face, auburn hair streaming back, your naked, pregnant body... your voice calling my name. I couldn't leave you." He pulled her onto his lap, wrapped an arm around her, reached underneath her sweater and splayed his hand over their son and held them both. Then released her. "I'm OK. Go back to work. Take Savage or Fields if you go out."

"Shadow, come." The dog trotted happily along after her, eager to go. She stopped in the closet to rummage for that painter's hat she'd taken from the Michaux cabin last May.

At HQ, Savage reported that he'd found no tape or recorder.

"Do you think Greer crawled down the embankment after it?" Mac asked. "Chris said he felt heat on his back; she probably pushed him in."

"Something like that." Savage studied her. "How's Snow?"

"Very ill. Feverish. If I call his doctor, will you swing by, take him in?"

He smirked. "Coward."

"He won't go for me," Mac said. "We had that discussion over lunch."

He nodded. "Call."

Erin quickly listed Chris's symptoms and fought for an afternoon appointment. "Otherwise, he'll wind up in the hospital with pneumonia."

"He wasn't inoculated this year?" asked the receptionist.

"I doubt ever. But he's already wheezing. It's far beyond a cold." She briefly related his fall into the frigid Susquehanna.

"All right. We had a cancellation. If he can be here in a half hour."

"He'll be there at 1:30 p.m." Mac nodded at Savage, who hustled out.

In her office, she hefted the phonebook, punched in post office numbers to ask about returned mail, a dead letter office that housed undeliverable mail. "I'll visit every post office if I have to, but..."

The postal clerk said, "Well, it depends on where the letter or package was mailed from."

"Probably Carlisle, Camp Hill—or maybe Hagerstown or Frederick, Maryland."

"I can't speak about out-of-state locations, but our area's dead-letter sites are Mechanicsburg and Harrisburg, because a lot of mail is routed through there. Oh, and New Jersey; don't ask me why. You'd have to call those other post offices to find theirs."

"Thanks so much." She ended the call. "Come on, Shadow, let's motor. Damn, let's get you some water first.

Hope it's not Jersey." Grabbed a bottle for both from the break room. Sonja emerged from Mac's office. "I laid your mail on your desk. Got a package. How you doin'? Girl, you look ready to pop!"

In response, Mac crossed her fingers. "Soon! I'm fine, but Chris is sick."

"No wonder! Swimming the river in November will do that." Sonja patted her on the shoulder. "Holler if you need anything. I'll send Ozzie over with a casserole this weekend. No, maybe soup."

"Woman, you're so thoughtful. Thanks. He loves homemade." Mac smiled. The package came from Kaufman; inside nestled a black vest labeled CPD K-9 stamped in white on either side. "Here, Shadow, you have a vest. Damn, it's Kevlar, too." Mac wrestled it onto the dog, who chewed on it, eventually accepting it. The vest had been donated by a woman in New Jersey who started a campaign to protect K-9 officers. The note inside: Bring Shadow in for refresher course next week. Call first. CK

First, she drove to Harrisburg Post Office, went through her spiel again there. Once she flashed her creds with Shadow beside her, the clerk acquiesced and ushered them into cavern at the back of the building stacked with packages of every shape and size, piles of magazines, letters and manila envelopes, some padded, some torn open. Stacked on shelves, floor to ceiling and tossed in huge rolling bins.

She pulled the cap from her purse. "Shadow, find." And let her smell.

Both pawed through boxes. Mac moved bins; climbed on the ladder to scan addresses while the dog nosed everything within her range, from one end of the room to another. Three frustrating hours later, nothing had materialized. Her hands were filthy; dust coated her. "Well, Isola said it was a long shot. Think Savage and Chris are home yet?"

Stopping at Boscov's for a vaporizer and a sleeping wedge, she was late getting home—after dark, a hard frost crusting the grass.

Arriving home, Erin procrastinated while Shadow loped around back to tend to business. She followed, waited, and then whistled. When she finally opened the door toting Won Ton Soup, scents of bacon wafted her way. Savage and Chris sat at the kitchen table eating dirty eggs scrambled with bacon, onion and hash browns —cheese melted over, laughing over a ribald cop joke about holes and whores. A jar of homemade chucky applesauce stood between them. Both canted heads in her direction and pushed chairs back. "Don't get up. Glad to see you can talk." She set the soup in the fridge. "Save me any?"

Chris grabbed his crotch. "You bet. Ready for some meat?" She didn't look at Savage who guffawed as he tipped his beer to his lips.

"Looks like I already have," she quipped, helping herself to dirty eggs.

After thanking Savage when he left, Chris showered and Erin assembled and filled the vaporizer. She climbed behind him and massaged his neck, shoulders and chest with Vicks, working it in thoroughly. He drank some cough syrup and swallowed his meds with steamy lemon-ginger tea sweetened with honey. He stuck a breathing strip across his nose; beneath the strip, Erin added a thin line of Boroleum, topped with peppermint oil. And then used her acupressure tool to stimulate sinus points the way Dr. Kiehl used acupuncture on her during her sinus treatments. Chris endured her ministrations patiently, collapsing onto the wedge and pillow when she finished. She let Shadow out and then inside. "Bed." Having completed her own ablutions, she eased under the duvet without waking him.

***

Next morning, Erin unearthed Abby's dog-eared case study to read while eating and getting ready for work:

The Absent Mother

Women have anticipated, endured and braved motherhood for eons despite the reservations, dangers and sacrifices involved—as a rite of passage, necessity, or even accidentally. Some weather it well; others fail in small, forgivable ways; nonetheless, children adapt and thrive. For a small percentage of mothers, that 'wholesome neglect' translates into indifference, emotional or physical abuse, or favoring one child over another, which has a lifelong effect on the other's self-esteem. Multiple studies following children of divorce K-twelve have catalogued the long-term damage. Those children were more reticent, prone to nightmares, slower to make and keep friends, more often depressed, lonely, angry, and frustrated than their peers. They are wary of dating and marriage, fearful of repeating their parents' errors. Often they reported being sullen and resentful towards authority. Others broke laws, joined gangs or turned to drugs for solace.

Personally, I withdrew and observed, using that reticence as a shell to protect my psyche at first. After relocating, I began to mistrust others. Although I felt alien in Pennsylvania, people fascinated me. I watched how careless they were, how confident of their own privileges, content and preoccupied with materialism. How ignorant of the dangers around them. I kept to myself whenever possible, going home alone to complete my homework before Dad got home from work. We fixed dinner; I did dishes. He checked my homework and corrected my math errors. In school, I tested well, received A's. On weekends, we walked or took day trips to educational sites like Natural History, Smithsonian and Air and Space Museums, the Hershey's Chocolate Factory, Amish country, and the Eastern shore points during summers. In high school, working summers at odd jobs for college, I honed my survival skills. People were cardboard props who appeared on my stage and exited. When others submitted to their base urges, I reined in mine. My shell hardened. Only I mattered. I planned.

Children of divorce are so amorphous—grains of sand that drift and shift with every wave. Removed from our homes, shuffled among parents and other relatives, dropped at libraries, shopping malls, the neighborhood pool, foster homes, orphanages—anywhere will do. Yes, we adapt; we're resilient, too self-absorbed to worry much about the world outside of childhood and adolescence. Anxious to please our peers or sibs, many flirt with drugs; take unnecessary risks, like the Finch children running freely in their community. Hence, they saw the world raw—Atticus shooting a rabid dog, defending an innocent man and talking down a mob. Huck Finn had similar adventures, with Jim as the surrogate dad. Peter Pan simply flew away with the Darling children to Never Land, his development arrested.

Now Millennials are entering adulthood, degrees in hand while the Baby Boomers are aging but working longer, and the Greatest Generation are taking their final bows. And what do we inherit? A stagnant economy, a financial scandal and housing implosion, high unemployment, a divisive, inert government and bloated bureaucracies, and a society tilting toward—well who knows what? Will America devolve into a nation of lords of the flies and fight one another for survival of the fittest? Have we learned nothing from two millennia of history? Or will we reiterate Stevie Smith's narrator's tragic end: "I was much too far out all my life/And not waving but drowning."

***

Mac blew out a breath. *Did this case study reveal a classic sociopath who seems rational while rationalizing her antisocial behavior? That ordinary people—others—are mere props who "make [their] exits and entrances" and that evil within is as deadly as the evil demonstrated in criminal behavior? Or just a learned or innate narcissism? Does the writer feel alienated or superior, aloof from the masses but intelligent or arrogant enough to succeed?* She shook her head, called Shadow and kissed her husband goodbye after fixing him tea and toast.

At HQ, Sonja handed her a message from Carlotta Coffey, asking Detectives Snow and McCoy to stop by her apartment. She ducked her head into her LT's office to let him know she was headed out. Since Fields had arrived early too, making coffee in the break room, she asked him to ride along. Shadow didn't need to be told; she sensed her handler was on the move.

When they arrived at Lyons's domicile and mounted the stairs to the second-floor apartment, Coffey invited them inside. Mac introduced Fields. "I received a note that said you wanted to see Snow and me, but he's ill, so I stopped myself. How can we help you?"

Coffey handed them a yellow form from the USPS. "This came in the mail today. They brought a package by, but no one was here to accept it, so the mailman left this notice with instructions to pick it up during operating hours." She pointed to the print at the bottom. "I usually work eight to five, including Saturdays, and can't go get it. I know it's irregular, but if it's Alison's, well, she's incarcerated..." Her voice petered out. "I don't even know where." She twisted her fingers together, staring at the yellow notice like it was poison. "I know it's not police business, but if you could pick it up and deliver it, I'd appreciate it."

Mac accepted it, trying to act naturally while her heart surged, a timpani in her ears. "Sure, no problem. I'll have to find out where the court placed her, but I can do that." She smiled at the tenant. "And thanks for calling, for cooperating with our investigation."

As they clambered down the steps, Fields grumbled, "You didn't need me for this."

"Snow told me to take you or Savage and Shadow everywhere I go. Let's just drive over to the Mechanicsburg Post Office and get this package. Can you find out where Alison Lyons is sequestered?"

"Harrumph. I guess. Hurry, though, I have to accompany the LT and Imhoff to the drill site. We have some arrest warrants to serve."

"For obstructing justice?" She asked as she drove to the post office.

He nodded. "Oh, yeah. West Enterprises is not gonna be happy about an idle well."

"Shouldn't take more than a few minutes. Shadow, stay." She pushed her flat palm toward the dog's nose. Within five, she returned to the vehicle, setting the securely strapped box on the seat beside her and pulled out into traffic. She'd looked at the address immediately and sucked in her breath. Stamped across the face: Return to Sender. The return address had been hand-printed. *Why*, she wondered when everyone had those free self-adhesive address labels. But the addressee must have moved without leaving a forwarding address: Mrs. Dale Evan. She hoped this was what she had been searching for. The Pathfinder was still in the lot at HQ, so Fields tore inside to join the others motoring north.

In her office, without the slightest compunction, Mac pulled on gloves, cut the seal and opened the package. Inside, nestled in white tissue lay a beautiful pink mohair sweater with tiny a fleur de lis etched on each silver button, the top one missing. She laid it open on her desk and snapped several photos and then placed it in an evidence bag—tissue and all—and sent it off to the lab to be tested for blood and any other foreign matter, along with the little glassine that held the thread and button found at the Murphy crime scene.

16

On the way to work, Mac accepted a call from Lightfoot.

"Did you get my message?"

"Yes. How did you know we're looking for Sienna Greer?" she asked.

"Chatter on the scanner. I know her. She named Ahnai as the reason for her divorce. She drives a water tanker for West Enterprises. From what I gather, she saw them together at the job site."

"CSU will take her domicile apart; we got a search warrant."

"Meanwhile, she'll cut and run." Lightfoot seemed certain.

"If she hasn't already," admitted Mac. "I would have."

"Do you have her home address?" asked her stepfather.

"The one at the RV site?"

"No, their permanent address. I'll pick you up in an hour."

"I'll need to inform the Chief and take my partner."

"Bring Shadow and provisions."

Mac knew she should tell Chris, but... She told the Chief she had a lead on Greer's likely whereabouts and gave him the address Lightfoot had given her. March said, "Take Fields; he's in Conference One."

Popped her head in the war room and said to Fields, "You stayed? Chief says you're going with me. Sit tight until I take Chris some lunch."

"Chief partnered us, so I'm here to serve," he grumbled facetiously.

First she stopped for soup and sandwiches and ran home for Shadow. Since Chris was sleeping, she left a note about the soup and that she had taken the dog for an assignment. "Get better, babe."

Returning to HQ's parking lot, Zach was waiting—freed from the paper work, but letting her know he preferred going with LT Stuart. Lightfoot's Ram pulled into the parking lot. Though a tight squeeze with three in the cab, Mac in the middle, and Shadow in the half cab, they headed north armed with coffee, sandwiches, apples, bottled water and dog food. Mac noticed a rucksack in the bed similar to Savage's. Behind the extra cab space hung a rifle, shotgun, bow and what looked to her like a blowgun—a hollow tube of bamboo.

Heading north on 15 toward Williamsport, Lightfoot told the detectives about the Greers. Husband and wife worked for West Enterprises, he as a Field Tech and she as a roustabout and then truck driver. They met Ahnai on her first inspection of their drill site; Dean accompanied her to explain operations, describe the equipment and show her around. She wanted to inspect their wastewater impound construction and intake hoses into the river. Asked questions about pollution prevention because she shared her concerns with him. "I remember her saying that Chief Seattle said that 'dogs don't soil their own bed,' but humans apparently do. And then Greer and Ahnai began canoeing the river together.

"Sometimes we went out as couples, but that ended when it became obvious Greer and Ahnai... And I'm a mean drunk." He shrugged. "You've heard we can't handle alcohol well. I punched him out when he felt my wife up on the dance floor at a local bar.

"We sometimes hunted together, too." Lightfoot's eyes never left the road; they panned the lanes, watching traffic flow, shifted to the rear view mirrors occasionally as he talked. "Sienna broke off contact."

"Whom do you mean by 'we'?" asked Mac.

"Both couples."

"Does she have the strength to string and shoot a bow?" Mac wanted to know.

Lightfoot turned his eyes to hers with a what-do-you-think look. "She's strong and capable, bigger than her husband: almost six foot. She's good with tools and numerous weapons, including the bow and rifle. Wicked temper and a sharp tongue to boot—pun intended."

"Did you make her arrows?" Mac asked.

"I did. And a bow adjusted to her height. She carried them in a golf bag with her clubs." In an hour and a half, they passed Bucknell College on the right and then Country Cupboard on the left. Lightfoot kept the nose of the truck pointed north. They passed a relatively recent strip mall, smattering of local restaurants, a furniture store and a candle factory. Sped past market stands displaying mounds of pumpkins, squash, and apples and a custom-built log cabin company—the display model lit up. Two-story windows allowed passersby an impressive view of pine logs inside. A massive stone fireplace dominated the center.

"And what do you have planned today?" Mac asked.

"You know that this trip is highly irregular—civilians weren't supposed—" Fields stated.

"I'm not an ordinary civilian. As a forest ranger, I can make an arrest," Lightfoot corrected him.

"On what grounds?" Mac asked.

"Attempted vehicular manslaughter." His hazel eyes made contact again. "I think that's how you phrase it. How is your husband?"

"Home with bronchitis, which I hope doesn't become pneumonia."

"So Greer did it?" Fields asked.

From the door pocket, Lightfoot handed Mac a glassine with dried blue paint scrapes and another with loden green.

"From her tanker and Chris's Jeep?"

Lightfoot shrugged. "Your lab can answer that. All their trucks are blue. If we find her, you can ask her."

"She won't admit pushing a cop into the river," Fields said.

Mac agreed. "The guilty never do. Do you think she's capable of it?"

Lightfoot nodded. He'd pulled his hair back and clubbed it as the nape of his neck. "A worthy adversary. Where she lives, she has the element of surprise." Grim lines creasing his forehead and bracketing his nose and mouth telegraphed his concern. The truck veered west onto Pentz Lane through forested land and climbed a steep incline. The sounds of industry, traffic and people faded away with the valley. Pines, pointed pyramids of firs, and densely packed spindly hardwoods provided the only scenery for miles. The truck veered north. "If she makes for Raccoon Park, she'll have 7500 acres to hide in."

"What's Raccoon Park?" asked Fields.

"In 1945, the CCC started developing the lands. Six thousand acres are dedicated to hunting, fishing, boating, horseback riding, and hiking trails. In the winter, add ice fishing and cross-county skiing. There's a 120-acre lake, with State Game Lands and the Allegheny Forest to the west."

"You seem well-informed," Fields said.

"I should be. I'm in charge of the wildlife here."

The truck churned up an incline where they could see a house high on a bluff facing the valley about 300 yards distant. Fronted with bowed glass and stone, it looked like a transparent half Saturn built into the cliff, a balcony ringing it. A winding road at the base led them to an access road. Lightfoot followed it to the end and turned off the ignition.

"We can't get any closer?" Fields asked. He fidgeted with the cooler, the gelled peaks of his hair tickled Mac's cheek as he reached behind, handing each half an overstuffed deli sandwich. Shadow sniffed the air appreciatively; she stirred restlessly, her neck and nose inching forward. Mac broke off a piece and fed her pup.

"No need." He pointed beyond the house to a level spit of land at the hilltop where a police chopper had landed.

Figures moved freely about the space—on the balcony that jutted over the cliff, inside and out. Lightfoot reached over Mac, pulled binoculars out of his glove box and put them in her hands. She adjusted the wheel but didn't really need them to see Snow, Savage, Stuart and Imhoff on the balcony conversing with white-clothed crime scene techs.

"Chris has bronchitis! Why is he here? Damn it. Sienna booked." Mac guessed. "Now what?"

"Want to join them?" asked Lightfoot.

"Better not. Looks like a crowd as it is." Mac also wanted to avoid a confrontation with Chris, who'd take her off the case, perhaps put a written reprimand in her file. Not to mention making a scene with Lightfoot, a recurrence of last weekend in Gettysburg.

Lightfoot keyed the engine, backed down the lane to a turn-around and headed south, hooked a sharp right and circled back a graveled drive and pulled up in front of rock cluster jutting fifteen feet into the air, surrounded by indigenous vegetation. A twelve-foot mountain laurel sprawled across the front. Oak, maple and spruce stood sentinel beside the rocks. White pine peaks peeked at them from the other side. They sat in the cab as the engine ticked down.

"Let's get out, stretch our legs." Mac was tired and stiff from the cramped quarters and long drive.

"What gives?" Fields cracked the passenger's door and climbed down, turning to assist Mac. The scent of pine resin pierced the air, and musky dried leaves lingered. Tiny particles of snow drifted down, melting as they hit the sun-warmed rock and the Ram's hood.

She let Shadow out, poured water into her hands for the dog to drink and than swallowed the remainder of the bottle herself.

"We're supposed to find something here." Mac felt anticipation pooling off of their guide.

"Look closely through the laurel." Seeing nothing from her current angle, she shifted left. Nothing but jagged rocks and boulders heaved up by a glacier, pitted by eons of rain, sleet and snow. Moving into the bushes, her eyes roved over the monolith. Shoving between them, Shadow found a shadowed crevice—about five feet high by two wide.

Fields whistled low as he entered the chamber behind the dog.

Hazel-green eyes considered her bulk and Lightfoot shook his head. She couldn't squeeze through. "Did you bring a camera or camcorder?"

"Ask Zach."

"Does your warrant cover the cave?"

"Is it Greer's property?" Mac asked. He nodded. "Are we likely to find something incriminating?"

He tilted his head at her. Wind riffed his hair. Rounding the truck, Lightfoot flipped open his rucksack and rummaged around and extracted an expensive-looking camcorder. He motioned to the crevice, crouched and then darkness swallowed him.

Mac thought about her girth, hips, plus the protruding bulk of her son and shook her head, sighing. From the rear, the hive of industry above muted, she ambled around the rock, studying the surroundings. She guessed they'd entered either an armed fortress or a survivalist's cavern stocked with provisions. At the back of the formation, a clothesline, stretched between two trees, had faded from exposure and frayed in places. Exposed squirrel and birds' nests swayed in the bare branches. Buck scrapes scarred one slender tree. Leaves were scattered about; rabbit pellets dotted the ground. Some turkey feathers had caught on a thorn bush. Trees stretched as far as she could see on undulating hills leading to Raccoon Mountain Park and Lake. She rubbed her arms for warmth and rounded the rock formation. Climbing into the driver's seat, she noticed that Lightfoot had left keys in the ignition. Unsure if she should, Mac breathed, "Oh, well," turning it over. It caught at once. Tepid air leaked from the heat vents. After several minutes, she switched it off. Still hungry, she fished a Payday from her purse and munched quietly. Minutes ticked by. Awkwardly, she felt in back for her thermos, unscrewed the lid and sipped hot decaf mocha. "Umm. Life's little pleasures."

A half-hour later, dog and men emerged, Fields wearing a smug smile, carrying bagged CD cases and a box labeled computer paper. Lightfoot carried his camera, which he dropped in her hands as she scooted over. Shadow jumped in and climbed to the back of the cab, and then Fields slid in beside her. Erin peered into the viewfinder; shelves of canned goods, a small Weber grill, and a kerosene heater stood beside a folded card table. A row of lanterns waited on the cavern floor. Three five-gallon Kerosene cans guarded a tall, metal gun cabinet—the door bearing an industrial-grade padlock. At the back, several cots lined end-to-end, a rolled sleeping bag on each. Hanging open, a cabinet revealed an unopened case of bottled water.

"You knew this was here," Mac said.

Lightfoot said nothing.

Fields moved the evidence bags to the back with Shadow.

"Leave it," She admonished her sniffing, curious puppy against chewing on anything and turned to Fields. "What did you collect?"

His face beamed. "One, video with Ahnai talking to the camera about the thousands of environmental violations committed by energy companies. She claims that EPA laws were essentially gutted by something called the 'Halliburton loophole' that Dick Cheney pushed through Congress when he was VP." He saw the questioning look. "Meaning the gas industry doesn't need to abide by the regs."

"Are you saying that nobody is monitoring or regulating the wells?"

"No, the SRBC does and there's federal oversight, but people assume the EPA is the watchdog protecting our environment. They aren't; basically the agency's hands are tied. Anyway I got photos—"

"That's OK, we can watch the video at the next briefing; tell the Chief. What else you got?" Mac felt irked that she was physically unable to see the find herself.

"A box of documents supporting her claims: forms, letters from people who can light their water faucets, accusations of spikes in cancer near wells, animals losing hair—all sorts of things, though some of these anecdotes are from out West. Plus lab reports of known carcinogens used in active wells in five states, including Pennsylvania. This box contains documented evidence. And that's the tip of the iceberg: CDs labeled Cover-ups, Kickbacks, Payouts, and officials siphoning funds from royalties. She identifies herself, her job, irate that men are damaging Mother Earth."

"What's the purpose of the film? And why does Greer have it?"

"No one said at the beginning. Could be Slaughter filmed herself in case anything happened or maybe a document—" Abruptly jolted, his head cracked against the window. The Ram veered right, perilously close to the drop-off—no guardrail. Lightfoot corrected as the left front tire flattened; he heaved open the driver's door; swinging out wildly. Grabbing his rifle with one hand, Mac with the other, he shoved her down to the running board behind him, the open door a shield. Shadow howled and wiggled free, growling at the tire. Zach slid out, groggy and wobbling. Mac pulled him down beside her. An arrow protruded from the left front tire. "Shadow, come!"

The three scanned what forest they could see. Lightfoot motioned for silence, his eyes raking the ground, the middle distance, and then up into the trees, listening intently. He inspected the front tires—the right just inches from the edge. Shook his head as he extracted a spare, rolled it to the front, let it fall. Locating the jack and a lug wrench from his tool chest, the Native American tested the firmness of the ground. "Want to give Snow a call?" he asked as he positioned the jack, and helped Mac and Zach up. Shadow sniffed the arrow, the tire and ground but held her stance.

Mac shook her head no.

Lightfoot nodded in response with a stern glance that brooked no argument. Fields got photos of the arrow embedded in the tire.

Sighing, she pulled out her cell and pushed number one. "Hi. It's me. Uh, we had a flat, will probably be late getting home."

"Was wondering when you'd call to inform me of your field trip. I have a lock on your cell. I'll be down shortly." Within minutes, he'd descended the cliff, throwing her a disparaging look. Eyes and nose still red and puffy, a coughing attack racked his frame; he turned away from them and buried his face in his elbow. Then his eyes took in Fields and Lightfoot, who was jacking up the truck. "Do you any need help?"

Lightfoot shook his head and said, "Got it, thanks." Leaning into his twist with both hands, forearm muscles straining, he wrenched the first nut free. Moved around the wheel.

"Fields, you can ride to Sunbury in the chopper where Savage has his vehicle. I'll join Lightfoot and my wife," his voice sliced the syllables.

"Sir, we have evidence from the cave. What about chain of command?" Fields asked, his face concerned.

Snow registered surprise. "That was a direct order. I'll handle the evidence. There's a path, then thirty steps up to the balcony." He gestured behind him and turned to Mac. "I'm taking you out of the field. You're on desk duty until your maternity leave." Finally, he asked Lightfoot, "Did you touch anything?" Fields stomped off in the direction from which Snow had come, stung by the curt dismissal.

"In the cave?" the man answered, responding with a quick headshake.

Snow nodded, snapped on latex, lifted the flat tire—arrow intact—into the truck bed, took Mac's arm and marched her around to the passenger's side. Brusquely helped her in. "Call your dog." Chris barely controlled his thunder.

"Shadow, come," Mac said abruptly.

He climbed in beside her. Lightfoot returned to the driver's seat, carefully guided the Ram back to the center and steered it down the mountain. The atmosphere was chilly despite the close quarters. Erin crossed her arms, and then cradled her belly, seeking a comfortable position.

When they turned right onto R 15 South, Lightfoot finally spoke. "I called Mac."

"Why not call me?" Snow asked brusquely.

"I called CPD; your Chief said you were home on sick leave."

Snow waited. The silence stretched out while he pulled a handkerchief from his pocket and blew his nose. "I'm listening."

"I was in Conference One when I got his call," Mac said. She felt his heart beat rapidly against her shoulder.

"We'll have our conversation later," Snow said.

"I anticipated that you'd subpoena Greer's house but might overlook the cave. The couple were survivalists—before the husband moved into our camper." He tilted his head toward the back. "That changed everything." With eyes focused on the road, he shook his head. "Sienna said she kicked Dean out first, but that hardly matters now. Well, a woman scorned..." He let the sentence peter out. "Fields videoed the cave, collected evidence. Ahnai was blowing the whistle—on persons unknown. You can see it for yourself and draw your own conclusions."

Snow sniffed, then huffed out a breath. "Did you bring any water?" He asked Erin. She thumbed to the back. He swung an arm behind and fished blindly around Shadow, who licked his hand. He hooked an insulated cooler, lifted it up and over the seat onto his lap. Unzipped it and took out a bottle, offering it first to his wife, who shook her head and then the driver who accepted it. "If it's not the last one."

Chris pulled out another, popped off the lid and drank. "Remains to be seen if any of that evidence is admissible in court. A good attorney will claim it's fruit of the poisonous tree. Why didn't you wait until we could run it through the proper channels?"

"Because I don't want to be arrested for killing my wife. I assumed Sienna had fled into the forest. The hunting, trapping equipment, bow, arrows and tent are gone."

"Would you swear to that in court?" Snow watched Mac from his peripheral vision—an alabaster statue with eyes locked on the road.

"Yes."

"Anything else I should know?" he asked.

"The subpoena covers their property. Cave's on their property. Treat it as a crime scene; see it for yourself." Lightfoot's jaw clenched.

Snow wasn't willing to let it go. "Do you love my wife?"

Two heads swiveled sharply to stare at the detective, as though his mind were addled.

"You have a fever, so I'll let that pass. No, not in the way you imply. I don't know her well but consider her a daughter."

"You're not related to her."

"I am her stepfather," he contradicted.

"You're not old enough. I'll bet you're not a day over forty."

He leveled eyes at Snow. "What does age matter? Time is infinite; we are finite, but our people do not measure every second, minute or hour. For us, time is elastic rather than linear—a brief gift for which we give thanks. Erin is my wife's firstborn, therefore my kin. That will not change. That's a connection your culture honors as well."

Snow mulled the words over for several miles while tears slid down Erin's cheeks. He nodded as Lightfoot crossed the Susquehanna and headed toward Carlisle. "If you could leave your tire at HQ and drop us off there, I'd appreciate it."

***

At home, each went about his or her chores—the domestic routine, making a simple soup and salad supper. After letting Shadow out, Erin kept busy baking apples, perfuming the air with cinnamon and nutmeg. Chris gathered trash, carried it out, tidied the living area, threw in a load of dark clothes and showered, appearing at the dinner table dressed in sweats, smelling of sandalwood. Without a word to one another, they ate. Then Erin fed the pup, took her shower, washed her hair, pulling out bits of bark, pine needles, and a twig as she worked her fingers through the tangled curls. Rinsed, towel-dried. Brushed her teeth. Pulling a red flannel nightgown over her head, tugged her pillow from their bed and turned toward the blue room.

Chris blocked her path. "You'll sleep with me."

She turned around, pulled down the duvet, tossed her pillow back on her side, lay down on the very edge, and crawled in on her side, rigid. Chris walked to the other side, tossed his sweats aside and slid in. Four feet separated them.

"I'm sorry." Hints of honey and peach radiated from her hair and skin. Silence. "You need to either tell me where you are or phone HQ your ten-twenty. I was worried. I don't understand why you wouldn't tell me.

"Imhoff called when the subpoena came in for Greer's house and rig. Savage and I drove to meet him and then flew to the drill site. The truck was parked nose in with all the other tankers and trucks at West Enterprises, apparently returned to the company. Williamsport CSU went over the rig, scraped green paint off and sent it to their lab. Cigs in ashtray probably bear her DNA—not much else. We got a ping off the cell tower on your iPhone —you were on the site."

172

He heard her breathing slowly but thought she might be feigning sleep. "Please don't go to bed angry. I'll never say another word about Lightfoot. I can't help how I feel; I want to handcuff you to the bed and…" He sighed, leaving the sentence unfinished. A tickle in his throat started him coughing. He sat up. Swung his feet to the floor and turned on the vaporizer. Slogged to the bathroom for a slug of cough syrup and took his antibiotic. Rummaged around for the Vicks, dabbed it under his nose, coughed again. His reflection looked like a drunk on a bender. Pressure squeezed his chest; he tried to beat the phlegm loose to no avail. Rubbed his chest with the mentholated goop, pulled a clean tee on and dragged his sluggish body back to bed. Plumped up a pillow on top of the wedge. Crawled in, facing his wife's back, reached across to lift a strand of damp red hair to uncurl, and then fisted a handful. "Throttle you!"

She'd scooted to the center of her side—her scent like warm honey more alluring now that he could breathe. "At least meet me halfway." He pulled her against him; she stiffened. "So you're not asleep. God, how I love you! I'm sorry. I won't embarrass you again." He slowly slid her gown up and ran his hand along her exposed thigh. He shut his eyes and rubbed around her distended abdomen. He kept petting, caressing her body, hoping she'd back into him. Erin didn't respond; her back's rigidity warned him. Although she did not speak, she didn't pull away either. This night, that would be enough. "Well, at least you're not mad at my hands."

17

The landline jangled. Snow reached for the handset. "Snow here. Yes, sir. Where? He's bringing her in?"

Erin sat up as Shadow padded into their bedroom nosing her nose. "OK. Let's go out." On the way she tapped the coffeepot's start button. Soon after Shadow was scratching at the back door. Erin scooped a cup of dry food into the dog dish. Filled her water dish. Returned to the kitchen for coffee. Opened the fridge, examined the contents: OJ, milk and eggs. She broke and beat eggs, heated a sauté pan, poured them in. Added leftover asparagus spears and topped them with shredded cheddar. No hurry. Nothing for her to do but scut work in Conference One.

Chris appeared, seeming somewhat better, pocketing his cough syrup and meds. Pouring coffee in a travel mug, he gulped down his omelet standing up. "Thanks for breakfast." Tugged on his CPD parka, added a watch cap and gloves, pocketed his gloves, kissed the air beside his wife's hair. "Remember, desk duty. When I call in, I want to hear your voice on the phone; update the boards and follow paper trails. Pour over photos. You need to attend Benedict's arraignment—see that ADA opposes bail. Interview her if you can; a confession would help. This afternoon, you and Savage have a date with Michaels. He can drive you to the TV station. I'll take Fields." He headed toward the door.

"Yes sir." Mac saluted him. "Where are you going? You're too ill to work."

He stopped and turned to face her. "We're speaking now? HQ. Lightfoot's bringing in Sienna Greer. Don't know when we'll be back, but I intend to charge her with attempted homicide and interview her. We don't have enough to hold her on the murders." Then he left without his lunch.

Erin shrugged, tossed his sandwich, apple and juice box in her bag. Showered and dressed as quickly as her bulk would allow. "You better come soon, baby; it's getting cramped in there." Out the door and in the car, she and Shadow motored through town, stopping at Dunkin' Donuts for a coffee and a decaf pumpkin latte, arriving at HQ before eight. She dropped her lunch into the break room fridge, bid the office staff good morning and ambled into the war room. Studying the white board, Mac bulleted updates: Greer's attempted homicide, subpoena on her property, cave contents—Fields had left his camcorder on the table. Mac sat down heavily to watch it more closely, trying to connect what she was seeing to the three homicides. *What if we're looking at this wrong? Maybe it's not the vengeance of a scorned woman, but silencing whistleblowers? So was Greer the killer, the accomplice, or part of a frame? Ahnai was stabbed and dumped in Letort. Why? Was it expedience, convenience or an opportunity to get rid of a troublemaker? Not personal but a professional hit—like the gas industry covering up the violations, the pollution, and the danger to people, communities, or the environment? Except the knifing felt personal.*

Locating another white board, she wrote this theory and questions from the perspective of a cover-up. The phone rang. "Detective McCoy."

"Ah, the voice of Mona Lisa herself—the enigma of the CPD."

"Agent Howard. How can I help you?" She smiled at his hyperbole.

"I'm on my way to Carlisle. Ask March if he'll hold the briefing until I arrive. A Williamsport station just announced the arrest of Sienna Greer, our person of interest in her husband's death. We saw Snow's dramatic rescue, too. You two know how to grab the headlines. I'm crossing the Pennsylvania line now. Thanks." He disconnected.

Savage waltzed in. "You and me again, babe." He read her white board. "Take the load off." He pulled out a chair for her, and then dropped into the one next to her. Picked up the camcorder and watched the cave surveillance. Drummed his fingers on the table. His hair recently barbered and shower-damp, face shaved, he wore a navy suit, blue shirt with a pinstriped grey tie. He looked Mac over. She'd worn her favorite teal pullover and the teardrop earrings—one that fell off in the kidnapper's cabin having been recently returned to her—and brown slacks with boots. Hadn't bothered with make-up because TV had people to do that.

"Ready for your television debut?" he asked.

She shrugged. "I'll defer most questions to you. How is your ex on an interview?"

He lifted one shoulder. "She asks sharp, leading questions, tries to trip you up or get you to admit to more than you should—fishing for a scoop. Avoid any personal guesswork. Keep to the facts you know; avoid the devils or details you're unsure about."

"You sound like Snow." She sipped her latte, relishing the spicy heat.

"Snow? You two haven't made peace yet? He climbed out of a sickbed haring off to Williamsport to track you down. Couldn't you give him a call? Why are you running around with Lightfoot anyway?"

"Back off, Savage. He wouldn't have sanctioned the trip. For your information, I'm working a case. And I left him a note."

"Were working a case. Work a little harder on your marriage. Please. I don't like being dragged onto choppers for a tracking expedition. Convince him you don't have a thing for your Native American."

"MYOB." She stood abruptly, huffed out of the room to walk and water Shadow, tugging on the leash, before they left for the courthouse. Gathered coat, gloves, leash and dog. Savage blocked the doorway—a huge X, one eyebrow raised, arms extended and legs opened. "Where are you headed?" Dark moody eyes followed her.

"Don't worry, I have my supervisor's permission." She ducked under his arm, stepped over his leg. Shadow followed. Mac stopped at the Chief's open door to give him FBI Agent's message. "Howard wants to question Greer about her husband's death, sit in on the briefing."

"He'll need to get in line. Snow's assault is more recent —one we can win. The lab confirmed the paint samples you gave 'em match her rig and Snow's Jeep. Peeled rubber on the road matches the wear on her front tires. Plus Snow's an eyewitness and you heard what went down. You headed out?"

"Snow ordered me to Abby Benedict's arraignment, so we'll miss the briefing. Savage and I have an interview this afternoon with Michaels—some crime forum." Chief nodded and motioned her out as he ducked his head to sign papers. "We'll return as soon as we're done taping."

Outside, Savage escorted her to the unmarked Bronco, handed her in, Shadow leaping into the rear, and eased around to the driver's side. Folded his frame into the seat while Mac rooted for a bottle of water and pocketed treats for the pup. Checked for the K-9 vest. Hoped the camera would pan to her pup and Michaels would ask questions about her training—a topic she could speak comfortably about.

A few reporters sat in their designated press spaces. Benedict and Wilhelm were seated at the defendant's table, ADA Lawson to the left. Heads turned when the door opened. Mac shuffled down, took an aisle seat, gave her dog a sit signal, then stay—handing her a twisted rawhide stick. Savage sat across the aisle. Benedict threw her a disdainful, condescending look while straightening her Peter Pan collar and pouting. The bailiff said, "All rise, Judge Adam Lewis presiding." The white-haired man filled his black robe; he took his seat, lowered the gavel and began proceedings.

"Counselors, approach the bench." Lewis put his hand over the mic and spoke quietly for a few minutes. The lawyers nodded. He motioned for them to return to their places.

To the gallery, Judge Lewis said, "This is an arraignment where the DA's office will offer the complaint, the indictment and any other information germane to this issue. The defendant will offer a plea. At that juncture, we will set a trial date and address bail and other necessary judicial decisions that arise. Counselor for the state, ADA Lawson."

Chase stood, sliding his chair back and approaching the bench, straightening his tie. He turned to face the defendant. "The Commonwealth of Pennsylvania charges Abigail Flowers Benedict with the homicide of Mindy Murphy with malice aforethought."

Benedict jumped to her feet. "Your honor, I object."

"Are you serving as your own counselor?" He looked at the sheaf of pages before him and zinged a glare at defense counselor. Wilhelm rose, restraining Abby's arm in an attempt to return to her seat, but the defendant shook it off and remained on her feet.

"No, sir. I object. I didn't have malice afore—" she said.

"Then please be seated and avoid any further outbursts. Wilhelm, first and only warning: contain your client."

"Yes, sir." She pressed the coed's shoulder to force her to sit down.

"Further, I consider this defendant a flight risk and since this is a homicide case, I hereby request bail be denied and that she be remanded to the Cumberland County Prison until her trial," Lawson continued.

Abigail whispered furiously into Wilhelm's ear.

Mac caught the words "...entitled to special treatment..." and "damn detectives wouldn't listen. I'm innocent." The indignant young woman was insulted to be treated like a common criminal or frustrated others wouldn't comply with her wishes.

Lawson concluded his litany of offenses as though he hadn't been interrupted. Finally, Judge Lewis turned to Defense Counselor. "How does your client plead?"

"Not guilty, your honor," Wilhelm responded.

"Then trial will proceed..." He checked the calendar. "...on Monday January 8, 2008."

"Wait!" Abby shrieked.

"You wish to address the court? Change your plea?" The judge looked hopeful, his eyes assuming interest, white brows raised slightly, his forehead furrowed. He waited patiently.

"Yes. No! I didn't kill anyone. You don't understand! I can't spend Christmas—"

Down whacked the gavel! Lewis leveled the defendant with an impervious stare. "I find you in contempt of court! A $300 fine. Dismissed. Next case!" The bailiff called the next number on the docket, as the guard hustled Benedict out the side door—to be incarcerated until the next year.

Wilhelm skittered up the aisle in a smart black pantsuit and white blouse, which complemented that white diagonal slash across her hair. "She's demanding to see Detective Snow."

"Sorry. He's out on sick leave," Mac said. "And working three homicides at three different locales. Not happening." She stood to go.

"Then will you talk to her?" Wilhelm asked.

"Why?" Mac gathered her purse, clicked her tongue to bring Shadow off the floor where she'd been contentedly chewing during the interlude. "Can't today. I have a TV interview scheduled in an hour." She checked her watch. "And I haven't eaten. I'm also restricted to HQ." She fished a card out of her purse and extended it to the woman. "I should be back at my desk by three p.m." With that, Mac turned and exited the courtroom as Savage held the door for her. "Have her call me."

"Want to grab some lunch?" he asked.

"I brought a sandwich."

"Save it for tomorrow. We're headed to Harrisburg; we'll grab something on the way. Pick your poison."

"No, thanks." She reached for her insulated lunch bag, peeled back the cello and munched on her turkey and sprouts on wheat. "Feel free to stop where you like. I'm trying to eat healthily." She licked stray mayo off the corner of her mouth.

"Since when?" he asked. "Ah, since advent of baby." His eyes fell to her tongue and then dropped to her swollen belly.

He stopped for a burger and fries, which he ate while driving to the studio across the river in Harrisburg traffic. Cars and semis rumbled over the bridge while the Susquehanna chugged sluggishly on it way.

"Don't drop anything on that spiffy suit," Mac warned.

"Didn't know you cared. I clean up pretty well, wouldn't you say?"

"Think *you* just did. But, yeah, you look good," Mac agreed.

At WHTM, both had make-up applied, mics pinned to their lapels, were escorted to a sitting room and later ushered into the studio. Seated in chairs with Elena Michaels opposite Mac, Shadow at her feet and Savage beside her. Hair and make-up people fussed, brushed, pinned and patted, then tore away the bibs. People bustled about, some at controls, conversations echoing from other rooms. Facing bright lights and a cameraman counting down on his fingers, Mac's eyes followed the wires that snaked across the room. The cameraman moved closer. A light turned green. Down went his pinky. Michaels put on a wide camera smile, greeted the audience, "Welcome to the Carlisle Crime Forum! Our guests today—CPD Detectives Reese Savage and Erin McCoy." As Michaels lobbed easy questions their way, the detectives appeared relaxed. They summarized Carlisle crime stats, number and categories of crimes, mainly Breaking and Entering, Burglaries, Armed Robbery and Homicides.

"If people are really interested, they can look on our website for the list of criminal offenses and numbers we commonly experience," Savage said.

"What about homicides? Our community has faced several this year alone."

"That's not uncommon," Mac added.

"I understand this is your first year with Homicide?" Michaels said, turning to Mac. "Have the men been treating you well?"

"Yes, most have been accepting, even encouraging. A number of good-natured jokes in the beginning, that sort of thing."

"If you don't mind my saying, you look too young to have attained that rank so quickly."

"I spent eight years in uniform. My credentials are solid, and my arrest record corresponds with any male officer's." Mac kept her tone even, though the broadcaster had promised no personal questions. "You have my resume; it speaks for itself."

The broadcaster cued the cameraman. "And when did you acquire this K-9 partner?" The camera panned to Shadow sitting at Mac's knee—head up, brown eyes alert with curiosity, roving from speaker to speaker.

Mac summarized Shadow's training to date, briefly described the obstacle course, the dog's duties and the advantages in having her on the squad—decreasing the time and danger the detectives faced, clearing a building within minutes and searching. "She'll be tested for certification in March. Afterwards, Shadow will have additional training in rescue and recovery as well as criminal detection and apprehension."

Michaels turned back to Savage, changing the subject, "You still have an open case from last year, Mindy Murphy's homicide?"

"About 20% of murders go unsolved. Hers was filed as a cold case because new ones occur, but we work on them when a lead surfaces."

"Do you have any new leads, Detective McCoy?" Her hair circled her face and ended in points just below her chin.

"We do. Today Ms. Abigail Benedict was arraigned for Murphy's murder."

"I assume she pleaded not guilty?" Michaels asked. Both detectives nodded.

"So can you share those new leads?" Michaels' eyes brightened, pleading for some juicy tidbit.

"We are not at liberty to discuss an on-going investigation." Mac knew the standard line would not deter Michaels, hoping Savage would field the next one. Her throat was dry, the hot lights growing uncomfortable. She sipped water from a glass sitting on the table near her hand.

"Surely, you can talk about already documented evidence. We know Murphy was bludgeoned with a blunt weapon in the Benedict driveway last May, that she was Lindy Flowers' sister and from Ohio. Can you affirm or deny that this concludes the 'needle-pricker's' reign?"

"We can't know that; the world is full of pricks," Savage smiled.

"You should know," Michaels rejoined. "We'll cut that," to the camera.

"Yes," Mac said, since Savage had been on the scene of only Murphy's homicide but deployed during the others. "The killer died in a freak thunderstorm last summer after fleeing another crime scene. Murphy's is related, but her case had a different modus operandi and perpetrator."

"You allege that Ms. Abigail Benedict, whose father was murdered in his Carlisle home last year, killed Mindy Murphy?"

"She was arraigned this morning," Savage said. "She and her sister were at the scene. The particulars will be presented at her trial in January."

Michaels faced the camera's eye and gushed dramatically, "We have to wait until *next year* to learn the outcome of the Mindy Murphy case. What evidence led to her arrest?" she asked her ex.

"That's January eighth. The wheels of justice may turn slowly for spectators, but the legal process has safeguards to protect the innocent as well as convict the guilty," Savage sidestepped her question.

"You refuse to say why she was arrested? Isn't it a matter of public record? Therefore, the public has a right to know," Michaels insisted.

"Arrest and arraignment are just the beginning of the judicial process. You'll know when we know. The lab is currently processing evidence. DNA evidence takes time," Mac added. The hair against her neck felt damp. Perspiration beetled uncomfortably between her breasts. The baby bumped her diaphragm, knocking the breath out of her. Luckily Savage noticed her discomfort and took the next question.

"Can you tell us the status of your current homicide?" The reporter held her index finger in the air. "We know Ahnai Lightfoot attended the Fort Hunter Corn Festival and participated in the ceremony at the former Carlisle Indian Industrial School's Native American cemetery. She was murdered and her body dumped in Letort. But she's not local?"

"The current investigation is on-going," Savage said slowly.

Michaels turned to Mac, sketched-on eyebrows stretched up.

"We know that she's originally from Cherokee, North Carolina, but lived in Pennsylvania for over twenty years and worked for the Susquehanna River Basin Commission as a Field Agent for the last decade."

The reporter smiled, satisfied. "What does a Field Agent do?"

"Monitor and test the Susquehanna waterways and tributaries. That includes oversight of the Marcellus Shale Gas Industry's active wells, cataloguing and giving citations for environmental violations, among other things." Mac took a breath, deciding that Michaels could do her own research.

"And the other two homicides? Why is the Carlisle Police Department interested in them? Aren't they out of your jurisdiction?"

"We think they're connected," Savage said.

"In what way?"

"All three individuals were tied to West Enterprises, an active Marcellus Shale drill site near Williamsport."

"Who were the others?"

"Dean Greer, a Marcellus Shale Field Technician and Gary Hauck, the Safety Coordinator at West Enterprises. It's on the police blotter." Savage sounded weary.

"Thank you, Detective Savage. We'll inform our audience," Michaels retorted. "Detective McCoy, can you say whether you have a person of interest or any suspects for Lightfoot's murder? Or perhaps you're looking at the same person for all three deaths?"

"She went by Slaughter. No, ma'am, we cannot comment on that," Mac said firmly.

"Can you tell us if you're satisfied with the progress CPD is making on these cases?"

"We find and follow the evidence, Ms. Michaels," Savage intoned and then smiled enigmatically and addressed the camera directly. "That's a loaded question —asking us to evaluate ourselves."

"Yes, we are satisfied because we *are* making progress," Mac claimed. "It's hard work slogging through and sifting evidence, chasing leads, which can be frustrating and dangerous. Because we're determined to do our job and make our communities safe, we court doubt and darkness daily." She glanced at her watch. "And if you'll excuse us, we have an interview to conduct." She touched Shadow's shoulder to release her. The dog stood, her K-9 Officer vest clearly visible; the camera panned to her for the last shot, and then returned to Michaels' head and shoulders.

"Well, thank you for taking the time from your busy schedules to attend our Crime Forum and answer our questions. This is Elena Michaels reporting." She covered her dismissal well, shook hands with both and smiled into the camera. The cameraman backed away and gave the cut signal.

Elena smiled. "Thanks for your time; we'll edit and add the interview to the crime forum to be broadcast tonight and tomorrow night. Is Snow available for an interview later? I'd like an exclusive interview with Benedict."

"No, afraid not, but I am," Savage smirked at his ex; she ignored the comment. "You're welcome to her, just clear it with our personnel and her defense attorney Denise Wilhelm."

Savage winked at Mac as they walked out. "Nice save, especially your closing. Thanks for cutting it short; she'd would've asked questions all day, and we were both heating up under those lights." He laughed at his own innuendo.

"You're welcome." Mac clipped the leash to her dog's halter as they left the studio.

Savage called HQ with an estimated TOA.

18

Entering HQ was a descent into Hell. Standing an arm's length from his captive, Lightfoot held Sienna Greer's arms, her hands shackled behind her back, her feet hobbled by restraints. Windblown hair stood about her head, twigs and leaves tagging along. Wild, wide eyes —pupils dilated—she hurled obscenities at him and anyone else who approached. Torn, dirty, disheveled flannel shirt and ripped jeans testified to time spent sleeping rough. She tried to shake Lightfoot off. "You son of a bitch whoreson, dragging me across the damn state. I know my rights, asshole! Camping, minding my own business and this damn redskin ropes me from behind like I'm a heifer. Tell him to let me go!"

Lightfoot's buckskin pullover had been ripped, one of the rawhide laces pulled off; his left eye had purpled; his cheeks bore raised welts from scratches, a bite mark visible on his right hand. He waited patiently but stood back from his captive.

Sonja, the CPD college intern and new secretary Paula Flood stood flummoxed, wide-eyed and open-mouthed, staring at Greer, then Lightfoot—uncertain of the protocol.

LT Stuart tried placating her over Shadow's deep growls. "Ma'am, if you'll calm down, we can explain why you're here—" FBI Agent Howard leaned against the wall, slightly amused by the outburst and discord.

"You pigs can all go to hell! I'm not talking. I want a lawyer. Get your stinking hands off me, for Chrissakes!"

Savage quickly reached around Lightfoot and pressed Greer's carotids with thumb and forefinger. Within seconds, she toppled forward, unconscious. Both men half-dragged, half-carried her into the interrogation box.

"She's an Amazon," Savage moaned while he shackled her to the table and floor.

"Strong and prone to outbursts, too," Lightfoot admitted wryly.

Snow stormed onto the scene and stopped suddenly, glancing from Lightfoot to Mac and Agent Howard.

LT Stuart stood in the doorway, shook his head and frowned at Lightfoot. "Was this necessary? Who is she?"

"Sienna Greer. She pushed me into the Susquehanna," Snow said.

"I arrested her for violating the fire regulations at Raccoon Mountain Park and brought the fugitive in for questioning," Lightfoot said.

"Ah, yes. Put up a fight did she?" Savage smiled and pointed to the bite. "Maybe you should get rabies shots."

"Didn't think it gentlemanly to knock her out," Lightfoot said.

"Whatever works." Savage shrugged. Shadow pushed into the interrogation, sniffing Lightfoot's hand.

Snow's glance slid from Greer to his wife with Lightfoot.

Mac turned to Lightfoot. "If you'll come into my office, I have a first-aid kit for those nasty scratches. We should scrape her fingernails. You can file assault charges," Mac said, retreating into the hallway.

Lightfoot shook his head. "I'll do." He smiled at her, followed her out, and hugged her briefly. "How are you and your husband doing?"

She shook her head as she led him into her office. "He misunderstood, thought I—"

"I know. You will work it out. He's a good man."

Mac nodded, dug the Canon out of her backpack, and turned it on. "Thank you for the risks you took on our behalf. I appreciate your help. Greer might have escaped otherwise."

"My motivations are purely selfish, I assure you. She would've had the wind at her back had she not backtracked to shoot my tire. What are you doing?"

"Photographing your injuries."

"That's not necessary."

"She assaulted you! Let me at least get the bite mark."

He shook his head. "No. Then I'd have to testify." He took her camera and placed it on her desk. Backed into the hall. She followed. He withdrew a suede pouch from his pants pocket, uncurled her fingers and closed her hand over it. "That's for you. Enjoy your harvest celebration. Tell me when my grandson is born." He leaned down to kiss her forehead and turned, silently slipping out the side door.

She refused to look around to see if anyone were watching, slipped into the conference room, closed the door, and peeked into the pouch but pocketed it. Noted Greer's arrest on the white board. Finally, personnel at the station resumed their customary tasks. She called a crime scene tech to collect the skin from their suspect's nails and do a DNA test. Organized the scattered papers into chronological order, putting together a timeline of the victim's movements and charting them on the computer to see if they intersected with the other victims or main suspects. Sonja brought in the lab reports of the paint scrapes Lightfoot gave her: a match to Greer's truck and Snow's Jeep.

When her legs cramped, she eased herself out of the chair and retraced her steps to the interview room. She called Shadow and escorted her outside. After that, Mac refilled her dog's water bowl and pulled a juice box and an apple from her lunch bag. Heard Greer's voice on her way back to the conference room, haranguing the stranger, presumably her lawyer, sitting beside her.

She opened the drawstring and dumped the contents on her desk: an eagle feather, plus small wooden carvings of a badger, bear and beaver. How did he know her runes? She smiled, pleased to have the talismans. Mac returned her wee animals and feather to their pouch, the pouch to her purse. Then resumed her task, finding dates when the men's schedules overlapped and when Dean

Greer accompanied Ahnai on assignments but no times when all three... *Not that that was necessary. What if there had been a partner? Still... what if I track Sienna's movements?* Mac called West Enterprises requesting Greer's work schedule and gave the secretary CPD's fax number. She jotted, wondering who would interview the suspect. Perhaps she could. She looked up—into her husband's eyes; he'd been watching her, registered her surprise at seeing him. Her dog lumbered up to greet him. Since they were alone, Chris pulled her into his arms and breathed in her essence. Then stepped away. His eyes were still watery, his nose stuffy, and his chest congested, but he could smell honey and lemon. He took a swig of cough syrup, returned it to his pocket.

Mac said, "You should be at home in bed."

"I'd like nothing better, with you beside me, me inside you. Savage and I are going into the box. You may observe," he said. "Would you please have Sonja bring in water and coffee? And would you bring Shadow in? What did I misunderstand?"

Ah, he'd been eavesdropping. "I'm not interested in Lightfoot. I resent your questioning him—discussing me as if I weren't there. How could you say such a thing? I love you; that's why we married, I thought. You can't be jealous of every man I talk to. The meta-message suggests that you don't trust me."

"What's a meta-message?"

"It's the meaning behind what you say."

"I say what I mean," Snow stated truculently.

"OK, then, it's the message behind what you say."

"For example."

"Yesterday you asked my stepfather if he loved me. The meta-message says that I might be attracted to him too, that you're jealous, or that you don't trust me. I don't know which is worse."

"That's not accurate. I wanted to know his intentions, but we'll let it go for now. And I apologized."

She handed him the lab report on the paint, then preceded him into the interrogation room. Mac signaled Shadow to sit and held her open her palm near her nose. "Stay. Watch." Snow stalked into the box as she left and slammed the door. Mac did as he bid. When their admin returned with the drinks, she whispered, "I saw tall, dark and beautiful give you that kiss. The first day he walked into HQ, I thought he'd walked off a movie set."

"Native Americans have been part of our culture, and we theirs, for centuries. You know history; Europeans were the invaders." Mac looked into Sonja's teasing eyes. "He's my stepfather, so get any notions out of your head. I'm a newlywed."

"Not like him, honey. Oh, my! Snow's jealous? That means Ahnai Lightfoot was your mother!" Eyes widened, she mouthed "O" while knocking on the door and sliding into the box with the requested drinks while Mac pushed a cushy chair in the adjoining room to observe experience at work. Then started the video.

The detectives busied themselves with laying legal pads on the table, setting out the recorder, making noncommittal organizational noises. Snow searched his pockets for a pen, and asked Savage if he had one. Of course not, they were stalling. Mac held one out as Reese ducked out of interrogation.

"Start already," Mac whispered.

Snow parked the pen in his front pocket, offered the suspect and her lawyer drinks. Greer asked for a soda; again Savage exited and reappeared with a Coke from the vending machine. He winked at Mac as he reentered, popped the top, pushed it to the middle of the table. With shackles clanking, a sullen Greer reached for it, muttering thanks. Shadow sat a few feet to the prisoner's left, growling deep in her throat.

"We all settled?" Snow looked at each person—the lawyer in his shiny black suit, Greer in worn, torn flannels—and threw a glance at Savage, thumbed the recorder on. He identified the case number, Mirandized

Greer, identified those present, pausing so the lawyer could say his name. "Let me introduce my wife's K-9 officer. Let me warn you, if you make any sudden, aggressive moves or even raise your voice, and I give her the signal, she'll jump over your lawyer and shred your arm to ribbons. Hope you're not left-handed." He bluffed; only Erin could command the dog.

Greer threw Shadow an ominous glance. Shadow responded with a menacing snarl—her wrinkled snout bearing sharp, white teeth.

"Because you took the recorder from my Jeep, we have to start over. Why don't you tell us what happened?"

"That damn Indian tracked and trapped me—"

"You're a fugitive who committed a felony—attempted vehicular manslaughter," growled Snow. "You were driving that rig that pushed me into the river, so save the unrighteous indignation. Why did you shove my Jeep over the embankment?"

She looked at the lawyer, who was cleaning his glasses fastidiously. He nodded for her to answer.

"Expect me to admit to a felony? What kind of lawyer are you?" she asked him. "That could a been anybody, even a man wearing a wig."

"You're reaching. Who would the court believe—you or a decorated Senior Homicide Detective?" Savage asked.

She shrugged. "Marcellus Shale has a hundred tankers and trucks. Could've been anyone."

"Let's try something easier," Savage suggested. "What happened between you and your husband?"

Greer threw Savage a torrid glance. "Oh, nothing. He was the perfect husband—handsome, a throwback to the 1940's with his matinee idol looks. Others on campus chased after him, so I felt lucky when he wed me. We were married for twenty years; our daughter's a sophomore at Bucknell. Had a few good years until he started slacking off: snorting, scratching, mumbling, burping, crunching, snacking, drinking, smoking and complaining. I didn't clean, cook, dress or do anything to suit him. Yet he never noticed how irritating he became—a constant noisemaker. Couldn't listen to a TV show without him interrupting, getting up six times for popcorn, soda, chips or beer or to go to the john.

"One day, five years ago, in walks Sacajawea reincarnated. Tar-black hair down to her butt, coffee-bean eyes in a perfect face, beaded shirt, jeans, doeskin boots—the whole shebang. Didn't pay much attention after that: Dean said she worked for SRBC, and he was a Field Tech for West's—no biggie. Later we met her husband Jason and their kids. Didn't see them much, as they lived in Sayre; we live near Williamsport. Long story short, Dean changed. Cleaned up his act, ate better, lost weight, started jogging, lifting, and started dressing like he cared. But not for me—for that Indian bitch. Canoeing with her downriver like something out of a romance novel."

"How did you find out?"

"I caught them in my rear view mirror last year as I was backing a tanker out on a water run. In the trees that ring the drill site, he hiked her skirt up for a quickie. They didn't even notice me."

"Did you approach them?"

"Hell, no. I told Jason, but he gave me some mumbo-jumbo about a millennium of matriarchies and clan mothers decided whatnot if a woman wanted to move on or preferred another mate."

"He wasn't upset like you were?"

"Not upset—sad maybe, but resigned. They were basically separated anyhow—what with him on Raccoon Mountain tracking wildlife all over and living over his studio in Sayre. They had separate residences. But that damn bitch wrecked my marriage and broke up my home."

"You don't fault your husband at all? And so she deserved to die?"

"Not really. He'd have no defenses against that siren. I hated her, but I like my job. I'm outdoors in Nature; I like driving, hanging out with the guys. Meeting in bars on weekends—eating pub grub. Letting off steam with a few drinks. We all have a good time together."

"I don't get the connection," Snow said. "Why not report him?"

"Dean has seniority; he's my immediate supervisor—in charge of setting and organizing frack tanks, water distribution, our schedules. Collecting and testing the water, among other things. I didn't want to jeopardize my job by making a stink. Like, he could fire me."

"You got even instead," Savage suggested.

"Damn straight. I kicked him out of the house we spent a decade building. Pretty nifty, huh? Our bay window had to be ordered from Pittsburgh and shipped here. You searched it, right? Find anything interesting? Sniff my undies?" she sneered and sipped Coke.

"So you don't admit to killing Ahnai Lightfoot or your husband?" Savage asked.

"She went by Slaughter. Why don't you ask her?" She guffawed. "Get it? Slaughter? Nah, you wouldn't be asking if you had anything solid against me."

"No," Snow admitted, "But I do." He tossed the lab report on the scarred table, flipped it open and revealed the paint scrapes. "And before you repeat the hundred trucks bit," he turned over an eight by ten glossy of her rig's license plates. "This truck's front end is damaged. Ah, more green paint marks. You still haven't explained why you ran me down."

She was staring at the plates and lab reports, befuddled.

"One more thing." Snow's eyes locked onto their prey. He tossed a grainy photo of Greer driving the rig at a Lewisburg intersection—time stamped, five minutes behind the loden-green Jeep, which had also been caught on camera—blurred because it had slid to a sudden stop.

The lawyer leaned forward to study the documents, turned his head sideways to observe Greer with those thick owlish glasses, twin brown cowlicks sticking up, a round face with a weak chin. He blinked several times. "You didn't mention this. I can't represent you if you don't tell—"

"You are under arrest for attempted vehicular manslaughter, assault with intent on me and one count of physical assault on Jason Lightfoot. You will be detained until your arraignment and held without bail until your trial." Snow repeated because she seemed stoned. "Add one charge of drug use; your eyes are dilated."

"We're done here," Savage said. "Too bad you didn't cooperate. We could've shaved off some jail time. Oh, a local news chopper got it all on tape. We're saving that for trial."

"You bastards. I'll see you in hell first, cock—"

"This is just the beginning," Snow interrupted. "We found your cave—confiscated evidence suggesting our victims were murdered by someone who wanted to cover-up a scathing documentary, rife corruption at your drill site, or perhaps throughout the industry. Or silence a whistleblower." He stopped the recorder as a knock sounded at the door.

A crime tech entered with swabs, a file, tubes to draw blood, and glassines on a rolling cart, bagged clothes on the second shelf. Greer refused, drew back, clawed. At the door, Mac said, "Shadow, guard." Her pup had waited patiently for her moment. She sprang forward, jumped on the lawyer and clamped her jaws on Greer's arm. The woman subsided immediately while counsel sputtered impotently. Snow and Savage exited the box.

"That's better. Open!" The tech swabbed inside her mouth, took a hair by the root, scraped the fingernails of both hands and used tweezers to lift a leather string from her flannel shirt. She combed the suspect's hair, collecting the debris. "Now undress and put all you clothes in this bag." She placed another clear plastic bag containing a clean prison jumpsuit on the table and waited for Greer to peel her filthy flannels off.

Mac released Shadow but had her stay close. She tapped the two-way when Greer had changed. Savage reentered.

Kerri swiped an alcohol pad in the bend of Greer's arm, tied a rubber tube above, and said, "Make a fist." With a quick stick, she pierced a vein and drew two vials of blood. Savage collected the coke can and handed it to the tech. "Here's another sample and get a bite impression, too."

As Mac released Shadow and walked out, Agent Howard sauntered in.

"My turn now." He introduced himself to the defendant. "Might want to hold up your call for transport for a few," he said to Snow, observing from the doorway.

Snow snapped his cell shut with finality. "We're trying her first," he warned Howard. "You can call the Chief when you're through." To Savage he said, "When the fed's done, put her in a holding cell until the van arrives." At the Conference room door, Chris watched Mac list the basics of Greer's interview on the board, Shadow—an apt pupil—at her side watching Mac write as though she could read English.

"Mac, let's go home." The bags under red-rimmed bloodshot eyes, the weariness on his face and the stoop of his shoulders said it all.

19

After a dinner of chicken cordon bleu, roasted vegetables, and pears poached in apple wine, the couple settled in for the first free evening in weeks. Chris sorted through the DVDs, the Hamilton's wedding presents, selected "Inside Man," set up the DVD player while Erin loaded the dishwasher.

He ambled in to offer help, but she'd finished and wiped the counters, island and table. Opening the pantry, he stood contemplating its contents. They stocked the usual staples: pasta, coffee, crackers, granola bars, peanut butter, a few snacks and stocked the freezer with meats and vegetables. His mother's home-canned goods were shelved in the garage, along with Shadow's treats and dog food in plastic bins. "Where's the popcorn?"

"Are you serious? We just ate!"

"Remember, we're eating for two," he quipped.

She folded the dishcloth and laid it across the drainer. "Please. We can add it to the grocery list."

"OK. How about peanut-butter crackers?" he asked. "I put a movie in."

"I need to shower first; I feel yucky. If you'll lay out the breakfast things." Erin sighed, rubbing her lower back with both hands.

"Then I have a better idea; we'll both shower." He grinned at her, as it had been weeks.

Erin cocked her head at him, arms akimbo. "What about that scene you made in the truck yesterday on the way home?"

"Are you still mad about that?"

"I'm angry that you chained me to the conference table for doing my job. You're also making professional decisions based upon personal feelings; that's not fair."

She walked the long way around the table to avoid him and padded to the bathroom, shedding clothes along the way.

"Correction. I removed you from the field because you refused to obey orders. Had you been any of my men, I would've written you up for insubordination. Luckily, you had Fields with you. Second, you promised me last summer you'd work at HQ until you delivered. I'm uncomfortable with the risks you're taking." He pulled off his dress shirt and tee. Unbuckled his belt and dropped his trousers. "And, finally, Elena moved out when Savage chained her to the bed overnight, so I wouldn't use that word—"

"Don't change the subject and don't make me angry again. What's the matter, you don't trust me?"

"Oh, I trust *you* all right," Chris answered.

"Then please don't think I'm after every man with whom I have a conversation. And what about the risks you take? You could have drowned in the river. Lucky for you, we were on the phone and could pinpoint your location." She had stripped to her underwear. "And Savage roped a chopper. Otherwise you would have died in that frigid water." Tears blurred her vision as she reached back to unsnap her tight bra.

He thought about that. "You're right. I'm sorry, but I can't promise it won't happen again. It's the nature of the job."

"Where was your partner?"

He looked at her. "Oh I see. Sauce for the gander."

She was too tired to argue, instead turned into the bathroom.

Since he hadn't heard "no," he joined her.

Afterwards, warm, clean and ravenous, Snow made banana splits topped with hot fudge and trail mix and carried them to the living room. A gleaming Erin sat on the couch knitting the blue baby blanket, which reminded him to stain his latest project in the barn. Her eyes lit up at the unexpected treat and laid her work aside. He sat down beside her, propped his feet up next to hers on the ottoman and started the movie. They had reached the point when the bank robbers pulled off the heist, when both cells phones sang. Chris tapped the pause button.

"Snow." He listened to the brief explanation. "I'm not coming out tonight unless there's a homicide. Let the prison personnel handle it. We can mount a search tomorrow. Call Imhoff and then Williamsport police for assistance. Hell, call the FBI. How did she escape?"

Erin pushed her call button. "Hello. McCoy here." She listened to a crying Abby Benedict, pleading to see her. "This prison garb doesn't fit! The food in here is rancid. My cellmate is a tattooed psycho, and the guards are sadistic. This is horrific and humiliating! I wouldn't treat Goldie like this. I'm begging you. I don't deserve this. Can you at least transfer me? How many times must I repeat that I'm innocent of this charge! Please, I'll cooperate if you come see me and move me."

"All right, tomorrow at nine a.m. Depending if what you share is helpful, I'll talk to the warden."

"Thank you very much." Accompanied with an occasional sniff.

"Until tomorrow, then." She disconnected and sent a TM to Sonja, noting her appointment at the prison and then emailed Cumberland County Prison, requesting the visit. By the time she was finished, she noticed the movie had turned itself off. She looked up at her husband, who lowered himself to the oversized ottoman and took her feet in his lap, rubbing his thumb up her instep. "Who was that?"

"The prison. Greer escaped." Her husband said dispiritedly.

"What? How? After all that commotion and effort at HQ?"

He sighed in consternation. "Yeah, exactly, especially after Lightfoot dragged the hellcat down here."

"Are we going after her?" Mac made a motion to get up.

"*We* are not. She's a prison escapee. The state police and FBI will handle it, set up a dragnet. CPD will assist tomorrow."

"How long has she been gone?"

He shrugged. "She was there at dinner. It's not lights out yet, but she can't be found on the premises. They're locked down, looking for her."

"What if they don't find her? Lightfoot claimed that she'd head for the Allegheny Forest. She had everything imaginable in that cave: food, water, weapons, and camping gear. Did you seal it before we came home?"

"I didn't see it. I'll call Imhoff first thing in the morning. Maybe he or Savage can get a chopper. If she pulled this off, she had help inside or else is incredibly lucky or terribly innovative."

"And if she escapes the dragnet?"

"On foot and in a prison jumper?" Chris snorted. His hands massaged her calves, working out the kinks; then saw her abdomen bulge out. He laid his hand on that spot and felt his son's heel. His eyes melted and gazed into her jade ones, watching him. "You are my treasure, now and always. If I could, I'd give you the world, the moon and stars. Forgive me." He pulled her up and wrapped her in his arms. "Let's go to bed. We can watch the movie another night. We'll have plenty nights at home after our son arrives, when we're on leave."

Mac trailed fingertips across his jaw, down his neck, along his chest and down his torso. "Did you take time off in the middle of a triple murder investigation?" She looked up in surprise and looped one arm around his waist, his skin radiating heat.

"I did. Chief gave me two weeks. LT Stuart volunteered to oversee the investigation until I return. Or we may solve it before the baby's born."

"And what if they can't find Greer? What if she makes it to the forest?"

He pulled down the duvet and slid into bed, too weary to assimilate a coherent answer. "Let's talk about it tomorrow." Plumped up two pillows. And laid his head down, sniffing the freshly laundered pillowcase. His mother must have sent her cleaning lady to the bungalow. He'd been too busy and distracted to notice until this moment.

"Oh, clean sheets. Your mother spoils us!" But Erin was thankful at the generous gesture. She kissed Chris good night, turned her back to him and scooted closer to be spooned. Exhaustion won out over frustration with the day's events; they slept.

In her dream, three men on horses struggled up the side of a mountain while snow sifted down on trees, the men's hats, and the horses' flanks. Wispy fog curled sensuously around the riders. A slice of moon lit the path —little more than a deer trail. Black tree skeletons stood in stark relief against the white backdrop like an Ansell Adams photo: a serene scene except for the saddlebags, bedrolls, rifles and the bow and quiver of arrows slung across the last rider's back. The men wore heavy winter coats, scarves and gloves, as well as durable boots. The last rider sat comfortably in his saddle, rocking slightly with the horse's gait. He led a packhorse, laden with provisions on either side. Its hooves slid backward, but the rider pulled him forward, turning around to encourage the animal or perhaps assure its safety.

The other two, Snow and Savage, turned to watch Lightfoot coax and soothe the packhorse until the animal regained his footing. Then the all riders faced forward, riding into a forest primeval in the winter silence unaware of the danger ahead. She wanted to warn them but had no voice—only eyes. A panther crouched on a tree limb on the path ahead waiting for the men to ride beneath her. The yellow eyes glowed in anticipation, her mouth held an arrow, her paws dripped blood.

Mac awoke with a start, her heart drumming a tattoo in her chest. "It was just a dream." She sighed, patting her heart, and felt cold at her back. She heard her husband open the back door to let her dog out and smelled coffee, dripping into the carafe. The clock's digital numbers read six forty-five. Erin rolled out of bed to execute her tai chi movements, a practice she developed since her running hiatus. Finally ready to face another day, another challenge, she padded out back, whistled for Shadow, fed and watered her. She ate a granola bar absently, dressed automatically in a warm pantsuit and stretchy turtleneck sweater while her husband seemed occupied with his own deliberations. Driving Silver, she left home first for the drive to the prison to visit Abby Benedict and later planned to work the war room.

She assumed her husband would conduct his own search for Sienna Greer, but she'd call Lightfoot anyway.

20

At the Cumberland County Prison, Mac showed her ID and left her pistol before she entered, telling the guard she had an appointment to see Abigail Benedict. Another guard patted her down and then led her through a series of locked, barred doors into a waiting room. A third promptly opened a door, escorting a shackled Benedict, her hair limp and untidy, the jumpsuit a size too large for her frame.

"I'll be right outside the door. Call me when you're done," the uniformed guard with tousled bushy hair and facial scruff said.

Seated on the other side of a plexi-glass window, Mac waited, knowing this inmate had plenty to say. Benedict started, "Criminals in here are from the streets: drug dealers, embezzlers, prostitutes—I didn't know Carlisle has or tolerates—thieves, DUI offenders—"

Mac cut her off. "Let's focus on what you have to tell me about the Murphy case."

"I'm telling you! I'm working on a Master's thesis; it's publishable, I'm sure. I'm engaged to a doctor—or was until you yanked me out of the line at the airport. I have —had—a future until you ruined it. I thought we were friends. Maybe I should talk to Detective Snow instead."

"Stop whining." Mac heaved her body up to leave because she refused to sit through a catalogue of the woman's customary boasts. When Mac's hand twisted the doorknob, Benedict's voice stopped her. "OK! OK! Please don't leave. I'll talk."

Turning around and leaning against the door, Mac waited.

"If I talk, will the court be more lenient?" Benedict asked.

"I can't make any promises, but I'll tell them that you cooperated if you tell the truth and admit your part."

"I didn't kill Mindy Murphy. Honest! But April—I mean Alison—and I were there—at the house packing stuff up to sell on EBay, donate to Goodwill or give away; the house was dark because I'd had the utilities turned off; nobody lives there anymore. We were using those battery-operated emergency storm lanterns and heard footsteps. Headlights poured through the front windows. My sister went out the back door and circled around front. I charged out the front with Goldie to the driveway to see who it was. I'd never met the woman. Claimed she wanted the rest of the money owed to her sister—her inheritance. I shouted for her to get out, 'You're trespassing on private property.' She refused to leave; we argued. Then she threw a punch. So we were fighting and scratching and whack! Alison clobbered her from behind—like that Detective Fields when she kidnapped you. But she meant to knock her out and call police."

"So why didn't you?"

"She died."

"You should have called 911 or the police. A doctor might have saved her."

Abigail shrugged indifferently and repeated. "I didn't know her."

"Really? So you didn't think to report a murder? Didn't she look just like Lindy Flowers?" Mac said.

"Who? Oh, I hadn't seen my aunt for fifteen years. How was I to know? To me, she was a stranger trespassing, robbing me of the little I had left. Now, what can you do for me? Can you get me out of here?" Her hand swept behind her, her face a moue of disgust.

"I'll see what I can do," Mac said. "Is there anything else you want to tell me?"

"My attorney and I'll use the Castle Doctrine as my defense. April Alison and I were defending my home from invasion—and an armed robbery."

"What exactly was Murphy armed with?"

"Wicked fingernails." Abigail's grimace and flat eyes signaled naïveté, arrogance or assurance of her rights. "The jury will know I am alone—without father or fiancé—thanks to the bumbling CPD, and find our actions justified. They will exonerate me, and then I'll fly to Edinburgh to join Rye. Just find a lenient judge. And I'm going to write editorials to send to your local paper with my concerns about my treatment and the conditions here. They treat me like those criminals, but I'm not!"

Mac nodded as she walked out. She'd wait for the lab report on that pink sweater before she made any overtures on that woman's behalf. Followed her escort back through the doors, stopping and waiting while he unlocked and relocked each one, each gate clanging shut with a depressing metallic nihilism. Preoccupied, she reclaimed her belongings. Shaking her head, she muttered as she walked into the clear, crisp November day. "Narcissistic to the core. 'Methinks the lady doth protest too much,' but what if she's telling the truth? If so, that leaves only one other option."

Mac swung home, collected Shadow, and phoned Sonja to tell her that she was taking the dog to Kauffman's for K-9 training. Then speed-dialed Chris to let him know where she'd be. Reached voicemail. "When I'm done with K-9 training, I'll work in the war room," wondering why he wasn't at HQ.

21

Thanksgiving dawned cold and clear, frost-frozen. Erin called her folks to see if they were coming.

Her dad answered. "Liam went home with his roommate, so it'll be Janelle and I. We're bringing a jelled cranberry salad and candied sweet potatoes. Be sure to tell Erica."

Next she phoned her mother-in-law to relay the message, adding that she and Chris were bringing a pecan and two pumpkin pies. After breakfast, Chris made pie dough for three pies, rolling each out to fit into the deep-dish glass pie pans. Erin located the sweetened condensed milk in the pantry, took the thawed pumpkin from the fridge and mixed the ingredients together. Setting that bowl beside the pie plates, she quickly beat the eggs, sugar and syrup into another, added nuts and lined that up next to the pumpkin mixture.

After Shadow's workout, Erin showered and took a nap because she felt mild cramps, her stomach unsettled. After her catnap, she ran her pup through the obstacle course and rewarded her when she found the "corpse," a CPR dummy smeared with blood that her father-in-law had hidden in the hunter's blind.

By the time the family gathered for dinner, the senior Snows' elegant table was groaning with traditional dishes, plus Dreena's squash casserole speckled with Parmesan and fresh parsley. Instrumental music emanated from the TV. Kyle and Kayla entertained the adults with their anecdotes about their school's harvest celebrations. Kyle described their upcoming Christmas play as they passed the dishes around the table after grace.

"Oh, look it's snowing out," Kayla breathed excitedly. "I should've brought my ice skates."

"Pond's not frozen," Kyle said to his sister and continued, "We're doing *The Best Christmas Pageant Ever*. I'm Joseph. A girl named Maria will be Mary. Funny, huh? May we use your baby for Jesus, Aunt Erin?"

"Of course not," Snow answered good-naturedly. He helped himself to candied yams and mashed potatoes. "He's not even here yet. Even if he were, he'd be too young to leave his parents."

"Speaking of baby, I'm surprised you two are here. I'd thought you'd be in the hospital doing the Lamaze breathing exercises," Jack remarked. "When is your due date again?"

"Today," Erin smiled tightly, trying to ignore the intermittent cramps.

"Well, both of mine were late," Dreena said, smiling at her offspring. "But they've made up for it since by running us ragged to and from their school, soccer, swimming and church activities."

"And I help you with your work too!" declared Kayla. "Running errands, picking up stuff, decorating and fluffing pillows."

"All that fussy girly stuff," Kyle shook his head in disdain.

Jeff changed the subject before his kids started nitpicking. "This cranberry concoction is fabulous. I can taste oranges and nuts, too, but what flavor is the gelatin?"

"Raspberry," Janelle said. "This recipe has a pleasing balance of flavors without being overly sweet like the canned sauce."

"I like everything!" Jack smiled. Being a bachelor, his meals were either quickly thrown together, bought in a restaurant, or the heat and eat variety.

"You're being quiet, Chris," Erica observed.

"Work was a bit hectic. Just catching my breath and enjoying the feast, mother. Everything tastes great. The turkey and filling are tender and moist. Thank you all."

COURTING DOUBT AND DARKNESS

His glanced at Janelle and Ethan as well. "And the yams are cooked to perfection."

"And Dreena's squash casserole is new to us. The Parmesan really adds a unique spark! It's really tasty," Ethan said.

"Thanks," Dreena seemed pleased with Ethan's praise. "Every year, one of us is charged with bringing a new dish to vary the traditional menu a bit. Your turn next year, Erin and Chris."

Erica nodded and added, "Thanks to Chris and Erin for bringing the pies. That really helped lighten the load—well, until we eat it." She rubbed her stomach and sighed, signaling she had eaten enough.

"Let's go cut them now. Would you make coffee, Jack?" Professor Snow stood to collect the plates from those who had finished. His middle son accompanied his dad to the kitchen.

Dreena jumped up and scooted her chair away from the table. "I'll help, Erica. Finish your meal. Come whip the cream, hubby." Jeff ambled good-naturedly after his wife, patting his stomach. "Not sure where I'll put pie, but we can walk around the block later."

"Pap, can I have plain vanilla ice cream instead?" Kayla scooted out to the kitchen where the adults were cutting pies, dipping ice cream, and spraying whipped cream. "Oh, may I spray? I know how!"

"Sure, pumpkin. We have apple, pecan and pumpkin. Who wants what?"

Ethan studied his daughter from across the table, still pushing food around her plate, as others indicated their dessert choices. She was too quiet, or was it preoccupation? "We thank all you cooks! It's a great repast!"

"Erin, are you not feeling well? You've just picked at your dinner. Is something the matter?" Erica asked quietly. Her eyes darted to Chris.

"Just a wee bit crampy, and I'm not very hungry. I can hardly breathe."

"Contractions?" Erica inquired, concerned.

Janelle nodded; Ethan scrutinized his daughter's face more closely. "Shall we take you to the hospital?" he asked.

"I'm not sure." Erin breathed deeply after a contraction released her from its vice. "This is my first." She shook her head. "No, it could be hours yet. Chris can take me, but if you want to come to the hospital later, that'd be fine. Chris can call you when the baby arrives."

"Maybe we'd better go home, get you a warm bath," Chris said.

"Don't be silly. Not before dessert. Could I please have a sliver of pumpkin pie with whipped cream?" she asked. Chris excused himself to get it and returned with Erin's and a generous slice of pecan pie a la mode for himself. "I might have bronchitis, but it hasn't affected my appetite. And who knows? We'll need the extra fuel if we're up all night waiting for our new addition." His eyes radiated bonhomie and excitement too expansive to contain. "Just think—a son! I can hardly wait." He embraced his wife and kissed her full on the lips. Then he turned to his in-laws. "Please stay at the bungalow. We have a guest room, and I doubt we'll be back tonight." He extracted a folded paper from his pocket and handed it to Ethan. "That's the security code. Help yourself to anything you need. If you'd just let Shadow out. Her leash and halter are hanging on hooks right inside the mud room."

"Thanks," Ethan's eyes dropped to the paper, then he pocketed it, stood and hugged his daughter gently, and then gave her shoulders a quick massage. "We'll come down in a bit. Good luck, babe."

"Thanks, dad."

"Call if you need me," Janelle said.

Chris and Erin said goodnight and walked to their bungalow, pausing when a contraction seized.

22

Shouldering through the front door, Chris had developed the habit of clearing their bungalow first. He twisted around to look for Erin; she was holding onto the post at the entryway. "Would you get my luggage?" She pulled her purse strap over her head and left shoulder so she didn't have to hold it. She panted through the contraction. On his way to the bedroom, he called home to tell their parents they were headed for the hospital. Next, he called night service to let Erin's obgyn know they were heading to Carlisle Regional. He ushered his wife into his Jeep, rounded to the driver's side and tossed the compact wheelie containing Erin's nightgown, a change of clothes, nursing bra, toiletries and the baby's clothes in back. She tugged her purse off and dropped it to the floor to snap her seatbelt.

Adrenalin pumped through Chris's veins, urging him to hurry. Skidding through a three-point turn, he headed north on 74 toward I 81.

"Let's get there in one piece," Erin said through gritted teeth. Head down, breathing, and timing contractions, Erin wasn't watching the snow cascade upon the freezing interstate and missed what Chris saw. At the top of the next rise, a semi lumbered in slow motion across the median, the tanker slipping even with its cab, tons of steel creeping stealthily toward them.

"Erin, we have to get out of the car." He pulled the Jeep to the shoulder, reached across her and flung open the passenger door.

She swung her feet around, hesitating. "Why? The hospital's the next exit." Then the sliding tanker caught her attention. "My suitcase!"

He eyed the jack-knifed ten-ton skateboard sliding toward them, blocking both lanes, the driver's mouth a horrified circle framing a voiceless scream. Chris twisted, grabbed her suitcase from the back and heaved it out the open door. "Oomph." He slid behind her and pushed her out. Not prepared, she tripped, her foot tangled in her purse strap, which came along, tripping Chris, who wrapped his arms around her and rolled, tying to cushion her fall, so he'd take the brunt of the impact. The tanker crumpled the Jeep as it swept pass, metal scraping metal, carrying it fifty feet more before exploding, angry fingers of flames climbing into the night, eating air. Smoke mushroomed over the flames.

Three hundred and fifty pounds of their combined weight crashed upon Chris's left shoulder, arm and wrist. Unyielding frozen ground cracked bones twisted beneath them. His feet fought for purchase along the slick surface. He cradled his wife's belly with his right arm; his left held her shoulders, neck and head against his chest until they stopped rolling. Then he gently released her, his hands going limp when his head smacked rock.

"OMIGOD! Chris, wake up. I can't do this by myself." Heat and fumes roiled from the tanker, gas fueling the flames climbing higher in the night sky, engulfing the semi. Erin dug frantically in her purse, numb hands seeking a hard rectangle in the scrambled contents. Finally, fingers closed over the iPhone and pushed 911. Tears and falling snow blurred her vision. "Officer down. Unconscious. Send an ambulance."

"What's your location?"

"I-81 between S. Hanover and College Street. Jack-knifed semi tanker exploded; driver feared dead. I'm in labor. OH!" Another contraction bore down—a fierce clamp gripping to a count of ten—stealing her breath. Simultaneously, pain and pressure punched her kidneys. Sharp pains knifed up her back.

"Mac, is that you? How far apart are contractions?" Flood asked.

"Paula? Woo. Woo. Five minutes."

"Yes, I'm moonlighting. Stay on the line. I'll walk you through."

"I can't deliver this baby myself!" she yelled.

"An ambulance is in route. Keep the line open. How's Snow? Can he help?"

"Unconscious."

"Check his airways to see if he's breathing."

"Oh, God. I don't know." She crawled to him, checked. Dusted snow away from his face, and lowered her ear to his lips. "Yes. I need to turn him—"

"Don't move him. Can you cover him?"

A dark shadow loomed over them. The man doffed his jacket, dropped to his knees and dumped his rucksack. Tugged out an aluminized blanket, shook it out over Snow, leaving only his face exposed and laid down the other half for her and helped her scoot onto it. "Are you hurt?" He ran his hands over her head, neck, limbs and body, resting on her abdomen.

"Stay on the line," Paula advised calmly. "An ambulance is on its way."

"Savage!" she hissed, but the shiny foil-like surface blocked the snow burn even though the flakes tumbled upon them all. Warmth permeated her bottom. Hands slipped her sweats down her legs.

"Prop you knees up and spread them out." He dumped some sanitizer in his hands and scrubbed, up and down, along his fingers. "More."

"No, don't touch me! Not here. Wait for the ambul—" Another contraction contorted her abdomen, pressure pinched her back, pain zipped up her spine. She panted— short and shallow. As his fingers entered her, she gasped. For a few moments, the pleasure outpaced the pain— damn her traitorous body—as he stroked. "Ahh. Stop, Savage..."

"No need for modesty now; I'm applying baby oil. Damn woman. How long've you been in labor?" He placed a hot hand on her stomach. "Tell me he's head down."

She nodded, gritting teeth. "Seven hours, maybe longer."

"He's crowning. Let's hope you're fully dilated." He reached over, tapped Snow's leg. "Wake up, 'ole man, your kid's coming. Bear down hard when I say so. Not yet, not yet. OK, push with everything you've got. Push!"

Erin threw her head back, a primal, gurgling yodel wrenched from her throat, surfacing as a long howl. She pushed against the slope to thrust her pelvis out and shove through the pain. Sweat prickled her forehead despite fresh snow burning her bare limbs cold. She grabbed her husband's arm; a muscle twitched. She yelled, "Christopher Snow!" His fingers interlocked hers as he fought with the thermal sheet and rolled onto his side, groggy and lightheaded, cradling his broken limb.

"Hold up, don't breathe!" Savage stopped to untangle the cord from the infant's neck. "Now push, put some muscle into it!"

She heaved, held and bore down.

"Hold up. I need to tug a bit on his shoulder. OK, push hard!"

Again, she clutched her husband's hand, gritted her teeth and pushed. Suddenly, labor done, she felt an immediate release, the weight and pressure gone. Only searing pain remained. Her eyes sought Chris's; his were trained on the squirming, slippery boy that Reese expertly turned face-up, holding him like a football. Quickly, he suctioned his nose, rubbed the little rubbery form vigorously with snow, wrapped him in his quilted flannel jacket and thrust him at Mac. "Nurse him." He washed his hands with snow, finally wiping them on his pants.

Sirens whined along York Road, the noise climbing as they screeched to a halt; the wailing stopped abruptly, silence rupturing the air. The lights flashed a warning to the few oncoming motorists.

"My bra's too..." Chris unsnapped it, lifted it out of the way, and the baby latched on, but nothing came out. Erin panicked. "Nothing's happening!" Chris leaned over his son's head and put his own mouth over her nipple, a sensation she knew, so she relaxed. When her milk spurted, she guided it to the baby's mouth. He clamped and suckled while Savage once again pressed steadily on her abdomen; a final contraction, and the afterbirth surrendered. Quickly, he tied off both ends of the cord and sliced through it with his sanitized pocketknife, dropped it into a plastic bag and packed snow around it.

EMT Hemmer climbed the embankment, carrying one end of a stretcher, a woman with a matching jacket on the other end, placing it parallel to Snow. They attached a neck brace and ran their hands gently over his body, stopping when he winced. Hemmer knelt down to snap a temporary cast on his left arm and wrist, saying, "One, Two Three, lift."

Snow grunted his objection. "Stop! Take Mac and the baby. My neck's fine; my wrist's broken." The precipitation slackened a bit. The EMTs slid down the embankment, ignoring his command, loading him in the first ambulance. Snow aimed his last remark to Savage, "Thanks, man, for delivering our son."

His friend returned a sly smile. "Your wife helped." Then Savage scooped mother and son into his arms and carried them to the next ambulance as the other driver opened the rear doors. "Get the cord. It's wrapped in a gallon baggie and packed in snow."

After depositing them on the bed, he backed out to climb the slope to halt on-coming traffic as the LT's Pathfinder ground to a halt across from Savage's Bronco —thus blocking all traffic from the south-bound entrance. The ambulances veered away.

More emergency responders roared in from the north, pulling into the median. Fire trucks doused the flaming tanker with foam—streaming white arcs burying the twisted metal while soft lazy discs sifted down. Stuart and Savage set up cones and flares. They gave stalled motorists an estimation of their wait time. Numerous vehicles tried to squirm out of the lane, but arriving camera crews blocked their exit. A crane on a flatbed lumbered slowly down the interstate, forcing cars to the interstate's shoulders. The leviathan waited until the firemen finished, to lift the pieces of hot, charred metal and haul them away as traffic backed up for miles. For the moment, men and machines left the corpse inside the cab alone.

Sirens screaming and lights whirling, patrolmen in Black and Whites blocked on-ramps along I81—flares sizzled like fireworks. Wind gusted the falling snow into mad pirouettes that dropped visibility near zero. The temperature fell almost as fast, glazing the road black.

Once the crane had the charred metal loaded onto the flatbed, leaving the cab, the fire trucks followed the crane. Fire marshal Lane Rusk stepped down from his truck, lugging his equipment with his assistant, setting up a portable light to a generator to study the skid marks, collect evidence, and examine what had occurred. He flicked on his mag light and started walking. "Damnit! I was afraid of this. Not much to see in this storm."

"Shall we wait it out?" asked Russell Garret, Rusk's right hand man—actually a carrot-topped, freckled-faced kid fresh out of college.

"Yeah, back in the truck." He removed his helmet, pulled his candy red Tacoma off to the shoulder, unscrewed his thermos, poured two cups, handing one to Garrett. "It's gonna be a long cold night, Rusty."

Assistant Fire Marshall Garrett shrugged. "I'm in no hurry." He inhaled the coffee, and then tipped it back to taste. It crawled down his throat, hot and bold. "Damn this shit's good—robust. You make it?"

"I did."

"Thanks, boss."

"Don't mention it." Rusk smiled despite the full night's work ahead, wandering what had happened. He sipped slowly, making it last. Once the flatbed had pulled away and the cops directed traffic off the interstate, they climbed out of the cab.

23

At CRMC, the hospital ER staff swung into motion, taking the baby, checking his vitals, adding drops to his eyes, pricking his heel for a blood sample, weighing him, and hauling him away to be circumcised and foot printed. Later, a pediatric nurse swaddled him and gently topped him with a blue knit cap.

Mac's obgyn examined her patient, gave her a localized anesthetic to stitch the tear. "Whoever delivered him knows the birthing process. I'm stitching a small, ragged tear. The stitches will dissolve in about ten days. If they give you discomfort, take a sitz bath—" showing Erin the shallow teal plastic container with a rim. "Fill with warm water, add a tablespoon of Epsom salts, place on the commode and sit in it until the water turns tepid."

As the doctor spoke, nurses covered Erin with several warmed blankets, informing her the IV contained mainly sugar water to replace fluids and an antibiotic, since her birth had occurred in a non-sterile environment.

"I want to see my husband." Though exhausted and sore, Erin couldn't rest until she knew he was OK. "I want him in the room with me."

"That's highly irregular," the nurse shook her head.

"Then have Dr. Singer discharge me, and we'll go home. I need him. He'll insist on seeing his son. Family is allowed to stay in the rooms! Ask my doctor."

"But he's a patient."

"With a concussion. That's hardly a health threat to the baby." Erin failed to mention bronchitis.

The nurse thinned her lips but complied.

Wearing a mask covering nose and mouth, Chris was waiting in her room with their son in his arms when she arrived. Once Erin was transferred to her bed, Chris sat down next to her, a hard cast, wrapping around his thumb, encased his left arm from hand to elbow.

"Chris, you broke your arm? Oh, no! Here I'd been so absorbed with—"

"And wrist. That's OK, babe! You were delivering a baby! You're amazing. Look at him. Tiny red scratches on his cheeks, but not bad, considering his hasty entrance into the world. He weighs nine pounds!" He hefted his son a little and resettled him on his lap. "And he has golden auburn hair. He removed the little cap to show her and then unwrapped his blanket so Erin could see him. "What do you think?"

She smiled. "He has your body; look at the barrel chest and meaty thighs, long legs and big feet. How long is he?"

"You forgot something." His eyes danced mischievously, as Erin rolled her eyes. "I'm kidding! Twenty inches. No wonder you were uncomfortable. He has your nose." The father laid his son on the bed and swaddled him again, leaving only the baby's face exposed. He gentled Ian into her arms. "I'll hold him if you're tired."

"He hasn't opened his eyes." She felt the stitches pull as she shifted, then settled. Her doctor couldn't give her a sedative because she was breast-feeding.

"They're blue. He's fine, full of mother's milk." Chris brushed Erin's damp hair away from her face, leaned in and gently kissed her dry lips, her cheeks and eyelids. "Would you like ginger ale, coke, decaf coffee? A sandwich? Or would you rather sleep? I'm at your service." He smiled happily, all vestiges of their ordeal absent from his eyes, gratified and thankful that Erin and their son were safe, healthy and now sheltered from the storm.

"Can you find a chocolate shake at this hour? Water will do for now."

Holding a milkshake, Ethan and Janelle McCoy were waiting at the door, quietly impatient to see their first grandchild. "Don't want to intrude, and we won't stay long because the entire Snow family is camped in the lounge down the hall." He handed Erin the shake with a kiss and took his grandson from her so she could drink it. Rocked him gently for a few minutes, kissed his forehead and passed him to his wife, who laid him on the bed, unwrapped and checked him over quickly, kissed his cheek, walked the floor with him humming "Rock a Bye Baby" and then reluctantly returned him to Chris.

"He's absolutely beautiful. Is it true that Savage delivered him on the banks of I 81?" asked Janelle. She turned to Erin. "How are you, dear?"

"Yes, sorry to say. I'm OK; I've had an episiotomy of sorts," Mac said. "How did you know that?"

"He just arrived, handing out cigars and talking to reporters."

"Hmm." Mac pulled the creamy concoction through the straw, savoring the smooth velvety consistence of the chocolate shake but remembering the embarrassing scene by the side of the road.

"He delivered a number of babies in Afghanistan," Chris said.

"And how are you?" Janelle checked her son-in-law's pupils with a penlight. "You've had two close calls this week—a dunk in the river and a fall, with snow on Snow. You're concussed."

He laughed. "Yeah, thanks. They checked me out here, Janelle. I'm fine, except for a few broken bones." He indicated the cast.

"Oh, my. There's some time off for you. OK." She relented. "We'll keep the hearth fire burning. The snow's abated, I think. Let's go, hon. Let the Snows see their newest family member." They filed out as a similar scene was repeated with Chris's family—all filing past the bed with comments about whom he favored, suggestions for baby's care, names, and whispered endearments to the sleeping infant. Kyle sighed sadly, telling his sister, "He would've been a great baby Jesus."

"I could email the paper with the news of his birth if—" Erica offered.

Chris preempted his mother's query. "No, we haven't officially named him yet, but you'll be the first to know." His dad and brothers clapped him on the back, offering congrats and jesting about fatherhood, jarring the baby awake. He startled, his body jerked, and his mouth opened and turned his head. Quickly Chris shifted him to Erin's right side. "OK, everyone, good-night. I imagine we'll be home tomorrow." The baby glommed onto his mother's breast, and he'd worked his arms free, fisting them under his chin as he nursed. Chris lay down and watched, content and awed. "Not bad for a shot in the dark, huh?"

Erin jabbed him with her elbow but smiled and watched the earnest little boy nurse, face scrunched into a prune. She tugged off the cap, touched the silky auburn waves and snuggled back against the pillows, her husband by her side.

24

True to Chris's word, the three went home on Black Friday. Waiting in their bedroom was an oblong pine cradle woven like a basket, slung between two wooden X-shaped supports connected by a curved rod that ran through the bars secured across the top. A locking device held the bed still. Once unlatched, the cradle would rock. On the right, a plastic box played lullaby music while it rocked.

"Oh, Chris, it's beautiful. When did you make this?" Mac had never seen anything like it. A thick oval mattress covered the bottom and quilted cotton bumper pads dyed to look like denim cushioned the interior.

"Whenever I couldn't sleep nights worrying about you." His wry smile reminded Erin of the first time they met. His forehead wrinkled in thought as he ran his hands over his finished piece. "It took a while. It's thirty inches deep, forty long. Do you like it? Look, when he gets older, I can remove the crossbars, put them under the cradle to raise it to bed level. Then I can reach over, change his diaper and lift him over for you to nurse. Then back in the cradle he goes. I'll turn on the music. When he gets a little older, I have a red, white and blue mobile to attach. Open this—it's a CD player—and you can switch the music. I added this plastic runner around the rim in case he chews. It's better than a crib—his head won't get stuck."

"You've thought of everything," she murmured. "I love you," turning to him as he lifted her nightgown.

"I can't—" she whispered, with her parents across the hall in the guest room.

"I know. I just want to touch. It's been weeks," he murmured.

Around eight the next morning, Ethan let Shadow out and watched her as he savored his first cup of joe. Janelle moved quietly around the kitchen so as not to disturb the new family, although she could hear whispers, a quiet conversation—and the baby's one squawk. Ethan returned to mince and sauté onions, green pepper and chop ham. Tossed all into the pan to wilt. Scrambled and added eggs. After the eggs had set, he grated cheese over while Janelle zapped bacon in the microwave and made coffee and toast. By the time the new parents emerged, breakfast was ready. Chris no longer sounded like a seal. Erin, her hair tumbled and tangled, looked tired but satisfied, smelling milky. They laughed when Ethan said he had to run out earlier for leaded coffee and handed Chris one.

"Thanks. This'll help me wake up. Boy what a night! I thought we were goners. I'm sure the incident will give me nightmares." He gulped the black coffee. "Wow! Bet this can walk by itself!" and added creamer.

"One we'll never forget, either," Janelle said, looking relaxed in a pea green sweater and slacks she'd worn yesterday—her hair French braided rather than pulled back in her usual casual knot. "But everything turned out fine. We're going to run up and thank your parents for their hospitality—a memorable Thanksgiving—that's for sure."

"You look like you're ready for the road," Erin said.

"I have the day off. We're going Christmas shopping at the Outlets and then home to decorate." The McCoys put up two trees—a real one in the living room and an artificial one on the solarium that could be seen from the road and the alley behind their house. They festooned lights along the gutter around the entire house, since people could see it from the Ragged Edge and the parking lot adjacent to the coffeehouse.

"Thanks for coming and helping out," Mac rose gingerly to hug her parents.

"Do you need me to help you with the sitz-bath?" Janelle asked.

"I'll help her," Chris beamed at Erin. "We'll do fine, but thanks."

"Last night, I made lasagna, and Erica brought down some Thanksgiving leftovers—turkey, filling and pie." Janelle eased Erin's hair back off her face and smiled encouragingly.

"Thanks, we appreciate it; I'm not quite up to cooking yet."

"Are you going to tell us what you named our grandson before we go?" Ethan's arms encompassed wife and daughter.

"Ian Christopher Snow," Erin tilted her head up at her dad. "We talked about Ethan but thought it might be confusing with two of you."

"Ian's a fine Irish name for that wee strapping lad. I'm thrilled you all survived your ordeal whole—a miracle really—well, except for Chris's broken bones. And those will heal in time."

"I expected a 'Reese' in there somewhere," Janelle teased Erin but looked to Chris for his reaction for a hint to Savage's delivery.

"Yes, well, I'll think of some other way to reward his valiant efforts," Chris shrugged. Erin was still wigged out over his former partner touching her—even out of necessity. "Besides, the Jeep is totaled, so I need to contact our insurance company; then wait for an agent to declare it, and look for a more family-friendly vehicle with the replacement money." He sighed, rubbing the side of his nose. "I'm thankful we all survived. It was a close call. The poor driver of that rig didn't... the terrified look frozen on his face."

"I was only aware of Chris shoving me out of the Jeep and rolling halfway down the embankment," Erin admitted. "Luckily we're on leave and have the time to adjust, though I don't know about Christmas shopping. It's all rather daunting." She sighed and looked dazed.

"But we'll manage, and we'll spend Christmas day with you."

"Great!" Ethan said. "We'll have the whole family together then. See you, babe. Congratulations again to you both." Erin eased herself down on the kitchen chair—the new memory-foam cushion gently yielding.

"We'll just do the dishes and clean—" Janelle said.

"Thanks, but I can do that. You've done enough!" Chris insisted, smiling. "And thanks for making breakfast. We really appreciate your support. Enjoy your day shopping. We'll be fine."

"Please call if you need anything at all." Janelle hugged Erin, having left a gift of baby essentials like infant nail clippers, thermometer, nasal aspirator, cream for diaper rash, and a baby neck support in the laundry room for them to discover later, items hospitals' newborn kits didn't include. Ethan had tucked in money and gift cards. Out into the brisk cold—the last day in November—they went, Janelle anxious to get to the Outlets when they opened to take advantage of the best deals. She had a list and Ethan promised to help until he went to work; they expected a crowd at The Ragged Edge because an author had reserved an upstairs room for a book signing on the Civil War.

Once Erin's parents left, Chris loaded the dishwasher, cleaned the kitchen and checked his email for any updates. His broken arm itched, so he found a straw to stick up his cast and scratch the irritated skin. When Erin stepped out of the bathroom wrapped in a towel, he stood in the doorway, tempted, but she walked to the cradle to check on the baby. He consulted his watch. About that time—every four hours a feeding, so he stepped away to make that phone call and watch the news. With any luck, they'd caught the fugitive.

Shadow moseyed in, dropped down beside the recliner, looking forlorn. "Ah, need some attention, puppy?" Chris stroked her back. "Don't know what to do with yourself or make of the baby, do you?"

Greer made the noon newscast. News choppers hovered like dragonflies over the nerve center at the base of Raccoon Mountain. A camera shifted to the reporter on the ground. "Police and FBI search for fugitive Sienna Greer began last night when news of her escape leaked out of Cumberland County Prison. An anonymous source claims she had help; a prison guard said only one truck delivered clean laundry and collected dirty linen during that time. The van driver must have loaded her in with a hamper of sheets. Assuming they drove to Williamsport, locals predict the fugitive could lose the police in the mountains.

"Wildlife ranger Jason Lightfoot is expected to lead the authorities into the mountains after the fugitive. Although refusing an on-camera interview, he affirmed that he'd been hired by local police to track the fugitive, charged with attempted vehicular manslaughter against Carlisle Chief Homicide Detective Christopher Snow. Lightfoot had no comment on Snow's condition.

"With me is her employer, Mr. Otto Kraus, West Enterprise's Williamsport drill-site supervisor." Below her knit hat, strands of long brown hair whipped across her face in the stiff winds. She swiped at them with a gloved hand and turned to Kraus. "What can you tell us about Sienna Greer? Is she connected to her husband's death or the second victim, Gary Hauck?" The mic went to Kraus, who explained that both Greers had worked for him for a number of years, seemed happily married, got along well with the other workers at the Marcellus Shale drill site.

"Tell me something I need to know," Chris whispered as he stroked the dog's neck. His cell hummed on the kitchen island; he hauled himself off the recliner to answer it. Savage offered congrats and asked about Erin and junior. Chris thanked him again and promised to get together to celebrate but didn't invite him over. "You know, we're both sore but recovering, so I'll buy your dinner and beer at your choice of restaurant when I get back. You watching the news?" The dog disappeared.

"No, man, I'm packing provisions—heading up north to stand in for you—going with Lightfoot's hunting party. Imhoff and Agent Howard plan to go along too: a regular posse. The tracker won't take ATVs or four-wheelers into the mountain. No roads where we're going, he claims."

"Well, he should know. It's his territory," Snow said. "Thought Stuart was taking my place on this case."

"Nah, the LT will manage it from HQ, since Mac's out too. Sorry, gotta run and gas up the Bronco, then head north for the summit. Lightfoot parked his RV within sight of Greer's house. Later."

"Wait, wait. What's Lightfoot using for transportation?"

"Horses."

"In that case, better you than me," Snow admitted. "Thanks for keeping me in the loop."

"How long you on leave?" asked Savage. "You should be heading up this search party. I'm too old for this," he groused.

"Nah. I'm off for two weeks. Think you'll wrap this up by then?"

"Not if she's as good a survivalist as Lightfoot claims. Take care, bro."

"Good luck." Snow disconnected and ambled into their bedroom to watch his son nurse. Tenderness swamped him, so he took the baby and shouldered him to burp him while Erin relaxed between sessions. Lust struck him where it hurt, but he'd ignore it until Erin had stopped bleeding and the stitches dissolved.

A milky burp escaped; the baby blew a tiny white bubble as his head bobbed against Chris. His right hand cupped his son's head; his little behind rode on the cast. Ian smelled of baby powder and his mother. He returned him to Erin, who switched sides; the kid latched on, this time his little fist on his mother's breast. Chris kissed Erin gently but retreated to the living room to catch the rest of the news. In about fifteen minutes, he'd return Ian to his cradle bed and perhaps join Erin in bed for a nap while he mulled over whether to join that hunting party.

"Don't have to worry about supper, either. I'll stick Janelle's lasagna in the oven and make a salad, with a slice of apple and pecan pie left from Thanksgiving."

"Hey, Shadow, bad dog!" Erin yelled. Snow bounded into the bedroom. "What happened?" His first was concern for his son, sleeping across Erin's lap. Startled by his mother's sharp voice, he woke bawling. Then Snow's eyes strayed to the open walk-in closet. Inside, the dog had shredded Erin's mules into bits of rabbit fur.

"Leave it!" Chris snapped at her, then led her out, made sure she had water and locked the baby gate in the mudroom doorway. "Did anyone feed Shadow this morning? I think she's put out. I'll exercise her later."

"I'm not sure. Let me call Dad." A few minutes later she relayed. "Yes. Who was that?" Erin asked after she handed the sniffling baby to Chris.

"Savage. He's part of the search party going after Greer." He walked the floor, shushing. Then tried humming, and finally sang softly.

"Oh, really?" She'd reached for a wide-tooth comb to wrangle the tangles from her hair and sighed, watching father swaddle his son. "So you think they'll find her?"

He lowered his voice. "Oh, I think so. She can only hold out so long with police from three cities, the FBI, and your intrepid stepfather hunting her while the media hover overhead." Chris watched his sleeping son exhaling little puffs, his little chest huffing in and out.

"Lightfoot's going? Then they'll find her, but who knows when. Are they using helicopters?" she asked.

"The media is. Lightfoot's leading the search. No, the forest is too dense."

"Horses?" she asked, looking him in the eye as he climbed in bed with her.

"So you knew." He pulled her into his arms and they rubbed noses.

"Guessed. I had a dream about it."

"Just let me hold you, little mama." Burying his nose into her hair, he inhaled; she snuggled against him, threw an arm across his waist, sighed against his chest, closed her eyes and slipped into slumber on the scent of sandalwood. Once Chris dropped his head to the pillow, he was gone.

***

Erin's iPhone buzzed on the bedside table. Groggily swatting at it before Ian woke, she mumbled hello and stumbled to the kitchen.

"Congratulations you two. The Chief just announced that Savage delivered your baby night before last along the freeway. You really know how to create a splash! There's a photo of you and Snow and the smashed Jeep on the front page of *The Sentinel* as a sidebar to the tanker fire on I-81. A short paragraph underneath starts with your 911 call and—"

Erin groaned. "Please tell me you're joking. Why did you really call?" She lugged the lasagna out of the fridge while she preheated the oven.

"I'm serious, girlfriend. I'll save the paper for your baby book. What an entrance! Anyway, thought you'd like to know that the lab report on that pink sweater just came in," Sonja said.

Mac slid the casserole in the oven, her attention riveted to the conversation. "And?"

"There are three blood types on it—one matches Mindy Murphy, the others Alison Lyons. The epidermis under her nails belongs to Abigail Benedict with some drops of her blood on the cuff. Dr. Chen says the blood splatter on the sweater, mostly condensed near the top, is consistent with a skull fracture."

"So Abby was telling the truth. She fought with Murphy, but Alison delivered the killing blow. That's the solid evidence I've been waiting for," Mac commented.

"Dr. Chen concurs. Do you want to call the ADA or shall I? Should we send a copy to Wilhelm?"

"I'll call Lawson. I'm going to suggest we try the sisters together. No, we'll wait until discovery to relay this information or Lawson can decide. Add the report to

Murphy's file; please lock the report in my office drawer and email me a copy. Would you also ensure that the sweater's still locked in Evidence? Maybe file it under Flowers. Thanks." She set the timer.

"Sure thing. How is baby boy Snow?" Sonja asked.

"Ian's doing well—mainly feeding and diapering every four hours. Sleeps a lot, but that's good. Gives me a chance to shower and do a few things before the next feeding. He's cranky if he has to wait to be fed, but Shadow tore up my slippers in protest earlier."

"It's a struggle getting born—*and* delivering a baby. You sound tired, but that's normal. Is hubby helping with Ian and Shadow?"

"Better not let your boss hear you call him that. Yes, he's doing practically everything else. He holds his son, burps him, changes his diapers and sings to him! Chris made a darling cradle for him; it's really unique—shaped like a bassinet without the hood. He and Erica do most of the cooking. So I'm fortunate. Still, it's hard to carve out time for Shadow.

"Feel free to call or email me about my case, so I'm not completely out of the loop when I return," Erin said.

"Have you been watching the news?" Sonja wanted to know.

"The manhunt for Greer? No, I don't have time, but Chris feeds me the highlights. Well, we both took catnaps, and I need to start supper because Ian will be up at eight," she said. "Thanks for calling."

"Take care. Miss you both. Over and out." Sonja disconnected.

Chris returned smelling of fresh, cold air, his cheeks wind-scoured from walking Shadow, whose tail thumped excitedly. Her nose sniffed the air. Chris snuck into the bedroom to check on the baby while Erin chopped veggies for a salad for dinner. Back in the kitchen, he swooped his wife off her feet and planted a playful but meaningful kiss on her lips.

"What's that for?" Erin smiled at him as he gentled her to the floor.

"Because I love you. Tea or coffee?" he asked.

"Iced tea, please. You seem pert today. What gives?" she asked.

"Shadow ran the obstacle course for me and found the bloody rag in 2.45 minutes. And then we jogged two miles. It's cold, but the sun's shining. I found a Christmas tree. I'll cut it tomorrow."

"Great. She needs to pass that test in March. Thanks, but I need to work with her while you watch Ian. Seems a shame to kill a tree," Erin added. Shadow plopped down beside her chair, offering support. She stroked her back. "Good girl. Did you give her a treat?"

"Yes. We planted fifty evergreens for Christmases a decade ago. When we're done with the tree, we'll toss it out back for a bird shelter or a new hideout for Shadow's finds. Besides, we need to pull you out of the doldrums."

"I'm not in doldrums," Mac argued. "I'm just tired."

"If you say so. I'll bring down the Christmas ornaments tomorrow; we'll have a tree-trimming party! And I have another idea: I'm going to buy a pump and bottles. If you can express some milk, I'll take the four a.m. feeding so you can rest. I can usually fall asleep easier after being awakened. Besides, there may be times you'll need to run to town, and mom could come watch the baby—but only if and when you want to," he amended. "At some point you'll need a break."

She sipped her tea and set it down, a genuine smile beautifying her features—his exuberance contagious. "You would do that for me? They're expensive. Then you'll be tired when you go back to work."

"Let's just try it. We can always adjust the schedule; I could take the midnight feeding if you're worried. Let's eat; smelling that oregano and cheese is driving me mad!" Erin let the dish set while she made garlic bread. While they ate, he summarized Savage's call, and she, Sonja's. "I can do these if you want to relax." He gathered and scraped the dishes while Erin put on a Tai Chi DVD and exercised for half-an hour. She screened out external noises and meditated for an additional fifteen minutes. Heard the dish and clothes washers humming in tandem. Chris reappeared with her parents' gift basket. He sat down beside Erin, and they went through each item.

"What's this?" Chris help up a package with a bulb base and an opening in a conical clear plastic top.

"Nasal aspirator. To suction mucus out of his nose when he's congested. Savage used one the night Ian was born."

"But he won't catch a cold if he's breast-fed; he'll have your immunities." Those bourbon eyes lit his face; he'd been reading.

"I don't have an immunity to sinus infections, but you're right, he'll have my immunities while he nurses. And I don't plan to expose him to too many people while I'm on leave, either. What's in the wash?"

"Baby clothes. Yes, I used Dreft. Next load, towels."

"And I'd like to do our sheets then."

"All right. Then I'll run for groceries. Need anything that's not on the list?"

"Deodorant and a pack of Pampers. Maybe swing by Kaufman's for Shadow's dog food?"

"Got it. Be back soon." He pulled her up, kissed her again because she needed it, donned his parka, easing it over his cast and breezed out the door, temporarily relieved of his work responsibilities.

The next morning, he and Shadow returned with a seven-foot pine, which he stood in the living room in front of the sunroom's sliding glass doors. A carton he'd unearthed upstairs held glass, homemade and crystal ornaments. Erin brought a shoebox with the ones her dad had given her when she left home, but she'd hadn't bothered to put up a tree when living by herself. After Chris put on the lights, they threaded garlands of fresh cranberries and popcorn and draped them around the tree. Added the mix of red bulbs, crystal angels, and a drum Chris had made in elementary school from a thread spool and matchstick.

"Oh, that's so cute!" Erin was thrilled he'd kept ornaments from his childhood. She added a little Santa on a ladder and an elf on a sled from her box, and a crystal drummer boy—her favorite.

Chris recognized them. "'Ba-rump-a bump-bum.' You've been to Chocolate World."

"Several times. First time, we walked through the actual factory; then they renovated it with those revolving cars. Talk about a scent driving you mad; chocolate permeated the entire town."

"I remember that! They probably changed that factory tour for insurance purposes."

They spent the afternoon and evening decorating and sharing anecdotes of Christmases past, breaking only to care for Ian—showing him the tree—walking Shadow and eating. Cocooning in front of the fire without dire interruptions from work or personal animosities—real or imagined, theirs or anyone else's—attuned their attentions to one another and family. They discussed Christmas gifts.

"I bought a number at the Gettysburg College seminar in October." She pulled her red tote out of the closet and showed him the earrings, stuffed animals, the paper airplane kit for Kyle, the pipe for his dad. "If you buy wrapping paper, I can wrap them and put them under the tree—or maybe upstairs in case Shadow feels neglected again and is tempted to rip them apart. Then Christmas prep won't seem like so much all at once."

"Think I'll order gift baskets online for my parents, Jeff's family and Jack. What would your parents like? I can order theirs from Amazon, too or Harry and David's or the Florida orchards."

"Food's always good. Wine. Or personal luxuries they wouldn't necessarily buy for themselves but nothing impersonal. They may have a wish list on Amazon. I have their password, so I can check."

"Good idea!" Chris moved behind her to massage her neck and shoulders, and then her back. When she turned into him in invitation, he lowered himself to meet her. "Ah, I can massage the front as well."

"I can't resist sandalwood," she whispered, her lips against his.

"I can't resist you—so soft, clean and glistening. I'll try to go slowly."

Erin pulled him down with her, dropping to the carpet.

And so they planned their first Christmas as a family in this niche of rare private time until the next phone call shattered their domestic bliss.

25

She'd tucked her cell into her pocket while padding out to the rocker. The call came on Erin's at ten p.m. while the baby was nursing. "Hello. McCoy."

"Erin? How are you and the baby?" asked Lightfoot.

She paused and then said, "Fine, thank you. We named him Ian Christopher. We're getting to know one another, but something tells me you called for another reason. Are you at Raccoon Mountain?"

"Yes. I need to speak to your husband. Sorry, I need him here, but I wanted to say congratulations, thanks for my first grandson and welcome to parenthood. It's a blessing with many joys and sorrows."

She sighed but warmed to the genuine warmth in his tone. "Thank you and we're honored: not many kids have three grandfathers."

"You knew I was going to call?" asked Lightfoot.

"I had a dream. Chris was riding with you in the mountains."

"Ah, a shaman in the making. Is he there? It's rather urgent."

"Sure, just a moment." She handed the iPhone to Chris, who'd been in the bathroom but wandered out, curious about the late call.

He plopped into an armchair. "Hello. Snow here." He listened to Lightfoot. "How bad is he? Will he live?" Then stood, waited. Erin could hear the low pitch of Lightfoot's voice but not the words. "Who shot him?" She sighed again and hefted the baby onto her shoulder, thumping his back until she heard an explosion of air and put him on her other side. "Greedy little pig," she smiled at him. His lake blue eyes locked on hers, his hands fisted beneath his chin as he nursed, his auburn hair golden red in the lamplight. Her husband was silent for a time, his eyes on her, sad and beseeching at the same time. She nodded, resigned to the fact that she'd be alone for a while—until Greer was apprehended and returned to CPD custody.

When he ended the call and laid the cell down, he shuffled his clothes into his duffle bag. "Someone shot Savage—blew out his knee. By the time they found him, Imhoff was using his pistol to tighten the tourniquet while Savage was fighting a PTSD flashback. A news crew airlifted him to the Sunbury Hospital. Lightfoot needs a replacement to go after Greer."

Erin made a motion to rise with the baby, but Chris took him, burped him, checked his diaper, changed to a dry one, swaddled him and placed him gently in the cradle. She followed, turning on the CD player. Chris drew her to him. "I'll get Dad to take me to HQ to get a four-wheeler. You may need your car."

"Take Shadow. She'll locate Greer quicker and easier."

"I will not. She's the reason I can leave; she'll protect you."

Erin gave Chris a bemused look. "I don't need protection."

"I'll feel better if she's here. I hate to leave you by yourself with a newborn, but..." He reached behind her neck eased her face to his, kissing her long and deeply because he needed to. Then tore himself away and resumed packing.

Erin shrugged, trying for nonchalance. "Duty calls. If I need help, I'll call your parents or my dad. And Danelle's coming up to take baby photos for our Christmas cards. Sonja will probably stop by too. I'll be fine. And I need to write Grandmother. When are you leaving?"

"Sorry, babe. Tonight. May I take the weapons in your trunk? Lost mine. I'll need my sleeping bag, hunting socks and vest..." She heard him mumbling while thumping up the stairs for his gear.

She found leaded coffee in the cabinet, started the pot. Washed out the thermos. Packed a turkey sandwich, threw in a couple apples and bananas, a bag of trail mix and a few granola bars. Stuffed the food into an insulated lunch bag with a cold pack. Tucked in two bottles of water. Passed it to him when he trundled downstairs. He gathered her into his arms, kissed her again and said, "I'll be back as soon as I can. Love you."

"Love you more," she whispered, and then watched him go.

***

By the time Snow pulled in front of Lightfoot's RV, he'd eaten the sandwich, an apple and banana, shoved the rest into his parka pockets. The search party was ready to go, having eaten and rested in the interim. Snow unloaded his gear and locked the CPD's SUV. Lightfoot updated him.

"We tracked her for several miles until Savage got shot. So we can make pretty good time until we reach that point," Lightfoot said.

Howard was staying in the RV to request more equipment and manpower. "Someone needs to keep an eye on her house," he said. "And I have an agent on the cave. I assume your people took out some things?"

"Where were you when that went down?" Snow asked Imhoff and nodded in Howard's direction, ignoring Howard's inquiry.

"On the other ridge. I thought someone was shooting at me, so I returned fire with my pistol." He tapped his holster. "Savage was shot with a rifle." He tipped his hat and turned his horse toward the trail.

Snow wondered why Imhoff told him more than he'd asked. He stood before the chestnut gelding; it stomped and snorted—the vapor visible in the near-freezing temperature. Snow took a deep breath to fortify his nerves, tied his sleeping bag on back of the saddle, slid Erin's forty-caliber carbine rifle in the leather holster provided, slung the shotgun case with ammo over the pommel, fit his left boot into the stirrup and hoisted himself onto the animal's back, groaning inwardly at the strain on his broken arm. Lightfoot alighted his mount and led the way into the deep freeze.

A crisp crust of snow crunched beneath the horses' hooves. Snow needed his three layers. Riding single file, he pondered what each man had said and not said. Moisture condensed and froze like silver filigree on the few withered oak leaves clinging to the trees. As they climbed higher, pungent pine resin pierced the air. Hooves clomped uphill, saddles creaking, the occasional falling acorn plopping against the ground. The biting cold stung his nose, so Chris tied his handkerchief around his face. Snow dust sprinkled everywhere like sifting powdered sugar: Winter's gift of sweet silence and sharp contrasts! Lightfoot clicked to his horse; they loped along, quickly covering ground they'd treaded before. They rode for an hour until Lightfoot signaled stop, dismounting, leading his Quarter horse by the reins. He motioned them all to dismount and led the animals to a fast-running stream where the horses drank; the men refilled canteens.

They pushed through the misty night—midnight blue above with stars winking pinpricks of light. "Here's where we had to turn back. If Greer shot Savage, she meant to immobilize him, put more distance between her and us. During the day, the news or National Guard choppers overhead pinned her down; she's probably hiding in a cave, one of the few places the thermal imaging wouldn't penetrate.

"We need to spread out. Look for branches broken off around knee level, prints in the snow, deer trails, recent notches on trees scored by humans, bent grasses, leaves disturbed or trampled weeds. Or branches cut or snapped from evergreens for a lean-to. Look under trees too. Try not to use a flashlight, but if you must, cover it and aim it down in case anyone is trailing from behind to pick us off one by one. She may not be alone. Crossing the summit means she's leaving her comfort zone, which makes her more desperate and dangerous."

"She's heading for the Allegheny Forest?" asked Snow quietly.

"Uh-huh. We must find her before she gets that far."

"Will the choppers return tomorrow?" Imhoff asked.

Lightfoot shrugged. "I assume; you heard Howard. He plans to put his people down on the other side of the mountain—trap her in the middle."

"Did he say how many agents?" Imhoff again. He tilted his canteen for a long drink.

"Twenty, I think." Lightfoot's watch cap was pulled down to his eyebrows and over his ears. He'd wrapped a wool scarf around his neck. He wore a padded flannel shirt, bomber's lined jacket, snug leather gloves, jeans and boots—seemingly comfortable in this milieu.

"Let's fan out and get to it," Snow said, feeling for his mini-mag in his right pocket. "Do you plan on riding all night?"

"Patience, kemosabe." Lightfoot smiled. "We'll ride until first light, stop and eat, sleep, rest the horses and let the feds take the morning shift.

"She won't be able to get by all of us," Imhoff stated.

"Don't bet on it." Lightfoot moved right, motioned Snow left and Imhoff straight ahead. A half hour passed before Snow found blue jean threads snagged on a thorny bush. He looked ahead for a path, saw none but smelled urine and saw a crumpled tissue nearby. He whistled. Jason was beside him within minutes, but Imhoff had ridden ahead.

Snow pointed to his finds. His guide nodded and gave him a thumbs-up, leaning close to his ear. "Something's off with Imhoff's story. He and Savage left together to scout ahead. Howard and I stayed to check the rocky cliff back there, looking for a cave or recession—even a shelf can provide shelter and a hideout." He strode farther, scouting, and then retraced his steps to where Snow stood thinking.

"Looks like she took a piss break," Snow concluded. "I'll watch your back if you watch mine."

The ranger nodded and returned to his horse, untied him, mounted and shoved up the mountain pass. Snow followed. His hand clasped his cell in his pocket, his fingers itching to call Erin, but what could he say?

Hey babe, I love you but don't know when I'll see you again.

I hope to be home by Christmas.

Your stepfather and I are finally bonding.

Nah.

He pulled his cell out and thumbed her a TM: "Look through all evidence." Then he stopped, sent it to LT Stuart instead. "Let's run background check on Imhoff, see who he interviewed at the drill-site." He had to kick his horse gently to catch up with his stepfather-in-law.

The party continued its search following the earlier pattern. Stop, dismount, reconnoiter and scan for clues that a person had traveled this way. When the horizon rimmed a faint peach, they stopped. Building a small fire in the curve of a rock face for warmth, the men ate bread, cheese and apples, unsaddled, tied and fed the horses oats, and then bedded down for a few hours.

When the choppers buzzed over the eastern ridge, Lightfoot rose to settle the startled horses that neighed and thrashed, tugging on the reins tied to tree branches. Snow rolled and stumbled up to help—groggy and stiff with cold but instantly wary. Lightfoot threw a blanket over his mount's head, grabbed the reins and jerked down while rubbing the horse's neck, talking to him calmly. Snow followed suit with the gelding he rode.

"The mare's missing." Lightfoot frowned grimly. "One of us should have stood guard." He strode onto the mountain path, glanced back and forth, peering vainly into the distance obscured by fog, shaking his head. "A cloud dropped down."

Snow was slower to respond. His eyes roved their campsite—a natural cove amid boulders screened by thin, scruffy trees. The fire had gone out. The wind bit into his face; he twisted one-eighty, but, sure enough, Imhoff was gone. "Imhoff took your horse?"

"Looks like." Lightfoot scattered the ashes with his boots, dribbling his own water on it to ensure it was out, canting his head to one side, listening. Then tucked in and zipped his jeans. "Mother, it's freezing. Let's go." He saddled the horse, his hands working efficiently despite the biting wind. He cinched it snugly while Snow rolled their sleeping bags, tying the ranger's on while Lightfoot saddled the other horse.

"Where?" Snow's eyes peered into the foggy mist.

"Forward. Either he wants to get to Greer first or warn her about the FBI swarming up the other side. Why would he go back?"

"Couldn't tell you. What do you suspect he did?"

"Shot Savage. Unless Greer's closer than we think. She had a twelve-hour lead—maybe more, unless someone shot my tire to give her time to escape."

"You mean as a diversion?" Snow asked.

"It's an old trick. Feint one way—go another."

"OK, say you're right. Why would Imhoff shoot Savage and then scramble back to help? And where is the rifle?"

"You're the detective." Lightfoot pushed ahead, eyes casting to one side then another, scanning the forest, looking and listening for signs of his mare. "Hope to hell the sun burns this off." He waved his hand.

"Suppose there's another explanation, like he scouted ahead, but his horse threw him. Or he fell."

Lightfoot shook his head. "Buttercup's too gentle. She's never bucked, but what you suggest is possible. Keep your eyes peeled."

"Yes, kemosabe. What are the other horses' names?" asked Snow.

"Mine is Sampson. Yours is Ronin, and Anya named the mare Buttercup. Ahnai's pinto back home is Spice." He spurred his horse forward. "I'd whistle for her but don't want expose our location."

Snow remained quiet, waiting and searching for Imhoff. He pulled out his cell: no message, though it was early yet. Perhaps Imhoff checked out, and they were chasing a wild goose. *As a cop, what possible connection could he have to this string of homicides?* He spotted a cell tower on the horizon; the sun glinted off the metal. Speed-dialed Erin. "Hey, babe. How you doing? Is it too early?"

"No, I just fed Ian. You sleep under the stars last night? Having a grand adventure, cowboy? Find anyone yet?"

"What sleep that could be had. I don't recommend rock or frozen ground for a mattress. You and Ian OK?"

"I'm fine. He had a restless few hours at midnight. Misses his dad, I suspect. The LT called. Why are you running a search on Imhoff?"

"Did he find anything?"

"He said none of his detectives are at HQ. And his computer skills are limited. Said he's busy fending off the media. This Greer story is a national sensation. The FBI trackers have helmet cams—apparently feeding the media footage while climbing Raccoon Mountain in the snow. Very telegenic. Howard never misses an opportunity."

"All right. Did *you* find anything?" Snow knew his wife would be too curious or industrious to let his request slide.

"Nothing suspicious. Born in Williamsport in '75, he's been on the Sunbury force for seven years after attending college and the Hershey Academy. Married, one child. Wife runs a day care center from their domicile. Average number of arrests early on, mainly DUIs, B&E, drug busts. A citation above and beyond the call in a shootout earned him a promotion. His father was the mayor there for three terms, now retired. His mother's a retired librarian—civic-minded, sits on the board at the library and school board. Two siblings: male and female, realtor and teacher, respectively. Need a search warrant for much else."

"Thanks. Nah, no evidence, just a hunch."

"OK. Any trace of Greer?" she asked.

"Not yet. And to answer your meta-message, I don't know when I'll be home. Couple days, I'm hoping. Don't know how anyone can stand to be out in this weather for long. It's brutal. Who knows how long my cell will last, so I'd better sign off. Love you."

"Love you, too. Are you wearing Kevlar?"

"I am. Love you more." Snow snapped the phone shut.

"Quite a night you two had Thanksgiving. Erin and the baby are all right?" Lightfoot asked.

"Thankfully, yes. Thanks for asking. Mac ran a check on Imhoff. He checks out. Though we'd need a subpoena to look at financials."

But the man didn't answer; suddenly Sampson leaped forward, galloped and whinnied, pulling up short and dodging into the brush. Lightfoot slid down, looping the reins around a branch, clicking his tongue. Buttercup turned and picked gingerly through the undergrowth toward her owner. Quivering all over, she rolled her eyes and stomped. He caught her reins, talking to her gently, but she needed no encouragement. She ploughed ahead, stopping abruptly alongside Sampson.

Snow eased off of Ronin, brought him level with the others. Together he and the ranger scouted the area, looking for evidence of Imhoff. They broke through a clearing of sorts. Low, grey clouds blowing from the west portended more snow. At cliff's edge, the wind whipped dry leaves before the storm. At the edge, four horseshoe prints were three feet shy of the ledge; then the ground sheared away. Lightfoot pointed at them with his flashlight. "See the first two are planted, dug in? A full stop, throwing him." Carefully stepping to the edge, they looked down. Imhoff lay still about twelve feet down, on an outcrop of rocky soil thick with weeds and stunted trees. The slope continued its steep decline for at least 300 feet, and then sloped before another drop-off.

Snow flipped open his cell, called Agent Howard to relay the man down. "We'll need paramedics—" He looked to Lightfoot for coordinates, but then remembering, continued, "About a fourth mile southwest of the cell tower near the summit." Waited a beat, listening. "No place for it to set down here."

"There's a campsite with open space a mile ahead," Lightfoot said. He walked back to the horses and pulled a coil of rope off Sampson's pommel.

"Don't think we should move him," Snow said.

Undeterred, the ranger looped one end of the rope around a stout trunk, knotted it, stepped backward to the edge and said, "I plan on moving myself. Let's see if he's still alive." He tested the rope, tying the other end around his waist and rappelled down, dropping onto the rock ledge. Kneeling, he checked for a pulse, and gave Snow a thumbs up. Lightfoot moved his hands slowly over Imhoff's body, testing for broken bones. Then he eased down beside the unconscious detective, crossing his legs beneath him, leaned against the mountain slope and waited.

Snow hiked back to the horses to see if they were still tethered to the tree. All stood, heads down, waiting patiently. Sampson gave him a withering glance. While debating his next move, absently plucking a thin offshoot off a branch to reach in and scratch his itching wrist, he heard voices climbing the slope from the west. Heads, then shoulders popped into view and finally uniformed men with caduceus insignias on their jumpsuits carrying a stretcher hustled his way. "Where's the officer down?" the rangy one with dark, razor-cut hair asked. The quiet one had a jagged scar along his cheek, powerful forearms and thighs; he carried a duffle bag with a red cross emblazoned on either side.

"Over the edge," Snow cocked his head, turned and led them to the spot where he'd left Lightfoot. The one with the kit slid the rope through its handle, than disappeared. The second slid over the embankment, sliding the stretcher along. The ranger climbed up soon after, trotted off and then returned with Sampson. He freed his rope from the tree, winding it around the pommel. A tug on the line, then Lightfoot lunged against the horse's chest, urging the animal back. Muscles straining, man and horse pulled the injured man slowly to the lip. Snow swung the stretcher onto solid ground with his right arm.

Lightfoot called, "Whoa, Atta boy!"

Unhooking the stretcher, Snow tossed the rope back to the waiting paramedics, who reappeared one after the other, dropped to their knees to administer aid to a nasty gash on Imhoff's forehead and cut and burned palms—as though he'd grabbed roots or branches to stop his fall—left eye swollen shut, he wore a neck brace and a splint stabilized his left arm. However, he *was* breathing without assistance. Once the men started an IV drip, the beefy guy Velcroed the drip bag to his bicep, and then they double-timed back the way they'd come. Later, churning rotors beat the wind and whipped treetops sideways; the whirring receded as it flew south.

Lightfoot and Snow pushed on—stopping at the campground to refill canteens and bottles. The ranger pulled out keys, opened the steel door to the concession stand, heading for the kitchen. Though the thermostat had been turned down to sixty-five degrees, that felt warm compared to thirty outside. Once he flicked the light on, he made a pot of steaming coffee, found some powdered creamer and sugar in an overhead cabinet and pulled out two cans of tomato soup. Chris poked around, in the stainless steel freezer/fridge combo. He drew out a slim block of cheddar, cut off the mold from either end. Some economical soul had frozen bread in groups of four slices. Within minutes, he'd grilled bread, sliced the cheese onto it, and they were eating hot sandwiches, soup and coffee.

"How about another?" he asked the ranger, who nodded. Chris repeated the steps, finishing the cheese. "Just as well; it wouldn't last much longer."

Lightfoot ate without comment, and so Chris let him be.

Jason stood. "If you clean up, I'll feed the horses." He pulled an institutional-size container of oats from a steel shelf, unearthed two totes from a pantry and walked out, where they'd left the horses, hitched to the front porch posts.

Chris took his time throwing away trash and twisting the bag closed, washing the coffee mugs and soup bowls, drying and returning them to the cabinet. He dusted crumbs into his hand and dumped them into the sink, rinsing them down the drain. Lightfoot secured the door. The men led the horses over to a spigot, twisted the faucet; water gushed into a bucket below. Jason let each horse drink his or her fill. They rode around back to a covered crib of split firewood; they filled one tote with wood and the other with oats tied them onto either side of Buttercup's saddle. The men mounted and resumed the trail and rode on for several miles to the rhythm of the horses' movements and the swaying of creaking saddles.

"Any idea where Greer might hide?" Snow finally asked.

"Other than holed up in a cave, I don't have a clue, but that's my best guess."

"Then I guess we'll ride until we meet the FBI." Snow scanned the surrounding, looking for a mound of stones, a rocky cliff or overhanging canopy that might serve as a hideout. He looked up among the trees for a hunting stand—even a crude tree house could serve as shelter, though that would be too obvious. "Lightfoot, I'm—"

"You can call me Jason."

"Jason, I'm sorry I jumped to the wrong conclusion—"

"That's OK."

"How do you know what I was going to say?"

"About my feelings for Erin the other day in the truck." Jason's head swiveled back to look at Chris, who nodded, and then faced forward once more. Glacial air knifed through their jeans; drops of condensation on their hair turned to ice. Faces stiffened. Fingers holding the reins grew numb. Tiny ice particles dropped from the sky, coating the snow.

"Don't feel bad. If not for our kinship, your comment might have had merit. You know the song about marrying a beautiful woman?"

"You'll be unhappy the rest of your life."

"I learned that from experience. Every man wanted Ahnai because she was their fantasy in the flesh, like some exotic Pocahontas with a perfect face with doe eyes, lithe limbs—a classic beauty like Jane Seymour or Jacqueline Smith. But Ahnai," he stretched three distinct syllables, "was right: I can't see her in your wife. Don't assume that Erin is like other women, though."

"And how do you know her so well?" Sharpness in his tone.

"I don't. She loves you—that I know. Do you know her runes?"

"Her what?"

"In our culture, we recognize all life as sacred—animal, plant, mineral—as well as human. We believe we have spirit guides that teach us about dangers to avoid as well as rituals to follow for a fruitful life. We ignore those guides at our own peril. Well, Erin has a bear to the north, a badger to the east, beaver to the south and an eagle to the west. All are powerful images. For example, the bear warns her about external and internal dangers. The badger will fight to the death; the eagle has eyes to see far ahead. Ask her to tell you."

"I know the story of the good and bad wolves," Snow said.

"And you see the significance of that story?" Jason asked.

"Yes—the one you feed fuels your life. So how do you know this? Did she tell you?" Chris wanted to know, his concern implying that Erin would share something so personal with Lightfoot rather than him.

"No, she told my mother."

"She's met your parents?"

"You have too, at the seminar in Gettysburg. My dad carves the tiny animal figures; my mother weaves baskets and makes other crafts like pinecone and cornhusk wreaths and dried herb bundles. They both convert dried gourds to birdhouses and make pinecone and grapevine trees and wreaths—they're very crafty." He chuckled. "And the income's adequate to meet their needs."

"They travelled all the way from Sayre?"

Jason answered with a nod. "All over the east coast."

When the man stopped talking, Chris mulled over his words.

Numerous times, they left the trail and rode through brush and around trees to inspect rock formations. When one looked promising, they dismounted for a closer inspection—running eyes and hands along crevices that might form an opening to a hideout.

"You realize this is like hunting for bee in an arbor or a hive?"

"You mean wasp. If not here, where?" Jason replied, exasperated.

"Does she have a cabin or vacation home? An RV parked someplace like your wife did?"

Jason shook his head no, or he could just be examining every shadow that might shelter a recessed nook where their fugitive might hide. "Not to my knowledge."

"Would she ride or be on foot?" Snow asked.

"Could be either. She won't use the ATV, though."

"I can see why. Or suppose she did and travels at night, then camouflages it during the day? Throw a few branches and leaves or camo netting over it."

"We could still hear it at night."

"If we were close enough," Snow countered.

A sound like a figure brushing through grass silenced them. They halted the horses to listen if it reoccurred. Could be a deer, rabbit or even raccoon. Drifting snow outlined trees in stark relief, yet obscured other forms, making day seem dusk, as the sun dodged behind the cloudbank that Canadian winds drove relentlessly southeast. A swishing sound like cloth rubbing—moving away. Jason dismounted to follow, tossing Sampson's reins to Chris. As he melted into the tree line, Chris slid off Ronin to stretch his legs and relieve his sore ass. He led the horses off the path and secured the reins in the shelter of the pines, staying put in case whoever Lightfoot was tailing doubled back to free or steal the horses. On foot, they would have a tough time getting back to base camp.

"Was this the second—or third day out? Since the paramedics took Imhoff, shouldn't the FBI agents be close behind? We're riding east to west. Will we have to also canvass the rest of the 6,000 acres from north to south?" Snow's musings caused him to miss the commotion at first. The ranger was dragging a protesting female from the protection of the trees to exposure on the path.

Coltish legs kicked and thrashed; she repeatedly tried to jerk away, struggling to free herself, but Lightfoot had a solid hold on the restraints on the girl's wrists. Long, streaked hair whipping side to side hid a long, narrow face. She stopped struggling when she saw Snow. Wide blue eyes were lined with kohl, lids shadowed in lavender. Her new clothes looked vintage Lands' End, but the pale girl was not an outdoors aficionada. The way she brought one foot up, then the other, gingerly lowering each meant her new Western boots were pinching her feet.

Snow kept his hands in his hip pockets; she might bite his fingers. Though he wasn't certain of her identity, she had her father's build and complexion but her mother's eyes. Snow smiled. "I'm Homicide Detective Christopher Snow. And you are..."

She spat in his direction, but he'd anticipated it and sidestepped.

"Detective Snow, meet Ms. Lillian Greer," Lightfoot said, "Sienna and Dale's daughter. What are you doing up her alone, Lily? Shouldn't you be at college?"

Silence.

"Do you a have a campsite close by?" Snow asked.

No answer.

"All right." Snow shrugged—no difference to him. "You are under arrest for aiding and abetting a fugitive from justice; your mother's a felon who attempted vehicular manslaughter on a police officer. You have the right to remain silent..." He Mirandized the young woman.

"Let's go." He took her other elbow; both men marched her to Buttercup and helped her mount. Lightfoot tied her hands around the pommel, holding the horse's reins. "Let's go back. We've got a prisoner." Throwing a leg up and over his horse, Snow felt his Glock shift in paddle holster at the small of his back.

"You can't hold me. I haven't done anything," Lily finally said.

"Oh, contraire, I can. You'll be arraigned later this week, printed and photographed. You'll not only miss Spring Semester, you'll likely be expelled, and, if you're over eighteen—as I think you are—then your arrest record will follow you for the rest of your life—a black mark that will bar you from most decent jobs, nullifying that pricy college education." They turned the horses around, jockeying until Lily rode between the men. Snow saw her eyes flicker in surprise at something ahead, so he reached in his hip pocket and pulled out his sling shot, loaded it with one of the smooth bird's egg-sized stones he kept in his coat pocket.

A woman stepped out ten feet along the path, bow in hand, a notched arrow ready. Hands behind the pommel, he said, "Ask yourself if you really want to shoot. Sure you're a good shot, but your daughter's also in the line of fire. And who knows what a spooked or injured horse will do? You tried to kill me once; you won't get a second chance." Before Greer could take a breath, the detective aimed the slingshot and fired, hitting her bow hand. She let go, howling, the impotent arrow plunking to the ground. He dismounted, holding the rein in his left hand, the cast held behind him to protect it. Cuffed the metal behind her back with both women screaming police brutality. Lightfoot stemmed the bleeding knuckles by wrapping his handkerchief around them tightly and knotting it. Then they hefted her up behind her daughter.

"Do you want anything from your camp like food or a sleeping bag?" asked Lightfoot considerately. "We barely have enough for two."

Sienna Greer gritted her teeth and shook her head, trying to signal her daughter by resting her shaking head on her shoulder to signal her to keep quiet about their secret hideout.

"Oh, my cellphone! Sorry, mama, I need my smart phone."

Her mother groaned.

"Where is it?"

"Back down that deer trail maybe thirty feet. You'll see the fire."

"You left a fire unattended? I could arrest you for that."

"I think Snow beat you to it," Lily quipped.

Snow checked Lightfoot's hands to see if they were gloved.

Lightfoot deftly reined Sampson left; they forged through the undergrowth until man and beast were lost from sight.

Snow repeated the arrest and Mirandized Sienna Greer again. "And save the theatrics for court. After going away for the attempt on my life, you'll be tried separately for each homicide."

"What's he talking about, mama?" Turning slightly, catching her mouth against the fur on her blue parka. Shaking her head again, Sienna Greer was conserving her energy, trying to stay conscious, preparing for her defense or perhaps planning another escape.

Loping back to the mountain pass ten minutes later, Jason held the cell out to Lily, who thanked him and pocketed it. He wore his wife's quiver with distinctive green arrows and raven feathers on his back. He reached across to take Buttercup's reins from Snow, wheeled back and loped in the direction they had come. The CPD detective lingered long enough to slash a deep X into the tree that led back to their cave. He was sure the women hadn't been camping rough because their clothes were dry but smelled dank. At the campsite that overlooked a lake where they'd stopped for sustenance before, they reined in again.

Tired and hungry, Jason and Chris ate the last of the granola bars and trail mix, halved the last banana, made more hot coffee, because one or the other—weapons ready —must watch over these wily, angry women all night. Wearing the restraints in front, Lily loaded ice into a baggie and gave it to her mother for her swollen knuckles. Then the daughter heated hot water in a teakettle. Snow motioned her back with his Glock and streamed the steaming liquid in the mugs for her. Lily carried it over where Sienna lay on a cot, her left hand elevated with the ice pack on top.

They sipped reconstituted dry soup and ate already-buttered peasant bread that they had put together like a sandwich to avoid smearing. Lily also had an apple, but her mother had succumbed to sleep after her captors gave her ibuprofen for pain. Sienna looked drained, her face crumpled in defeat, but her daughter, unfazed by her arrest, munched contently on the fruit, her eyes as frosty as the snow outside.

26

By the time they reached the base of Raccoon Mountain, they were wet, tired, and edgy from insufficient sleep. Sienna and Lily Greer made no cooperative gestures; both remained surly and combative, the mother sure the men erred in arresting her, still denying the charge, the daughter convinced of her mother's innocence.

Special Agent Lionel Howard greeted them affably, offered hot food and drink from Lightfoot's RV: hot chili, corn bread muffins and coffee and tea. A medic examined Greer's injury, doused it with alcohol—causing the woman to yowl while he stitched the torn flesh and rewrapped it in sterile gauze. "I'll give you an antibiotic and ibuprofen. You need to see your family doctor—"

"Not happening," Snow interrupted gruffly. "She's going to Carlisle to be arraigned and tried for attempted manslaughter."

"I'd prefer to take charge of Mrs. Greer, escort her to Washington to stand trail for the murder of our agent, Dean Greer."

"Do you have enough evidence to hold her on that charge?"

"No, because I didn't kill my husband." Greer gritted her teeth. "However else I felt, he was Lily's father and beneath his many irritating habits—he was a good man and father." She elevated her leg on the dining bench.

Howard considered this. "Yes, everyone claims innocence. Lab's still processing what we found at the house and cave."

"How dare you search my cave! Did you have a search warrant?" Her face reddened at the invasion of privacy. "Bad enough you pawed through everything at my house, leaving it a wreck, but my cave too?"

"What were you looking for?" asked Lily. "I'm sure if you would've asked, Mom would have given it to you."

"Murder weapons and anything tying her to her husband's death."

"And did you find what you were looking for?" asked Lily with asperity.

"As a matter of fact, yes, we found photos..." Lightfoot began but thought he'd better not speak for the police.

"Photos? I didn't have any photos!" Sienna screeched. "Had I seen those, I probably would've kill—" Then she stopped, realizing she might incriminate herself.

Snow argued, "My case can proceed immediately. I witnessed her most recent crime, and since the Sunbury detective is laid up, I will personally escort her to the Cumberland County Prison after her arraignment to await trial. I also have solid physical evidence: time-stamped photos of her tailing me in her rig and its plates, paint scrapes of her rig on my Jeep, her fingerprints on the door. She stole police evidence, left the scene of a crime and failed to stop and help the victim." He looked around the table at the others, a challenge in his eyes. "Lightfoot also found stolen goods at her hideout."

"Well, my duty's done here, so if you'd all vacate my RV, I'd like to take my horses home," Lightfoot voiced wearily.

"Sorry, but we still need it for a day or two longer. If you can haul your horses with your truck, I'll have one of my men return this RV—where do you want it?" asked Howard. "And I'll put in an expense voucher to insure you're aptly compensated for any inconvenience we've caused."

Lightfoot shrugged. "At my studio in Sayre." He gave them a business card, the address listed. He stood, pulled Snow up, shook his hand and clapped him on the back. "We solid? I'd like to visit soon."

Snow canted his head sideways and nodded slowly, as if just coming to a conclusion. "Solid. Sure. Next time you swing down our way. And thanks for your help. Otherwise, we'd still be on the mountain."

"No problem. It'll be after Christmas." Lightfoot waved, ducked through the doorway to back up his truck, hitch the horse trailer behind.

Snow looked at Howard, waiting for an answer.

"All right, you win this time. Take her. Depending on what sifts out, we'll come to collect her for a federal trial."

"I'll help Lightfoot first."

"Why's he palling around with you? You need a guide?"

"Raccoon Mountain is his jurisdiction—thought you knew that. Besides, he's family."

"Enlighten me."

"He's Erin's stepfather." Snow also ducked as he stepped out of the camper gingerly, his gluteus maximus aching from days in the saddle. For once, the agent was left speechless to ponder over that one.

When Snow turned to Carlisle, he escorted Greer to CPD's unmarked Bronco, tucked her into the back behind the screen after checking to see that her hands were secured behind her back and her ankle restraints had not been compromised. He dismissed Lily Greer for the moment, directing an FBI agent to take her home or back to college, whichever she preferred.

"Neither!" The young woman wailed. "I want to stay with my mother."

"Sorry, no, she's going to jail. If you insist, I'll charge you too." With the last word, Snow climbed into the driver's seat and drove as far as Sunbury to visit Savage and check on Imhoff. He assigned a police detail to guard his prisoner. "No one is to talk to her, release her for a piss break or even so much as to open the door. She's armed and dangerous." He locked the vehicle. The officers gave him a befuddled glance.

Savage had been attended to, discharged and sent to an orthopedic surgeon for a consultation, Snow learned. He called his partner's cell, but it went to voicemail.

"Stopped by the hospital to find you already gone. Give me a head's up, and I'll come get you if you can't drive. I need an update; I'll inform HQ as well. Get better, man. See you soon."

Imhoff looked beat under the fluorescent's unforgiving glare. He could nod or shake his head, but his eye was swollen and bruised; his jaw was wired shut, and he wore a cast on his arm. Snow held up his left arm so Imhoff could see his own. "I've got one too."

Imhoff groaned something incomprehensible.

"An accident trying to deliver my wife to the hospital. We have a boy, and they're fine. Look, you can't talk now, but I've got Greer in custody. Thanks for your help. I'll remind the Chief to send you a check for consulting. For now, take care of yourself." They fist bumped gently.

"I can't stay, but let me know when you're well enough to talk or travel; we'll get together for a beer." Imhoff nodded solemnly, and Snow returned to the Bronco. He drove home in a daze, his hands and feet automatically honing on home. Eventually, Greer grew weary of haranguing him about filing criminal and civil suits against him, CPD and the city of Carlisle for police brutality, denying her the constitutional right to a lawyer before questioning, and planting evidence, blah, blah.

By the time he'd dropped her off at the prison and drove home, he was too tired to do anything but shower and plop into bed. But Erin insisted he eat a bowl of beef vegetable soup; he watched Ian sleep while the mild warmth settled in and filled his stomach. After he climbed into bed naked, Erin rubbed peppermint salve on his saddle sores, massaged his knotted muscles using a special liniment and also tended to the one that rose to greet her.

Turning over gently he murmured, "I haven't seen anything as beautiful in four days." He stroked her hair, kissed her and hugged her to him, breathing in the delicious scents of honey and lavender. She slid out of bed to restart the CD. "What did you do to your hair?"

"Danelle trimmed, straightened it and put in golden highlights." Loose waves had replaced tight spirals; the gold made her face look younger, more vulnerable and exposed the freckles along her hairline. Erin sighed. "How I've missed you! Your warm body, your presence, your help! I couldn't do this baby project or live without you." Her eyes glistened.

"Did Mother come down?" he asked, thumbing away her tears.

"Every day to watch Ian while I worked Shadow. She's so dear. Yesterday, she brought an entire meal with her—there's enough for you.

"Ian was fussy, so she bathed him. Shadow was a bit cantankerous, too, so I need to work her daily, despite the weather. But I wrapped Christmas presents, and Danelle got some good photos of Ian for our Christmas cards. I'll show you proofs tomorrow because your eyes are crossing."

"I'm tired and sore, babe. Four nights with four hours of sleep each night—maybe. Hunting, riding, searching for—"

"I know, honey, sleeping on hard rocky ground in the snow, no less. Poor baby. You are amazing—and you got your woman!"

"How did you know?" Chris nodded. "Your stepfather called."

"That he did. I invited him to dinner next week when he visits. And ADA Lawson and I have a meeting with Abigail and her lawyer scheduled tomorrow, so let's get some shut-eye."

"But you're on leave," Chris objected.

"And so are you. Hope you get comp time for hazardous duty. Besides, Savage is out on indefinite medical leave, so that leaves me."

Her jade eyes, framed by long russet lashes, filled with tears, but she blinked them back. Her scrubbed cheeks and her milky breasts against his chest in a warm bed! "What more could a man ask for with you in my arms and a beautiful son tucked into his cradle?" And their sleeping son's music gently lulled the couple to sleep.

27

Abigail's arrest was beginning to penetrate the fog of over-confidence she'd displayed to hide her misgivings. Other than the occasional taunts from other cells, she was left relatively free from harassment or harm at the Cumberland County Prison where DUI offenders and others charged or found guilty of lesser crimes could participate in the work-release program. But the noise was incessant, even after lights out—people teasing, taunting, threatening, yelling or complaining—grating metal doors, sliding trays, whining fluorescent squares in the halls, squeaking wheels of carts toting the candy bars, cigarettes, magazines and used paperback novels for sale.

She would save her energy for her defense.

For hours at a time she'd stare straight ahead, ignoring everything, earning the moniker "Psycho." Not that she cared what riff-raff behind bars thought. Funny, how one could be reduced to basic survival skills. She had no make-up, books, radio, TV, computer, weapons or cell phone. Bereft of her material possessions, she felt naked. "I've fallen so far, so fast!" Exposed to chance, the haphazard violence and the leering of guards. She had no way to access her money either: April Alison was also behind bars, and Rye had flown to Edinburgh without her.

"But I will be exonerated. I fought in self-defense. Defended my own property, and AA hadn't meant to swing hard. But leaving the body looks bad. I need a good excuse for that. Did McCoy really find the pink sweater? If so, April will be in prison for a long time. But what has it to do with me? Nothing." She smiled, and then frowned. "Did that nosy detective find anything incriminating in my case study?" Shook her head. "No matter, I'm resilient, determined and creative. I can do this." She refused to cooperate, speak, eat or sleep but sat on her cot, back against the cold, porous blocks, waiting until her lawyer contacted her.

Until then, she plotted. If she kept her wits about her, she'd beat this. No one had ever bested her before. *Why, my considerable talents have served me well this far.* She believed the lies she lived, would study the law herself—if she could gain access to the library and could represent herself. "Just get out!" she coached. "My M.A. work is essentially completed, my case study turned in. I'm positive I passed all my finals. I'll become a lawyer and show them all. Maybe even a judge, to dispense my form of justice. The first will be that crafty, lying detective McCoy.

"First, have Wilhelm find out about that sweater and move for a separate trial for me.

"Second, make a timeline of my campus, extracurricular and community activities like volunteering for Habitat for Humanity and time spent with Rye. Communicate my aloneness—my father killed, mother AWOL, well not technically, but absent nonetheless.

"Third, argue that AA planned while I cleaned up afterward, like Michael Clayton. I'm the janitor." She giggled.

A window high in the cell admitted weak light. The shift was changing, so more clanging metal and banging doors! A breakfast tray slid through the opening. Alone once more, Abby crawled off her bunk, her back against the wall until she reached the tray. Scrambled eggs looked half decent; the aroma made her mouth water. A dot of soft oleo had melted on the toast. She picked up the tray, crossed back to her bunk and ate slowly with the plastic fork. She'd need energy for this.

Breakfast over, a guard opened her door, shackled her, motioned her out and escorted her to a private interview room. In walked Denise Wilhelm, her and April's lawyer, looking crisp and fresh in a black pantsuit with silver stripes, complementing that wild white skunk's stripe in her hair. Set her overstuffed tote and briefcase on the floor beside her and pulled out Abby's file—already several inches thick. "How are you doing? You look thin and haggard. For trial, we want you to look healthy."

"What about jail is healthy?" asked Abigail.

"Look, you need to cooperate, work with me here. I think we can get a reduced sentence if we plead justifiable manslaughter and save the taxpayers the cost of a lengthy—and sensational trial—on the heels of your sister's. The DA's office is recommending you and Alison be tried together for Murphy's murder, but frankly, I'm opposed to that: guilt by association. If you were fighting in self-defense, and she actually killed Murphy, then—"

"But April's already in jail," Abby said, unclear for once.

"For the McCoy kidnapping. This is a separate and far more egregious charge, which could keep her in prison for life. But let's focus on you."

"All right. Then I'd rather take my chances in court with a separate trial. People around here will identify with my plight—my father killed, people robbing our home and my fiancé abandoned me. Pennsylvania has the Castle Doctrine, right?"

"A version of it." Wilhelm nodded, shuffling through her notes. "Anything else I need to know before our meeting with the ADA and the arresting detective? I brought you some clothes to change into after you shower." She pulled a plastic bag from her tote and handed it over.

"Yes, McCoy claims she has a pink sweater that proves who the murderer is. Can you find out if she's bluffing?"

Wilhelm paged through papers. "Yes, ADA Lawson mentioned it, said the lab has a pink sweater with flowered buttons. Were you wearing it?"

"Uh... It's April's sweater."

"What will it reveal?"

"It will have my, April's and Murphy's blood on it."

"Why didn't you call 911 immediately? Trying to save her would have helped convince the jury you are innocent of murder. That's going to go against you."

"We panicked. April didn't mean to hit her hard, just wanted to stop her from attacking me. I had scratches and marks all over my face and arms. Murphy drew blood first. She refused to leave the premises. Screaming about Dad and me stealing her sister's inheritance."

"Did you take photos of your injuries?" the lawyer asked. Her client shook her head regrettably, an important detail overlooked.

"How do you know she meant to rob you?" asked the lawyer.

"Because she'd been in the house—I found my Cabbage Patch Doll and cradle in her car."

Wilhelm frowned at that. "A doll? Where were you at the time?"

"Downstairs, packing up the den, marking things to be sold. We heard noises upstairs—footsteps creaking on the hardwood. And my car was in the garage; the lights were out. Guess the house looked empty."

"You didn't recognize her as family?"

"She's not my family. How was I to recognize her if I hadn't met her?" Abigail shrugged.

"Why would she take the doll?"

"The cradle mattress was stuffed with cash. My dad was rather eccentric—didn't trust banks. Afraid that rubbed off on me."

"OK. You're willing to risk ten to twenty in prison if the jury finds you guilty?"

"Or, if they exonerate me, I'll be free?"

"That's right. Free to continue your life."

"After I pick up all the pieces. All right, I want a trial." Abigail collected her clothes and called for the guard while Wilhelm waited, going over the packet the ADA had handed her that morning. She'd check the court calendar and argue for a speedy trial because her client was not guilty of anything except defending her home against invasion.

When Abigail reappeared, she'd showered and changed, looking wan but decent, as they left with an armed escort for the ADA's office.

ADA Chase Lawson, Detective Erin McCoy and a court stenographer were already seated when Benedict and Wilhelm arrived. After brief introductory remarks, Lawson outlined the charges against the coed and her options. For the record, McCoy reiterated Benedict's apprehension and arrest, explaining, "Savage's absent because he incurred an injury in a shooting incident while chasing a fugitive." Without notes, McCoy delineated the evidence the CPD had collected at the Benedict domicile. "There's ample blood, tissue, and hard physical evidence to bind this case over to trial and show that Abigail Benedict and her sister did willfully take the life of Mindy Murphy."

"Is there also evidence that a robbery was in progress?" Wilhelm asked.

"Yes, we found some of Benedict's possessions in Murphy's vehicle."

"Well," Chase summarized. "So don't you feel a plea bargain would be in your best interests? You'll do less jail time, and I'll note your cooperation with the police."

"And deduct time served?" Wilhelm reminded him.

He sighed and glanced at McCoy, then at Benedict and nodded.

"I do not agree. I'd prefer a trial." Benedict sat straight in her chair, her hair a nimbus of frizz framing a determined face and defiant demeanor. Hazel eyes bored into Mac's. "I want my freedom."

"Let me remind you, if found guilty, you'll do more time as an accessory to murder who failed to report a crime, fled the scene, withheld evidence and numerous other counts," Lawson warned.

"I understand, but I won't be found guilty."

"I'd like the trial scheduled in January, as my client is guilty only of defending her home against invasion," Wilhelm claimed.

"So you're saying your defense is justifiable homicide based on the Castle Doctrine?" Lawson made a note of it. McCoy said nothing, but her lips thinned.

"Not guilty, based on the Castle Doctrine. And I'd like to congratulate Detectives McCoy and Snow on the new addition to your family. How is he? Where is he?"

"Thanks. He's fine—with his Dad."

"Aren't we going to talk about bail?" asked Abigail.

"Sorry, there's no bail for murder." ADA Lawson stood, gathered his files and bid them a good day. "Plus, a note in your file claims you're a flight risk, as you previously left Carlisle during the investigation of your father's homicide against the advice of police detectives."

The inmate was returned to lock-up, seething at McCoy's good fortune and her own decline in this debacle. Fuming in frustration that Wilhelm would feel pleased at the cop's good fortune but seemed unconcerned with Abby's dismal situation. "I've tried to please others, befriended that cop because she'd been reared by a single parent too, and for what?"

***

Hurrying home because her breasts were leaking, Mac scooped the baby up and fed him while Chris fixed pannanis and coleslaw, with mini chocolate-dipped cones for dessert. He insisted on cleaning up too, so after she put the baby in his cradle, Mac went upstairs and typed her report of the meeting with Lawson, Wilhelm and Benedict. Emailed it to LT Stuart, the Chief and Sonja in case anyone else needed a copy. Chris joined her to write up his report on the Raccoon Mountain search, the Greer arrest and escape, mentioning Savage and Imhoff's injuries in case they were busy with rehab and couldn't file their own reports.

"I'm concerned that Savage hasn't called," he said as he hit send.

"Oh shit, I forgot to tell you," Erin whirled around in her desk chair. "He did; he's at that rehab place over by the hospital—I forget the name. Wait, I'll run down and get the note."

"No, I'm coming down with you. I'm finished here. I'll need to go visit him. Should have done it already." He hustled down the stairs after her and took the note from the pad.

"He said to call first, in case he was doing PT or something. I'm sorry."

"When did he call?" Chris asked.

She looked at the clock. "Before I left this morning. Were you outside with Shadow?"

"I guess. I took Ian to work, too. They gave us a money tree and a dozen Krispy Kremes. I put them in the garage when I brought Ian in. I'll take a few for Reese, OK? Do you have a Get Well card?"

She kept a box of all occasion cards for such events. Erin trudged back upstairs and returned with a humorous card about watching where the doctors and nurses put things and handed it to Chris. He'd bagged several donuts, kissed her, signed the card and tugged his coat from the closet while dialing his cell. "Hello, Savage? Hey, Snow here. How they treating you, man?" And then the door thumped shut.

"Well, shit on a stick. You could've asked me to go along. Oh, well, I guess we couldn't take Ian. Speaking of —" She tiptoed into the bedroom and peered into the cradle. The baby had somehow freed his arms from his swaddled blanket. One thumb in his mouth, the other was cradled under his chin. She wanted to pick him up and take a bite out of his little pink cheek, but instead, threw a load of his laundry in the wash.

While waiting, she took Shadow out to do her business and spent some time brushing her, talking. "I'm sorry, girl, that Ian takes so much time, and I can't spend it all with you, but come March, when you pass your K-9 certification and I return to work, we'll be solid again, I promise." She walked through the baby gate that kept Shadow in the mudroom when she heard Ian fussing and ran to change and let him nurse. "You're just like your daddy, little man." Energy sagging, she held the baby in one arm, made coffee with her free hand and trotted out to the garage to grab and nuke a glazed donut.

The baby stayed awake after his last burping, so she bathed him, dried and combed his wavy hair, and put a flannel romper on him to cover his arms. By the time his lids closed, Erin was hungry enough to think about supper and went to the fridge to investigate. "I can't let Chris and his mom do all the cooking. Oh, shrimp. I'll make carbonara." While cooking the angel hair and grating the cheese, she mentally planned a menu for the day Jason Lightfoot came to dinner while cracking and beating eggs. "Something simple but tasty, maybe comfort food like spicy turkey meatballs and mac 'n' cheese. We'll invite Savage, too." Then she realized she had no idea what he'd like.

28

Snow eased into Savage's room, where he lay prone on the bed, his leg swathed in bandages, staring out the window. His eyes blinked rapidly, so he knew someone had entered his room but made no move to see who it was. Chris sat the bag of donuts on the tray table and dragged a chair into Reese's line of vision and sat down. "How ya doing old man? Resting up for a marathon?" Then he turned his head to see the naked trees swaying in the December wind. A small bird sailing in for a landing missed the limb, collided with the window, and dropped to the sill, stunned. After a couple of minutes, he shook his tiny head and tried again, alighting on the nearest branch.

"I wasn't supposed to return," Reese said.

"Sure you were. That's what all COs tell you—just in case. You made it home, and I'm glad you're back." Chris eased to the edge of the bed.

"Some of us survived; others returned, shattered shells of their former selves, minds numbed by the macabre violence, the living nightmare of war. Nothing's the same. Civilians seem obsessed with the mundane or too absorbed with their electronic toys to notice spring green, summer's bounty or fall's chorus of colors." Savage motioned Chris up, levered the bed up and gestured his friend to sit again.

"You didn't mention winter's wonder. We can't control what others do or don't do. You returned to your old job, which the Chief held for you. It must be similar to the military—often dirty and dangerous, but somebody's got to do it. We court darkness daily—not knowing what we're walking into. While the risk is constant, we have to embrace life. Second, you look hale and hearty—body parts intact at least. We can't see PTSD. But your family, friends and neighbors are all still here, willing to help when we can." Chris put an arm around Reese. "You have to help yourself first."

"Did they tell you?" He picked up the bag and smelled it. Opened it, one glazed confection disappeared in two bites. "Thanks, man."

"Sure. The CPD staff gave Mac and me a dozen. Who and what?"

"Imhoff and Lightfoot. I heard a rifle crack—and bam! I was back in Iraq—the abominable heat, over a hundred degrees day after godforsaken day—desert as far as you can see. IEDs exploding underneath you. Suicide bombers. I shut my eyes and flash! Every vehicle that approached the Green Zone—even ones with families—could carry death. We'd clear buildings two, three or ten times, but the Taliban would keep coming back like a black plague. Some suicide bombers wore women's burkas—everyone covered and furtive. Risk and danger in every dark corner, stress and tension constant."

"Thought you were doing well; are you getting counseling? Or help from the VA? Or TAPS?"

Reese snorted. "Nah, the VA's good at dispensing pills and useless encouragement. TAPS is in Virginia. I don't think many people know how to treat PTSD, and there are too many vets suffering to adequately address the problem. And I was doing better, spending my days off at the Ragged Edge."

"With Ethan McCoy?"

"Yeah. He's been through it. Man's learned how to cope. Don't know how he managed taking care of his kid like that—"

"Kids. Erin and Liam."

Finally Reese made eye contact. "Yeah, I meant a baby. Couldn't be easy with bombs, gunfire and men's screams echoing in your grey matter." With Savage's coffee-dark eyes weary and bloodshot, his baggy eyelids smudged with insomnia, and his scruffy beard, he looked rough.

"Did he tell you how he coped?"

"Sure. He had to quit drinking and smoking when Liam arrived. Let's see, he said walking the floor singing marching songs. Playing music. He's tried acupuncture, marijuana, yoga, and meditation. Jogging. But a lot involved the kids: swimming, soccer, basketball, softball, backyard football, cooking, shopping, taking the kids for doctor check-ups and visits, ice skating, movie matinees and scouting the Civil War battlefields. Visited gravesites. Mainly keeping busy with household projects: digging, repairing and painting. His wife helped, too."

"Yes, Janelle's a nurse. She'd know what to do."

"Well, sometimes she'd have to inject him with a sedative. Once she doused him with a bucket of snow so he'd realize where he was."

Chris laughed. "Now that's a novel idea. Hey, we could try that on you. Seriously, what do the docs say? What's on the agenda with your knee?"

"They had to replace it." Savage looked at his knee like an alien had invaded it.

"No shit? Already? Now what? Rehab for how long?"

Reese shrugged. "We take it a day at a time. It hurts like a son of a bitch—they don't tell you what's going in—only how marvelous the bionic knee will be. This, PTSD and the heart attack—CPD will soon put me out to pasture."

"No, they won't. Put you behind a desk for awhile until you quit limping."

"Can you see hyper me sitting behind a desk pushing paper? I'd rather eat my g—"

"Now cut that shit out. That's not like you. Haven't you heard forty is the new thirty? You'll meet someone new, remarry and have kids. A lot of interesting single women out there yet like Erin's BFF."

"Easy for you to say." Reese glanced at his best friend again. "You bedded, wed and had a child within six months."

"You know better than that. It takes nine." They both laughed. "Funny, Mac had been on the force for three years or so, and I hadn't even noticed her until she was promoted to Homicide and wore street clothes. I trained her; we worked together for a few months. At our first interview on our first homicide this year, a shooter breached the domicile and tore loose with a 9mm clip. Bullets ricocheted all over. He hit me, but I nailed him in the leg before going down. One civilian was shot. Mac crouched, pistol ready, and when he ran out of ammo, she swiveled into view and clipped him under the chin.

"She stayed with me, brought me home and nursed me back to health, which wasn't easy. She never once complained. One day, just like that," he snapped his fingers, "I had to have her. Asked her to marry me, but she didn't give me an answer, so I walked away from the relationship. Long story short, she returned from Quantico, and—"

"Yeah, I heard about that scene at Growlers! Some brassy woman."

"Thought you didn't like her." Snow leveled his eyes at his friend.

"Nah, I just wish you'd waited. Matter of fact, I told her getting knocked up was the oldest trick in the world." Reese held up his hand to stop Chris from protesting. "I got over it. She's touchy, often pissy, but she loves you—I can see that. I've heard Ian's a cutie, too."

"See, what would I do if you didn't have my back? You delivered my son in a snowstorm. I owe you, just name it. And if anything ever happens to me, I want your solemn oath that you'll look after my family. We can make it official; you're Ian's godfather. Erin's best friend, Danelle, is his godmother."

"Ah, shit man, why'd you go and do that? Now I gotta get better."

"Damn straight, soldier. Come on, have you been on your feet yet? I'll walk you around." Chris stood up.

"No, you can't yet. My PT will be by after lunch to show me the routine, and then we'll see."

"It is after lunch," Chris checked his watch.

"Well, I haven't eaten." As if he'd buzzed her, a volunteer wearing an elf hat sailed in with a tray of food, greeted them both with "Happy Holidays," deposited the tray and whirled away. Looked like turkey, dressing, green beans and cranberry sauce. "Great! I missed Thanksgiving dinner. Wonder if I can have pumpkin pie, too."

Chris sat down. "Do you know who shot you?"

"That crazy Greer dame?" He tried the turkey.

"That sounded like a question, Reese. Don't you know?"

His partner shook his head. "Hell, no. You were up there; with the fog, cold and snow, visibility hovered at zero."

"Apparently someone could see pretty well."

"Maybe with night-vision goggles. One minute the rifle cracked the stillness, then my knee gave way, and I dropped to the ground. Must've hit my head and passed out; when I woke up, I was seeing my past and a solider was using his service weapon to tighten a tourniquet around my leg."

"Did you know him?"

"Never seen him before in my life; he wasn't in my unit. Guards carted me out on a stretcher. I passed out from the pain. After they flew me out and I came to, I realized it was Imhoff. We'd been scouting for Greer earlier: he along the north ridge, I along the south. Did you find her?"

"We did. Well, we arrested her daughter, and the mother steps onto the path with a loaded bow. I didn't have time to pull my pistol and rack one, but I shot bow and arrow out of her hand with a slingshot."

"I don't believe it! Damn, I missed the excitement."

"You can have it. I'd rather have been at home in bed."

"It's a little early for another baby, isn't it?" Reese smiled.

"You know what I mean. On the trail, we slept rough for two nights and spent a night, coming and going, in a concession stand at the park." Reese's eyebrows shot up. "Lightfoot had a key. It had a state of the art kitchen, a bit of food in the fridge. And he made hot coffee so we could stay awake. Best part was bedding down out of the freezing cold, wind and snow."

Reese kept smiling. "I know exactly what you mean." He rang his bell. When the perky attendant reappeared, he asked for pumpkin pie.

"Coming right up," she sang and zipped out and returned with a generous portion topped with whipped cream.

"Thanks a lot. Now this is what I need! Want a bite?" Reese asked.

"And deprive you of your Thanksgiving dessert? No, but thanks."

They spoke of other matters until the PT appeared—blonde hair in a ponytail and wearing a long-sleeve blue tee, with Physical Therapist in an arc across an ample bosom, and loose cotton cargo pants—bouncing in the doorway. "Ready for you first session, Mr. Savage?" She smiled, showing dimples.

For a moment, neither man spoke, so unprepared were they for *this* physical therapist. She had to be a college graduate but looked like a teen. Her Sketchers squeaked across the floor. "If you'll excuse us, Detective Snow, we'll be gone about forty-five minutes. Then we'll shave and hit the shower. You can wait or..."

Snow cleared his throat. "Excuse me. Do I know you?"

"No sir, but I read about your son's birth in *The Sentinel.* I recognize you and Detective Savage from the photo."

"Pleased to me you, ah, Miss..."

"Tracy Winters, sir. Nice to meet you, too."

Winters turned to assist Savage while Snow saw himself out, still shaking his head at the younger generation, her words about Ian's birth ringing in his ears. "What should've been private has become public discourse." He drove home submerged in a kind of twilight suspension. Cocooned with Erin and Ian in the cozy bungalow—the Christmas lights ablaze in welcome, Chris felt freed momentarily from that time construct that demanded his attention. "And I intend to enjoy the holiday with my family."

Erica Snow closed the front door quietly but started, her hand going to her throat when she looked up. "Oh, dear, you scared me."

"Don't you recognize me, mother?" An eyebrow rose quizzically.

"Of course, Chris, but my mind was elsewhere. Sorry, a senior moment. Anyway, Erin's out back with Shadow and the K-9 trainer. I just put Ian down. Beef stew's in the fridge. Please come up to the house tomorrow. We'd love your help with the Christmas cookies." She wrapped her scarf around her neck and put her hood up as she gave her youngest a smooch on the cheek and jogged up the driveway.

"Of course we'll help." Chris had always helped with the baking but usually made his at the bungalow. "Oh, you want to cuddle Ian, and I don't blame you." He smiled as he let himself in and armed the security system. First he checked his son, who was sleeping on his side, two fingers in his mouth. Slipping into the bathroom, Chris shaved and showered and then pulled on sweats, closed the bedroom door. In the kitchen, he put the stew on simmer. Turned on the oven. Opened a can of rolls, separated them into triangles and formed crescents. In they went, a clay plate beneath them, and set the timer. Ladled homemade chunky applesauce into dessert cups heated some granola and sprinkled it evenly over each.

Erin came in flushed with wind-bitten cheeks, Shadow right behind her. Chris gave the dog a rawhide chew wrapped in dried chicken and duck; she plopped down in front of the oven as the timer went off. He retrieved the rolls, setting them on top of the stove. Having stowed her coat, hat and gloves on hooks in the mudroom, Erin reappeared and wrapped her arms around her husband. "Hmm. You smell good enough to eat."

"That's by design. Let's have dinner while it's hot." He dished the stew into bowls and slid the clay slab and rolls into a basket lined with linen, setting them on hot pads on the island.

She needed no encouragement. "I'm famished. We just spent two hours 'attacking' Corey. He's teaching Shadow how to go on the offense."

"I hope she was gentle. She has wicked teeth."

"He was wearing a padded suit. Actually, she's pretty aggressive."

"I wouldn't have my women any other way." Big brown eyes leveled on her wide green ones, the deep cinnamon lashes—an added spice. Her touchably soft ivory skin... "My what delicious stew! Just like mother's."

"That's because it is. I would've slapped together some sandwiches."

"Yes, well, comfort food works when you're tired and hungry." He scooped the rest of his stew out of the bowl with a bit of roll.

"Hmm, you warmed the applesauce. I'm so lucky to have you." Her mouth tipped into a warm smile while she studied his expression.

He nodded in acknowledgment of her appreciation. "As am I. I'll show you when we finished here. But let's not disturb Ian." He pulled her into the living room where a blanket and pillows lay before the fireplace, the logs cracking and spitting occasional sparks, the fire settling into a low, slow burn, blue and red flames dancing across the log.

"But I need a shower," Erin said.

"I need you more." He pulled her close and kissed her with feeling. "My heart aches for you." He planted kisses at the top of her forehead. Her hair smelled like pine and fresh air. Slowly, he removed one garment, kissing her neck, her shoulders, removed another and kissed the length of her body, stopping with her toes. She wiggled and squirmed, pulling him up to her lips, tasting their toasty invitation, wanting him. After their lovemaking, he asked, "Do you feel up to helping with Christmas cookies tomorrow?" Chris asked.

"OH!" Erin popped off the floor, hitting his chin with her forehead. "Sorry." Patting his injury. "I love baking cookies. At Christmastime, we made snicker doodles. Dad let me press walnuts in the middle, and gingerbread men and butterballs rolled in confectioner's sugar. Some call them Russian tea cakes."

"Cookie-making is a day-long marathon at the farmhouse. Usually I make peanut blossoms—with Hershey kisses. And the kids like the good 'ole stand-by, tollhouse cookies. Then we eat the broken ones or mulligans, as Dad calls them. Did you make other kinds?" Chris asked.

"Oh, yes—rolled sugar cookies and sand tarts. Once we tried stained glass cookies—with Jell-O, I think, but they were a disaster. Liam likes the ones Professor Mellow made—with oats and M&Ms. We do cinnamon rolls for Christmas breakfast. Dad will either make something like a quiche we call a Christmas pie or bake oatmeal with fresh fruit compote. But you'll see. We're having Christmas dinner with the McCoys."

"Yes, we are. And I'm really looking forward to that, but we need to finish our Christmas shopping first. Let's take a morning to run into Camp Hill. Mother can watch Ian."

"I just don't want to take advantage of Erica while I'm off. She does so much for us as it is."

"She's eager for us to take advantage. She's just so happy to handle a baby again since her other grandchildren are hundreds of miles away."

A lusty "w-a-a" turned into a throaty squawk.

"Speaking of whom," Erin rolled up but Chris beat her to the bedroom. "I'll change him first and bring him out to you."

Erin sighed and lowered herself onto the rocker to wait.

When Chris eased the baby into her arms, Ian latched onto her swollen breast like a pro; Erin sighed when the milk let down.

"How's the pump working?" He sat on the ottoman and lifted her feet to his lap and stroked them gently.

"It pulls, which is a sensation I have to get used to. When my leave is up, I'll pump regularly, since I want him to have breast milk for at least a year. Hmm, you have an hour to quit that, maybe two."

"Yummy," Chris smiled as he watched. "You have no idea what a turn-on that is."

"Hmm. Yes, now you have to share them. How's Savage?"

"Hard to say. I'm concerned about him. The doctors had to replace his knee—he calls it bionic. He's depressed as hell, thinks he's washed up. He's in pain and he's not sleeping well, but my greatest concern is the PTSD. Said your dad's been helping him cope with it. Unfortunately, much of Ethan's coping involved you and Liam's care and activities, so Reese will have to develop other coping strategies. I'm encouraging him to seek counseling, but..."

"I thought he was seeing Dr. Drummer."

"Guess he quit going. Anyway I asked him to be Ian's godfather. I know Danelle is his godmother and—"

"Do you think he's capable of that role if something happened to us?" Erin asked; her brows wrinkled in consternation. "You said yourself—"

Chris interrupted. "Let's not worry about it now. We have four parents, three uncles and their families to help. They'd take precedence. It's our family's first Christmas together, so let's enjoy it."

"And Jason Lightfoot," Erin reminded him. "He's coming to dinner Friday." They watched the lights winking on their tree—emitting its pleasing pine scent. The cranberry and popcorn garlands hugged the tree naturally. Lights reflected the crystal and glass. "Maybe we'll pick up a few more ornaments for that last layer of branches. What do you want for Christmas, babe?"

"Nothing. I already have you and Ian, our families, and home. Shadow may pull ornaments off the low-hanging limbs." Shadow's head perked up at the mention of her name, so Chris took her out. He returned after locking the gate to the mudroom and returned to his seat.

Ian had nodded off, so Erin pulled him off, sat him up facing Chris and thumped him on the back while his dad put his index fingers in Ian's hands to see whether he'd grab and hold, which he did. Ian released them when he discovered the other breast. Erin said, "Like father, like son." She laid her head back, rocking gently as Chris continued to massage her feet and calves.

This time, Chris plucked Ian off, using his finger to break the suction, turned and lifted the slack bundle to his shoulder, patting his back and carrying him to the bedroom, singing, "Bye baby bunting, Daddy's gone a hunting/To catch a bad lady, and put her in a shady..." Erin smiled at the improvisation, relieved that they'd put Greer behind bars until her trial. She heard lullaby music. Before she could rise, Chris pulled her up, scooped her into his arms and carried her to the shower, stepping in to help her again.

Tomorrow—cookie day.

Friday—Christmas shopping and a leisurely lunch to buy a new car because they had received the replacement check.

Saturday—sleeping in—one could hope.

Sunday, they'd scheduled Ian's christening because family and friends would be home for the holidays. Reese and Danelle standing beside the parents over the baptismal fount, friends and family seated in the front few pews. Ian snoozed until the water woke him; his little hands fisted and arms flailed the air as he wailed. The minister returned him promptly to his mother's arms. Afterwards, their parents hosted a buffet dinner at the farmhouse with shepherd's pie, BBQ wings, roasted baby vegetables, tossed salad and cake with ice cream. Adults toasted Ian's birth with champagne; the kids lifted their stem glasses of sparkling ginger ale into the air.

The last-minute Christmas shopping had been easier than selecting a new vehicle; that afternoon they walked away from two car lots because the salesmen held firm on prices, despite the vehicles being nearly a year old. "We conduct January sales and slash prices during the car show; you can get a really good deal then."

"Really? In a week or two? And besides," Erin said, "we're more interested in safety and a roomy back seat. Do we really need all these extras?" She turned to Chris in exasperation. "We should do an online comparison of prices, mileage and safety features before we buy. I have to go home, feed Ian and fix dinner." She waved her hand in dismissal at the front of a sedan with polished wooden panels, knobs and gauges like a Cessna.

The salesman shrugged indifferently.

Chris leaned toward the bigger SUVs rather than the so-called crossovers anyway. Put off by the man's attitude, he said, "You know what? We can survive another couple of weeks with one vehicle, so let's go. This is too big a decision for an impulse buy."

29

Christmas Day began with opening Ian's gifts: a candy-cane sleep set with "Baby's First Christmas" embroidered on the front. Eagle sweats. The adorable round hedgehog his mama bought at the Gettysburg Native American seminar, a soft tool set from his dad, and a play gym with rattles, a "mirror," large beads and other attachments. Finally, they opened a toy cell phone; beeping sounds startled Ian. His little bow mouth downturned, his lips quivered—unsure what to do.

"Let's set this aside," Chris said, as he laid him on his play mat, shaking the rattles, rings and other things to show the baby.

Erin gave Chris a back scratcher to reach his itching wrist. Binoculars when he hunted again. "Or whenever you need them." He opened the leather case, aimed them out the sliding glass doors and adjusted the knob. "Might work better outside." A new hunter-green vest to replace the down vest the Susquehanna had ruined. And a Homedics back massager.

Chris plucked several small packages from the tree for Erin. The first was a beautiful navy cloisonné necklace shaped like the Earth with the continents etched in tan and pale green and matching earrings with crescent moons dangling tiny stars. She was amazed to tears, remembering his words. "You gave me the world, the moon and the stars!" she exclaimed, put them on and threw herself against him with a bear hug and long, slow kiss while Ian tried to reach the rings on his blanket.

"Careful now before you start something I have to finish." Chris smiled and handed her an unwrapped basket, which he'd hidden behind the tree, full of Bath and Body Works lotions, bath gel, a natural sponge, body spray and a new fleece robe.

"Oh, you darling! Now I won't need your robe after I shower!"

"Yes, I'd like mine back so I don't have to run around naked all winter."

Then they bundled up, greeted the cold, clear day and hustled up the drive to the senior Snows for a Christmas brunch of baked French toast with strawberries, bacon and turkey sausage, fried apples, wassail spiced with apple wine, a clove-studded orange slice floating in each punch cup. They finished with Christmas cookies and coffee topped with whipped cream. They exchanged gifts afterwards. Although Jeff and his family wouldn't arrive until dinner, Jack gave Ian a set of his illustrated children's books—all signed. "Oh, they're lovely. And that's so generous!" Erin was delighted with her son's books. "He has his own bookcase already!"

Erica adored her silver dream catchers. "These are finely crafted!" And threaded the wires through her ears. The senior Snows bought Ian stuffed animals—all Christopher Robin's friends, the A.A. Milne book collection and a set of DVDs about Pooh and Friends. They gave Chris and Erin a gift card for dinner and a play at Allenberry, plus a generous check, "to cover any extra for that new car you're looking for," his dad said. After brunch, he stuffed his new pipe with cherry tobacco and enjoyed it in solitude on the solarium.

Chris loaded his family into Silver for the trip to Gettysburg, with Shadow leaping in last. "Down, girl." She nestled beside Ian's car seat.

At the McCoys' house, they enjoyed Christmas dinner —an informal yet traditional meal: honey-glazed ham, mashed potatoes with sour cream and chives, green beans almandine with roasted red peppers. Ethan served a chocolate Yule log with ice cream for dessert. During dinner, he tossed out questions about the origins of Santa Claus, the Christmas tree, and other holiday traditions.

"Santa comes from St. Nicolas; everybody knows that," said Liam.

"The jolly, chubby American Santa all decked in red was designed by Thomas Nast in the 1800's," Erin offered, as she passed Ian, in his own Santa outfit, to her dad. "But Europeans honored the tradition—based on a generous priest who donated coins to the poor, I think."

"Cute little buggar. Actually, the jolly elf is much older than that." Ethan laid the baby in the cradle created my one ankle crossed over his other knee, his large hand cupping his back. "There were two. Saint Nicholas was a bishop; the other, a Christmas sprite—perhaps descended from Dionysius—created mischief, instigating rowdy revelry. And Native Americans recorded visitors from the north with gifts."

"Don't you think the spirit of light—generosity, peace and good will are more important than the men of history or legend?" Janelle interjected. Her family nodded. "I heard the legend about a bishop tossing coins down chimneys of the poor because he wanted his gifts to be anonymous." She took the baby and rocked him in her arms.

"This is all news to me, but thanks for our stockings and the Kuerig and the K-cups assortment. They're really a good idea." He referred to the oversized quilted ones under the McCoys' tree stuffed with personal, practical gifts like leather belts and gloves and knitted scarves, plus IOUs for babysitting and several restaurant gift cards. Ian's was overflowing with baby toys, bibs, an infant manicure set and a stuffed baby seal. Even Shadow had one with homemade biscuits, treats, beef-hide knots and a squeaky toy.

"I bought most of my gifts this year from the Native American seminar at Gettysburg College," Erin admitted.

"Thinking ahead! You always were the most organized one of us," Janelle smiled. "We bought everything on Black Friday. They had some really good deals. And thanks for bringing all these cookies, the wine and cheese and other gifts. Gracious!"

"They're great," Liam took several. "I really like these little pecan squares. And the wallet with money—perfect!" He popped the entire bar in his mouth and chewed slowly while folding the bills into his new wallet bearing his initials. "Thank you both!"

"Chris made those! They taste just like pecan pie." Erin hugged her husband.

"So you cook, too?" Ethan asked. "I enjoy putting a recipe together and providing a decent, home-cooked meal."

"Oh, yes. I was a bachelor for fifteen years, though Mother does sneak a pot of soup, stew or marina sauce into our fridge from time to time. We made the cookies at the farmhouse and store them in tins in the solarium where they'd keep for weeks if they last that long, with everybody home for the holidays."

After Liam took Ian for a few minutes, he said, "Oops, he's leaking."

Chris took him, laid him on the waterproof mat in the living room while Ethan and Liam stepped out for a cigarette. After Erin nursed the baby and Chris let Shadow out for a romp, they collected their gifts, thanking all again with warm hugs and kisses then set out for Carlisle.

"Seriously, we're going to do the stocking thing for my family next year. They're much more manageable and practical," Chris said.

"I'm just so happy that we had a stress-free holiday away from work."

"Yeah, me too. And you did a fine job selecting gifts."

"You helped!" Erin turned around to check Ian, who was sleeping zipped into the blue bunting Janelle had made him. He looked bug-snug warm wearing his Santa hat.

"One day. You did the rest. I appreciate the appropriate gifts, especially for my parents and the kids.

When we get home, we'll heat wassail and tip a cup of good cheer for a happy new year. I have a feeling we're going to need it."

Erin plugged her ears. "If you're segueing into work, I can't hear you." On January second, Detective Snow would report to work, while Erin's maternity leave lasted until March. Shadow's certification was scheduled for Saturday of the second week—way too far ahead to worry about it.

Chris kept his eyes on R 15 and the odometer because cops patrolled it regularly and waited until Erin dropped her hands to her lap to finish.

"Not just the open homicides, but the two trials, and Savage will need our help, too. I'd like to spend some time with him."

Erin said, "I know he'll adjust to his knee in time. It's a pretty common operation, though painful, I'd imagine."

"It's not his knee that worries me," her husband answered. He reached for her hand and nibbled on her knuckles while stopped at the red light to turn onto 74 N.

"Why, did you talk to Dad about him?"

"I did. He advised me to keep him engaged in life, said you'd be happy to make him dinner once a week. We could have Danelle and Sydney over at the same time to spend some time with Ian."

Finally arriving home, they unloaded the car, Ian and Shadow first. While Erin let the dog out, Chris returned to Silver for the gifts and stockings, tucking them under the tree. "Let's see how long this holiday hiatus lasts," he said to himself and then snapped on the kitchen light to warm the wassail before he noticed Ian still strapped in his car seat, eyes focusing on the lights. Chris freed and changed him, checked the time, warmed a bottle of his mother's milk and fed him four ounces, rocking and singing softly to gauge the baby's reactions. "Is that a smile I see at the corners of your milky mouth, baby?" he teased. Ian reacted by kicking. By the time Chris had burped Ian, Erin returned to finish the job.

If the baby cooperated by sleeping soundly, Chris wanted to try his back massager, shave and shower and then take his wife to bed.

30

The phone jarred Chris out of bed on New Year's Eve morning. He stumbled to the kitchen to unplug and answer his cell. "Detective Snow."

"Yes, sir. This is Martin Feldman. No one here at your station will allow me access to my client. I've driven from Williamsport. So I'd appreciate it if you'd meet me at the prison and escort me—"

"Excuse me for asking," Snow answered. "But I don't know you. Who's your client?"

"Oh, pardon. I've represented Sienna Greer's family for years. To have her incarcerated over the holidays when she heretofore has had no serious record—"

"I don't mean to be rude, sir, but you'd better check that record again: two DUIs and an assault on her husband, but he didn't press charges. Besides, she drove me in my Jeep into the Susquehanna. She's guilty of a felony this time."

"She said you accused her of murder."

"That hasn't been proved. We charged her with attempted vehicular manslaughter of a police officer. But, yes. I'll meet you at the prison in thirty minutes." But first, he stoked up the fire in the living room because he could hear his son stirring, washed his hands and changed the baby's diaper, rolling the soiled one into a tight wad to throw away. Their bed was empty, so Erin must be out with Shadow. He held Ian in his left arm, toasted bread with his right hand. Pulled the peanut butter out of the pantry and a banana from the fruit bowl. Shadow's dish rattled.

Ian let out a squeal when he turned his head to Chris's chest and met flat flannel.

"Here, I'll take him. You have to go to work?" Erin asked.

"Apparently no one will let Greer's lawyer in to prep for trial."

"And how did he get your number?"

Chris checked his watch as he sliced half the banana onto the peanut butter toast. "Maybe Sonja's on call. I'll only be gone about an hour. I also need to swing by Savage's place or call to see how he's doing. He's on leave until Dr. Drummer reinstates him; he won't until Reese seeks treatment. I intend to drag him to the shrink's office like he dragged me to the doctor's when I had bronchitis."

She rose up on tiptoes to kiss her husband but kept mum on his mission and carried Ian into the living room for his eight a.m. feeding.

She needed to check her email, do laundry—always, and prod her husband into choosing a vehicle. But she had nothing special planned for the day. After putting Ian back to bed and showering, she was eating granola sprinkled over berries and yogurt when a knock at the door surprised her. She hustled to open it before the person could ring the bell and wake Ian.

"Well, ADA Lawson, you have a habit of showing up unannounced."

"I apologize, but I got this weird call from a guy named Feldman natting on about Constitutional rights and due process. CPD has a skeleton crew there; no one knew this character. I'm looking for Detective Snow."

"Get in line. He went to the prison to escort Feldman to Sienna Greer. He claims to be her lawyer. Did you check that first?"

"No, but I will, if you let me use your coffee table and I could trouble you—"

"Yes, I'll get you a cup of coffee, but Chris won't be back for awhile. He also went to see how Savage is doing."

"Did the Greer woman shoot Savage?"

She shrugged, handed him a mug. "This coffee has a backbone."

"Thanks, I like it strong. Can you help me with any background? Feldman's stopping by my office at ten." Lawson's fingers danced across the keyboard. "Yep. A lawyer in Williamsport, a partner in the Feldman and Dirkson Law Offices—meaning he's been practicing for years."

Erin perched on the recliner with her second cup of coffee, this one decaf from her parents' gift box. She smiled; they must have overhead her and Chris's on-going leaded/decaf discussion and the effect of caffeine on infants. "I'll help if I can. I was on the phone with Chris when Greer pushed him into the river. The Jeep stopped at the edge, but Chris was injured and either fell or was pushed into the Susquehanna."

So she spent some time giving Lawson the background on the West Enterprise drill site, the Slaughter, Greer and Hauk homicides, the reason the woman ran him off the road. "We assume she took her recorded interview out of his Jeep and left Chris to die in the frigid water. He doesn't recall what specifically was so damaging on the tape to go to such an extreme measure to silence him."

"Did she admit to killing anyone?"

"No, she maintains her innocence, but there's enough evidence to put her away on AVM," she said. Lawson jotted notes on his laptop while she spoke, asking questions intermittently. "The homicides are still open, and though we found incriminating evidence on her property, she swears someone planted it there, trying to frame her."

"Anything else?" Lawson asked.

"That's about all I can reveal until lab reports return. If you call Chris's cell," she handed him one of her husband's business cards, "he'll tell you what he can, so you can pass it on to Feldman and Greer—or not. Word of warning?" Lawson nodded while packing up his laptop. "She's a real head case with a vicious temper. She will kick, bite, scratch and punch, so stay away and insist she's shackled. She's escaped from prison once; Chris and Ranger Jason Lightfoot had to hunt her down."

"Oh, I think I saw the FBI climbing a mountain up north. Was that Greer?" Chase whistled. "Thanks for the warning. I'll try to stay calm."

"Keep something at hand you can use as a defensive weapon." She smiled her encouragement. "Good luck and let me know what transpires. I expect Chris home for dinner." She walked him to the door, let him out and armed the security. "Now what to fix for dinner?"

The landline rang. Erin rushed to pick it up. "Hello."

"Hello, dear," Erica Snow said. "Hope I didn't wake the baby. Won't you join us for dinner this evening? I'm making the traditional pork and sauerkraut with mashed potatoes. If you're going out, we'll watch Ian."

"Oh, thanks. I was just wondering what to fix. Chris is out, but I expect him home by dinner. What should I bring? We're staying in this year."

"Just yourselves. I'm thawing an apple pie for dessert. See you tonight. Did you enjoy Christmas dinner with your folks?"

"We did. It was very informal with Dad quizzing us on Christmas traditions, especially Santa and of course everyone had a different opinion. They were delighted to see Ian and handed him around like he was a Christmas present."

"We all are just thrilled to be grandparents. He's such a good baby."

"Thanks, Erica. Yes, most of the time. What time would you like us to be there? Are the others still there?"

"Oh, no. They all went home. It'll be just the five of us, unless Chris wants to bring Reese. How about six? Until tonight, then. Goodbye."

Erin nursed the baby, bathed and dressed him in his new pajamas and played patty cake and teensy, weensy spider until Chris stormed through the door, riled about his encounter with Sienna Greer.

"What happened?" asked Erin.

"Wacko tried to choke her lawyer: he suggested a plea agreement, which could mean a lighter sentence, then she lunged at me, clawing and cursing." He shook his head in disgust.

"What did you do?"

"Put her in a choke hold until additional officers could come and restrain her. The prison put her in solitary. Feldman ordered a full psychological on her. Do you buy that she has a disability?" His voice rose, incredulous.

Ian squalled at his father's tone of voice. At once, Chris became contrite. "Sorry, son. I'm not mad at you, precious." He lowered his volume significantly and tone softened considerably. He plucked Ian off Erin's lap and rocked him gently, singing, "Swing, Low Sweet Cradle," omitting Chariot from his version. Within seconds, Ian had switched to cooing. "Couldn't you just eat him up?" Chris glanced from the sweet-smelling baby to his wife, his bourbon eyes wide and luminous. Returning the baby to his mother, he kissed both—the first tenderly, the second passionately. "And you too."

"Greer could be bi-polar; her moods seem high or low. Don't think I've ever seen her on an even keel. Though I don't see her often," Erin said.

"Mitigating factor may bring a lesser sentence."

"Or send her to a psychiatric ward," Erin added.

"We'll have to wait and see. But isn't Benedict's trial in January, too?"

Erin's eyebrows drew together. "Yes, Wilhelm requested a speedy trial, claiming her client is innocent. They're using Pennsylvania's version of the Castle Doctrine as her defense in the Murphy homicide."

"That may work. Look, I better run—"

"Be home by six. Your mother invited us to dinner—pork and sauerkraut. She said to bring Savage."

"He's still in rehab, but 'I'll be back,'" imitating the Terminator; Chris grabbed keys and coat and slipped out the door.

"And it's off for a nap for you, little man." Erin carried him to his cradle, hoping he'd be pleasant this evening for his grandparents. "I'll need to review the Benedict file in case I need to testify," padding up the stairs to locate it, she returned to the kitchen to read.

31

After the holidays, the mood at HQ was subdued; people wandered around in a trance, slow to react to questions, conversation or the phones. It usually required a few days for detectives, officers and staff to click into the routine. A number of people called in sick, so the Chief sent Fields to ride with the newest beat hire, Officer Tanya Storm.

Snow poured a mug of coffee, tossed a dollar into the kitty, because Sonja made decent coffee. He sauntered past his office and into Conference One, where all the data on their three open homicides were stored. Taking his time, he stood in front of Board I with Ahnai's photos, timeline and list of suspects. Board II belonged to Dean Greer, despite his murder occurring outside of CPD jurisdiction, which made him think of Steve Imhoff, who'd fallen off Chris's radar over Christmas.

"Damn. I forgot to inquire about him," so he called Sunbury and learned he'd been discharged from the hospital. He dialed the detective at his home number, and his wife said he was sleeping and suggested he call back around five-thirty or six, dinnertime.

"How is he? I'm Detective Snow with the Carlisle Police Department, one of the officers who found him. Are his injuries serious?"

"A broken arm and jaw are serious, don't you think?"

"Is his jaw still wired?" he inquired.

"Oh, no, thank god! For weeks, he could only drink liquids through a straw and lost ten pounds. Now he's on a semi-solid diet, but it'll be awhile before he returns to work," she said.

"Tina, isn't it?"

"Christina, yes, sir."

"Will you just tell him I called? I don't want to disturb his dinner on New Year's Eve. I'll call him back next year —say, January third or fourth to check on him again. We wish him the best."

"Thanks. He's finished consulting with you, right?"

"Yes, well, the cases are still open, but we think we have a suspect in custody. That's all I can say at the moment."

"OK. I'll tell him. I need to check on my five-year-old. Please excuse me. Goodbye." Sounding harried rather than rude, she disconnected.

"Finally, Board III—Gary Hauck, on whom we have the least information," Snow observed.

"You talking to yourself again?" LT Stuart asked in the doorway. "Happy New Year. Mac and baby fine?"

Snow saluted with his mug and nodded. "Yes, thanks. To you, too. Just thinking aloud. I'm going to comb through Slaughter's files to see if I can locate more on Gary Hauck, the Safety Coordinator—find a connection between him and the other victims. I'm sure there is one."

"And Slaughter and Greer?"

"My bet's on whistleblower and lover. The evidence is pointing to Sienna Greer, who has the best motive for both."

"All right, let's get busy. Give me half the pile, and I'll look online and make some phone calls to get a more complete picture or some hard evidence."

"Thanks." They both sat down. Snow divided the pile, sighing. Nobody liked to wade through the paperwork, but it had to be done, and CPD was short-handed at the moment with Mac and Savage out. And usually the killer left a trail, and many leads came from analyzing the paper trail, determining his pattern and little slips or inconsistencies.

"How did your interview go with Greer?" Les asked.

"It wasn't my interview, sir. Just got her lawyer access to her, but she went berserk when Feldman suggested a plea bargain. Then she came after me for putting her behind bars. Our second meeting wasn't any better than the first."

"Let's go over what we know," Les suggested. "From the top."

"Just the two of us? At least let me call Mac. She can brainstorm."

"All right, if she's available."

Snow speed-dialed his wife, asked if she could take a conference call. "We want to review what we have on Slaughter, see if we can somehow connect the dots."

"Sure. Ian's asleep, and I've been doing some research on my own on Sienna Greer during down time."

"Got anything new? I'm putting you on speaker phone."

"Not yet." Mac didn't want to reveal her hand just yet—that Imhoff and Greer were related, perhaps in on this caper together, which would explain a lot.

"OK, Mac, I'll check off what we have and turn her white board over if we introduce something new. Let's start. Go!" Les volunteered.

"Ahnai was killed with an ice pick, the others with arrows that Jason Lightfoot makes, which is why Howard arrested him first. All were murdered the same week in October: Ahnai on the former Carlisle Industrial Indian School grounds, Greer at Lightfoot's RV parked near Winfield and Hauck at West Enterprises drill site. Slaughter (to distinguish her from her husband) worked for SRBC; the others for WE at the drill site. Dean Greer, a Field Tech, was having an affair with Slaughter, which could be a motive for Sienna Greer for two reasons: jealousy over the affair and the evidence that Slaughter was documenting West Enterprises' violations and suspected illegal activity."

LT Stuart's face registered surprise at Mac's working knowledge.

Snow added. "Yes, Geer seem worried about job security. The site super, Kraus, denied knowing about the monetary notations in Slaughter's files. The other workers reported similar stories about their observations of Slaughter, Greer and Hauk. The men bunked together at WE's RV campground. Shadow, Mac's K-9 officer, uncovered our victim's clothes buried under the men's camper."

"How were the *three* connected?" Stuart asked.

"Perhaps as whistleblowers, someone shut them up so they couldn't finish that documentary. One or both could've been receiving kickbacks or royalties from the gas—only way to explain the $10,000 in the OJ container in Greer and Hauck's RV," Snow suggested.

"Do we know that the dollar notations are in Slaughter's handwriting? Why blackmail Ahnai? Just about everyone knew about her affair. Did Sienna kill Ahnai and Greer to retaliate? She denies it. Did Hauk kill Greer? Then who killed Hauk? Not enough information on him. Same MO for the men. Or did someone else murder all three, then try to pin it on a scapegoat?" Mac asked. "Obviously, Jason Lightfoot—who has a solid alibi—and Sienna Greer, who claims she's being framed."

"Great questions," Les said. "But we need answers. What do we know?"

"Who buried Slaughter's clothes under the RV? Who benefits most from the three deaths?" Mac said. "Sorry, LT, more questions. Let's assume it's someone connected to the Williamsport well: the industry, the employees or the landowners.

"Let's strike off Marcellus Shale because they haven't launched an internal investigation yet. And the FBI are involved. Employees could likely find work at another active well. For my money, I'd say whoever is receiving the royalties. They'd have the most to lose if the well were shut down."

"Was Slaughter working with a filmmaker? Do we know who is he? Wouldn't that change the scenario?" asked Snow.

"More questions." Les dropped his aching head into his hands, his sandy crew a bristling bottlebrush.

Mac summarized. "We know Lightfoot brought Sienna Greer to CPD for questioning. She was arrested, arraigned, and incarcerated in the CCP but escaped to Raccoon Mountain. Imhoff, Savage and Lightfoot tracked her, but an unknown suspect shot Savage, so Chris was recruited for the search. They apprehended and retrieved the fugitive and her daughter. Greer has refused to cooperate. The FBI rescued Imhoff and flew him to the Sunbury Hospital." The LT made checkmarks against the known facts, while Snow noted new questions they hadn't investigated.

"Can you call the Williamsport lab to see if there were any prints on the bills? Did Dr. Chen submit a report on Slaughter's clothes? Anything foreign found on them belonging to someone other than the victim? Has anyone seen Imhoff's report on Dean Greer's murder? Who's the lead on Hauck's?" asked Mac.

"Mac, not so fast, I'm trying to jot this down. I'll comb through what's on the Conference table, then start calling these other people if we don't have their reports. OK. We know that all victims were stabbed or shot through the heart. While heartless—pardon the pun—the murders were not about torture or getting attention. Seems the killer simply wanted them eliminated," Stuart said.

"We also know none struggled, so perhaps did not see or expect an attack. Or they knew the killer. Do we know that Slaughter's husband and son are not guilty?" Snow asked his wife.

"Yes," Mac answered.

"Clearly, we need more eyes and hands on these cases. I'll call Agent Howard; have him send several of his best men up for the duration. We just don't have the man or womanpower," Les said to the speakerphone, "to handle this ourselves."

Snow groaned. "Let's give it one more day."

"OK, sure, but Mac, Savage, and Imhoff aren't able to work the field," Stuart argued. "I'll call Fields back in; he has a good handle on all the interviews and the evidence found in the cave."

"Afraid you'll have to excuse me. The baby's stirring," Mac said. "If I come up with anything new or Earth-shattering, I'll email it to you both. Bye and good luck. Chris, we need a Greer interview. Or did you find the original interview in the cave? Or let Dr. Drummer hypnotize you. I'm working on a family connection. Bye." Then silence.

"How about it, Snow?" asked the LT. "Let's talk to Sienna Greer again. We'll try another tactic—like leniency on her assault on you if she can give us something concrete on these homicides."

Snow groaned. "How lenient? This whacko belongs in jail or a psych ward."

"Don't think we need to be that specific. If she realizes she's going to spend a dime plus behind bars, we might be able loosen her tongue with a carrot."

"More like a burger and beer." Snow sighed and checked his watch and then pocketed his digital recorder. "Speaking of... Can we stop for a sandwich first? I need fuel."

"Why not. Come on. I'll drive." Stuart called up to the front office to tell Sonja they were going to the prison.

The prisoner's hair was stringy and matted, face pale and splotched; her body shed unwashed odors. Her stained jumpsuit was missing the top two buttons. Fingernails had been chewed to the quick, and her wrists and ankles had been scrapped raw by the restraints. She sank in the chair, surly and disinterested.

"What's the meaning of this?" demanded LT Stuart. "Why isn't she decent?"

The guard shrugged indifferently. "She's been in solitary, attacks—claws and bites—anyone who approaches her. We've had to sedate her more than once."

"Find a female guard to escort this prisoner to the showers. Get her a clean suit or do I need to involve the warden?" Les asked sternly. "Is Brandi Brown on duty? Did you consult a doctor or psychologist?"

"Yes, sir. No, sir, to the second question."

"Please page her."

Within five minutes, Brown arrived and exchanged pleasantries with Stuart. She'd been a teen prostitute who chose to accept an education rather than incarceration, so Les personally supervised her rehab, HACC coursework and arranged her internship with CPD. She'd spent that time living with the Stuarts. "I'll have her back in fifteen minutes." She, too, was nearly six feet and solid—had clearly spent time in the gym toning up.

"We'll call her lawyer, inform him we're questioning her."

Feldman answered on the first ring. "You will not question her without my presence, and I'm currently in Williamsport. It would take me two and a half hours to drive there. Sorry, you'll just have to reschedule. Try calling my secretary first to check my availability."

"Do you have a speakerphone?" Les asked.

"Of course," Feldman answered.

"Then, if you have a half hour, we'd like to ask your client questions to review what she knows. If she opposes a plea bargain on Snow's AVM case, perhaps we can bargain if she gives us something concrete or useful on the homicides," Les said. They waited several minutes while Feldman put them on hold.

Brown escorted Greer back into the interview room. The prisoner looked much better showered—still scrunching her damp hair in place with her hands, restrained with zip ties—wearing a clean jumpsuit. Her wrists and ankles had been wrapped with gauze. Snow started the recorder. The LT explained that her lawyer was on speakerphone and made their pitch about leniency before the court for her cooperation.

Greer said nothing for several minutes. She shrugged and then asked for a Coke. Les nodded, so Brown disappeared and returned with a can of soda from the staff vending machine, popped the lid, which she kept, and set the drink on the table near Greer's right hand.

The first few questions were easy enough: name, address, home, status and her health—same ones Snow had asked her in Williamsport weeks before. She seemed to relax as she sipped her soda, turning it around, as if to seek solace.

Snow ran over the usual questions about work, her duties, marriage and family, relationships with her co-workers, friends and boss. "How long have you been employed by West Enterprises?"

"Ten years."

"So the Williamsport well has been operational that long?" asked LT.

"No, first we had to clear the site, build the drill derrick, dig and line the impound and retention ponds. The boss obtained spacing units, permits and negotiated with a dozen different agencies just to set the well in motion."

"Spacing units are..." asked Stuart.

"The space—acres—required for horizontal drills for the area."

"The Marcellus Shale industry sets up the equipment, supplies the trucks, tools, and hires the personnel to make it operational?" Snow asked.

She refused to look at the detective, sipped her drink slowly, then put the can back on the table and made eye contact with LT Stuart.

"He makes it sound easy, but essentially that's correct," she said.

"Do you know any people who oppose the Williamsport well?" asked Les.

Greer shrugged again. "Lots of people sign petitions, send editorials to the newspapers and write their legislators and the governor." She laughed. "It's already a foregone conclusion; the well is usually erected and fracking shale by the time the locals find out. Can't stop progress."

"You don't feel your health is compromised working there?" Les asked.

She shook her head. "I really hadn't thought about it, but we all need the jobs."

Snow said, "Do you know whose camcorder shot Ahnai Slaughter reporting on this or any of the active wells? Was a filmmaker at the Williamsport well anytime in the past few months?"

She looked at Snow then, considered him for a minute. "No."

"So you didn't find the camera we found in your cave on your mountain property?"

"No."

"Anyone approach you or ask any employees questions about the Marcellus Shale industry, your well's operation, the violations or citations received from the Susquehanna River Basin Commission, the state or federal agencies?" he asked.

"You did. And so did some reporters from TV stations and *The Daily Item.*"

"What did you tell them?" asked the LT.

"Nothing. That's not my job. I drive trucks. We have PR spokesmen for ads, commercials and such."

"Did you harbor ill will toward your husband for any reason?"

"No, Just the Indian woman—Slaughter. Wouldn't you if your wife were screwing around?" She glared at Chris.

"Definitely." Snow pounced. "Did you kill her?"

"Nah. And I didn't kill anybody else either. My husband supported us, helped pay Lily's college tuition. Why would I do something so stupid?"

"Anger, revenge, retaliation," Les suggested mildly. Greer shook her head vehemently.

"Let's move on gentleman. Stop fishing," Feldman interjected. "My client does not have to answer questions that may incriminate her."

"All right. Do employees have an interest—shares—in the Marcellus Shale industry?"

"Some do." She blinked rapidly, glancing away.

"Have any employees acted suspiciously in regards to the victims Slaughter, Dean Greer or Gary Hauk?"

"Slaughter had no friends there, but most accepted she had a job to do and left her alone."

"So the violations, her citations or the repercussions didn't disturb you?" Snow tried to keep his tone even.

"No. They didn't stop production. Didn't affect our jobs or salaries."

"You overheard no conversations or threats toward any of them."

She shook her head but not convincingly.

"You have to answer audibly," the lieutenant said.

"Once Hauk was yelling at Dean about spending too much time on the river with the SRBC broad."

"For the record, do you mean Ahnai Slaughter?" the LT clarified.

"Yes."

"How did your husband react? And why would he care?" Snow asked.

"He said, 'I'm a Field Tech; my job requires me to be in the field.' Then walked away. Not much rattled him. Hauk depended on Dean to keep him informed."

"So he didn't fear for his life?"

"Not to my knowledge. We've been separated for over a year."

"Because of his affair with Slaughter?" Stuart asked gently.

"Yes," she hissed.

"Do you know anyone who might benefit from the deaths of these three victims?" Snow moved along.

Again, she studied him, hesitating. He waited her out.

"Whoever silenced them," Greer replied, jiggling her Coke can.

"So you didn't benefit from your husband's death?" Snow wanted an honest answer on the record.

"Well, yes. I get the house and his $50,000 life insurance policy." She'd anticipated their next question.

"Do you have a mortgage and college expenses?" Snow made a note to subpoena their financials.

"No, he had another policy that paid off the mortgage in case of his death. No, Lily has a full academic scholarship, though we pay for books, clothes, and other expenses. She has her own car."

"Do you know who killed Slaughter, Dean Greer or Gary Hauk?" Les asked bluntly.

"No."

"Anything else relevant that you want to share with us? Now is the time to do it." Snow laid it on the table.

"Hauk wasn't liked. People don't trust a brownnoser; he wasn't one of us." She said and paused, deliberating then continued, tugging on the gauze. "Word was the bigwigs greased his palm to let safety issues slide, keep Slaughter out of their hair."

"Like who?" Les asked.

She shrugged. "People with money."

"Can't you be more specific?" Snow prodded. "Owners? Lobbyists? Politicians?"

She shrugged again. "That's all I'm gonna say." She turned her head and motioned to Brown. "Can I go back to my cell?" Brown caught Stuart's nod and escorted her out.

"Goodbye, gentlemen. See you in court." Feldman disconnected.

Back at HQ, the men removed their coats and dug into the data again. The Chief recalled Fields and rotated officers so rookie Storm would not be patrolling alone. When Fields arrived with three cups of cappuccino and donuts, they updated him on the gist of Greer's interview. While they talked, he rubbed his temples. "So was this similar to your first interview with her?" Fields asked Snow.

"I just don't remember, but I followed protocol so must've covered the same information. Nothing clicked that warranted plowing me into the river, if that's what you're asking."

"What are you saying?" Fields asked. "That these cases are not someone lashing out emotionally but political hits?"

"Not necessarily," answered the LT. "It's another angle. Let's just keep open minds. We're mining this data again. Snow, you highlight pertinent information we've overlooked that's not on the boards. Fields, star the margins of any sentence that points to motive, and I'll circle the suspects. Find out who interviewed Hauk's wife or partner, if he has one." He picked up the phone and pushed Sonja's extension. "Locate a transcriptionist to put our case interviews on paper." He paused. "You really have the time? Fine. Oh, check through the email attachments—see if Dr. Chen sent a report on Slaughter's clothes. If so, print three copies for us and email one to Mac. Thanks."

Sonja knocked, and then entered carrying the box of tapes. "Just made a fresh pot. Don't let it go to waste. I put the intern on the email request. That'll probably take some time. And so will this." She exited.

Chris put the papers aside to rest his eyes, take a whiz, and get a refill. When he returned, he unearthed Imhoff's report on Greer's homicide: "Anonymous 911 call from Winfield about noise across R 15 at the RV site. Deceased 45 yr. old male has one arrow shot through the heart, back bruising and scrapes from sliding down RV, legs extended in front of body, arms and hands slack at his sides. Death instantaneous. No rigor. Coroner's report affixed—concurred with the detective's conclusions with medical terms—like perforated pericardium, left ventricle, lung, etc. Estimated TOD: inconclusive, noting cold weather a factor, probably between four p.m. and midnight. X-rays revealed no medical reasons contributing to his demise.

"Deceased dressed casually in clean jeans, sweater and jacket, boots, socks and underwear. Recently showered and shaved. Dirt on the seat of jeans and under fingernails was consistent with soil beneath him at the crime scene, common elements found in the Susquehanna Valley area.

"Searched RV, found Greer and Slaughter's clothes, personal items like razor, toothbrush, his and her prints and accessories like camera and laptop. Several prints from Jason Lightfoot, RV's co-owner as well."

Essentials present but not an exhaustive report. Snow made a note to call Carl for more details, especially about her camera and laptop.

32

At home, Mac had just settled Ian in his cradle. In the kitchen, she put the soup kettle on a burner, added some EVOO and butter. Chopped onions, celery and carrots. Added flour for a roux. Stirring, poured in a carton of chicken broth. She chopped, diced and added potatoes, and then turned the burner to simmer. Opened two cans of clams and set them by to add last with the half and half. Popped dinner rolls in the oven and debated: "Salad or sandwiches?" Opened the fridge to see what was available. "OK bagged spinach, hard-boiled eggs, grape tomatoes, and turkey bacon." Except for the bacon, she tumbled the salad together quickly and stored it in the fridge until Chris arrived.

First the back door opened; a whistle lured Shadow out; she returned rather quickly, her tail tucked between her legs. Poor dog disliked pooping in sub-freezing temperatures. The dog flopped down in front of the warm oven, wiggling back until her rear touched the stove and looked up expectantly, amber eyes imploring to be fed.

Erin felt a cold wind at her back; the door thumped shut. Chris wrapped his arms around her. "Brr, you're freezing."

He pulled away and slipped out of his parka and sport coat, tossing both on hooks in the mudroom. "So warm me up!" He smelled of cold and coffee. Erin reached up as he picked her up; his cold lips locked on her warm ones for long minutes while he tried to slip his hands under her knit top, but she hopped down. "No cold hands on my warm skin, thanks buster! Besides, supper's ready." She padded to the stove and dumped the clams—juice and all into the soup, stirred, added cream, fresh pepper and parsley and then cocked the lid so steam could escape and turned the burner to low. Nuked bacon. Hustled to the garage to get Shadow's food.

Chris set the table while telling her what happened after their conference call. He opened the fridge for the salad, whisked honey-mustard vinaigrette together and poured water. Tapped power on their new Keurig and laid out a decaf mocha cup for Erin, a medium brew for himself. Shadow padded to the mudroom to eat.

"Did you learn anything new from Greer the second time?"

"Not really. She gave routine, guarded answers. Admitted that she benefitted from her husband's death—house and insurance, but that's not unusual. My brain keeps niggling and nibbling at my conscious. I can't remember, but she must have said something incriminating during that first interview. What's this? You mixed potato and clam chowders together? And more chicken broth than cream, so it's lighter."

"I used half and half. Do you like it?" Erin stopped, her spoon suspended part way to her mouth.

"Of course I do. It's just different." He forked a hard-boiled egg quarter off his salad first, then bacon and finally spinach. "A spinach-salad kabob."

"You forgot a tomato." Erin smiled as he chased a slippery tomato around his salad plate.

"It's like you." He smiled in return. "What's for dessert?"

"I didn't make anything. You know, Dr. Drummer could try hypnosis—"

"You said that already. Let that idea go. We'll try another way."

"I already have."

"Like?"

"Don't know if I'm ready to reveal my hunch. I need to research; it's still in the discovery phase."

He shrugged, pretending disinterest as he gathered the plates and bowls. He stopped, ready to return her bowl or dish up another serving. "Unless you want more?"

She looked up. "Of course I want more—oh, soup, no thanks. I'm trying to track down—" Ian let out a wail that made them both jump.

"I'll get him." He was off like a scalded cat.

"What on earth?" Curious, Mac rose to see what caused their son to make such a panicked angry sound.

"He's all tangled up. Maybe he's done being swaddled. Let's give the kid some freedom." Chris gently untangled baby from blanket, unsnapped the flannel romper and changed his diaper with expert swiftness, wiping the little butt clean and dusting baby powder onto his bottom. "And he's sweating." Erin handed Chris dry pajamas. He stretched the fleece up over feet, then legs, and poked the baby's arms through while Ian fussed. Snapped him in. "Bottoms up, baby!" Chris lifted him up over his head. "You're flying!"

"How was he lying when you found him?"

"On his stomach." Chris cradled Ian in his left arm, tickled his chin with an index finger. Ian threw his head back. "Don't break my cast, son." Chris moved the baby to his shoulder.

"I didn't put him to bed that way." Erin stared at Ian.

"He must've turned over."

"Not at seven weeks. The baby books says—"

"Don't guess he read that book. Did you turn over, Snookems? And tie yourself up? Silly boy."

"Well, that's pretty amazing!" Erin returned to the kitchen for her cup of coffee, laying out several finger éclairs to thaw while Chris played with Ian.

"Well, he weighed nine pounds at birth!"

She heard singing and the baby's gurgles of pleasure at his father's voice.

"That baritone sold me, too." She chuckled at the memory of Chris singing at his closing party and on their wedding day. When the baby's tone transformed to a squawk, her milk flooded in. She set her mug carefully on the wooden plant stand beside the rocker, sat down and let the flap down on her bra. Chris laid Ian in her arms; he latched on hungrily. Swinging back to the kitchen to make and doctor his own coffee, Chris returned then collapsed onto the recliner, which sighed and creaked under his weight.

"And here I thought you wanted my body," he observed.

He'd heard her after all; man had ears like a bat. "I want it all." Her eyes raked over him and came back to rest on his warm bourbon eyes, alight with mischief.

"Once that kid's done with dinner, you're going to get —" He interrupted himself. "What were we talking about?"

"I don't remember." Her arms were busy burping and repositioning Ian to the other side. "Funny, how Ian commands all one's attention."

He didn't question her. "I'm going to hop in the shower after I fetch you an éclair or two. And I'll let Shadow out while you shower, hmm?"

She smiled into her coffee.

The next day she planned to follow the trail of the West Enterprise well to find out who owned the rights to what lay beneath the land. She'd learned the land belonged to a holding company called S. Stephens, LTD., which usually meant a lawyer had set up a company for a group of individuals to hold the assets and divvy them up accordingly. For the moment, however, she wanted her husband.

33

Shadow poked her cold nose under Erin's arm and blew, then lifted her nose to her chin and licked. "How'd you get out of the mud room? Did we leave the gate open?" Her hand felt behind her—no warm, bare body; her head swiveled to the cradle as she sat up. No baby. Back went the duvet. Down thumped her feet. Shivering, she struggled into her robe, rounded the corner and sprinted to the living room. Chris had started a fire. Fully dressed for work, he was feeding Ian—fully absorbed in the baby. She backed away, found a K-cup regular cappuccino in the pantry, powered up the machine, poured the cocoa powdered tube in first and made a frothing mocha. "Yum, yum."

"Fee, fie, foe, fum, I smell a coffee mocha and a milky mum!" Chris swung Ian back and forth. "Ready?" and lofted him into Erin's arms without actually letting him go. He finished his own coffee, kissed his son's head and his wife's lips. He tucked his pistol in his shoulder holster, slipped it over his head, and donned a brown tweed sport coat and then his parka.

"Going anywhere special today?" Erin asked because he usually wore a paddle holster in the small of his back.

"Just work. Bye, babe and baby. You two have a good day. Oh, you can have your car back now." He laid the keys to Silver on the kitchen island.

"Oh? Have a safe day. Don't forget to wear your vest, then." Erin hefted Ian up to her shoulder to burp.

"Yeah, Savage is picking me up. I'm bringing home an Explorer tonight."

"Ah, that explains why your lunch isn't packed."

"We're going out for lunch. It's his first day back—at his desk."

When the door whumped shut, it was the loneliest sound. Once she'd tucked Ian into his cradle with a regular baby blanket—no more swaddling for him—she stripped the bed and pillows to wash the knit sheets—a winter addition, as they usually slept without sheets during the summer. Chris swore they made him sweat. She stuffed them into the washer and started it. The landline was ringing.

"Hello?" Erin caught it before it went to voicemail.

"It's cold but a lovely, sunny day. Would you like me to come down and sit with Ian for a couple of hours while you stretch your legs, work with Shadow or have a girl's day out with Danelle?"

"Thanks, Erica, that'd be lovely, although Danelle's working. I can run to the mall and then get some groceries. We'll see about Shadow. She's bored with the course. I need to think of new obstacles for her. Chris left my car. He's picking up his Explorer today."

"That's great. You need your car! Whatever you'd like to do is fine with me. Shall we say ten?"

"That's perfect. Thank you." Erin really had to do something special for her mother-in-law one of these days. "Wonder if she'd like a massage?" Putting the kitchen to rights, dressing warmly and checking the fridge to ensure a bottle of her fresh milk was there, she tucked her keys in her coat pocket, collected her backpack to toss into the car and let Erica in when she heard footsteps crunch on the gravel. "Come, Shadow." The dog looked at her quizzically as though she wasn't sure. Erin snapped her fingers and repeated the command in a lower register. "Come now." The dog lumbered up from the warm hearth.

"Have a good time, dear. And take your time."

"You too. I will. And thanks for being a great mother-in-law. Bottle's in the fridge when he wakes up. Clean clothes in the changing table."

"And thanks for giving me a grandson I can spoil." Erica closed the door with a quick wave.

Erin turned over the ignition; the car thrummed to life as her iPhone pinged. "Hey, babe, can you come to work for a few hours? None of the detectives are available to man the war room. Mom won't mind if—"

"Did you ask your mother to babysit Ian?" Erin asked accusingly. "So you could go joyriding in a new SUV?"

"Hell, no. I'm working the case. We're driving to Winfield and Williamsport to follow up on your suggestions, matter of fact. Like why there's no report on Hauck's homicide at the Williamsport station. And I need to speak with Imhoff."

"Why can't Savage do it?" she asked petulantly. She'd wanted a few hours to herself.

"He's at the courthouse testifying at the Benedict trial this morning, the Greer trial this afternoon. Please, babe, I need you here in case..."

She sighed. "Sure, OK." Last time he'd asked her to do that, she'd abandoned the station to arrest Abby Benedict at BWI. She still felt guilty that he'd wound up in the Susquehanna, kissing death, because of her insubordination. "I'll be there in fifteen."

Once at HQ, she slid her backpack onto her shoulders and pushed her way through the front. "Hello and thank you all for the money tree and donuts—everything's fine. Ignore me. I'm still on maternity leave—just doing Snow a favor. I'll be in Conference One. Any questions regarding the current cases can be routed through to me." First, she detoured to the break room for coffee and then meandered into the conference room intending to organize and straighten. Apparently Sonja had done that. Secondly, she opened her office, carried Shadow's bowl to the break room for water. From her bottom drawer, she extracted a beef hide chew for the dog and a snake— formerly a draft stopper—for her to play with. Satisfied her pup was settled and could entertain herself for a while, she returned to the war room.

A pile of transcripts was stacked on the corner of the table. She picked up the top one, Greer's second interview, and read it. "I wonder what she told Chris originally that she omitted from this one." The second in the stack: Otto Kraus's, the West Enterprise well super. Then his secretary—a woman whose terse manner and stick body Mac remembered well; however, her answers seemed forthright and tallied with the others. No one had actually seen anyone near the impound pond where Hauck's body was found. Only a few remembered seeing him at the site the week before. "You'd think the Safety Officer would be on the job every day." She moved on because Ahnai Slaughter was CPD's main concern. Greer fell under the purview of Sunbury Detective Carl Imhoff. *Why hadn't anyone interviewed him on finding Greer's body?*

"Where's Greer's autopsy report?" She found Imhoff's one-page summary and frowned after reading it. Chief March would demand a complete report—wasn't Imhoff consulting? The coroner made no mention of the condition, evidence or anything else about Greer's clothes. No one had attached a crime scene report, i.e., the $10,000 that she'd found. "What's his name—Sid? Had anyone interviewed the 911 caller? It's not difficult to trace the person through the phone number." She picked up the landline, called Sunbury Dispatch, identified herself and gave her shield number, requesting the phone number of the 911 caller the night Greer died. "Imhoff has been consulting with the CPD but is out on medical leave, and I'm wondering if anyone contacted or interviewed the person who called in the homicide." She gave her the CPD landline and her cell numbers. "I'd like to speak with that person today. Thanks."

Sonja knocked, entered. "We're sending a lunch order to Panera Bread. Would you like something?"

"Oh, yes. I'll have a combo—chicken orzo or noodle soup with half a turkey Panini." She dug into her purse to find a ten and handed the bill to her admin. "Thanks." She smiled distractedly in her direction.

By the time Mac had scanned through the interview transcripts, Sunbury called back with the phone number of the Winfield resident.

She thumbed numbers, hoping whoever called in the homicide would be home and had witnessed something. "Seven rings. Perhaps no one—"

"Hello?" a timid, shaky female voice asked. From the tremulous voice, Mac guessed a senior citizen or someone recovering from an illness.

"Hello, I'm Detective Erin McCoy..." and briefly explained why she wanted to speak with her.

"I'm Verna Gribble. I've been retired for twelve years from the Lewisburg Area School District. I was a guidance counselor at the high school for twenty-nine years until my health quit on me."

"Last October—" Mac had to look up the date. "—when you called in a homicide at the RV across R 15 along the Susquehanna, did you see or hear anything, Mrs. Gribble?"

"Will this conversation be kept confidential?"

"Well, I'm not a lawyer, but for the time being, yes. I'm just seeking information at this point." *No need to scare the woman about testifying.*

"Funny you should ask. I saw the camper from my bedroom window because most of the leaves were gone by then. We had a terrible storm a few nights earlier, but that night was balmy, so I had my windows cracked open. Maybe you remember... Anyway, a murder of crows shot from their roosts along the tree line. Something disturbed them. That's why I looked that way. I heard a whoosh— like air whistling through. Then a projectile, like an arrow, zipped across my vision, but there's no hunting at that time that I know of. Too early for turkey or deer season, I think."

"Did you see anything else? Was it dark then?" Mac nodded her thanks when the intern brought in her lunch.

She opened the soup and spooned in deliciousness while she listened.

"No, the sun was setting: a blue sky, the horizon a rim of salmon. I thought I heard a shout—or a man's voice, then something heavy thumped to the ground. It was strange because a Native American woman stays there from time to time. That's all I remember."

"Did anyone talk to you about what you witnessed?"

"Oh, yes, a young man. I couldn't believe he was a detective; he looked like a teenager."

"Can you describe him?"

"Blond hair like straw sticking up on end but short on the sides: broad forehead, heavy eyebrows, and clear blue eyes. Average height for a man, maybe five-nine. Cute rather than handsome, if you know what I mean. A bit stocky—sturdy, not heavy."

"Do you remember his name or what he said?" asked Mac.

"Oh, yes. Carl Imhoff. His father was the mayor of Sunbury for years, though the family's originally from Williamsport. The detective asked questions like you're asking, dear. And how do I know you're a detective? You sound so young."

"Do you have a computer?" Mac asked. "Why didn't you say his name?"

"You asked me to describe him. Of course I have a PC. I may be retired, but I'm not a dinosaur." Gribble chuckled.

Mac directed her to the CPD website and told her where to find her name and gave Mrs. Gribble her badge number if she wished to call and confirm. "Or call the CPD police station at this number and ask them to connect you with me."

"Well, that's proof enough. Now, what were we talking about?"

"I asked you if you knew what Detective Imhoff asked, and you said questions similar to mine. Anything else you can tell me?"

"One thing. It's not anything he did or said, but he rang my bell about ten minutes after I called 911. I didn't give my name."

"He could have back traced the call like I did," Mac said but wondered how he could have reacted that fast.

"I worked in Lewisburg, which is ten miles from my house; Sunbury's even farther south. How could he have gotten here so fast?"

"I see your point. I'm not sure. Perhaps speeding with sirens, lights flashing."

"I heard no sirens and saw no flashing lights, and no cars stopped here that night. I just wonder how he got here so fast. Never mind, young lady. If you're finished, I have to fix dinner and go to choir practice. Thank you for calling, even if the topic was unpleasant."

"You've been most helpful. Thank you. I have one more. Has anyone else interviewed you about that night?"

"You're the second. Good afternoon. I'll call you if I recall anything else," Mrs. Gribble said.

"Thanks. Have a good day." Mac disconnected, savoring the last of the hot soup and then attacked the half sandwich. She took a quick break to walk and water Shadow after lunch. "You need a diversion, don't you, girl?" The shepherd had opened Mac's bottom desk drawer and tugged out a knotted rope and unearthed a bone. Chewed the rawhide down to a nub. Erin took a bathroom break herself. Then called Erica to tell her she'd be awhile yet and explained where she was and what she was doing.

"Oh, bummer. You're working! Shame on Chris! Don't worry; Ian's fine. He's playing on his busy mat or whatever you call it. Take your time."

"Thanks so much." Mac was so grateful Erica was so generous with her time and signed off, knowing she didn't have to worry.

She booted up her laptop, barging her way past layers and levels of information until she found an article in the 1998 *Daily Item* about West Enterprise's construction site

—a new well in Williamsport. The accompanying photo showed several smiling men and women wearing hardhats striking shovels into the ground. Another article explained how Marcellus Shale drilled and fractured the shale to free the gas. The caption identified the man in the middle, former mayor Stephen Imhoff flanked by Martin Feldman and Mrs. Marie Imhoff, who stood by her brother-in-law and sister-in-law, Ken and Sarah Imhoff. "Sienna's parents. She has her mother's wiry hair and her father's build."

"Wonder if Feldman and Dirkson established the company S. Stephens, LTD. that owned the mineral and gas rights and if it's a family business." She hunted through the hundred photos spread out across the table. "Found it!" She examined it with the magnifying glass that looked suspiciously like hers. The close-up of Detective Imhoff talking to Sienna Greer was no cop interview. Both were smiling at one another, unaware of the camera. Carl's thumbs were tucked into his front pockets; Sienna leaned against the blue fender of her rig, one hand resting on the detective's arm. Not only did they know each other, they were cousins. "I'd bet my badge on it."

But she didn't have to. She'd call the newspaper to find out how far back their records went. Maybe they'd have the year—twenty-two years ago—on microfiche. The phone startled her out of her reverie.

"Hey, babe, you still at work?" asked Chris. A susurrus of air shushed over his words, making hearing difficult.

"Just following orders," Mac answered.

"OK, thanks. Savage is on his way from court. He can relieve you, and I'll be at HQ within the hour because I couldn't find Imhoff. We had a late lunch scheduled, but he was a no-show. Did you find anything that would shed some light on our homicides?"

"Not exactly."

"Darlin', don't be mysterious. We need a break, and I'll take one of your hunches I can follow up any day. Spill it."

"I'll tell you when you get here. No, I need to feed Ian. We can talk tonight at home when we have some privacy."

"OK. Bye. Love you," Chris whispered across the line. She shook her head, looked at the receiver and set back in its base. Sensing someone else in the room, she looked up into the ice blue eyes of Carl Imhoff.

"Mac, you here by yourself? Where's everybody?" he asked.

"On assignment, on patrol or in court. I'm not really here, still on maternity leave and was just about to gather up my things and…"

He pulled his weapon and trained it on her. "Figure it out, did you?"

"What are you doing, Imhoff? What am I supposed to have figured out?" Mac asked. Playing dumb had never been her strong suit.

"I overheard your conversation with your intrepid husband. He's like a pit bull and you're a terrier. Once you set your teeth in an idea, you won't let it go. Let's hear your hunch."

"I have a few questions. Why did you stand him up for lunch today?"

"I wanted to be alone with you. The two of us are going to take a little trip up north. You've been working too hard; you need a vacation. And I really can't afford you going around my stomping grounds wagging your tongue with little old retired ladies who should mind their own business."

Mac nodded. "You bugged our phone when you were here consulting and have listened in to CPD business since."

"See how astute you are? Someone really should sweep and debug the station on a routine basis. But, listen—"

He was interrupted by a knock on the door; he sat abruptly to hide his pistol. Sonja entered and glanced at both detectives, sitting across the table from each other, stiff as starch. She laid collated papers beside Mac's elbow. "The other transcripts you requested." Her finger tapped the pile. "Why don't you go home, Mac? You look exhausted. I'm sure Detective Imhoff will mind the store until Savage or Snow returns." Mac felt for her iPhone in her pocket, pushed the first button to speed dial Chris and put it on speaker, hoping he'd listen, hiding it behind the stack of transcripts while Sonja talked, something she loathed doing while conversing with somebody because it was rude.

Imhoff canted his head toward the door, a gesture only Mac saw.

"I'm packing up now." She stood and stacked some files together. "Thanks for these, Sonja." She looked up and smiled, willing her admin safely out of the room.

"I'm going home early, but the night receptionist will be here in about thirty minutes. Good night. Kiss the baby for me."

"Goodbye, Sonja. I'm going home soon. Hello to your family."

Mac and Imhoff were alone once more.

"You really don't think you'll get away with this," Mac said.

"I walked in here without any problem, didn't I?" he answered, his smirk revealing he had covered his bases. "And you'll walk out with my gun in your back as soon as I've confirmed what you know. I have it leveled at you under the table. Sit down."

She noted an incoming and pretended to sneeze, shoving books to the floor to cover the weak "Hello?"

"Excuse me. I need a tissue." Bending over her backpack to retrieve one, Mac said loudly, "Just listen! What do I know about you?" Mac asked Imhoff as she acquiesced.

"No, not just me. The whole situation." He leaned back in the cushioned chair, stretching his legs out as if time were no matter. "Father Time has never lost a game."

Mac shrugged and mimicked his body language. "Neither has Mother Nature."

"Toss me that photo you were studying so intently." His tone held iron. "Ah, Sienna and me. Tell me what you see." He lobbed it carelessly onto the table, changed his mind, and wadded it up and stuck it in his coat pocket.

"A family resemblance. That's no detective interviewing a 'person of interest' in *your* homicide. That means either you know Greer didn't kill her husband or you know who did. Maybe you did it yourself. If you were on the crime scene in ten minutes to question the neighbors, you were already there. I just don't know why you'd kill your cousin's husband. Or perhaps you were both in on it, which would explain the two different MOs. Plus, on Raccoon Mountain, you shot Savage and either Sienna sent you over the cliff for killing Dean, the horse threw you or you jumped to throw suspicion off of yourself."

"Why would I be stupid enough to break my jaw and arm? And why would I be considered a suspect?" The tomcat was enjoying toying with his mouse.

"It worked, didn't it? No one suspected you. Maybe you misjudged the distance? Who else could omit pertinent evidence from the scene or the homicide report? Chief March would never approve such a sketchy, incomplete report. Nothing mentioned about evidence found on Greer's clothes, of his things in Ahnai's trailer, and no word of the $10,000 found in his RV in Williamsport. Is Sid dirty, too? There's no Sid crime tech at your station and no report filed on Hauck's homicide, either. Look at our comprehensive reports on Slaughter. And the Sunbury coroner merely rubber-stamped your conclusions without offering anything different of his own. That's not an oversight, that's negligence."

"Temper, temper, Red." Imhoff laughed. "A rookie lecturing a seasoned detective. I have to hand it to you; you have moxie and a head for the business. But, pray, continue." He gestured with his gun hand, now leveled at her chest. No contest. "Sometimes a fall is just a fall. Tell me what else you suspect."

"You know I can't do anything unless I have concrete evidence. Why don't you tell me what you know? We can take turns," Mac returned.

"I don't think so." That Cheshire smile and irises going dark and flinty warned that she was testing his patience. Good. "If you've learned this much, you have evidence."

"Nothing inconvertible. You've been very thorough and left no trail—no connection to any of the crime scenes. Though I must tell you, I found the ice pick blade sticking in the bridge. Clever. Actually, the setting sun found it. Were your prints on the handle saturated in Ahnai's blood?" The landline extension was blinking; someone was trying to reach her. She hoped he or she investigated.

"Your stalling is beginning to bore me." He looked at his watch, frowning. He stood up, backed to the door and cracked it open, listening for telltale human sounds. Left it ajar. Too early for the night shift. Mac bent over to pick up her backpack, but Imhoff barked, "Leave it! Let's go!"

"But I may need it 'cause I don't carry a purse. Everything's in it."

"Like a Glock or Taser. No tricks, just come along, real slow and friendly, and I'll leave your mother-in-law and baby out of our little tryst. Otherwise, we'll go to your place. I have everything in the car we'll need. Tell you what. I'll give you a sporting chance once we get to the mountain—a ten-minute head start."

"Raccoon Mountain? My husband and his partner know that mountain; they were there, remember, and they'll call my stepfather to search for you. You think you're clever—that because you're a cop, you don't make mistakes. But we found your bloody prints on the hundred-dollar bill we kept from the juice box in Greer and Hauk's trailer," she bluffed.

"Won't do you any good. We'll be long gone."

"Then you might as well tell me why you killed them. It's not about an affair, a vendetta or revenge, at all, is it?

It's about silencing those who threatened your royalties because you and your family are raking in at least hundred thou annually. And Ahnai threatened to blow the whistle and shut down your little operation? Weren't you making enough on royalties? Paying employees like Hauk to falsify safety data, since that drill-site alone had over a thousand reported violations? Were you giving them kickbacks to spy on one another, then eliminating the threats?"

Imhoff lunged at Mac, catching her arm. She jerked away and whistled. A ball of snarling fury soared at the man's arm. Shadow clamped razor-sharp teeth on his gun arm and bit down with about 1200 pounds of force, shaking her head sideways, clawing him with her feet, shredding his legs with her hind legs. He dropped the gun, but, despite the shepherd's vicious attack, Imhoff was reaching for it. The sound of a bullet racking in the chamber ricocheted around the room, as Snow, trying to catch his breath, pushed the barrel against the back of Imhoff's head, Savage a step behind. Afraid Imhoff would shoot Shadow, Erin dug into her pack's front pocket for her Taser, but Savage had already cuffed the man's good arm to his belt.

"Shadow, release," Mac ordered. Quickly, Snow restrained the man's ankles, while Shadow stood over the body, snarling and growling vociferously, blood dripping from her teeth and gums. The detective's eyes rolled up, his eyelids fluttered, and he stilled.

"Call Cujo off!" Savage ordered. He opened his cell and pushed 911. "We need an ambulance at CPD Headquarters. White male, Detective Carl Imhoff, unconscious but breathing on his own, mauled by K-9 Officer Shadow McCoy." He smiled at Mac. "Lacerated arm, broken radius and—hell—it's too bloody for me to assess correctly. He'll need a police escort and guard." He paused while the Dispatch operator talked. "Yeah, I will. Hold on. Mac, are you hurt? You're turning green. Bloody

hell." He dropped his cell on the table and ran to catch
Erin, who'd fainted.

Snow's foot pinned Imhoff's right wrist to the floor.
"Shadow, down. Sit. Stay." When she obeyed, his eyes
widened. "Good dog, good girl" and rubbed her neck in
reward, as he had no treats on him. When he looked up,
he stared at Savage. "What are you doing with my wife?"

Savage held out his arms for Snow to take Erin. Chris
sat on the conference table and held her across his lap.
She snuggled against him, her warm head tucked under
his chin. He suspected she was conscious but weak or in
shock, and therefore content to do nothing more.

"Help me stem the bleeding. Your dog did a number on
his arm. I can see bone and muscle." Savage lifted the
first aid kit from the wall, dropped to his knees, tossed
the entire bottle of alcohol over the exposed wound,
waking Imhoff, who yowled at the pain and damage.

"Let the fucker die," Snow answered. "He was going to
kill my wife." He felt Erin smile shakily against his neck.

"Wouldn't it be better to see him pay for his homicides
with three consecutive life sentences? Know how
prisoners inside treat dirty cops?"

The paramedics arrived and took command of the
patient writhing on the floor. "You need to be still, sir, so
we can transport you to the hospital." He wrenched away,
nearly falling off the stretcher, batting away helping
hands, his right tucked impotently by his side. The
attendant didn't hesitate. He extracted a syringe from his
kit and shot it into the screaming patient, who quieted
quickly.

"He's a CPD prisoner wanted for three homicides, so
he needs to be restrained at all times with a guard with
him and another at the door."

"I'll go," Savage said. "Not much else we can do here."
He fell into step behind the ambulance crew as they
exited HQ with the suspect.

Another paramedic, the female who had attended Ian's
highway birth, took Erin's temp, BP, pulse and snapped a

tourniquet around her bicep; with gloved hands, she swabbed the bend once, stuck her and drew blood into a vial. "Ready for transport?" Shadow skittered from side to side, uncertain. She jumped onto Chris's knees. "Down girl, good dog. We're going home."

Erin shook her head against Chris's neck and clung to him, shivering.

The EMT shrugged and had Erin sign a paper admitting her refusal to go to the hospital, leaving a copy with the consequences listed.

"Really, I'm OK. I have to get home and feed my baby. I'll call my Obgyn. Think I'm anemic."

Snow took her home, settled her in the rocker with a glass of Shiraz. Erica was walking the floor with the wailing baby. "I've tried everything!" Sounding exasperated, her mother-in-law said. "He's clean and dry."

"And hungry," Erin held out her arms, and Erica deposited the squirming infant there. Once his mouth glommed onto his mother's breast, his cries stopped. "I'm so sorry he's fussy. It's past his feeding time, and I had only one bottle pumped, thinking I'd return in two hours."

"It's my fault, mother, I ordered her to work."

Erica stepped around the shepherd. "The dog's mouth is bleeding. Damn it, Chris, don't do that. You wife needs a break from work. Having a baby is traumatic. That's why she's on maternity leave." While she scolded him, he escorted her to the front door, helped her don her coat, and kissed her temple. Once the door was shut and secure, he said, "I'm sorry to have put you in that position. I would've killed him myself if he'd touched you, harmed you in any way." He fell to his knees, his dark amber eyes troubled, sad as Shadow's.

"It wasn't your fault. You didn't know where Imhoff was. If I had told you my suspicions, you would've turned around and come back immediately and maybe arrested him prematurely."

"Then why didn't you tell me? What did you piece together? That he and Greer were in this together?"

"Yes and no. They're first cousins. Greer's maiden name was Imhoff. Their family owns the land on and the mineral and gas rights beneath the West Enterprise well, plus all the timber on their hundred acres."

"How does a cop get his hands on all that?" her husband asked.

"All in the family. His dad was the mayor of Sunbury for three terms; his uncle's a contractor. My guess is that Marcellus Shale also employs the rest of the family members in some capacity. Feldman and Dirkson drew up the agreement. They're raking money in, but that's not enough because they're all living beyond their lifestyle. Did you notice the Greer's house? Imhoff didn't admit to killing anybody, but he doesn't have to; we may have his fingerprint on the payoff money, a partial print under Ahnai and Lightfoot's RV, where Imhoff was searching for a key. He was first on the scene, identified by an eyewitness, a Mrs. Gribble—whom we need to put into protective custody. She wondered how he could have arrived at the crime scene so quickly. So I checked his work schedule for each homicide—all occurred on his days off or when he was in the field. I'm telling you, he's our guy, but can you clean Shadow's teeth, feed and water her? But please get a blood sample for evidence first."

Ian was dozing quietly, one hand hugging his mother's beast, hiccupping from the crying bout. Chris broke the suction, put him on his mother's shoulder, kissed her head and hurried to the mudroom to tend to Shadow first. Once the dog was settled with clean teeth, washed paws, fresh water and dinner, Chris moved to the kitchen. In the fridge he found a cooked beef roast. He sliced and diced onions, celery and potatoes into the pot with some EVOO. Tossed in enough flour to make a roux, added beef broth and pot pie noodles from the pantry. Chopped and dropped the meat in, putting together a one-pot meal in thirty minutes, throwing in a box of frozen peas and mushrooms to add color. "There, Rachael Ray! And thanks, mother, for the roast."

He took the drowsy baby to his cradle, cranked up the lullabies, tiptoed out of the bedroom, gently closing the door. Back in the kitchen, Erin added parsley, plated the potpie and opened a home-canned jar of peaches. Tipping Shiraz in both their glasses, they spent the evening fitting the conundrum of the puzzling homicides together. Unfortunately, Hauk's role was a missing piece, as well as a direct link to Ahnai Slaughter's death.

"Mac, your reasoning is sound—that Imhoff killed Slaughter to silence a whistleblower—"

"Which would've shut down the well until the case was decided, which translates into lost revenue."

"Maybe. I was going to say 'silence a whistleblower to force Greer and Hauk to fall in line.' But we need solid proof. We don't have it."

"So get a confession from him."

"I'll try, but that lawyer is shrewd and calculating. I'm sure he's making money off the deal, too, but legal counsel is not illegal."

"Unless he's covering up Imhoff's tracks, skimming himself, or—"

"Just covering his ass. The man's past retirement; he looks seventy! But that's another issue."

"I'd like to focus on Ahnai Slaughter; she's our case. Think I'll meet with Michaels, let her write an article on what we know, maybe leak a little about what we need..."

"Erin, we've got to do this one by the book. It's complicated and interwoven with the Greer and Hauck homicides on several levels."

"All right. Let's get subpoenas and follow the money."

"We can do that. Oh, Savage saw Wilhelm at court today."

"When do I have to testify?"

He shrugged. "She'll probably serve you tomorrow."

"Won't Lyons and Benedict be thrilled," she said.

"They're being tried together?" Chris whistled.

She nodded. "Much to Abigail's chagrin. Alison seems indifferent. And damn, I didn't work Shadow today. Your Dad and I devised several different obstacles—one tunnels underground—Dr. Chen donated a finger for the cause—and exits at the next obstacle."

"Oh, I'd say Shadow had her share of action today." Chris chuckled. "Thank God!" He picked up Erin's feet and massaged, working his way up her calves but stopped. "I need to touch you."

"Did I say anything?" Erin looked perplexed.

"You had this funny look on your face," and then he understood.

Both said "Shower" at the same time; off they scrambled.

Next morning, Snow answered the door and let Wilhelm inside. "Erin!"

"I'm right here—Oh!" She padded into the living room in her robe, burping the baby and held out her hand for the subpoena. "When?"

"Tomorrow morning at ten sharp." The woman turned on her heel and huffed out the door in a lawyer's typical gesture of preoccupied busyness.

Erin lowered herself and the baby into the rocker for the second installment, switching him from left to right. "Except for his eyes—a deep lake blue and hair the color of a new penny, Ian looks like you. Isn't that an unusual combination?" She observed. "What are you doing today?" She looked up at her husband.

"Hmm. Three guesses." Snow looped his wine-colored tie into a Windsor knot, which contrasted well with his blue shirt and navy Dockers. Topping it with a wool tweed sport coat, he looked like he was testifying.

"I'd guess to interview Imhoff, but you're dressed for court."

"Right on both counts. Court at nine, Imhoff at eleven. Are you bringing Ian?" he teased.

"Actually I'm meeting Sonja on the courthouse steps with him; she's taking him to work. I'll pack two bottles of milk this time. Then I'll pick him up after I finish testifying."

"Want me to pick him up at noon and bring him home?"

"No, I can't ask your mother to watch him again so soon. I'm hoping court will be brief." She crossed her fingers and started giggling when he looked skeptical, eyebrow lifted. "There's always a first time."

He moved to the kitchen island to pack his lunch—his version of chicken cordon blue, two apples and a snack bag of Muddy Buddies, plus a bottle of water. "I'm begging you—stay calm and collected."

"I notice you didn't say cool." Erin smiled up at him.

"My red-headed wife?" He kissed her and disappeared out the door. His voice ghosted back to her. "Not a chance." The lock slid home.

34

Hurriedly, Mac dressed and bundled the baby in his bunting, finally flipping a blanket over the infant car seat. She packed the diaper bag, tossed a pbj and an apple into her backpack. Slipped her shoulder holster on, securing her pistol under her left arm. She threw on a hunter green jacket over a black turtleneck and slacks and scurried out the door. Sonja was waiting on the front steps of the courthouse, so Mac handed her Ian's car seat and the diaper bag. "I'll be there the minute they dismiss me from the witness chair."

"Not to worry. He'll be fine, won't you, baby?" She hustled him into her car idling at the curb, leaving the detective to mount the steps and enter the antechamber to the courtroom until she was called. While waiting, Mac reviewed the Murphy file. When her turn came, she walked into a packed courtroom, noticed Elena Michaels on the end of the media row. Walking sedately down the aisle, past the tables, and onto the stand, standing until ADA Lawson swore her in. They ran through the routine quickly, lobbing questions and answers across the room until they reached the pink sweater.

"You notified me several weeks ago that you found a pink sweater worn by the killer. First, how did you find it?"

"I first looked at the Post Office's dead-letter warehouse."

"What caused you to look there?"

"We'd looked every other possible place. I surmised she might have mailed it to one of her cousins rather than destroy it—a very beautiful, expensive sweater."

"We?"

"CPD detectives and the FBI."

"So it was returned?" Lawson asked, surprised.

"Well, New Jersey had it for awhile and sent pieces of the package to the Mechanicsburg Office where it was postmarked. In the end, Lyons's tenant Carlotta Coffey called me to collect it." Out of her peripheral vision, Mac noted Lyons' shocked and Benedict's dismayed visage.

"And why are you so sure this is the sweater the killer wore?"

"We found one unique button and pink thread at the crime scene. The lab identified three distinct blood types: Murphy's, Lyons's and Benedict's on the sweater. According to the lab, the sweater's a perfect match to the button and thread."

The courtroom erupted. Benedict yelled, "It's Alison's sweater!"

Lyons contradicted, "That's not true!" smacking her sister in the face—the sound cracked in the quiet courtroom. "You damn little sneak. I'm already in this godforsaken jail—"

"Order!" The judge banged his gavel, admonished the jury to discount the defendants' remarks, called them in contempt, and levied a fine on each. "Bailiff, escort the defendants out of the courtroom."

"Objection!" Wilhelm leaped to her feet. "It's a federal offense to open someone's mail."

"Objection!" countered Lawson. "Defense Counselor can conjecture all she wants but needs to frame her object—"

"Don't be so eager to assume, either of you." He turned to Mac and asked, "You did testify that the FBI was assisting the search?"

"Leading it, sir."

"And you had search warrants for both domiciles?"

"Yes, sir. There were three—Lyons owns a cottage at Rehoboth Beach."

"Objections sustained. Seems a moot point." Judge Lewis stated as he resumed his seat, the wings of his black robe sighing out. "Continue." He scowled at the media seats, his glare daring anyone else to further disrupt the proceedings.

Lawson took a moment to peruse his notes, regain his composure and the jury and gallery's attention. He cleared this throat and took a sip of water. "Did the lab report tell you anything else?"

"One, that the murderer wore the sweater. At some point, Murphy drew blood from Ms. Benedict; blood samples were on the Vic's navy shirt. She was bludgeoned from behind with a blunt object; it fractured her skull. Blood splattered backward onto the sweater. The person in front was fighting with the victim. Ms. Benedict's blood sample was located on Murphy's sleeves and around the neck," Mac stated.

"In your view, does that evidence correspond with the CPD crime scene scenario you encountered at the domicile, indicating the sisters' complicity in Mindy Murphy's demise?" asked the prosecutor.

"Objection," Wilhelm said from her chair. "Detective McCoy is not an expert on blood splatter. Second, 'complicit' suggests collusion, therefore premeditation."

The judge cogitated a bit on those statements, shrugged as though any rejoinder or ruling on semantics unnecessary or unworthy of an argument. "Rephrase, counselor."

Lawson first asked Mac what her B.S. degrees were in.

"I have a B.A. in English and Psych. Once admitted to the Police Academy, I earned a B.S. with dual majors in Criminal Justice and Science. And earned sixteen semester hours at Quantico."

"And how long did you serve on a police force before you joined the CPD Homicide Squad?"

"Four in Adams County, four in Carlisle before I joined Homicide."

"Detective McCoy, in those eight years, did you ever encounter blood splatter? Did you study this concept for your degree?" Lawson continued.

"Yes to both questions, sir, and at the Police Academy and Quantico."

Then ADA Lawson repeated the question, using the verb "responsible" in the place of "complicity" because the women had already admitted they caused Murphy's demise.

"Cross," Wilhelm said as she stood. "Just one question. Why would either Mrs. Lyons or Ms. Benedict put a return address on it if they wanted it to disappear?" A mumble of assent rumbled through the gallery, a point for the defense.

Mac smiled. "They didn't; Carlotta Coffey did when she mailed it; she assumed the lack of a return address was an oversight."

By the time they were finished, her milk was leaking through her turtleneck. She felt like she'd been forced through a sieve and had no idea where Chris was, so she drove to HQ to collect Ian, nursing him in her office. She pushed Sonja's extension and asked, "Can you tell me where Chris—"

"Interviewing Imhoff, as far as I know. He hasn't checked in, but that's not unusual in hospital or rehab centers. Shall I page him?"

"No, thanks, just tell him I went home, if he calls in. And thanks for minding Ian for me!"

"No problem, anytime. He's an adorable little boy. Wonder where he got that red hair? He napped awhile but fussed after his feeding; I sang gospels while changing his diaper, which quieted him down." By the time Mac disconnected, she had an incoming on her cell—Chris.

"I'll be late. Savage and I are escorting Imhoff to the CCP after the interview—with Feldman present."

"OK. Did you interview him yet?"

"We questioned him. When I listed the evidence, he went ballistic—clammed up after he insisted on seeing his lawyer."

Erin listened while she wrestled Ian's car seat into the back seat, strapping him in snugly.

"We can talk at home. Gotta go now. Love you," Snow concluded.

"Love you more." They disconnected. She smiled. Despite risk, pain and duty, Chris lived life wholly: mind and body open to the possibilities. He would entertain the probable and attempt the impossible. "I'll love you forever," she whispered. Hopping into Silver, she and Ian motored home, vowing to say no to any other intrusions while on maternity leave. "Can't say no to a subpoena, though."

***

Despite the ungainly cast encasing his right arm— wrist to elbow and two weeks of relative inactivity, the former police detective remained strong and agile. Anger radiated off him. The CPD detectives weren't so happy either. Presented with the evidence, Imhoff admitted nothing. He'd been well schooled in legalities. "I won't talk without my lawyer present. Besides, you guys are shoveling shit. I'm a cop; I know the tricks. Hell, everybody does with all the crime shows on TV." After an hour, they let him have his phone call.

An hour and a half later, in walked Feldman, smartly outfitted in a tailored navy suit and red power tie. Tossed down his briefcase like a deck of cards. He extracted a clean white handkerchief from this breast pocket and wiped his eyeglasses. "I haven't yet conferred with my client, so if you'll gentlemen will excuse us, and turn off the video, he and I will talk. I'll call you when you can begin the questioning."

"No can do. You've had two weeks to confer with your client—that's how long he's been a suspect. In addition, Imhoff was a cop; he knows his rights, has been Mirandized and will be incarcerated until his trial," Snow said unequivocally.

The lawyer frowned and scratched his chin thoughtfully, looking from one to the other. "What's he accused of?"

"Three homicides: Ahnai Slaughter, Dean Greer and Gary Hauk, plus an attempted coercion, threats, abduction and intimidation of a police detective," Snow reported.

"He's still entitled to confer with his lawyer." Feldman stood his ground. "With video off."

Savage nodded and stood, taking Snow's elbow. "OK. Fifteen minutes." On the other side of the two-way, he shut off the video and whispered to Snow, "Do you have your digital recorder?"

"Yes, I carry it with me. You know that."

"Well, with video off..." Savage shrugged, looking indifferent.

"All right. I'm going to my office to call the lab and have them fax me what they have."

"Was Mac bluffing when she said she kept a bloody hundred-dollar bill?"

"A hunch but the lab confirmed it. We kept Slaughter's clothes and a few other items germane to our homicide. But since Imhoff was the lead on Greer's and worked with Williamsport on Hauk's case—"

"As well as consulted with us on Slaughter," Savage added.

"I don't trust the accuracy or veracity of anything he touched, processed, said or reported. It's all tainted if he's guilty—even the evidence in the cave. Greer claims Ahnai's stuff was planted. I believe her. We need to lean hard on this guy; he's confident he'll beat the rap. And call your ex. Tell her Imhoff has been arrested and arraigned for the triple homicides—just the basics, though. Mac promised her a heads up, but she can do her own research and interview. The rest will get it in the police report a couple of hours later."

Snow glanced at his partner, frowning at Savage's hesitation.

"Or I can do that if you get the lab report," Snow offered, his brows wrinkled inquisitively at Reese's unwillingness to talk to his ex.

"No, I'll call Elena." He checked his watch to see if she'd be at the station or at her new digs—a condo near the TV station. Four-thirty. "She's on the air at five." He lifted his cell off his belt hook and pushed numbers, leaning back on the observation table while Snow hurried out.

Fifteen minutes later, they entered the interrogation room armed with the lab report. Savage entered first while Snow snapped the video on. Inside, he set the recorder on the scarred table and listed the attendees, case code and people present. Detectives Snow and Savage began questioning former Detective Carl Imhoff, son of Sunbury's retired mayor and a civics-minded mother, and first cousin to Sienna Imhoff Greer. Formerly, a star athlete who won a football scholarship to a Division III college, Imhoff married his college girlfriend. Father of a young son, he and his extended family owned the top of the mountain and the rights beneath West Enterprises' drill site. Financials revealed regular deposits into the holding company Stephens, LTD—twice as much annually as he earned as a Sunbury detective.

"Why did you have Dean Greer shadow Ahnai Slaughter? No need to deny it. We have the phone records." Snow waved the papers in the air. "Cell calls, from lasting from ten to twenty minutes for two months, to Greer's number; then they peter out."

"I didn't trust Slaughter," Imhoff admitted, after a nod from Feldman. "I suspected her of falsifying data, skewing water tests, snooping around—trying to shut down my well for personal or political beliefs. I asked him to talk her out of it, since she seemed partial to him and vice versa, as it turned out."

"Did you pay him for this assignment?" Snow asked, pitching softballs first.

"He's already on the payroll." Imhoff leaned back in the chair.

"But what do you attribute the $4,000 bump in his pay three months ago?" Savage asked.

Imhoff shrugged. "A merit raise. I don't know; ask Kraus."

"And what did you learn?" Savage said.

"The idiot fell for the Indian. He and my cousin separated, and then he moves in with Slaughter, canoeing up and down the river like teens in some idyllic movie—working and sleeping together." He laughed. "Here I thought the SRBC bitch was stabbing me in the back. Instead, she's toying with Dean and stealing my cousin's husband—he wasn't much of a prize. As it turned out, an unreliable employee as well. I knew when his reports and calls stopped all together."

"Then you had to pay Hauk to follow Greer and Slaughter."

"If it were your business, wouldn't you?" Imhoff returned.

"I'd verify first and leave surveillance to a pro," Snow said. "Did you also know that someone was filming Slaughter's findings? Your drill site had over a thousand environmental violations, mostly pollution, discharge of waste and violation of PA Clean Streams Law. And the feds were investigating? FBI claims Greer was one of theirs."

He shrugged again. "Hell, she kept Kraus awash in paper: forms, letters of violation and deadlines for correcting this or that problem. Notifications and calls from the SRBC for compliance dates. Threats to bring in the EPA, DCNR, etc. Otto didn't have time to supervise his employees. And I had a full-time job to do."

"Yeah," Snow nodded. "Stalking and killing the people you couldn't buy. Observing their habits, their schedules and movements. Guess it was pretty difficult for one person, but three police departments were working the cases, feeding you information. You even tapped the CPD phones."

"You have no proof of that," Imhoff said, sitting up higher in his chair.

"Careless of you to admit it to Mac. We debugged CPD, at your suggestion, and found Sunbury police-issued equipment."

"Phone taps do not prove homicide, gentleman." Feldman smiled.

"No, but DNA, fingerprints, murder weapons, and eye witnesses do."

"You mean Verna Gribble, that senile old busybody? You've got to do better than that." He smiled smugly while tapping his fingers on the table.

"Oh, she remembers your presence on her stoop vividly. Oh, didn't anyone inform you? We have her in WITPRO until your trial and arrested that goon you sent after her. He's in jail for attempted murder. She's a witness for the prosecution. She's the one who tipped us off."

"I deny any connection to that." He sat up in his chair, blinking, mental cogs wheeling.

"Denial doesn't change the facts. See the trouble with embracing risk is darkness shadows all your actions. You're stubborn, smart and savvy enough, but you made mistakes. I'm here to point them out." Snow opened the lab report and revealed close-up shots of Slaughter's clothes: doeskin leggings and boots, shirt, fancy shawl, and a black patent leather belt—an arrow pointing to the partial lifted. "A single Franklin with a bloody thumbprint, phone company's logs of your calls, a fingerprint found on an aluminum strip from Lightfoot's RV. Finally, fabric matching your SPD sweatshirt at the murder scene."

"But I was wearing gloves when I searched her RV," Imhoff said. "I was only looking for Dean's clothes or other belongings to confirm what Sienna had told me." He turned to the silent Feldman, who quietly gazed at the lab reports on the table before them. "It's my job—investigating."

"But apparently not when you returned the key to its place," Savage guessed.

"Oh, that's not all." Snow smiled grimly. "You entered Greer's cave with Slaughter's arrows and quiver in hand. You toss her cabin? Why, to frame your cousin? Lightfoot will testify that they're his wife's because he etched her initials inside the quiver and on each arrow. You didn't notice, detective? Are you framing your cousin?" Snow asked.

"And once we find the rifle that shot out my knee," Savage added, "We'll add another attempted homicide to your case."

"If I'd wanted to kill you, I would have," Imhoff snapped back and then realized he'd just made a grievous error.

"That was a trick!" Feldman interjected and jumped to his feet. "This interview is terminated. No questions that may incriminate my client. He's cooperating. Didn't I say that beforehand?" He turned to Carl. "Remain silent. Have you been arrested and arraigned?"

Imhoff nodded.

Savage and Snow nodded their heads, smiling. Though wounded, scarred and exhausted from their efforts in this case, chasing this criminal to ground, both seemed satisfied with the results.

"Court date set?"

Both detectives nodded affirmative.

"February fourth," Savage said after checking his daybook. "Judge J. Acorn. Where did you hide the rifle?"

"Don't answer that! That means no bail will be set. Sorry, son, you should have called me earlier."

"They wouldn't let me!" Imhoff exploded.

"CPD denied my client his one phone call for legal counsel?"

"We were in court, and so were you—Sienna's trial, I think."

Snow felt a smirk tickle his throat, so he grabbed his water bottle and glugged to cover it. The bottle flew as Imhoff lunged across the table and head-butted him, knocking Snow backward into the two-way. Sparks of white light blurred the detective's vision, pain hammered his left eye, the skin cracked, blood trickling from his split eyebrow down his cheek. Savage wrapped the prisoner in a chokehold until he sat down and Imhoff's head bobbed. Quickly, he lashed the chain over and under the chair, between the prisoner's legs and through the handcuffs, making it impossible for Imhoff to rise.

"You know I have to report this abuse of my client," Feldman said, gathering his things as he approached the door, shaking his head and lips thinned. "I'm surprised that you'd resort to such brutal tactics—"

"It's all on camera," Savage said. "Including the assault on Detective Snow." He slid across the table to aid his partner, but Snow, pressing a folded handkerchief against his wound, shook his head. "It's OK." But Reese peeled back the cotton square to see and nodded. The blood was congealing along the split left by an eyebrow ring Chris had worn in college. Still, Reese limped to the break room for ice.

Feldman slammed the door, grunting in disapproval, muttering to himself. "One right after another."

After his head cleared, Snow called Mac to explain he'd be late.

In the parking lot, he climbed behind the wheel, started the CPD's new Explorer with the separating grill while Savage pushed Imhoff—shackled, chained and hobbled—into the back seat, easing his head down to clear the hood. The prisoner jerked away, so Reese pinned an arm against his throat until he secured the seat belt. For good measure, he lashed Imhoff's head to the headrest with his tie. Then folded himself into the passenger's seat and nodded. They drove into the darkness, crossing the Army Heritage and Trindle Road intersection, following the road to the prison.

A furious Imhoff spewed invectives and threats at them. "You assholes are going to regret tricking me! I'm a cop, damn it! Is this how you treat a brother in arms? You can't make this feeble evidence stick, or you rigged it to frame me. I didn't leave any fingerprints anywhere; I always wear gloves, and I don't make mistakes!

"You don't have any idea who you're messing with! My family will ruin yours—will sue you for every last cent you have. And I'm going to kill that goddamn dog when I get out—be it when I'm acquitted or when I get out of here—in front of you wife. And then I'm going to fu—"

Snow jerked the SUV's wheel right; the vehicle shuddered, rocking to a stop. Fury propelled him from the vehicle. Rounding it, he yanked the rear door open, snapped the seat belt back and hauled Imhoff out.

"Go ahead. I'll sue your ass for police brutality, excessive force when I didn't resist—" Spittle flew from the prisoner's mouth, eyes sparked with fury. "You have no idea how hard I work to keep my wife satisfied. Think daycare makes money?" He snorted derisively. "Or a detective's salary? The woman lives to shop; what's a guy to do, huh? She's got my nuts in a vice, always on my case the minute I walk in—wanting this or that."

Snow unlocked the prisoner's chains, ready to defend a kick that never came. The desperate man looked at Snow, eyes pinpricks of dark blue, assessing, rubbing his chafed wrists. "Thanks, man. That's decent of you; giving me a sporting chance to leave, or will you shoot me in the back when I try to escape?"

Snow seemed to relent, stepped back and turned sideways. Spinning around, his fist—powered by the force of 220 solid pounds—collided with Imhoff's chin. A crack split the silence, and the man keeled backward into a drainage ditch. His eyes shifted, his brain assessing the impact. A primal moan keened through clenched teeth. Leaning aside to spit blood and a tooth out, the prisoner's injured arm was pinned beneath him, shooting pain up to his shoulder. He made no move to rise.

Chris yanked Imhoff to his feet, jarring the prisoner's mouth and arm. "Payback's hell! If you ever mention my wife or Shadow again, I'll kill you myself." He locked on the chains, hauled Imhoff over to the SUV and pushed him into the back seat—again anticipating a kick in the groin. Imhoff launched both feet, but Snow sidestepped, chopped the man's Adam's apple with his elbow. Imhoff wilted. Snow restrained him quickly, crammed his bloody hanky in the prisoner's mouth, slammed the door shut and climbed back into the vehicle. He looked at Savage, sitting quietly, as one acquainted with the night, his eyes on the falling darkness dropping over the Susquehanna Valley. No streetlights lit the two-lane road that led to the prison. "Did you have to take a piss, man? Took awhile."

Snow smiled grimly. "More or less." The detectives delivered their prisoner without further incident. Snow reclaimed his handkerchief. Imhoff remained strangely silent through the intake process but his and Detective Snow's injuries raised a number of eyebrows.

***

At the Snows' home in his reclining seat with the rattles across the bar, Ian's little feet thrashed to reach the noisemakers, but he found his legs could set them in motion, so he kicked contently. Mac smiled at his dexterity. Chris showered while Erin reheated his dinner. He shoveled two pieces of ham and broccoli quiche, a mound of red potatoes and cole slaw into his mouth without speaking while Erin sat opposite him with a cup of cocoa and two chocolate-covered graham crackers. After he'd eaten dinner, she asked no questions but applied peppermint liniment to his swollen eye and iced the injury.

"Are you in pain?" She reached across to take his hand; he clutched her around the waist and hugged her hard, his forehead against her midriff. Imhoff's irascible words echoed like a refrain. He tugged her onto his lap and kissed her intensely, biting her lower lip gently, holding on but holding back.

"Let me breathe, babe. Bad day at the office?" she asked him, sitting back to study his countenance. She peered at the cut over his brow and his purpling eye. "You've been fighting."

Again he nodded, not trusting his voice—Imhoff's threat still ringing in his ears, head throbbing, his knuckles raw from the impact with the guy's jaw. He kissed her again, tasting chocolate and smelling the scents of honey wafting from her hair, baby powder and amber lotion radiating from her skin. She rose slowly to get him a pain pill and water while he plucked Ian from his pumpkin seat, changed his diaper and put him in his cradle—somber blue eyes gazing at his father. Chris started the music, rocking the cradle until the baby's eyes fluttered, then closed.

When Erin came to bed shivering from the cold, she cuddled beside him, entwined her bare body with his; like roots, they drew sustenance from each other. He fisted her hair in his hand—auburn tendrils clutching like fingers—and clinched her around the waist, drawing her closer, his mouth finding hers soft and welcoming. She tasted minty. His hand slid down her back. Her essence engulfed him. Both working with a quiet intensity and abandon until, wordlessly, they joined.

35

At work the next morning, Snow anticipated the ribbing he'd receive from the guys. Savage, Fields and LT Stuart clustered around him in the break room, taking turns pouring and doctoring their coffee. Uniforms did the same, mumbling "morning" while filling their to-go mugs. Three new figures in tailored black leather, two carrying black helmets with visors nodded. One introduced himself while the second made another pot. The third tossed a couple of dollars into the kitty. "Gabe Summers," the tall one with a crooked nose indicated himself. "The coffee guru is Chase Rivers," whose hair, shades of black on brown like a ferret's pelt, was pulled back into a stubby tail. "The talkative one is Shannon Mahoney," who removed her headgear, revealing a prominent eyes, wide mouth and a fall of caramel hair. She turned and said, "Hello, boys," in an alto voice. "See you ran into something."

"Nah, a guy head-butted me. Did the Chief add a motorcycle unit?" Snow wondered aloud, patting for the pain pills Erin had slipped into his pocket as he left. Mahoney nodded and left with her team.

"You've been out for awhile or you'd have met them. They back-up the patrol cars, or if they get to a crime scene first, it's their case, except for homicide. They'll also pull drug duty. Eye looks nasty," Stuart observed. "You take up boxing lately?"

"It's better today. They look fresh out of the Academy."

"Nah, new hires but experienced; they hail from York." The LT stepped into Snow's private space to examine his bloodshot eye and bruising above and grey smudges beneath, with a butterfly bandage bisecting his left brow. "Did you see a doctor?"

Snow shook his head but stopped when pain split his injured brow and orbital rim. "Mac iced it." He stepped past the LT to refill his mug.

"Imhoff surprised, you, huh?" Fields didn't often get a change to razz his boss. "Gotta protect the head. A concussive impact can give you brain damage. There was a clip on the news about pro football and soccer play—"

Chief March loomed in the doorway in his usual crisp white dress shirt, black tie and slacks. "Snow, in my office!" He pivoted on his heel and returned to his office. Eyebrows raised but the others remained silent. When Chris entered, March barked, "Shut the damn door. Then sit your ass down."

His detective complied.

"Well, I'm listening. Let's hear your side of the story."

Snow shrugged. "Where shall I start, Chief?"

"My lead detective's brawling with a prisoner? Start at the beginning, smartass. Give me the highlights, and then go type a detailed report of the entire incident that will hold up in court."

Snow reviewed their interrogation, though the Chief had probably seen the video; he bet they all had. He skated over the ignominy of the head butt and went right to the moment Imhoff gave himself away with his insistence that he wore gloves, made no mistakes and admitted shooting Savage. "And that was his biggest mistake. I showed him the lab photos with some of the evidence. Feldman terminated the interview, and Savage and I escorted the prisoner to CCP."

"With a stop along the way?" March asked.

"You've already heard from Feldman?" Snow was surprised that the old man was in his office at eight a.m.

"No. I got mug shots from the prison infirmary, documenting your prisoner's jaw and missing tooth. He claimed police brutality, and his lawyer intends to file charges against you and sue our asses as well. Got anything to say about that?"

Snow leveled his eyes at March. "Yes, sir, the man assaulted me, threatened my wife and her K-9 officer—very graphically described how he was going to kill them —"

"And you couldn't restrain yourself? Running three homicide cases at different crime scenes, hiding a senior citizen in WITPRO, adjusting to a new baby isn't enough? How does this brawl look to the men you supervise? You're supposed to be a role model, set the tone for the entire Homicide Squad. I won't even mention calling Mac into work while she's on leave, putting her in the direct line of fire. The union will have a picnic with that one!"

"I needed—"

"Did I tell you to speak? I've heard quite enough. I can't believe it. This story will be plastered over the front pages of local newspapers because somehow Elena Michaels and God knows who else has already interviewed the prisoner! You'll be lucky if you don't lose your badge over this, Snow."

"The mitigating circumstances are all on the video!"

"Not *all*. You know better than to let a prisoner, especially a former cop who's shackled, goad you into retaliation. Hand in your weapon and badge. You're on paid administrative leave until IAD completes its investigation. You're damn lucky there are no witnesses. Dismissed."

Snow packed up his possessions and his files on his open cases, while mumbling to himself about the limits of the law, the need to pound the shit out of the bastard, withholding the fact of freeing the prisoner temporarily. He stopped by Savage's desk, cardboard box in his hands. "I'm on leave until IAD investigates Imhoff's charge and lawsuits."

"You expected a promotion?" Savage raised one eyebrow, looked up and lowered his voice. His dark eyes simmered with anger, but Chris refused to acknowledge crossing the line.

"You heard what Imhoff said," Chris huffed angrily. "I'll defend mine."

"I got your back—and Mac's and Ian's too. Don't try to be a hero."

"And let my wife and Shadow be threatened?" Snow said. "NFW."

"Don't push your luck. Now go home," Savage mumbled.

The intern, holding her hair back out of the way, had the copier going full speed, coughing out collated stacks of paper. He handed the coed a rubber band for her hair and said so long to Sonja, who was at her desk peering intently at her computer.

"What happened?" Pointing to her eye, her eyebrows drew together in concern. With her turquoise sweater sleeves pushed up, she was scanning court documents and taking notes. Before Snow could form an answer, Feldman pushed through the front door and served him with a subpoena and slapped a lawsuit on top, wheeled around and stalked out.

"That was fast." He looked at the papers in his hand. "The man must be late for court. His client head butted me in interrogation. I retaliated when he threatened Mac and Shadow. I'm on leave until further notice."

"Did you do that on purpose to have more face time with the wife and baby? You old fox! But I won't tell!" She held three fingers up as her eyes danced. "Scout's honor."

The detective looked querulous at first, and then a slow, easy smile reached his eyes. "My God, you're right!" and hustled out the door with his load lightened. "Spending more time with Erin and Ian—what luck! Anyway, I can work the case at home through Savage." He tossed the box into the Explorer's passenger seat, walked around the rear and nearly collided with Lightfoot, who grasped Chris's shoulders—holding him at arm's length to steady him and studied his eye, then dropped his hands.

"I was just coming to see you," admitted Lightfoot.

"And I'm just going home. Follow me. Erin will be delighted to see you. Or, if it's private, we can stop for breakfast, if you like."

"All right. Let's eat first. If you'd call Erin and tell her I'd like to see her and the baby, give her a chance to..." He opened his palms and shrugged. "...make herself presentable—women don't like drop-ins."

"Oh, sure. I'll meet you at the Carlisle Diner—great pancakes. You know where it is? Last booth against the windows—if it's available."

"I do." Lightfoot climbed into his truck to follow the Explorer. At the diner, a waitress brought coffee and took their orders. After she left, Jason told Chris he'd been served a subpoena. "I don't want to testify against Sienna because we were friends. Her husband was killed, so it seems disrespectful, like rubbing misfortune in her face." He held up both hands—palms out. "I know I have to, but I'm not going to be very helpful to your case."

Chris stirred the cream and sugar into the strong brew. "Don't worry. Just answer the ADA's questions. Tell what happened. I assume the prosecution wants to know about our search for Greer on Raccoon Mountain." He pulled out his cell; speed dialed Erin and explained he had Lightfoot with him. "We'll be coming by the house in about half an hour." He winced when she squealed her delight into his ear. "Bye, babe." He snapped the cell shut. "For some reason, you've made quite an impression on her," Chris said.

"I acknowledge who she is—her mother's daughter and my stepdaughter. Kin, remember? It's important." The hotcake stacks and bacon came out of the kitchen quickly; several flavors of syrup sat in a wire caddy on the table. Both reached for the maple; Snow handed it to Jason. They tucked into their breakfasts, trading questions and answers about court throughout the meal.

At the bungalow, Erin greeted them at the door, passing Ian off to his father to hug her stepfather and wish him good day. She pulled them both into the kitchen, where they drank more coffee and ate a slice of banana bread. Jason took Ian in his arms, touching his forehead, ears, and hands. He studied the infant's auburn hair and his vibrant blue eyes. Ian stared at Lightfoot solemnly, concentrating, his focus solely on the man holding him.

"I brought you something, young man. You've grown, and you look a little like both parents, but another ancestor's present, too, in those eyes. You have the fox's pelt but sky eyes." Then he looked up at each parent and smiled. "They're so pleasant at this age."

"He's fussy at times, but he's generally pretty good once his tummy is full and his bottom's dry, and he's sleeping most of the night." Erin smiled. "How's life going for you? Back to work and a normal routine?"

"Yes and no." He told her about the subpoena, about his reluctance to testify. "But your husband—"

"Call me Chris, Jason."

"Chris coached me on proper techniques." He handed Ian to his father. "Excuse me, please." Long legs carried him out where he pulled out Ian's gifts and strode back inside before the security alarm sounded. "Though it will be a while before he can use these." In one hand, he held a toddler-sized handmade bow, quiver and arrows with suction cups and a small bulls-eye target on a stand. In the other, he held a tom-tom. "So I brought the drum, too, so he can play it." He put the little drum between Ian's knees, took each of his hands and showed the baby how to beat the taut skin stretched across the top and bottom. When Jason withdrew his hands, Ian smacked at the drum repeatedly, often missing, but smiled at the sound.

"See?" Jason said. "A natural."

"Thank you, Stepfather," Erin said.

"Call me Jason, Erin."

"I thank you too. It's very kind to keep us in mind when you have so much on your plate," Chris said.

"You're welcome. Family first." Jason's lips tipped into a rare smile. His straight nose, hatchet cheeks, light copper skin and bone structure carried his heritage—a rugged man who wore his life, career and history for all to see. And his green eyes carried another ancestor, too. "Now, once I've answered their questions, will I have to return to court?"

"I doubt it. I assume that Feldman will call different witnesses or consider you hostile if you're not cooperative."

Erin added, "But he may also question you to try to undermine your authority or testimony. For many lawyers, court is a test of cunning, control and parroting the rules of law rather than honoring justice. Chris tells me to just answer the question and don't volunteer information. That's good advice 'cause I tend to add unwelcome comments."

"I will remember. Now, I must report to the courtroom at eleven. Thanks for the coffee, bread and your company. Please don't get up; I can find the door." He chuckled as he walked out, but Chris followed to rearm the security. Erin laid Ian on his play mat with the little drum. When Chris returned to the table, he locked his arms around her in a warm embrace. "I need to tell you what happened. I've been placed on leave pending IAD's investigation." He summarized the events from the night before and the morning's work, omitting why he beat the man, saying only that he resisted arrest. "I'll probably receive a reprimand, but the tape will show I had good reason to pop him."

"Poor baby. Your eye!" She turned in his arms, planted a hand on either side of his cheeks, and gently eased his lips to meet hers. She moved against him, unbuttoning and pushing his shirt off his shoulders. He smelled of sandalwood, his brassy light brown hair long enough again to tug, his brown eyes softening, watching her. He lifted her shirt over her head, grabbed her up, dropped to his knees and dumped her gently on her back in front of the fire. For a time, their light eclipsed the world outside with its worrisome ways, criminals and police courting doubt and darkness, while Ian burbled on his blanket, arms waving and legs kicking at plastic rings, rattles and keys. The drum rolled out of reach.

As if on cue, Ian started fussing, flailing his arms and kicking his legs—frustrated, angry or hungry. Chris scooped him up to change him and brought him back to the living room for Erin to nurse. He heard the dog scratching at the gate, so he pulled on sweats to let her out. When they returned, he scooped food and poured fresh water in her pans. "Good dog. You contained and detained the perp. I'll never complain about anything else you do. Ever." He hugged her and combed his fingers across her back, which arched under his hand. "I'll even leave the gate open if you behave."

He sighed into the recliner and slowly related the day's events. "So I'm off for a couple weeks or until the lawyers work out the logistics of who is suing whom for what. I expect the judge will throw Imhoff's charges out when she sees the head-butt in the video. Savage finally restrained the bastard. But I have to write the incident report about nailing him for retaliation. Nothing's worse than a dirty cop."

"Think the evidence is enough to send him away? What, three first-degree murders? Will the ADA seek the death penalty?"

"I really don't know, but our evidence is solid. A confession would help, but that won't be forthcoming. Feldman won't even put him on the stand. It could be a long trial, though, with all the elements and people in play, three different sites and two different MOs. The DA may try this one because the media has aired interviews with Greer's assault on me. Still, she may be involved in the others. Michaels interviewed Imhoff; I think she's working a different angle than he expected." He winced as pain zipped across brow. "And if our brawl gets out..."

"Elena's headline read 'When Cops Cross the Line!'"
Erin nodded, as she burped and switched Ian to the other
side. "Who wrote the police report on Imhoff's arrest?"

"Just the facts, ma'am," Snow quipped like Joe Friday.

"Savage," Erin guessed. Chris nodded. "So he's
adjusting to the desk duty, then?"

"Well, he also rides with me, mainly for company,
because he can't carry or work the field. I'd say he's
adjusting, not well, but he does a thorough job without
complaint. He said he has our backs."

"So he was with you last night when you took Imhoff
to CCP."

"Hmm. Swept our house for bugs lately?" Chris said;
Erin looked startled, then remembered the killer's
admission and ominous threat at HQ. Her eyes roved to
the lamps, the landline and overhead lights as she shook
her head and asked no further questions while her
husband searched, peeling off clothes as he made for the
bedroom. Minutes passed slowly, but when water
hummed in the shower, Erin sighed.

She spent the afternoon doing laundry and fixing
dinner while Chris spent several hours upstairs on his
report. Since the pocket door was open, she heard one-
sided conversations as he fielded a number of calls from
ADA Lawson, Sonja, LT Stuart, and Feldman. The
landline rang incessantly, so Erin leaped to grab it,
turning the sound down.

"Snows. McCoy speaking."

"Well, what do my wondering ears hear but the
honeyed tones of a dulcimer in tune—"

"Agent Howard, how are you and where have you
been? I'd have thought you'd be front and center on this
one, especially since the search for Sienna Greer. FBI
jackets climbing up Raccoon Mountain make quite the
photo op," she said sweetly.

"You know we let the locals handle the cases on their
turfs."

"To a point, but this call tells me you are about to make an appearance and an announcement; let me guess: you plan to take our prisoner to federal court."

"You are just too intuitive, Detective. I do wish you'd joined... Well, water under London Bridge. May I please speak with Detective Snow?"

"Of course, if you'll hold." Erin turned, slamming into her husband's chest. "Telephone, dear." She gave him the handset and returned to the kitchen, chuckling. All three knew very well Pennsylvania had the death penalty; District of Columbia did not. After two months of slogging through a pastiche of bits and pieces, searching the Carlisle Industrial School Grounds, the Indian Steps cabin, Slaughter's RV, the West Enterprise drill site, Dean Greer and Gary Hauk's RV, with Chris and Jason enduring Raccoon Mountain, and finally the confrontation with Imhoff and the collar, it all seemed so pointless if Howard swooped in and spirited Imhoff away. Not to mention attending The Native American Gettysburg Seminar, which she enjoyed immensely despite the tension.

She shrugged. "I guess as long as killers are put away, the outcome is validated by the work," she told her son while she bathed him in his own wee blue, inclined tub. She lathered him up, especially the folds in his neck and under his arms that collected dirt and lint, Ian kicking and splashing all the while. She laid the hoodie towel on the bathroom rug and wrapped him up, patted him dry and doused baby powder in those crevices. Taped him into a double diaper. "Into pj's you go, leaky baby doll." Erin fluffed his hair—several shades lighter than her own —with her fingers. Gathering him up in her arms, still on her knees, she waited a beat, wondering if she could lift, stand and hold him all at once.

"Here." Chris reached over her and hefted his son into his arms, shifted him left and offered his right to Erin to help her up. She thought he might tease her for being out of shape, but he smiled beatifically as though she'd done something miraculous. She smiled too in response, warming at the amber light in his eyes, the aura around his hair from the light.

Depositing Ian in his cradle, Chris settled his wife on the bed in front of him, lifted off her nightgown and massaged her shoulders until the tension eased, and then pulled her backward and continued rubbing until her body responded. She turned to face him and finished what he'd started, taking her time, languishing in sensual delight. Avoiding his bruised, sore eye, kissing gently at first, she raised the ante—lightly nipping then nibbling at his solid body, the muscles tautly braided over a strong frame. "Since no one has to rise early..."

"Sorry, babe; you walked into that one." He grabbed her hips and slipped into his one true home, a union that forged an unbreakable bond. "I'm glad I waited to marry you; you're truly marvelous," Chris whispered in her ear when she'd collapsed onto him, her hair tickling his face. He shifted her curls to one side. Erin tucked her face into his neck, inhaling sandalwood and peppermint.

"Do you want something for your eye?" she asked.

"Not if it means your getting up; let's just rest a bit and enjoy the moment." Ten, then fifteen minutes passed. Erin scooted to one side, lifted the covers over them and fell asleep, too.

36

Powdery snowflakes floated gently toward Earth, melting as they touched. Chris jogged to the end of the drive to get the paper, opened it on the way back to the bungalow. A full-banner headline screamed across the top: "Suicide by Cop in FBI Stand-off at the CCP!" by Elena Michaels and Martin James.

The article described how Imhoff had walked out of the prison the night before escorted by FBI agents—media cameras shooting the perp walk. Without warning, Imhoff had distracted his handlers by tripping, then a pistol appeared in his hand; he popped the g-men on either side and then turned the gun out, spraying bullets in an arc. Several people hit the ground, either injured or ducking for safety. He had no chance to run, as he was shackled in chains, the standard protocol:

> Before a full-scale riot ensued, Special Agent FBI Howard mimed a "Shoot to kill" order before former Sunbury Detective Carl Imhoff could further harm innocent civilians, prison personnel or other police.
>
> The prisoner died from a single gunshot wound to the head.
>
> "A clear case of suicide by cop," observed a bystander who wished to remain anonymous.
>
> Accused of a triple homicide in the deaths of SRBC Officer Ahnai Slaughter in Carlisle; West Enterprise's Field Tech Dean Greer in Winfield, and Safety Officer Gary Hauk at the Marcellus Shale drill site near Williamsport, Imhoff was arrested, arraigned and incarcerated in CCP.

Homicide Detectives coordinated their search with the FBI and Imhoff had been consulting with CPD until he became a person of interest in the cases.

CPD's Detective Christopher Snow and Ranger Jason Lightfoot apprehended fugitive, Sienna Greer, who's now on trial for attempted vehicular manslaughter of Snow.

Greer and Imhoff's family own the land, mineral and gas rights under West Enterprise's well. In a prior interview, Imhoff claimed, "I have the right to protect my property and family from whistleblowers, blackmailers and leeches who prey on those trying to earn a decent living."

Detective Snow, who also received injuries during a testy interrogation with the prisoner, had no comment; he and wife Detective McCoy are currently on family leave.

Imhoff's widow could not be reached for comment, though Agent Lionel Howard said he personally informed her of her husband's death at the CCP while his men were collecting possible evidence at Imhoff's Sunbury home and office but refused to elaborate.

At CPD, Detective Reese Savage indicated that the police had enough evidence to convict the deceased of the triple homicides.

His trial was slated for early February. While Imhoff's motive seems murky, his actions suggest he chose death over a protracted trial and a likely prison term. His final words in the exclusive interview at the CCP: "I will not go to prison."

Chris tossed the newspaper aside as he crossed the threshold. He stacked the kindling, slowly adding sticks and the one log in the basket to the fire. On the way to the garage, he let Shadow out. He could hear Ian stirring, but kept his eye on the dog, who skittered back in to escape the January freeze. Loading his arms with dry logs, Chris laid several on the fire and watched as they caught. By the time he closed the grate and stood up, Erin was padding to the rocker to feed Ian. These domestic chores, the necessity of food and shelter, their daily routine settled him. He smiled at his wife and kissed his son's forehead, and then he ambled into the kitchen to see what he could stir up for supper. For once, the time was right.

Once the Benedict/Lyons and Greer's trials concluded, the couple could finally breathe easily for a few weeks. Uncertain of the first because the defense intended to use the state's version of the Castle Doctrine but confident of the second verdict, he pulled ingredients from the fridge for a shrimp stir fry, then rummaged through the cabinets for the spices and condiments.

BIBLIOGRAPHY

500 Nations. Dir. Jack Leustig. Warnervideo.com. 1995.

Allen, Paula Gunn. *The Sacred Hoop: Recovering the Feminine in American Indian Tradition.* Boston: the Beacon Press, 1992.

Brosius, Shirley G. "Museum Offers a Glimpse into Cherokee Past." *The Patriot News.* O6 August 2000.

Cherokee. Cherokee Indian Reservation. Western North Carolina. www.cherokee-n.c.com

Deloria, Vine. *Custer Died for Your Sins: an Indian Manifesto.* University of Oklahoma Press. 1988.

Erdoes, Richard and Alfonso Ortiz, ed. *American Indian Myths and Legends.* New York and Canada: Pantheon Books (Random House, Inc.) 1984.

Gasland. Dir. Josh Fox. DVD HBO Documentary Films, 2013.

Landis, Barbara. "The Carlisle Indian Industrial School History." The Cumberland County Historical Society. 1996.

Maxwell, James A., ed., et.al. *America's Fascinating Indian Heritage: the First Americans: Their Customs, Art, History, and How They Lived.* Reader's Digest, 1995.

"Police Dogs, Handlers Learn Detection Techniques." *PN.* 29 March 2012.

Susquehanna River Basin Commission (SRBC) Information Sheet. "Natural Gas Well Development in the Susquehanna River Basin. 1/2013. www.srbc.net

Weatherford, Jack. *Native Roots: How the Indians Enriched America.* NY: Fawcett Columbine, 1991.

ACKNOWLEDGMENTS

Thanks to all family members and friends who encourage my writing. In addition, Sunbury publishers provided a wealth of information and assistance with online seminars, advice, tips and support. Feedback from consultants, readers and editors is always welcome. Thanks also to Amanda's valuable corrections, clarifications, suggestions and questions to ensure accuracy. The Internet is also a boon with its encyclopedic knowledge at writers' fingertips for research, interviews, blogs and social media. Other valuable resources I found at The Bookery, the Bosler Library's 'gently-used' bookstore. So kudos to the folks there for a good time, inexpensive sources and eagerness to share books with readers! Katherine Ramsland's *The Criminal Mind,* Sean Mactire's *Malicious Intent* and Michael Kurland's *How to Solve a Murder* offer important information, facts, history and insights. Again, I thank the police consultants who gave freely of their time and lent their expertise whenever I asked questions.

I owe a debt of gratitude for the talented writers in this genre whose books I read (David Baldacci, Brunonia Barry, Agatha Christie, Jeffery Deaver, Sir Arthur Conan Doyle, Julia Spencer-Fleming, Ariana Franklin, Tammy Hoag, Ridley Pearson, Louise Penny, E.A. Poe, Deanna Raybourn, Karin Slaughter, Charles Todd, Jacqueline Winspear, et. al.) before attempting the Carlisle Criminal Cases series. David Baldacci, the main speaker at 2012 Celebrate the Book Symposium in Carlisle, PA urged writers to follow their dreams. So I queried agents and publishers.

My college rhetoric and lit Professors Ruth and Lewis Barnes kept me writing, and my profession required continual practice, editing, revising and coaching students. My father encouraged me to realize my dreams.

Finally, I thank all you readers for following these adventures.

Any errors are mine alone, though I admit taking liberties with time and geography to accommodate my narrative but tried diligently to keep facts in all novels marshaled in order to lend them verisimilitude.

In my first mystery, *Dying for Vengeance,* Carlisle Homicide Detectives Christopher Snow and rookie Erin McCoy face a murder scene with little to investigate except a dead body. But they track down the sparse clues, slowly piecing the conundrum together, discovering an undeniable attraction to each other as the body count mounts and the chase quickens. The trail spiders across four states and numerable suspects before law enforcers from three states and the FBI close in.

Courting Doubt and Darkness finds Detectives Christopher Snow and Erin McCoy assigned to another complex case, tracking a pernicious, ruthless killer who thinks he is beyond the law's reach. The discovery of a body in the Letort Spring initiates a manhunt involving CPD's entire Homicide squad. Again, sparse clues and closing other cases stymie the team at first while Snow and McCoy's relationship is tested as they encounter difficult and dangerous challenges.

In the third, *Darkness at First Light,* our intrepid detectives traverse a graveyard for clues for a killer who left a trussed body on the cannon at the base of Molly Pitcher's (Mary Ludwig Hayes McCauley) monument. The killer's act initially points to a connection to Revolutionary War re-enactors, but as the detectives untangle a web of deception, other culprits appear. Please read on to learn of Snow and McCoy's continuing exploits.

DARKNESS AT DAWN

A Christopher Snow and Erin McCoy
Carlisle Crimes Case

Death is absolute darkness—solid and devoid of sense or
sensation, a psyche or any other living trait, a shock
nearly beyond human comprehension—and certainly far
from the realm of daily conversation—unless it's
somebody else's. But the abandoned shell tells much, as
Dr. Haili Chen, Cumberland County coroner and Fire
Marshal Lane Rusk hovered, waiting for a scrim of light to
illume the stark scene before them. Rusk's assistant,
Russell Garrett, lumbered among crowded markers
carrying a tripod and camera, kicking clumps of dirty
snow in his path.

Approaching sirens howled in the distance.

A female corpse dressed in eighteenth-century garb,
skirt and legs partially burnt from the waist down, was
lashed to the cannon in front of Molly Pitcher's
monument in the cemetery surrounded by a stone wall at
the corner of South Bedford and East South Streets. A
dove grey ribbon lifted the total darkness, revealing a
disturbing scene.

The previous night's downpour had swept the victim's
cap to the ground, freeing limp, mouse-brown curls that
hugged the cannon. Eyes—wide pools matching the grey
sky, gazed into the void, her face a mask of surprise and
terror. Fine crow's feet, a mole beside her left eyebrow
and a wide mouth pulled in a grimace bore witness to
death's brutality. A stout, stumpy handle protruded from
her chest. Her legs and wrists were tied together with
hemp beneath the cannon.

Rusk circled the corpse, examining the scene with a perplexed frown, heavy eyebrows drawn; his mustache quivered as he nosed the charred shreds of burned skirt and flesh. He scraped samples of the leg and cut a scrap of skirt to test. The woman had a decent build, as the wet, coarse homespun clung to her body; she wore no underwear.

"Where's Snow?" he inquired of Dr. Chen, to break the dreadful silence where winter still ruled, despite the calendar marking March. Fog hovered eerily, a silent white cloak. Chills shimmied through Rusk's open coat; he shivered and zipped it.

"On his way." She consulted her watch, set her leather bag on a nearby stone marker, with murmured apologies to the deceased, unsnapped it and extracted her thermometer from the inside flap where each sterile instrument was tucked into its own pocket.

"TOD?" He tried again, assuming she'd estimate.

"Hard to say without a temperature reading."

"Rain and sleet a factor," he commented as he caught the tripod that Garret had carelessly set on crumbling concrete. "Steady. Take your time," he directed. He'd hired the boy fresh out of college a few months ago when a semi shot across the median and totaled CPD Detective Snow's Jeep Wrangler, a horrific scene that had stopped traffic Thanksgiving night for hours while police and firemen squelched the fire. Rusk had read about the incredulous couple's leap for their lives and their son's birth on the slopes of I 81 in the paper the next day.

"The fire's a problem," the coroner said.

"Ah, you can smell the accelerant." Gasoline.

"Could have been a lighting strike otherwise had he refrained."

"He?" He disagreed but kept his opinions to himself. He knelt to tip a soil sample into a sterile container, capped and labeled it.

"Figure of speech." Chen waved his pronoun query aside.

Snow tromped up to the trio, slipped on a patch of ice but righted himself by grabbing the monument's pedestal. He nodded at Dr. Chen but stopped, staring openmouthed at Rusk's hair. "Bad hair day?" The hairs cresting each wave on the man's head had a slight orange cast.

"Tried highlighting with hydrogen peroxide while on vacation."

"They have kits for that in drug stores," Snow quipped.

"Are we waiting for Christmas?" Dr. Chen stomped her boots to keep the circulation flowing. Prongs of cold stabbed through them despite wool leggings under her traditional black slacks.

"Mac's got the camera," he said absently as he perused the body; it looked like a grotesque Halloween display. "An Amber Alert on the morning news. They flashed the girl's photo, so we'll be getting calls. Though we currently have no details."

"She's back on the job?" Dr. Chen voiced her surprise.

"Today." He stepped closer to examine the murder weapon.

As if summoned from the fog, a sleep-deprived, top-heavy Mac appeared, Shadow at her heel, nodded without speaking and pointed and clicked her Powershot. She rose over the corpse, snapped several shots from various angles, zooming for close-ups of the embedded weapon with blood congealed at its base. The air stung with a sharp rusty tang. Mac stepped back for full-length body shots, laying a ruler by the drowned cap and blue ribbon. Charred clogs lay beneath the cannon, one tipped sideways. She covered the immediate vicinity quickly, sensing the coroner's impatience humming just beneath the surface. Turning and photographing the surrounding graves, her eyes simultaneously swept the area for physical evidence. Finally, she caught images of Molly Pitcher's, or Mary Ludwig Hays McCauley's, towering monument. A statue and plaques summarized her valor at the Battle of Monmouth.

Shadow nosed the frozen ground, sniffed the corpse, sneezing at the acrid odor, rounded the cannon, and McCauley's pedestal—scouting. The K-9 officer strayed from Mac, her nose leading her from grave to grave, whether from curiosity or seeking, she alone knew.

Ignoring the dog, Dr. Chen waited for Snow's nod, gloved up and then took the body's temp, palpitated the hair for wounds, found a bump over the left ear and worked down the body, examining the exposed face, throat, and torso closely, then the extremities, moving her hands along the body but avoiding the burned legs until Rusk and Garret had completed their prelims and captured the scene. "We'll wait until we get her into the lab for the postmortem, but with active rigor, I'd say this homicide occurred within the last twelve to fifteen hours. And no, detectives, I cannot pin it down accurately until I get her on the table and obtain a liver temp." She waved at Hemmer—idling the meat wagon—to collect the body and picked her way gingerly across the slippery surfaces.

"Need any more time?" she asked Snow, who shook his head.

"Strange," Snow commented, scratching his weak arm from habit. The cast had been removed, so it felt exposed —even covered by his shirt and parka. His eyes raked the macabre scene again. "Looks almost like a prank, like the kids toppling cemetery stones except..."

Mac paused beside him, their elbows touching, adding, "It's not Halloween. Looks like a sacrifice, but the worn handle's rounded and stubby—hard to believe it penetrated the lungs or heart."

"Doesn't mean the knife is short. How can you tell?" asked Rusk, his hazel eyes settling on Mac's curly auburn hair twisted back and clamped hastily at the nape of her neck; stragglers had snaked free, framing her face. He smoothed his mustache with his thumb and forefinger, and then dropped his hand when he realized the nervous gesture.

"Well, I'm not a doctor, but the handle doesn't look like any knife, ice pick, or screwdriver that I've ever seen," she remarked. "Or anything I'm familiar with. It looks antique, blackened by age and cook fires, so I'm assuming it's a re-enactor's tool or utensil." She measured the handle. "Four inches."

"No point in speculating, though. Let's get your photos printed and get to HQ to set up a board and mount them. Any ID? Purse lying around?" He scanned the vicinity but saw nothing else. "On second thought, let's widen the perimeter, search for evidence. The killer may have dropped something in his haste to leave." He opened his cell, called Carlisle Police Headquarters and requested that Detectives Zachary Fields and Reese Savage join them. "And Sonja, please check the missing persons database or any news about a missing woman dressed as Molly Pitcher, likely re-enactors. See if there are any staged in the vicinity."

"Didn't realize there were Revolutionary War re-enactors," Rusk boxed up his shiny red tool kit, which matched his candy-apple truck, having already collected what he needed. He stood slowly, joints cracking. He wore jeans, a heavy tweed sweater under a saddle leather jacket. He dusted snow and grit from his pant legs.

"Yeah, there are. Someone set her on fire to destroy evidence and perhaps her identity, but the rain put it out," Mac surmised. "Covering it up suggests some degree of guilt, so the killer's not going to turn himself in, call the media or send us missives." Their breath puffed out in foggy moons as they spoke. In the dim sepia half-light, oblique sunlight filtered fitfully through gunmetal clouds. "They were sloppy, unprofessional: the double knots were hurriedly tied and they left evidence."

"Mac, check your phone for any Revolutionary War encampments around here. I think Pennsylvania's Fifth Regiment is headquartered in Bucks County, but I haven't heard of any events scheduled here. When exactly was the Battle of Monmouth?"

She glanced at her husband with unabashed admiration. "You remember the battle that Mary Hays manned her husband's cannon when he fell, injured? I'm impressed."

"Dad's an American History Prof, remember? Besides, she's a folk hero; everyone's heard of Molly Pitcher."

"Hmm. Then the killer's sending us a message," Mac mused while searching her iPhone. Scanning the text, she read, "Born and reared in Philly. Mary Ludwig moved to Carlisle in her twenties to work for a Dr. and Mrs. Irvine. Met Hayes here.' To answer your question, the battle occurred on June 28, 1778 in Freehold, New Jersey. Question is, did our victim live here? I doubt it. And we're assuming she portrayed Molly Pitcher, but we don't know that. Her garb could also be circa Civil War; re-enactors sometimes set up camp in Gettysburg early to train new members, rehearse—that sort of thing. Or gather for meetings, take minutes—you know, like any other organization. So we need to check motels, too."

"Four months early?" Snow sounded dubious. His eyes scanned for Shadow then spied her at the Baker marker, snuffling into the dead grass and pawing the snow.

"OK. Scotch that." She called Dr. Chen's office, left a voicemail message requesting a call if she found any sutlers' labels in the victim's clothing. "Wow! The clothes are really expensive: a hundred dollars for a gathered skirt like she's wearing, seventy-five for a scarf and fifty for the cap! She probably made hers herself. And she should also be wearing a wool cape."

"There you go, assuming a frugality—that she and her persona share the same socioeconomic group when in fact, our victim may have been comfortably middle class." Frigid air passed through his Dockers, so he shifted his weight back and forth, then dodged behind a headstone. "Did you get the shots of this blood trickle? She bled out here." He kneeled as he spoke to peruse the pattern closely, so he missed her jaundiced glance. Not even a rookie would overlook a blood drop pattern.

"Yet her hands were chafed. Maybe she shared her husband's hobby. I can't imagine living without amenities —like running water, a warm house with modern appliances. I've seen the Gettysburg encampments and reenactments. In July the woolens are hot, the campfires smoky, the tents airless." She lowered the camera and pocketed her iPhone and resumed searching, more to return circulation to her extremities than anything else. Inside leather gloves, her numb fingers refused to function, so she laid the camera on a nearby headstone and made a mental note to browse sutlers' sites online in more detail and visit Gettysburg's later. Stepping over gravesites, she checked to see what Shadow was investigating: a wadded frozen cloth—likely a handkerchief. "Good dog." Mac rewarded her, dropping the frozen ball into a paper bag.

The graves were jammed together closely without an apparent pattern—some too worn to read the inscriptions. She noted the names and dates, a number cotemporaneous with Mary Ludwig Hays McCauley. While they combed over the markers and monuments, a car door slammed nearby. Fields and Savage approached, each carrying two cardboard cups of steaming coffee. That brought Mac's eyes up. "Bless you! You brought us coffee!" She nodded her thanks at both her colleagues. Zach had a watch cap pulled over his sandy crew; Savage was hatless, his ears like ripe plums. Both wore their CPD issued parkas.

Zach handed her a cup. "Not just ordinary coffee for our prodigal couple—a mocha cappuccino for you." He smiled and bowed slightly as he handed hers over. "It's really hot, so don't burn—"

"And a caramel for you." Savage handed Snow his other cup.

"Thanks, guys—that's thoughtful." Snow sipped gingerly to test the temperature and then drank the hearty caloric latte. He pulled earmuffs from his pocket and handed them to Reese. "Frost bites ears and yours look sore. We need to cover every inch of this cemetery, and then the streets in the neighborhood. Knock on doors, ask if anyone saw a woman dressed in colonial garb—or anyone, male or female—in this vicinity last afternoon or evening between five and ten. We have no ID on our victim."

The warm brew flooded her mouth and throat with welcome heat, spreading through her stomach—the caffeine jolting her awake, the whipped cream tempering the heat. She was still nursing Ian, but Chris's mother, Erica, had the baby today and would use milk Mac had pumped the night before with more in the freezer should she be delayed. She'd learned that lesson when the Marcellus Shale killer tried to kidnap her from HQ. At home the baby had fussed, and a harried mother-in-law handed him over when she and Chris finally arrived home. Shuddering from the memory, she turned away to complete the grid. An hour later, she'd unearthed three old-fashioned hairpins, a sodden matchbook from The Rustic Tavern and a torn piece of black wool flannel caught on the wrought-iron gate. Chris was bagging the bowl of a corncob pipe as she approached with her evidence bags. Savage's boots clopped down the outside perimeter of the cemetery, shaking his head when he reached the wrought-iron gate—no witnesses.

"No one recalled any shouts or loud noises. One old guy asked who'd be out in last night's downpour?" He handed Mac a baggie containing the stump of a beeswax candle through the gate's bars. "Where's the boss?" he asked. His eyes dark as raisins, eyelids squinted to keep out the wind, which had picked up, while water swirling down the street pooled where wet leaves clogged the drain. He lit a cigarette and leaned against the wall.

"Did you know each cigarette you smoke takes seven minutes off your life? You do the math." Mac ignored his question but couldn't resist asking her own, since Savage had supposedly quit when he had a heart attack last summer.

"Yeah, so I'll miss the shitty years."

"What an attitude," Snow appeared around the corner shaking his head at his former partner. "Let's head back to HQ, analyze what we have. Where's Fields?"

"The boy scout?" Savage shrugged. "Probably helping the senior citizens—"

Fields checked the empty road, and then ran across to join the others. "I've got something! A couple dressed in Colonial costume grabbed a sub at the South Mountain Deli across the street." He nodded toward the tiny concrete-block building and raised an oil lantern in his gloved hand. "The owner said he thought they were married the way they talked to each other—arguing about their kids. They left this on the floor in front of the counter, so he didn't find it until he closed but remembered they fumbled around for enough change to pay for the sandwich and two drinks. It has prints! She called him Sam."

"Good work, detective," Snow smiled. Though often too talkative and clumsy, CPD's newest homicide detective showed promise because he tracked clues tirelessly. Since he seemed earnest and trusting, his interviews contained the most arcane and irrelevant information because he allowed people their tangents but now and then, he'd glean a gem of a clue. "Get a description on tape?"

"Better: I got their surveillance tape!" he crooned brightly.

"Good work!" Snow nodded. "Meet you at HQ." Savage had already turned over his Bronco's ignition, pealing away from the curb the second Fields had shut the passenger door and whipping a hard left.

The glowering skies spit icy sparks; sleet needled them. Snow motioned for Mac to follow him as curdling grey clouds massing overhead threatened more, while the wind kicked up debris, but she stopped to answer her cell, listening while approaching the Explorer. Halted abruptly, hand up, palm out. "Yes, sir, I can take that call."

Chris waited, one brassy brown eyebrow quirked, motioning her to get in the vehicle by opening the passenger door.

"Chief March wants Shadow and me to take the Amber alert missing persons case."

"Why?" he asked, his hand on the driver's door. "He has a lead?"

"A Carlisle woman called in to say it's her granddaughter. She's nearly hysterical. Chief thinks she needs a woman's touch, said it's a good opportunity for Shadow to prove her mettle. Shadow, come!" The dog leaped in—always ready to ride.

"I'll have to drop you," Chris said. "You can call—"

"And I will, after I've talked with the grandmother. You never know, maybe the kid skipped school to hang out at the mall with friends. Though you'd think the girl would've called if she could. Anyway, if she's been kidnapped, I'll have to focus on this case, so..." she ruminated as they drove to the scene.

"We can work out the logistics later. Love you." Snow patted her shoulder and reached across to open her door. She hopped out, let Shadow out, snapping the leash in the halter rings and hurried up the walk that curved like a comma toward a red brick and clapboard Cape Cod in the quiet, established neighborhood where generous lots separated the houses, most with blinds drawn on the cul-de-sac.

Made in the USA
Lexington, KY
02 December 2019